Kip Manley

CITY *of* ROSES

VOL. I

"WAKE UP..."

Supersticery Press
Manley, Kip
City of Roses Vol. 1: "Wake up…" / Kip Manley
ISBN 978-1-7349452-0-1

Originally published as individual chapbook nos. 1 – 11 from 2006 – 2011. Portions also published in *Coyote Wild* no. 3, Summer, 2007 (coyotewildmag.com) and in the 7th issue of Stumptown Underground, "City Folk" (stumptown.underground.com).

Art is a Gift

www.thecityofroses.com

Four Fifths

"Portland," says Ysabel, spreading marmalade on her toast, "is divided into four fifths."

"Four," says Jo. "Not five?"

"Four," says Ysabel. Leaning over her plate she takes a bite of toast, careful of her sleeveless peach silk top. "There's Northwest, Southwest, Southeast, and Northeast." Her finger taps four vague quarters on the purple tabletop between her plate and Jo's coffee cup.

"What about North?"

"What about it?"

"It's a whole chunk of town," says Jo, leaning back. The jukebox under the giant plaster crucifix on the back wall is singing about how you're all grown up, and you don't care anymore, and you hate all the people you used to adore. "Isn't it one of the fifths?"

"There's no one there."

"There's nobody in North Portland."

"But few of any sort," says Ysabel, shaking pepper on her omelet, "and none of name."

"Okay," says Jo. Stirring her coffee. "But it's still there. It's still a part of Portland. It's still a fifth."

"If you wish to be finicky, you might also note that there's no one technically 'in' downtown, either," says Ysabel, cutting a neat triangle from the corner of her omelet. "Or Old Town. So you might speak of six fifths. Or seven. But." She forks it up, chews, swallows. "I'm trying to keep things simple. For instance: the whole city is, technically, under my mother's sway."

"Because she's the Queen."

"Also, the Ban. Sometimes. But. Her power is concentrated in Northwest, and that fifth represents the practical limits of her demesne. There's too many mushrooms."

"What?" says Jo.

"In the omelet. There's too many mushrooms. And she *still* hasn't brought my soda."

the TABLE *of* CONTENTS

an INTRODUCTION

AT THE END OF THE NINETIES I spent a lot of time walking back and forth, between an office on Park between Washington and Alder, and an apartment next door to what would eventually become Robin Goodfellow's house, catercorner to that bright green house with the white columns where the Queen was going to live. And a lot of the time when I was walking back from the office to the apartment it was midnight, it was one in the morning, it was two. The route I took to avoid busy (even at that hour) Burnside took me through what we were only just derisively starting to call the Pearl, through the heart of what would one day become the Brewery Blocks, when it was all still, y'know, a *brewery,* and at midnight or even one or two a line of glass bottles would be clink-clinking against each other on a conveyor belt that ran high overhead across the street, from one stage of the brewing process in that anonymous white corrugated metal building there, to the next stage in the process, in that anonymous white corrugated metal building yonder. And somewhere on the side of that building long since dismantled was this thing, and I don't know what it's called, where the main power line comes in and down the outside wall in a sort of pipe that ends in several up-curled horns from which sprouts a thicket of much thinner cables that branch out to carry the power off hither and yon through the building. And sometimes there's one that isn't in use anymore, or yet, no cables sprouting, just those horns, empty, upturned, waiting. And walking past one night or early morning, the bottles clinking by overhead, I saw them and I stopped and I said to myself, I said *snakes,* I said *pythia,* I said *oracle*—

—and there she was, all of a sudden, sprung fully if not finally formed into the pinkish-orange glow of the streetlight: this Lori Petty-looking kid with spiky yellow hair and goggles pushed up on her forehead and black jeans and a white T-shirt with the sleeves ripped off that said, I dunno, maybe The Rodney Clock? And the mis-matched Chuck Taylors with the duct tape on the toe, and one work-gloved hand on her hip and a glimmering baseball bat in the other, and she's staring at those horns, and she very obviously expected them to stir and turn and *talk* to her—

Our protagonist, Jo Maguire, ladies and gentlemen.

Oh, the baseball bat was swapped out soon enough for an actual sword, and Guthrie got the T-shirt; the goggles went to my own iteration of Those Two Guys, Messrs. Charlock and Keightlinger (though they do different things than they did then); Roland got the gloves. I gave my hair to Becker, though it's my hair then, not my hair now; much as the Duke's drinking whatever beer I was drinking at the time; much as the Danmoore Hotel's still standing, and there's still an Indian restaurant in the Masonic Temple, and Macy's never came to town, and Henry Weinhard never left, and those bottle still clink-clink by overhead at all hours. —But some things are forever: the nail of my left big toe's still a dead grey curl of a thing, so I gave it to Jo, to ground her.

And all of it made up of nothing more than words upon words: words sparked and suggested by, overheard and stolen from Emma Bull and Ellen Kushner and Peter Beagle, John Crowley and Joanna Russ and Joss Whedon, Patricia McKillip and William T. Vollmann, John D. MacDonald and Christ I don't know, but also: words supported by Lisa Spangenberg and Barry Deutsch, picked over by and bounced off of Nick Fagerlund and Brenna Zedan, loving and loved by Jenn Manley Lee and Taran Jack, words that couldn't possibly bear up under the debt they owe, or contain their gratitude. And yet: here we are.

Portland, Oregon
2003 – 2011

(Ysabel? Come now. That would be telling.)

Also he knew something about writing, for when wandering the city he had visited public libraries and read enough stories to know there were two kinds. One kind was a sort of written cinema, with plenty of action and hardly any thought. The other kind was about clever unhappy people, often authors themselves, who thought a lot but didn't do very much. Lanark supposed a good author was more likely to have written the second kind of book.

—Alasdair Gray

The visible world is merely their skin.

—William Butler Yeats

NO. I
PROLEGOMENON

WHEN THE PHONE RINGS the rumpled blankets jerk and twist and spit out a hand. It fumbles about and finds the alarm clock and slaps the snooze button. The phone rings again. A head pops out, blinking, befuddled. Blond hair cropped close to the skull, a couple of locks here and there left long, dyed black, lank. The phone rings again. She falls on it, half-tumbling off the futon, snatches up the handset. "What," she croaks.

"Frankie," she says. She grabs the alarm clock. "Frankie. You have any idea what time it is. It's," peering thickly at the clock, she frowns, "it's a quarter of eleven. Fuck.

"Well, my alarm clock didn't go off. I –

"Frankie, I'd have to catch a bus, I'm gonna be late as –

Listening to the chirpy voice on the other end of the line she fumbles about for something in the litter of unopened junk mail and discarded clothing by the futon, comes up with a crumpled pack of cigarettes. "Fine, fine." She shakes it. It's empty. "Let me just – yes, Frankie.

"Yes.

"I said I would, dammit."

Jo Maguire hangs up her phone and puts her face in her hands and takes a deep breath in through her nose. "Fuck," she says.

It's raining. Under the bus shelter eyes half-closed leaning against the frame she coughs a thin little cough into a fist she jams back into the pocket of her careworn jacket, army-surplus green. One of her Chuck Taylors is black and the other is white and its toe is held on with duct tape. She wears khakis hacked off below the knee over grubby once-white longjohns. She doesn't have a hat.

In the window of the salon behind the shelter is an enormous poster filled with a dim watery light that is neither green nor blue. A waifish model wrapped in a white towel floats in the middle of it and looks supremely unconcerned at nothing in particular. Her red-gold hair spreads out behind her and above her, the only source of warmth. About her are gathered little emblematic piles of this or that, a sprig of something herbal, a mound of chalky stuff, a puddle of goo the color of molasses, shavings of some yellowish root or clay. Beneath her dangling feet the words, dripping with photographed water: Reinterpret the day off.

A number fifteen bus pulls up to the stop. Digging in her cavernous pocket for change, Jo ducks through the rain and climbs on.

It's a thirty-year-old apartment complex, small, maybe eight units in two two-storey buildings making a haphazard U around a small pocket of badly patched parking lot. Yellow siding and peeling brown trim and a sign that reads The Bedevere in faded Old West letters. Jo dodges a torrent from a broken downspout and trudges up a flight of cantilevered steps to a second-floor apartment. The door pops open almost as soon as she knocks on it.

"Well?" says the skinny guy, with dark hair down to his shoulders.

"I'm here, aren't I?" says Jo.

"Yeah, but you want to maybe come in out of the rain?"

Inside it's dark. One of those ubiquitous halogen torchieres stands unlit in the corner at a slight angle. There's an old vinyl couch like something out of a dentist's waiting room and a litter of dirty dishes and take-out boxes on the carpet in front of it. "Hey, uh," says the skinny guy, kicking an empty 2-liter bottle out of the way, "I hate to ask, but can I bum a smoke?"

"I'm out," says Jo, in the doorway.

"You're out." His voice flat, his head turning to kick a side-long look at her.

"Yeah, Frankie, I ran out last night and I haven't had the chance to pick up any more because I had to run all the way across town to find out what the hell you wanted and – "

"Geeze," Frankie's saying, "oh, geeze, Jo, I didn't mean you had to just run out, I mean, you could have had some coffee or something – "

"Oh. Thanks."

" – or picked up some cigarettes, you know, I mean, it's not *that* important – And I'm trying to quit anyway, you know? So maybe it's a good thing, you know? Maybe you should, maybe think about it too, I – "

"I've got to be at work in ten minutes. Which is a physical impossibility from this side of the river. Can we hurry this up?"

Frankie looks away. "I, uh. Got fired. A week, a week and a half ago."

The rain is loud through the open door.

"That's not exactly my problem anymore," says Jo.

"Don't," says Frankie, "don't be like that. The past few days, I mean, I've been trying, you know? Calling people, and look-ing, but – well, it's been hard, and I just – "

"Frankie," says Jo. "Just stop it."

"What?" says Frankie.

Jo looks away as he turns to face her there in the gloom. Her hands in her pockets. She takes a deep breath.

"Stop what?" says Frankie.

She lets the breath out, deflating. "What is it you want, Frankie?"

He makes half a chuckle like it's too much effort to bother finishing. "What, what do I want? I want things to be like they were. You know?" His hands swing up in two arcs before his face, his fingers sketching a little starburst in the air, poof.

"And maybe they were only like that for ten minutes, fifteen minutes, but still. I want. I..." His hands drop to his sides, his shoulders slump. "I want a lot of things. What I need, is. What I need is fifty bucks. You know?"

His eyes on hers, hers on his. The rain, falling. She's the first to look away.

He smiles. A little. Enough to bring out a dimple, there and there.

Leaning against the side of the bus shelter on Morrison and 20th, a wall of greenery behind her, the rain steady. Pulls her hand out of her pocket and shakes down the sleeve of the jacket so she can peer at her watch. 11:35.

"Shit," says Jo.

She lays her head against the scratched plexiglass. Closes her eyes.

Which is when the rain stops. As she opens her eyes, frowning, the light starts flickering, a little, as if – it's like the clouds above, the low solid milky grey ceiling, all that is breaking up, scudding away, a movie in fast-motion. Standing, frowning, she ducks her head out, looks up. Her hair shining. A fat drop of water hitting her shoulder unnoticed, sinking in, a dark splotch.

A short man in a dry peppermint seersucker suit comes walking down Morrison, whistling tunelessly, reaching into his jacket and pulling out a small cellophane-wrapped packet with a bright red circle on it. He has ruddy cheeks and a thick brown mustache and a summery straw porkpie hat. Jo looks down at him, her mouth framing a word she isn't yet speaking, as he shakes the packet once, deftly. A couple of cigarettes leap to attention and he plucks one, offering it to her with a courtly little bow, an exaggerated dip of his head.

"I, uh. Thank you," says Jo, and then after a moment she reaches up to take it. She smiles. It's a wrinkled little thing, an off-white ivory color, and it has no filter. She lifts it to her nose to sniff. "Nice," she says. "Flowery. What's – "

But the man in the peppermint seersucker suit isn't there.

She looks up and down Morrison, steps out to the corner to look along 20th. The daylight is changing again, re-murking. The movie running in reverse as a drop of rain falls striking the puddle that drowns the backed-up storm sewer, and then another and another and another. Jo runs back under the bus shelter. Laughing. The rain coming down as if it had never stopped.

A Narrow Office – an Unwanted Promotion
Waiting, Watching

A narrow office on the sixth floor of a building on the west end of downtown has indecisive cream walls interrupted by kelly green carrels, a couple dozen of them set up on top of long folding tables against that wall and the back wall. Each of them has just enough room for a computer screen, a keyboard, a telephone. There's maybe thirty stations, all told, and just about every seat is full.

"Is there someone home I *could* speak with? Your mother or father, maybe?"

The front wall has a bulletin board and a doorway into the office kitchen, startlingly white: formica and linoleum and fluorescent lights, refrigerator and white-handled microwave oven.

"Does anyone in your household work for a bank, an insurance company, a financial services company, or a market research firm?"

The other side wall, the one without a line of tables and carrels and dialers working phones, has a couple of tall windows and through them, past the last outriders of downtown's tall buildings, mostly older brick, a refurbished hotel, a stark new-build apartment block hanging over the highway's gully, past all that there are the west hills, suddenly close, soaked in shreds of low wet clouds like dirty grey cotton.

"And how would you rate that on a scale of very satisfied, somewhat satisfied, somewhat dissatisfied, or very dissatisfied?"

Up at the front of the office is a desk, an actual desk with a computer on it and a big harried guy in a lurid red-and-black plaid shirt who's running his hand through what little of his hair is left as Jo walks in, dripping. "Ahem," says the big guy, pointedly.

"Hey yourself, Becker," says Jo. "Where's Mike?"

"Quit."

"Quit?"

"Gave two minutes' notice." There's something on the screen that is apparently deeply puzzling to Becker. He frowns at it. "Apparently, Tartt was yelling at him."

"Tartt's always yelling at him."

"This time it actually sank in."

"Which," says Jo, "doesn't explain why *you're* sitting in the hot seat."

Becker looks up with a grin. It's a sour grin. "Hi, my name is Becker, and I'll be your supervisor this afternoon."

"You're kidding," says Jo.

Becker's eyes are back on his screen again. "If there's a joke, it's on me, and it's in terribly poor taste." He twiddles his mouse, clicks one of its buttons, pokes a couple of keys and definitively stabs Enter with his middle finger.

"You've been promoted," says Jo.

"So it would seem."

"Well, that's great! Congratulations!"

"Lucky me. The Peter Principle still works. Look, just sit down and start dialing so my first official act in a supervisory capacity isn't busting your late ass." He looks up again. "I just freed up a batch of Central phone numbers. Go bug a little old lady in Duluth, would you?"

"Power's gone to your head already," says Jo. "I like it."

"Shut up and dial," says Becker.

Jo shrugs off her coat and hangs it on the back on an empty chair. She spins it around so she can straddle it and leans her elbows on the back of the chair and boots up the survey on the computer. As it's pulling up the first phone number, she settles the phone's headset over her ears and adjusts the mike. She takes a deep breath.

"I assure you, ma'am," the thin young man next to her is saying, a thick clump of mascara smeared in the corner of his left eye, his rough-knuckled hands black-nailed and glittering with silver rings – ankhs, skulls, snakeheads, dice – "everything you say is held in the strictest of confidence." His voice is deep and silky smooth and as gentle as his smile, his little nod hello to Jo. His black T-shirt in white letters says Necrophiliac, M.E. "Your phone number was randomly generated. None of the financial information we gather is in any way associated with your name and address, which we don't even know, and won't ever ask for."

Jo punches her first number into her phone.

"Good evening," she says, into her mike. "My name is Jo Maguire. I'm calling from Barshefsky Associates, an independent market research firm. We're not selling anything; I'd just like to ask the person in your household who makes most of the financial decisions a few questions."

"You think you know what's going on," says Becker. "You think you've got it sussed." They're sitting at the table in the back, in under the balcony by the video poker machines. The jukebox is singing about those strangers who pass through the door and cover your action and go you one more. "I mean," says Becker, loudly, "sure, you're overqualified, but you're underambitious. So you put in the minimal amount of effort. You call out sick often enough so you can kid yourself that you don't really do this for a, for a *living*. That you're really between life-stages or you're finding yourself, you're working on your book or getting the band ready or whatever the fuck. It's just a way station. But. But. You don't fuck around so much that they have an excuse to *fire* you, God knows, because you can't afford to lose this, this *job,* and you do this, you walk this line, paycheck to paycheck you are the epitome of mediocrity, and what do they have the nerve to do?"

"They promote your ass to supervisor," says Jo.

"They promote my ass to supervisor," says Becker. "Why? Why me?"

"Scraping the bottom of the barrel," says the thin young man with all the rings, dumping a third spoonful of sugar into his coffee.

"Maybe," says Jo, "Tartt figures you already know all the tricks, so you're ready for whatever the rest of us will try to pull."

Becker face sours contemplatively. "Tartt's not that smart," he says. "Is she? Do you think – " He smacks his forehead. "Shit. Here we all are getting fucked-up drunk and you people are all going to call out sick tomorrow and expect me to cover for you."

"He catches on quick," says the short, older woman with the loose wattle under her chin and the whiskey sour. "For management."

"*I'm* not getting drunk," says the thin young man with all the rings.

"Shut up," says Becker.

"I will *not,*" a woman says loudly enough that they all look up. She's climbing out of the booth by the video poker machines, small black shoes kicking awkwardly at the end of long pearly grey stockings up to a short slip of brownish mushroom grey hemmed with yellowed lace. Black hair glossy in artful tangles swings as she reaches back for her coat.

"Sit down," says whoever's still sitting in the booth, and she looks away, and sighs, and then sits.

"Damn," says the thin man, appreciatively, and then, jerking back, glaring at Jo, *"Ow."* Jo smirks over the rim of her glass at him. "For that," says the thin man, "you owe me dinner."

Jo downs the last of her rum and Coke and thumps the glass down. "You keep that dream alive," she says, leaning forward, scooting her chair back.

"You aren't *leaving,*" says Becker.

"Bathroom," says Jo, standing. Grinning. "I'm not nearly drunk enough to pull off an epic hangover tomorrow."

"You guys," says Becker, and he sighs, heavily.

Jo snorts a laugh and steps away from the table, turning, colliding with the woman in the mushroom slip, who's climbed back out of her booth. "Whoops," says Jo, reaching out, catching the stumbling woman's upper arm. "Whoa."

The man who swarms out of the booth isn't tall but he is lanky, slick green track suit flapping as his long arm quickly plants a bicycle-gloved hand on Jo's chest. He leans into a shove that sends her pinwheeling into the back table.

"Hey!" barks Becker, as the thin man kicks back his chair, standing.

"Don't," says the lanky man in the green track suit. His voice is thin, reedy. He's young, for all that his hair is silvery white and closely cropped. Green sunglasses with jagged, sporty lenses ride up above his forehead. Blue and white headphones cling to his neck. "Do not touch her."

"The fuck?" snaps Jo, shaking her head.

"See," says the little guy in the dark suit. He's holding a flashlight and a book with some 19th-century-looking man on the cover, all pointed mustaches and ludicrously mesmerizing eyes. "Your problem is your diet."

"Really," says the big guy in the dark suit. He's sitting behind the wheel.

"Yeah," says the little guy, who's sitting in the passenger seat. What little hair he has is lankly grey, clustering around his ears and struggling in vain to launch a curl almost precisely midway between his brow and the top of his skull. "The mucus and stuff. Builds up from your diet. Meats and breads and stuff, it gets all, you know. Sticky. Mucus. Clogs up the entire pipe system of the human body."

The big guy has a beard the color of rich mahogany furniture, bushy enough to bury the knot of his skinny black tie. Most of his hair straining against the leather thong that pulls it taut into a clumsy club of a ponytail. "Mucus," he says. He wears a pair of classic black sunglasses. The left lens is covered with spidery words painted in white ink.

"Listen to this." The little guy flips back a couple of pages in the book that doesn't so much tremble as vibrate, thrum almost, in his jittery hands. "We took a trip through northern Italy, walking for 56 hours continuously without sleep or rest or food, only drink. This, after a seven-day fast and then only one meal of two pounds of cherries – Uh…" He turns the page, runs a finger down it. "After a 16-hour walk – "

"Cherries," says the big guy.

"Yeah," says the little guy. "See, he eats only fruit, right? Because it doesn't have any mucus. Mucus, see? Clogs you up. So. Cherries. Apples. Figs."

"I hate figs," says the big guy. "Heads up."

Halfway down the block out from the door under the red neon sign comes the woman in the mushroom slip, struggling into her camelhair coat. The big guy takes off his sunglasses and opens his door with a popping squonk. The little guy drops the flashlight and the book and fumbles for a pair of sunglasses. The owl's feather tied to one side hangs them up on his jacket pocket. "Friggetty fuck," he says. "It's her?"

"It's her," says the big guy.

"She's alone?"

"She's alone."

"Persistence," says the little guy sliding his sunglasses onto his face, owl's feather dangling to one side, "pays – shit."

"I see him."

The door under the red neon sign pops open and out at a stalking half-run comes the lanky man in the green track suit.

"Damn," says the little guy, one hand brushing the owl's feather away from his cheek.

"A knight?" says the big guy, pulling himself back into the car.

"Yup."

"The Chariot?"

"Who else?"

"Damn," says the big guy.

"Wait and watch," says the little guy. "Watch and wait."

The door under the red neon sign pops open one more time, and out comes Jo Maguire, Becker on her heels, the thin man bringing up the rear.

Halfway to the corner, she's stopped. His bicycle-gloved hands are on either shoulder, clenched under the faux fox shawl of her coat. "This is none of your concern, miss," he's saying. They're both looking at Jo, who says, "I just made it my concern."

"She's going to get our asses kicked, isn't she," says the thin man.

"Shut up, Guthrie," says Becker.

"You do not understand," the man in the track suit starts to say. The silver stripes down his sleeves and pants shine unearthly in the pinkish orange street light. He wears outlandishly puffy running shoes, strapped and gussetted, spotlessly white.

"I understand just fine," says Jo. "She said no. And that's it. That's the end. You let go. You walk away."

"Is this, this guy bothering you? At all?" says Becker to the woman.

"Yes," she says, simply, and steps back away down the sidewalk from his hands left hanging there in space.

"Lady – " he says, stricken.

"Back off," says Jo.

"Would you like us to walk you somewhere?" says Guthrie. "Bus stop, maybe?"

"Would I," says the woman, looking down, away. "Would I."

"Your car, maybe?" says Becker.

"I would," says the woman, looking up at Jo.

"That's that," says Jo.

"Lady," says the man again, as she says, "There is, you see, a party. I'd like to attend."

He takes a step closer to her, hands dropping. "Lady, *please.*"

"Of course," says Jo, her eyes on the man in the track suit.

"We'd have to walk," says the woman in the mushroom slip. In the windows of the jewelry shop behind her fantastically encrusted eggs glitter, hard greens and reds, brash golds, in the bright hard beams of little spotlights. "It's up in Northwest – ten, fifteen minutes away? If any – or all – of you would like to come?"

"I, uh," Becker starts to say, as the woman smiles at him and says, "I insist. To thank you for your chivalry."

"We'd love to," says Jo. Her eyes still on the man in the track suit, who steps back now, hands at his sides. Guthrie shrugs.

"Fuck it," says Becker, looking at his watch. *"I'm* calling out sick tomorrow."

"You are wrong, my lady, to do this," says the man. "But I will accompany you."

"Not if 'my lady' doesn't want you to, you won't," says Jo.

"Your mother," he starts to say, as the woman says, "He may tag along. I don't mind."

"I cannot leave your side," he says. Looking back along the cars parked on both sides of the street. The red neon of the sign above the bar's door gleams from the drops and streaks and puddles of fresh rain on windshields, hoods, chrome trim, the dark wet pavement.

"Shall we?" says the woman in the mushroom slip, brightly.

It's Raining Again – What She Says is True
In Carcosa – Terms

It's raining again, pattering softly unseen through the branches of the trees down Everett Street. Candles and Christmas lights wink and flicker from every window of the big white ramshackle house on the corner. The thin young man, Guthrie, pushes open one of the two front doors and staggers onto the porch, letting out a burst of music, a fiddle, sharp popping drums. Rings glitter from his fingers as he points, peering along the front of the house. Frowning. "See?" he says. There's a woman with stubby dreadlocks and baggy jeans, a plastic cup in either hand, leaning against the half-open front door behind him. "See? Out here the window is *there,"* and then he drops his unsteady hand, ducking his head back inside. "While in here, it's further down that way. See? See that?"

"Is it?" she says, holding out a cup for him. He takes it.

"Yeah," he says. "I mean." He frowns.

Inside the big front room the drum kit is set up between the fireplace and the keg. The drummer's head is ruddy. The singer, or at least a woman in a bulky fisherman's sweater and jeans who dangles a microphone from one hand, sits on a folding chair on the other side of the fireplace. The fiddler works the room, snarling himself in a jig, his red hair bobbing up above the circle of people stomping along and down again, his bow leaping into the air. There's someone up in the shadows at the top of the stairs, playing something of a rhythm line on a guitar. "Remind me never to play poker with you," says Becker in his big plaid shirt, leaning up against the wall, as the woman in the cat's eye glasses pulls a neat royal flush in hearts from behind his ear.

"You was the one hiding the cards, pal," she says. "Not me." She lifts her bangled wrist up, peering at a loosely buckled watch. "Now, if you'll excuse me – "

"That's, ah," says Becker. "My watch."

She cranks her eyebrow up higher but smiles a little nonetheless. "You maybe want to keep an eye on it next time," she says, reaching to take it off.

"I think you've maybe got the wrong idea," says Becker.

The drummer cracks his sticks three times over his head and rattles out a sharp popping parade-ground roll, syncopating as the guitarist sends a carillon lick ringing down the stairwell. The singer smiling twirls her microphone once wrapping the cord around her wrist catching it with a pop and as the fiddle picks up the lick flawlessly she stands and launches a song about how us Amazonians know where we stand, we got kids, we got jobs, why do we need a man? The room roars and kicks into a staggeringly varied assortment of dances. Jo leans against the corner under the stairs and lifts a hand to her mouth to stifle a rather large yawn.

"Enjoying yourself?"

Jo jerks her head to one side. It's the woman in the mushroom slip, holding two glasses just thicker than a finger and almost as long. She shakes a black curl out of her eyes as she holds up one of the glasses to Jo.

"Well?" says the woman, leaning close to be heard over the music.

"I'm, I'm sorry," says Jo. "It's just – you look familiar, somehow. Except I think I'd remember you. If I'd ever met you before, I mean." She takes the little glass almost full of something pearly shimmering in the dim light, just on the cusp of transparency. Lifts it up and tips half of it down her throat. "Damn," she says, blinking.

"Damn?"

"Good hootch. The booze," says Jo, in response to the woman's quizzical look. "Liquor. Moonshine."

"Our host brews his own."

"Does he."

"Though he doesn't use moonshine. Too common. He prefers ingredients less readily available. A maiden's virtue, say."

Jo grins and downs the last of her drink. The singer's singing about boiling up rice in a satellite dish.

"What's your name?" says Jo.

"Pay your quid, first."

"What?"

She's smiling, the woman. "Quid pro quo. Tit for tat. What are *you* called." A slim man in a blue sarong and a white shirt nods to her as he comes down the stairs, which she acknowledges with a quick smile.

"Jo," says Jo.

"Joe," says the woman in the mushroom slip. "Joe. A boy's name?"

"Nah, it's short for – "

"Don't," says the woman, raising a finger as if to shush her. There's a short man all in black behind her, talking to the man in the blue sarong.

"Don't?"

"You don't like it, do you."

"Well, it's," Jo shrugs, "it's kind of a dumb name."

"So don't tell me."

"Okay," says Jo. "I won't. So."

"So?"

"I've paid my quid. Now it's time for quo."

"Ysabel," says the woman in the mushroom slip.

"Ysabel," says Jo.

"More often than not. He's still watching me, isn't he."

Jo cranes her head a little looking over and past Ysabel's shoulder. By the front door the fiddler sawing his way between them stands the man in the slick green track suit, running a bicycle-gloved hand over his white-furred scalp. His jagged green racing sunglasses down over his eyes like pieces of broken bottle. "What's his story?" says Jo.

"Complicated."

"What is he, an ex? A stalker? The father of your love-child?"

Ysabel looks down, her lips pursing around a half-swallowed smile. "He watches over me. A protector."

"A bodyguard."

"Of sorts."

"I presume," says a short man, the man all in black, dark-haired, his beard neatly trimmed, a whisper of tamed curls just past stubble along his jawline blending flawlessly into his close-cropped sideburns, "that we are discussing the good Roland, Miss Perry?"

Ysabel turns. He smiles and ducks his head, a little. "You make me a liar, Robin," she says.

"Never, Miss Perry," says Robin, sipping from his tall black mug.

"Did I not just tell Jo that most people more often than not call me Ysabel? And up you step as bold as you please to prove it a lie." She smiles as she says this, sipping from her own thin glass.

One of Robin's shoulders lifts as his head tips down and away, his eyes looking over to crook a smile at Jo: an elaborately ambiguous shrug. "What she says is true, miss." Looking up. He is quite short, not even as tall as Jo. "Whatever that may be." The song clatters to a halt, the drummer rattling his toms with random rolls and fills, the guitarist wandering off quietly down a minor scale, the fiddler scraping a long droning note out of the guts of his fiddle.

"Robin is our host," says Ysabel.

"*Humble* host," says Robin, smiling.

"And this," says Ysabel, "is Jo. Who rescued me."

Jo nods. Then shrugs, smiling uncertainly.

"A pleasure, Jo," says Robin. "Rescued? From what?"

"A dreadfully dull evening," says Ysabel, frowning a little. Looking up at nothing in particular. A set of pipes has begun to drone somewhere further in the house. Coming closer. The fiddle scrapes into a new note and begins to wrap a slow pulsing melody around the unseen pipes. "Is this..?" says Ysabel.

The corners of Robin's mouth turn down, arching his little mustache up and out. "I merely asked them to play. I didn't tell them what."

The piper, pale, her clotted yellow-white curls swept back from her face, steps a measured march into the front room to the squeezing of her little pipes. The crowd – varied, lycra and fleece, glittered cheeks, khakis and sweaters, army pants and a black sports bra, a floppy mohawk, a tuxedo, a glittering minidress, a bared chest under swirls of bodypaint, pegged jeans and garish T-shirts, Roland's green and silver tracksuit as he makes his way across the room, sliding through them all standing quietly now, watching, waiting. The singer smiling as the piper slowly picks up the fiddle's melody over her drone. The drummer wiping sweat out of his face, swigging something from a red plastic cup.

"It *is*," says Ysabel, grabbing Jo's hand. "Come on."

"What?" says Jo.

"Lady," says Roland, there beside them, reaching out to almost but not quite take Ysabel's arm. "It is perhaps time we got you home."

"Not yet," says Ysabel, turning her back to him, her hands on Jo's upper arms. Her eyes closing. "Listen," she says.

There's been a shift in the song, gears changed. The guitar ambling forward now in a rickety rhythm line as the melody takes a breath and repeats itself, strong, assured. The drummer waiting, sticks still. Nodding to someone, hey. The singer looks out over the little crowd there in Robin's front room and lifts her microphone to her lips and says, half-singing, "Along the shore the cloud waves break, the twin suns sink beneath the lake, the shadows lengthen – in Carcosa...”

Jo frowns. “It’s not hooked up.”

Ysabel, her head tipped back, hair hanging heavy as she sways left foot to right and back, her hands still on Jo’s arms, smiles. “What?”

“The microphone,” says Jo.

“Strange is the night where black stars rise and strange moons circle through the skies – but stranger still is lost Carcosa...”

The drums pop then, once. Someone whoops. The piper’s playing two lines over the steady heartbeat of her drone, one marching a slowly quickening lockstep with the grinning fiddle, the other skirling after the guitar, each chasing the other, looking for the monstrous beats to come. The whole room tensely waiting, almost, almost.

“Songs the Hyades shall sing, where flap the tatters of the King, must die unheard in dim Carcosa...”

Jo closes her eyes. Ysabel’s hands fall away. Jo takes a deep breath.

“Song of my soul, my voice is dead – die though, unsung, as tears unshed shall dry and die in lost Carcosa...”

The fiddle and pipes are pruning, boiling the melody down as the guitar and pipes settle and under it all the drone and the threat of the drums.

“In Carcosa... lost Carcosa... dim Carcosa...”

A grizzled man pauses his bobbing head to shove his white-taped black-rimmed glasses back up his nose. Robin pinches off a blissful little smile and downs the last of whatever’s in his mug. A dark girl in patched overalls throws wide her arms her hands swallowed by bulky workgloves. Becker catches his breath and looks eyes shining at the singer as the woman in cat’s eye glasses eases a hand into the hip pocket of his jeans. The dervish melody has spun itself tighter and tighter until it’s almost nothing more than two notes pulsing on-off one-oh in-out *da*-da as the singer wails. The drummer lifts his sticks and hangs there, waiting.

“In Carcosa... lost Carcosa... dim Carcosa...”

Jo opens her eyes.

That first brontolithic beat unleashes something monstrous. The room whirls snaps leaps kicks stomps into motion, heaving as one with the avalanching rhythm. Jo is in the thick of it now arms high above her head yelling, yelling, Ysabel beside her, head down, hair flying, all of it so loud the music is almost lost, the band redundant all of them, madly now chasing some driving jig just barely out of reach. The fiddler's spinning widdershins in a circle of tossing people dancing about him, the piper's on her knees, cheeks blimped, pipes jerking; the guitarist still cannot be seen up in the shadows on the stairs but can most definitely be heard. The singer's head's thrown back, microphone lifted high above her, howling the wordless melody up into it, a drawn-out hopeless nameless vowel, and the drummer's making up for lost time. But Ysabel is gone.

Jo puts out her hand, stumbling, shoved to one side by the grey-haired woman in the Frankie Say T-shirt. Turns against the dancing crowd, bumbling against the lumbering boy with the wispy beard and the black leather trench coat. Ysabel's there at the foot of the stairs yelling something at Roland whose bicycle-gloved hand is clamped around her upper arm. Jo looks away rolling her eyes and is knocked two staggering steps towards them by the whipcracking arms of the man in the glittering vest. The band suddenly and out of nowhere hits a spattering of notes as one, a clarion, a fanfare, and falls back as suddenly into its churning driving almost-chaos. "Carcosa…" moans the singer, and Jo pushes her way between a woman in a white fur coat and a man whose long brown arms are fishnetted in hot pink. Roland pulls Ysabel after him towards the door. He's saying something about her mother.

"Do not mention my mother again this night," snaps Ysabel. "As a favor. To me."

"Hey," says Jo. Planting her feet.

Roland purses his lips and looks away from them both. Lets go Ysabel's arm and she steps back once towards the stairs as he lifts his hand to touch the bridge of his nose lightly, closing his eyes. He peels the green sunglasses from his face and his eyes are mild as he turns them again to Ysabel. "Lady," he says. "Enough. You have made your point." He holds out his hand for her to take. "But now we must be off."

"I'm not here to make a point," says Ysabel, just barely to be heard over the music. She smiles sweetly. "I'm here to enjoy myself."

"Okay?" says Jo. "So just go. Leave her – "

"Who are you?" says Roland.

"What?" says Jo.

"Who are you, that you should care about this?" He turns to face Jo now, and his eyes are no longer mild. "That she should be a concern to you?" He throws out a hand, encompassing the dancing room. "You don't belong here. Who *are* you, to interfere?"

"I don't know," says Jo. She shrugs. "I guess I don't like bullies."

"*I* am her guardian!" says Roland. "She is *my* charge. My responsibility – "

"You have a funny way of showing it," says Jo.

"Are you," says Roland, quiet now under the stomping feet, the roaring band, "impugning my honor?"

Jo snorts. "Honor?"

The band driving up out of nowhere hits its spattered unison again; and again – the syncopated, punch-drunk fanfare. In the moment of silence between the last note driven home and the first whoops from the suddenly motionless dancers the rip of velcro is shockingly loud. As applause breaks out all around them Roland strips the bicycle glove from his right hand and throws it at Jo's feet.

"Well?" he says.

"Well?" says Jo, frowning.

"What say you?"

"What say me?" says Jo.

"What say I," says Ysabel. Smiling. "Pick up the glove."

Jo, still frowning, not taking her eyes off Roland, kneels slowly. Picks up the grubby glove.

"Name your terms," says Roland.

"Terms," says Jo. Standing up.

"As the challenged. What weapons? Where? When?"

"Weapons?" says Jo.

"It's late" – the Merits of a Quarrel
a Wicked Thing – Awakening

"It's late," says the little guy in the dark suit, ticking off a point on his fingers. "It's trying to rain." He leans against the front of a black car. Meticulous lines of hand-painted white letters whorl up and over the fender. "There's, what, a half-dozen knights in there?" He begins counting off on his other hand. "The Chariot, of course. The Axe. I'm pretty sure the Mooncalfe. The Mason and the Helm. You said yourself you saw the Shield. And a dozen more in shouting distance." He looks up, frowning. "Did I mention the rain?"

"Swords," says the big guy in the dark suit. He stands on the hood of the car, both feet primly within concentric rings of cramped white letters.

"Yes, they have swords," says the little guy. "That's another problem right there."

"They're *bringing out* swords." The big guy peers through a pair of black sunglasses at the ramshackle house on the corner across an intersection clogged with traffic waiting on a red light. The left lens of the sunglasses is covered with spidery words painted in white ink.

"So I have to ask why they're bringing out swords to find out why they're bringing out swords?" says the little guy. Somebody's trunkthumping stereo kicks up a rattling bass line.

"The Chariot has gotten himself into a duel."

"All the more reason to ske-fuckin'-daddle. It's the Calfe again, isn't it." The light changes. The trunkthumper recedes down the street.

"It's the girl."

"The girl." The little guy looks up, alarmed.

"The girl from the café."

"You're shitting me. The Bride? He's going up against his own goddamn – "

The big guy looks down at the little guy over the rims of lowered sunglasses.

"Oh," says the little guy. "The girl. Right. The what, the gutter-punk. *That* girl." And then, "Oh," he says. *"Oh."*

"Precisely," says the big guy, peering at the house on the corner.

"She can't win," says the little guy. "There's no way she can win."

It starts to rain a little harder.

"Let the record show," sighs Robin, "that your body has entered the lists to make proof of your appeal, and so your pledges by law are discharged. Will you have grease, ash, and sugar?"

"I will not," says Roland.

Ysabel leans against Jo, one hand on her shoulder, murmuring in her ear. "Don't worry. He can't hurt you. It's against the rules. He won't let you hurt him. It's only a game."

"And who will stand as your second?" says Robin, looking up at the ceiling.

"I will have none here in that office," says Roland. Robin nods perfunctorily. A brief flurry of whispers and titters sweeps the room.

"And do you swear," says Robin, taking a deep breath, "you come no otherwise appointed, with naught but your body and the merits of your quarrel, that you have not any knife, nor any other pointed instrument, or engine small or great, no stone or herb of virtue, no charm, experiment, nor other enchantment by whose power you believe you may the easier overcome your adversary?"

"I do so swear," says Roland. His eyes calm and mild.

"A game," says Jo. Swallowing. "Great."

The party crowd has raggedly ordered itself along the walls, leaving clear an aisle that crosses diagonally from the foot of the stairs where Jo and Ysabel stand next to the door into the bright toothpaste-colored kitchen, held open by the piper, sitting on her heels, offering up a bottle of something-or-other to Roland.

Robin's walking down the middle of that aisle toward Jo, passing the barefoot boy in bone-white khakis holding two crossed rapiers on a fat velvet pillow. "Jo Maguire," he's saying, "save your honor and come in to your action which you have undertaken this day. Will you have grease, ash, and sugar?"

"She waives them," says Ysabel. "It's okay," she says to Jo. "A formality."

"And do you swear you come no otherwise appointed, naught but your body and the merits of your quarrel, not any knife nor other pointed instrument, no engine, stone, herb of virtue, no charm, experiment, or other enchantment?"

"Yes?" says Jo, as Ysabel says, "She does."

"And who stands as your second?"

"I, uh," says Jo.

"I will," says Ysabel. Another flurry, of whispers and gasps, and not so brief. Ysabel shrugs. "It's as good a way to discharge my debt as any."

"You may choose your blade," sighs Robin, snapping, and up comes the barefoot boy with the fat velvet pillow. Jo stares at the swords. "They are of a length," says Robin.

"Yeah, they're long," mutters Jo. "And sharp."

"It's only a game," says Ysabel.

"It's insane," says Jo.

"Don't worry," says Ysabel. "You'll lose. But he won't let you hurt him."

"That's *not* what I'm worried about," says Jo.

"I told you: he can't hurt you. It's against the rules. It's for *honor*," says Ysabel. "Your honor, nothing more. Which you hold lightly enough." Jo frowns, looking sidelong at Ysabel, who smiles. "Trust me," she says, as Robin says, "Your blade, Jo Maguire?"

And Jo picks up a sword, looking down at the candlelight and Christmas-light winking and chasing the basket of steel ribbons woven around the hilt. "This is," she says, "insane."

"Duelers!" calls Robin from the center of the aisle, and up comes Roland in his green track suit, blue and white headphones still clamped around his neck, planting his soft and spotless white shoes one before the other, his hips edge-on, his left arm up and back, bent so his fingertips brush the air behind his head, the tip of his blade fixed to a point in the air before his eyes. "Salute!" cries Robin. Jo in her plain black T-shirt, her hacked-off khakis, her grubby longjohns, fixes her duct-taped Chuck Taylors one before the other, her left arm back and out, her sword held up before her like a stick. Roland fluidly swirls his wrist and his blade in a circle, his head dipping. Jo nods in return. "Engage!" cries Robin, throwing up his hand, and everyone begins to cheer. Roland lunges. Jo leaps back, stumbling, ducking her head, yelling "Whoa whoa whoa whoa whoa!" She drops her sword clattering to the floor, arms crossed over her face, crying "You win! You win!"

The cheers wither into whispers and mutters.

"Pick up your blade!" says Roland.

"No!" says Jo. "You win! I yield, I surrender, that's it. Uncle." There are giggles at that. A stifled guffaw. Jo peeks out from under her crossed arms. Roland still in his stance has pulled his sword back to fix the tip at that point in the air before his eyes. "Congratulations, big fella," says Jo. "Way to go."

"You insulted me," says Roland, pulling up out of his stance, his arms relaxing, his blade dipping.

"And now I'm leaving," says Jo. "Deal." She turns her back. Becker and Guthrie and Ysabel stand waiting at the foot of the stairs. "Where's my coat?" There's a collective gasp as she catches herself mid-step. Arms up and out suddenly, grasping at nothing. Frowning, she looks down. The tip of Roland's blade has ripped a hole in her black T-shirt. A good two inches pokes out of her chest, a little to the left of center. "I," says Jo.

With a twist and a jerk Roland pulls the blade back out of her body.

Jo turns unsteadily to look back at him. One knee threatens to give but she does not fall. "I," she says. "Jo?" says Becker. She puts out a hand for something, anything, for balance. It isn't there.

"Ow," says Jo. She falls.

The outer office is dark except for the spark of a halogen desk lamp. The woman behind the desk wears a shapeless linen dress and narrow spectacles on a fine chain draped around her neck. She looks up from a yellow legal pad when the big guy in the dark suit opens the outer door. "Mr. Charlock and Mr. Keightlinger," says the little guy in the dark suit. "To see Mr. Leir."

"He's expecting you," she says.

The inner office is dark except for a white-shaded banker's lamp shining on a leather-topped desk. On the desk a silver pen and an ivory-handled knife with a wide blade of tarnished bronze. The man looking out the window at the street below has thick, unruly white hair, and wears a white shirt and a white tie. A cigarette is pinched unnoticed between the thumb and forefinger of his pale right hand. The window is open. Up from under the drip of the rain comes the washing susurrus of a street-sweeper.

"Well?" says Mr. Leir. His face is quite young under that white hair.

"Well," says Mr. Charlock, "the Chariot went and got himself into a duel. With a girl. A *mortal* girl. Which, well. He lost."

"Lost," says Mr. Leir.

"Struck her from behind. Yeah. He lost."

"There is now," says Mr. Keightlinger, idly twirling a lock of his beard, "a gallowglas."

Mr. Leir looks over his shoulder at them. Frowns. Looks down to discover the cigarette in his hand, which he lifts. Takes a drag, blowing smoke out the window into the rain.

"Well," he says.

"You," calls the old woman over her shoulder, her eyes on her fingers running along a brightly lit shelf of orange plastic prescription bottles, "have done a wicked thing." Finding the one she wants she plucks it down. Wrestling the top off she taps two pills into a mortar. "Sit up straight. You're indecent."

Ysabel does not sit up straight. Out in the darker bedroom she's curled up sideways in a wing-backed chair by the fireplace, her head leaning back against one wing, her legs folded up and tucked against the arm opposite. "You should concentrate on waking her up." Still in her mushroom-colored slip rucked carelessly up revealing the dark bands at the tops of her pearly stockings. "Assuming you can, of course."

"Oh, I can," says the old woman, huffing into the bedroom from the bright white bathroom, holding the marble mortar and pestle in both hands. She wears a heavy pink robe with a tangled garden of tea-roses embroidered on the thick shawl collar. Glossy white hair hangs loose before and behind her shoulders. "She's just shocky, is all. You'd be yourself, if you was her."

On the bed pillowed in a deep down comforter lies Jo Maguire, naked, asleep. An old scab mars one knee. The nail of her left big toe is a dead grey ridge. A tattoo down the swell of belly from navel to the edge of dark curled hair, an angular thing, abstract, a suggestion of beak and eyes. Her right arm folded, hand on her chest, fingertips touching a dull red welt just to the left of her breastbone. The old woman sits on the bed beside her brushing a lock of black-dyed hair from Jo's forehead. "I don't know why you picked this one," she says. On the nightstand by the bed is a glass of water. The old woman pours powder from the mortar into the water, which turns several colors too quick to be named. "She's in your mother's world, not yours. Or mine."

"I didn't *pick* her," says Ysabel. Fussing with the lace that hems her slip. "I didn't *do* any of this. It all just – "

"It just happened?" says the old woman.

One of Ysabel's narrow black shoes dangles half of a twitching foot. The other is on the floor before the wing-backed chair. "Yes," says Ysabel.

The old woman dips her fingers into the glass of water and then flicks them at Jo's face. Jo sits up suddenly gulping, the hand at her chest now a fist against that welt. The old woman sets the glass of water on the nightstand and picks up a small jar, a baby food jar with the label half-picked away. Jo doubled over heels kicking left hand clutching the deep soft comforter sucks down a ragged breath and another, her right fist grinding into the welt.

There is another welt, larger, more diffuse, as red, on her back. The old woman sniffs the baby food jar and nods, then scoops out a two-fingered dollop viscous and translucent which she plops on the welt on Jo's back. Jo jerks upright crying out, arms flailing, eyes wild. The old woman shushing her clamps one hand on her shoulder holding her still as she smears the rest of the stuff on the welt on Jo's breast. Jo screams. Shushing her all the while the old woman holds Jo's shoulders as Jo kicking tosses her head back hands digging into the comforter firmly in the old woman's grip. And then with a hitch Jo stops. Opens her eyes. Takes a deep sobbing breath. Sinks forward, curling around herself.

"Fucking hell," she croaks.

"There there," says the old woman. "You don't go through *that* every day."

Jo coughs and shivering pulls up one end of the comforter she's sitting on to wrap herself in. "My clothes," she says. Coughs again. "Where are my clothes?"

"Burned them, dearie," says the old woman. "Filthy things. You couldn't possibly appear before the court in *those.*"

"There were holes in your shirt," says Ysabel, who does not look up from the lace in her lap.

"You," says Jo, seeing Ysabel sitting sideways in the wing-backed chair. "You. You lied. You said he couldn't hurt me. You said. He – " Jo frowns. "Stabbed me?"

Ysabel's looking up and glaring at Jo as "There, there," says the old woman. "I spoke the truth," says Ysabel. "Roland made me a liar." She looks back down at the lace in her lap. "There *is,*" she says, "a difference. I don't see what you're so upset about."

"You don't," says Jo. Huddled under the awkwardly rucked-up comforter. "You don't see." Eyes closed. Deep breath. "I was stabbed. You. I have no idea where I am. Where am I?" she says, as the old woman says "There, there." Jo shakes her head. "What time is it? What do I – need to – I was *stabbed.* He – " Another deep breath, and something that's half a chuckle. "Do you," says Jo, and swallows, "have any idea how hard it is to find a decent plain black T-shirt for less than ten bucks?"

"You won," says Ysabel.

"What?"

"You won," says Ysabel. "You bested him."

"It's true," says the old woman, peeling back the comforter to peer at Jo's back. "Struck you from behind – a grievous breach of honor and decorum. To say nothing of your skin." The welt is gone.

"I won," says Jo.

"You proved yourself against his honor," says Ysabel, "and all his offices are forfeit for his blow. Including," and she looks up to meet Jo's eyes, "me."

Jo blinks.

"Rather, my keeping," says Ysabel. "He was my guardian. Now you are. I was his charge, his responsibility;" she shrugs. "Now I'm yours."

Jo closes her eyes, and when she speaks her voice is quiet and steady. "I want my clothes. Any clothes. I want a cigarette. I want some coffee. I want – I want to go *home*. If you," and she looks up at Ysabel, her voice rising, "think I am going to go along with this, with this – game – for even one minute, I – I – "

"Well," says the old woman, pushing herself with some effort to her feet. "*That's* a relief, and I don't mind saying so."

"I – " says Jo, frowning. "You. A relief?"

"Dearie," says the old woman, leaning against Jo's shoulder, "we were rather worried you'd accept."

"AN UTTER DISASTER" – AN UNEXPECTED CALL
NONE OF HER CONCERN

"AN UTTER DISASTER," says the woman with the pince nez perched at the tip of her nose. She purses her lips. "We may well be forced to raze it to the very ground and start from scratch." She adjusts her pince nez with knob-knuckled fingers taloned by sharp black-painted nails. "Perhaps," she says, "some sort of wig?"

"You are not," says Jo, "touching my hair." She's standing on a faded burgundy footstool wearing a short white chemise, lifting her arms so the old woman in her heavy pink robe can wrap a tape measure about her chest. Ysabel smiles, sitting on her bed in a short white robe, her hair heavily damp, one bare leg crossed over the other.

"Your first address to the Queen should be as her majesty, which thereafter ought be scaled back to ma'am." The tall man's narrowly somber face is lit by extravagant gin blossoms appling two-thirds of his nose and his sunken cheeks. His chin is restless behind the high white gateposts of his upturned shirt-collar. "*Never* avail yourself of that horrid redundancy, her *royal* majesty; it smacks of arse-kissery."

"I'm stumped," says the old woman, folding the measuring tape into her fist.

"As am I," says the woman with the pince nez.

"She may well refer to herself via the accepted fiction of the royal we, or may just as well stoop to the first-person singular; our Queen is rather charmingly erratic on this point of protocol. She has as yet shown no proclivities toward the *third* person, for which I suppose we ought give thanks."

"There is the dress the Princess wore to her cotillion. We could take in the bosom – "

"Too much crinoline," tuts the woman with the pince nez.

"You, however," says the tall man, "must keep in mind you address not merely a person but the people she rules. When addressing our Queen directly, restrict yourself to the second-person plural: 'you' and 'your' as decidedly opposed to 'thou' and 'thine.' I do *not,*" and his face cracks then into a small wry smile, "anticipate *this* point, at least, proving difficult for you."

"Whatever," says Jo. "Look, I'm not about to turn down a free outfit. But maybe you could keep it simple. You know? Jeans? A pair of pants, a nice shirt?"

"Out of the question," says the woman with the pince nez.

"Couldn't possibly, dear," says the old woman.

"*Not* before the Queen," says the woman with the pince nez.

"Actually," says the tall man, "it's not *entirely* without precedent, but I should advise – "

"The new girl, the amanuensis," says the old woman, snapping her fingers. "She ought to have a skirt and jacket that – "

"I think," says Ysabel, "you'll find what she's asking for in my brother's trunk."

A moment of silence follows, broken by a quiet "Your brother?" from the woman with the pince nez.

"Also," says Ysabel, "a pair of boots."

The woman in the pince nez turns abruptly then and mouth moued stalks out the door, followed after another silent moment by the old woman, bustling in her heavy pink robe.

"Thanks," says Jo.

"Cigarette?" says Ysabel.

"Dear God yes," says Jo, stepping down of the hassock.

"If I might be permitted to pick up the thread of my instruction from the moment I was forced to leave off?" says the tall man with the narrow face. "When the presence begins, Miss Maguire, you will wait in the back of the room until you specifically are called before our Queen." Ysabel opens a rattling drawer in a cluttered dresser on spindly legs and roots around, pulling out a small wooden box. "Allow her to direct the conversation where she will; she may well wish to make small talk." The tall man allows himself another narrow smile. "It is *not* without precedent." Ysabel opens the box and plucks out a slim brown cigarette, which she tosses to Jo. "Answer whatever questions she might have with candor, discretion, and wit, and you shall do fine."

"Clove?" says Jo, sniffing the cigarette.

"We are not entirely unpredictable," says Ysabel. "Majordomo, if you don't mind?"

"Actually," says Jo, "a light?"

The tall man turns his back on them, facing the bay window looking out on a small green yard, a lightening street. Ostentatiously adjusting his black frock coat. "A light?" says Ysabel. "Of course." She unbelts her robe and lets it fall, then fishes a matchbook out of the wooden box and pads across the room toward Jo. Clear crystal catches the dim light and flashes from the gold pin piercing her navel. The match pops into flame. "Where was I?" the Majordomo is saying. "Yes. She will broach the subject at hand in, ah, whichever way she chooses." Ysabel smiles as Jo leans forward to touch the cigarette to the match. The cloves crackle as they light. "Said subject, the matter upon which all this hullabaloo hangs, being the question of whether or not you accept the keeping of the Princess." Ysabel blows out the match and lets it drop, walking back across the room to the dresser as Jo takes a deep crackling drag. "That answer, of course, will be: no." Ysabel opens another drawer and pulls something filmy out of it, a handful of lingerie. A teddy. She lifts it over her head and shimmies into it. Tugs it into place. "The Queen will then exile you, and that will be that." Turns, arching one leg tiptoed bending a little awkwardly to snap the crotch.

Jo, blowing smoke, frowns. "Exile?" she says.

"Of course," says the Majordomo. "Refusing the office *must* be taken as an insult. But: the Chariot will be returned to his rightful place. The Princess will once more be held by someone who can keep her. And *you* will be free to go wherever else you may wish: that, as I said, will be that."

"Okay," says Jo.

In the long narrow office with indecisive cream walls and skinny green carrels each with a computer screen and a telephone and most with a waiting or chattering or yawning dialer, Becker sits behind the big desk up at the front, a cup of coffee in one hand, a telephone handset wedged between ear and shoulder. "What I'm seeing," he says, "is a room where Rob's here, and TJ, and Dorfman and Denice and Christian's here. Guthrie's here. Hell, *I'm* here. What I'm *not* seeing, Jo, is you. You aren't here. Why is that?"

On the edge of Ysabel's massive dark bed on the deep white comforter sits Jo, wearing a pair of tight black trousers and black knee-high motorcycle boots and an open white shirt with billowy sleeves and a wide flat collar. "Um," she says, into the gold and ivory handset of a princess phone on a silver tray held by a boy half-swallowed in an of-white tabard edged with gold braid.

"Um?" says Becker.

"Yeah, see, there was this thing. You remember the party? Last night?"

"Yes."

"And the fight?"

"You got into a fight."

"Yeah. With the guy? In the green suit? You tried to, ah, anyway. I have to sort some stuff out, this morning, which is why I'm running a bit late, and, um. What time is it, anyway?"

"Eleven thirty."

"Oh. It's later than I thought. Um." Jo frowns. "Can I, just – how did you get this number?"

"From the schedule."

Jo blinks. "The schedule."

"Yeah, Jo. We tend to keep all our employees' phone numbers on the schedule. So we can call them, if they don't show up for shifts."

"Oh," says Jo.

"Are there, are there cops involved? Do you have to see the cops about this fight?"

"What? No. The guy. You remember the guy? Who wouldn't leave that girl alone? And there was a, um. There were swords?"

Becker rolls his eyes. "Jo, just. Stop. I don't appreciate being screwed around with like this."

"I'm not trying," says Jo.

"If you can't make it in here by noon, then don't bother to come in at all today. Okay?"

"Becker, listen to me, I'm not – " Jo sighs, then reaches up to drop the handset back onto its gilded cradle.

"But five minutes remain until the presence, Princess, Miss Maguire," says the Majordomo.

"Yeah," says Jo, "thanks. Could you guys just, ah, leave me alone? For a minute? I mean, not Ysabel, obviously, it's her room, but – "

The Majordomo is holding the door open for the woman with the pince nez, who sweeps out, full burgundy skirts clutched in one black-taloned hand, followed by the pudgy page with the phone on the silver platter. "I will send someone to fetch you both," says the Majordomo, closing the door behind him.

"Well?" says Ysabel, sliding a dark red chopstick into the base of her ponytail.

"What the fuck is going on?" says Jo, tugging her blousy white shirt closed. "Becker doesn't remember the duel. At all."

Ysabel adjusts her tight black blouse, checks the fall of her somber grey skirt in the three-way mirror.

"Well?" says Jo. "He calls my number and reaches me here." Running a hand through her short, short hair, ruffling the random dark locks. "Are you forwarding my calls or something? And it was daybreak, what, an hour ago? Tops? And now it's almost noon?" Tugging the shirt again. "What *is* all this? Who are you people? And how the *fuck* do I keep this shirt on?"

"The ribbons," says Ysabel.

"Ribbons?"

"At the bottom. Wrap them around your waist and tie them off."

"Oh," says Jo. She reaches for the long ribbons trailing from the shirt's tails and ties them into a floppy bow over her left hip.

"How's that?" says Ysabel.

"I feel like a pirate." Jo looks down. Reaches up to touch the skin between the folds of the blousy shirt still hanging open. "A T-shirt would be nice." There just to the left of her breastbone. "Or a button, up here. Maybe a bra?"

"I've got it," says Ysabel, stepping into the closet. Coming out with a black vest, the front of it heavy with dense gold embroidery. "Put this on and button it up. You look fine."

Jo slips into the vest. "Your mother's a queen," she says. "And you're a princess."

"Yes," says Ysabel, adjusting the Jo's collar as Jo begins buttoning the vest.

"Of what?"

"The city," says Ysabel. "Well. This much of it, anyway."

Jo looks up into Ysabel's eyes. "So what is this? Some kind of family thing, some kind of old-country thing, like the Mafia? Or gypsies?"

Ysabel steps back. Folds her arms. "Who are you people?" she says, with a faintly mocking lilt. "What the fuck is going on? What is all this?"

"Pretty much," says Jo.

"It's *none of your concern*, Jo Maguire." Ysabel reaches out tuck a wayward black-dyed lock of Jo's hair behind one ear. Smiling she says, "Just go out there and say no and that will be that. Over and done. As if it had never been."

"Yeah," says Jo.

The music wherever it's coming from shimmers like falling water. Cascades of quiet fluting bells ring changes on a simple theme that's lost in all its mirroring roundelays. Jo stands to one side of the big back room, eyes closed, listening. Down two shallow steps on a soft white leather jetty of sectional sofa sits a wiry woman all in black with long black hair in glossy, artful tangles. A small black pillbox of a hat cocked at a jaunty angle. The Majordomo leans with some dignity over the back of the sofa to murmur in her ear as a big man straining the shoulders of a shiny blue suit waits patiently. By French doors opening on a small shaded garden stands Ysabel picking at the gauzy curtains. "You," says Roland, quietly, "are a disgrace."

Jo opens her eyes. Roland stands beside her, arms folded, his eyes on the Queen all in black. He wears a white shirt and a yellow tie and blue jeans and he looks down at Jo's gold vest, her blousy white shirt, looks up to meet her eyes. "In those colors," he says. "Do you know what it takes to wear those colors?" Jo says nothing. "To do what I do? To be what I am?" He does not raise his voice. "You must with shield and rod save yourself from nine spears cast at you all at once. Could you do that? You must shake off the hunt in a forest and come from among the branches unwounded, without a loosened strand of braided hair, and you must while running leap over a branch the height of yourself and stoop under one the height of your knee. You must be able to tune a poem by the rhymes and rhythms that make the worth of it." His smile is thin. "Can you do any of that?" he asks. "Mortal?"

"Comes now before you," says the Majordomo then, "Jo Maguire; and your knight, Sir Roland, the Chariot," and Jo pushes off the wall ahead of Roland, past the big man in his shiny blue suit, his face beaming, on his way up and out, down the shallow steps and around the white sofa to stand before the Queen. Jo frowns, looks over her shoulder to see Ysabel there by the French doors, her hands now clasped behind her back. "Miss Maguire?" says the Queen.

"I'm sorry, ma'am. Your majesty. I just – "

"The resemblance is remarkable," says the Queen, her head tilted just so towards the Majordomo's murmur. "Still. She *is* my daughter. What else would one expect? Thank you," she says to the straightening Majordomo. "I trust our Gammer Gerton has you fully recovered?"

"Ah," says Jo, "yes. Ma'am. Unless there's some side effect to that goop she used." Jo reaches up, touches the top button of her vest. Pinches it. Lowers her hand.

"Roland," says the Queen.

"Your majesty," says Roland, "I was intemperate – "

"You were a fool. Were it not for the prowess of your sword, we might grow tired of cleaning up your awkward messes."

"Ma'am," says Roland.

"Nonetheless, here we all are, and I have a lunch to attend. Miss Maguire. Through no fault of your own, you find yourself with the charge and office of our daughter's safety. This is yours to accept or reject." Wherever it is, the music trickles slowly to a halt, like a wound-down music box. "What say you?"

And Jo says, "Yes."

The Queen looks up to the Majordomo, whose Adam's apple bobs in a swallow behind the upturned gateposts of his collar. "You accept," she says, to Jo.

Jo looks at Roland, who stands unmoving, eyes closed. Ysabel behind her has covered her mouth with her hand. Jo takes a deep breath and looks the Queen directly in her dark, dark eyes. "I accept," says Jo.

The Queen sighs a short sharp sigh. "Very well." Roland shakes his head. Behind her upraised hand, Ysabel is smiling.

"WHAT WERE YOU THINKING?"

"WHAT WERE YOU THINKING?"

Ysabel stands on the sidewalk arms akimboed, angry eyes half-hidden by narrow black sunglasses worn against fitful, threatened afternoon sunlight. Jo still in those black boots, that floppy white shirt, the black-and-gold vest, comes down the steps from the porch of the old green house. "I don't know," she says, shifting a big black bag hung from one shoulder. "That you couldn't possibly fit all those shoes in this bag?"

"This is entirely *your* fault, Jo Maguire."

"I had no idea she would kick you *out,*" says Jo, dropping the heavy bag at Ysabel's feet.

"*Us* out," says Ysabel. "Us. You now have the keeping of me. You can't very well do that from halfway across town. And you can't stay here." She folds her arms, looking down the street. Mouth pinched. "So I go where you go," she says.

"Lucky me," snaps Jo.

"We told you how to get out of this, Jo." Ysabel turns to look at Jo over lowered sunglasses. *"You don't belong here.* We showed you the path out." She pushes the sunglasses back into place. "And you refused to take it. What were you thinking?"

"Maybe that I didn't want it all to go away," says Jo. "As if it never was."

"Lucky," says Ysabel, "me."

Jo jerks the heavy black bag up off the sidewalk and slings it from her shoulder. "It's going to rain," she says. She starts marching toward the corner. After a moment Ysabel starts after her. "Where are you going?" she says. "Jo?"

"Huh," says Jo, at the corner. Across the intersection is Robin's ramshackle house.

"Where are you going?" says Ysabel, catching up with her. The afternoon sunlight is changing, drowning in fits and starts. The trees down Everett Street begin to shiver their leaves.

"You go where I go, right? Well, I'm going to get you a hotel room. Get you situated, and we can maybe start trying to figure out a way to make this right."

"A hotel room," says Ysabel. "That's generous of you. With your ten-dollar T-shirts and your bummed cigarettes."

There's a break in the traffic. Jo doesn't start walking. "You," she says, "have money. Right? She said. Hopefully."

Ysabel says nothing.

"*Shit,*" says Jo. Then, "Your mother. She's got to come up with something for you – "

"Do you want to go back in there and ask her for it?"

The light one block up changes, and a wave of traffic starts down the street towards them. The first fat drops of rain are starting to fall.

"Her temper will pass," says Ysabel, looking back toward the old green house. "They'll come up with something. Have Roland challenge you, perhaps. And this time, you'll make sure you lose. Pass the office back to him."

"Great," says Jo. "Until then, you can sleep on my futon."

"What," says Ysabel, "I don't get the bed?"

Jo starts laughing.

Nevertheless, I venture to predict that the independent reader of these Prolegomena will not only doubt his previous science, but ultimately be fully persuaded, that it cannot exist unless the demands here stated on which its possibility depends, be satisfied; and, as this has never been done, that there is, as yet, no such thing as Metaphysics. But as it can never cease to be in demand,—since the interests of common sense are intimately interwoven with it, he must confess that a radical reform, or rather a new birth of the science after an original plan, are unavoidable, however men may struggle against it for a while.

—Immanuel Kant

NO. 2
FIDESSA

"July, July!" sings Jo in the shower. "It never seemed so strange, it never seemed so strange!"

Ysabel sitting in the open window lights a cigarette and takes a drag. Shaking out the match she blows the smoke outside. Stretches one long bare leg onto the skinny white faux balcony. She's wearing an oversized blue sweatshirt that says Brigadoon! She reaches up to pluck a crumb of tobacco from her lip.

"And the water rolls down the drain," sings Jo, opening the bathroom door. Her wet hair is plastered to her skull, black tufts smeared back against yellow fuzz. She's wrapped up in a Spongebob Squarepants towel. Jo plops herself on the foot of the futon and starts digging through a tangled nest of laundry. "Aha!" She yanks a pair of black tights free and holds them up. Sniffs them. Shrugs.

"You live in a pigsty," says Ysabel.

"What?" says Jo, standing up, tugging the tights up over her hips.

"You live," says Ysabel, "in a pigsty. You should have someone in here to clean it."

Jo looks up at Ysabel. Coughs up a single snort of laughter. "Yeah," she says. "I'll get right on that." She unwraps the towel and ducks her head into it, ruffling her hair.

It's a small studio apartment. There's a narrow kitchenette along the wall opposite the bathroom. The sink is filled with dirty dishes, empty Ramen wrappers, a half-empty ashtray, the remains of a case of Diet Coke. A petrified sprawl of old, dried spaghetti clings to the wall above the little electric range. Jo's futon takes up most of the open floorspace. In the corner by the window is a big black bag overflowing with shoes: high-heeled sandals with thin straps, high soft limp brown leather boots, spotless black and yellow and white athletic slip-ons. A small television set sits on a milk crate up above a welter of potato chip bags and more Diet Coke cans and a stray shoe or two.

Ysabel primly moues her mouth and looks out the window, at the green hills to the west, sweeping north. Past the scatter of highrises and apartment buildings, the great curve of the highway bridge looms over the river. The sky is high and white. It's going to be a hot and humid day.

"Damn," says Jo. She's pulled on a black T-shirt. There's a big red devil's face on it, sticking out his tongue. "I wish it would make up its mind and start with the rain already."

"It will," says Ysabel. "Soon enough." She leans back against the window frame, then looks up and over at Jo. "I'm hungry," she says.

"There's still some pizza left over."

Ysabel lets a mouthful of smoke leak out the window. "I don't want cold pizza," she says.

"So we can heat it – "

"I don't want *hot* pizza, either."

"Oh." Jo's digging around in the pile of laundry again, and comes up with a black denim miniskirt. "There's ramen," she says, wriggling into it.

"You know what I want, Jo."

"And I'm talking about what you can have."

"I *want*," says Ysabel, "to go to a restaurant. And have a proper meal."

"And I want a million bucks," says Jo, pulling on a couple of mismatched tube socks. "Isn't gonna happen anytime soon."

"You can't possibly expect me to survive on a diet of noodles and those," she shakes her head, "those *flavor* packets!"

"And Diet Coke," says Jo. "And cigarettes. And pizza."

"Jo," says Ysabel, grinding out her cigarette butt on the slat-ted floor of the faux balcony.

"I mean, you're perfectly free to go wherever you want." Jo fishes up one big black battered boot. "As far as a restaurant or whatever. Hell, *I'm* not stopping you."

"*Jo,*" snaps Ysabel, swinging around to stand up.

"What?" says Jo, and then, waving off Ysabel, "*Don't* tell me, I know, I know. I have the keeping of you."

"You do," says Ysabel, folding her arms across her chest.

"Like it was my idea," says Jo, sighing.

"It's not *my* choice, either," says Ysabel. "Nonetheless. I'm your responsibility. And I want to go to a restaurant and have a nice brunch."

Jo stands up, her leg canted a little, one boot on and one boot off. "We'll go to the Roxy," she says. "You can have an omelet."

Ysabel opens her mouth and then stops, frowning. She nods. "At least it gets us out of this – *apartment,*" she says.

"Whatever," says Jo, bending over to scoop up her other boot. "You might want to put on some pants first."

The man in the linen suit stands on the corner looking up at a big, blocky brick building. The cornerstone is marked with a Masonic compass and square. Signs advertising an Indian restaurant and a head shop hang over the front doors between green-capped white columns. The man in the linen suit ducks under a bouquet of tie-dyed shirts sales tags fluttering and steps into the hemp and bead and world crafts shop.

"Hey," says the kid behind the counter. "Can I help you?"

"Yes," says the man in the linen suit. He picks up a small statue, a whip-thin figure coiling into an improbable, prayerful pose. He smiles at it. His face is fleshy, and his rich red hair flops from a high widow's peak. He carries a long black artist's portfolio tube slung over his shoulder. "Tell his grace the Stirrup is here to see him."

The kid behind the counter picks up the phone and says something into it. The Stirrup looks up at a wall papered with overlapping Hindi religious posters. Ganesa looks down at him with soft dark eyes. If he's smiling, it's hidden behind his pink trunk.

"Go on up," says the kid behind the corner, hanging up the phone.

"Gaveston!" cries the young man who opens the door.

"Your grace," says the Stirrup.

"Come in, come in." His grace is barefoot. He's wearing pyjama pants and a floor-length dressing gown crowded with paisleys of purple and maroon and gold and brown. He leads Gaveston down a dark hall into a room filled with sunlight from tall, narrow windows. A low bed stretches across the middle of it. On the bed lies a woman, on her stomach. She has long blond hair and wears a pair of black lace shorts and has a pen in her teeth. She's frowning at the crossword puzzle in a newspaper.

"Please excuse the mess," his grace is saying. "I was just getting ready for the morning staff meeting."

"I had hoped," says the Stirrup, "that we might have a word in private?"

"Oh, don't mind Tommy," his grace says, sitting on the edge of the bed. He points to the squat man, wearing a black T-shirt and black jeans and standing to one side of the door. His long dark hair gleams in the light. "Tommy hears everything. That's his job."

Tommy grunts. The Stirrup looks at the woman on the bed, then looks back at his grace. Who winces sheepishly, and leans back next to her. Strokes the small of her back. Kisses her shoulder. "Darling?"

"What," she says, "is six letters long and means, the magic word? It starts with P."

"I have no idea," says his grace. "Maybe you could go look it up? Give us a minute, to talk business?"

Sighing, she rolls out of bed, scoops up her newspaper, and pads past Tommy down the dark hall.

"Well?" says his grace.

The Stirrup takes a deep breath. Shifts the weight of the port-folio tube hanging from his shoulder. "Your grace," he says. "If

you will allow, I shall see to it that – by this time tomorrow –
you will be a married man."

His grace frowns. Points at the doorway. "To *her?*" he says.

"Oh, no, your grace," says the Stirrup. "To the Bride."

"Oh," his grace says. He looks over at Tommy, who shrugs.
He looks up at the Stirrup. "Go on," he says. He smiles. "I'm
listening."

PORTLAND, DIVIDED INTO FOUR FIFTHS
BRAZILIAN BEER, THAI NOODLES – SHOOTING THE MOON

"PORTLAND," says Ysabel, spreading marmalade on her toast,
"is divided into four fifths."

"Four," says Jo. "Not five?"

"Four," says Ysabel. Leaning over her plate she takes a bite of
toast, careful of her sleeveless peach silk top. "There's Northwest, Southwest, Southeast, and Northeast." Her finger taps
four vague quarters on the purple tabletop between her plate
and Jo's coffee cup.

"What about North?"

"What about it?"

"It's a whole chunk of town," says Jo, leaning back. The
jukebox under the giant plaster crucifix on the back wall is
singing about how you're all grown up, and you don't care
anymore, and you hate all the people you used to adore. "Isn't
it one of the fifths?"

"There's no one there."

"There's nobody in North Portland."

"But few of any sort," says Ysabel, shaking pepper on her
omelet, "and none of name."

"Okay," says Jo. Stirring her coffee. "But it's still there. It's
still a part of Portland. It's still a fifth."

"If you wish to be finicky, you might also note that there's no
one technically 'in' downtown, either," says Ysabel, cutting a
neat triangle from the corner of her omelet. "Or Old Town. So

you might speak of six fifths. Or seven. But." She forks it up, chews, swallows. "I'm trying to keep things simple. For instance: the whole city is, technically, under my mother's sway."

"Because she's the Queen."

"Also, the Ban. Sometimes. But. Her power is concentrated in Northwest, and that fifth represents the practical limits of her demesne. There's too many mushrooms."

"What?" says Jo.

"In the omelet. There's too many mushrooms. And she *still* hasn't brought my soda. Her colors," says Ysabel, "my *mother's* colors," before Jo can ask her question, "are gold and white. Also, black and red. Sometimes. The rest of the fifths are parcelled out to those who owe her fealty." Ysabel takes another bite. Jo sips her coffee. "Southwest is the Count's, Count Pinabel. His colors are white, blue, and rose. He doesn't go over the hills much anymore, and most of downtown is open, unclaimed, so his is the smallest fifth, and the weakest power. The largest fifth belongs to Duke Barganax; he has the most knights enfeoffed – "

"Enfeefed?"

"Sworn to him." The waitress in a tight black T-shirt that says Merry Fucking Christmas sets a tall glass on the table next to Ysabel's plate. "Orgeat Italian soda with cream. Anything else?"

"Actually," says Ysabel, looking up, "this omelet – "

"Is fine," says Jo. "The check?"

"Sure," says the waitress.

Ysabel drops her fork clattering on the plate. Sits back. "I must," she says, *"constantly* remind myself that you know nothing of who I am and what your proper place is."

"Right," says Jo, leaning forward, her elbows on the table. "So you were saying? About this Duke, with the biggest fief?"

After a long moment Ysabel picks up her fork. "He has the most knights," she says. "Were it not for my mother, he would most likely have seized the Throne by now. His colors are red and brown, though sometimes he affects black and gold."

"Okay," says Jo. "So. Northeast."

Ysabel chews thoughtfully. "Some colors are rarely if ever seen," she says.

"And?"

"We almost never go to Northeast Portland."

"Yeah, but who's there? It's the fourth fifth. Who has it?"

Ysabel looks down and away, her heavy dark curls slipping from behind one shoulder to spill in front of her lowered face. She lifts them up and back with one hand. "The hair of her head hanging down to the ground," she says in a quiet voice. "Her eyes like stars, her hands of iron. The nails of her hands and feet like sickles. She changes herself to a dog, a cat, a fly, a spider, a raven, an evil-looking girl, and she enters the houses of the people and hurts the women and brings trouble upon the children. She brings changelings, and she has nineteen names."

"What the hell was that?" says Jo, after a moment.

"Northeast Portland," says Ysabel. "Black and grey and cold moon silver." She smiles brightly. "You might want to pay the woman, Jo."

The waitress is setting the check on the table. Jo digs through her black backpack and pulls out a folded wad of bills held by a medium-sized binder clip. Peering at the check, she peels off a five and four ones, then a fifth. "We should have just had the pizza," she mutters.

"Yes, but how much more pleasant was this?" says Ysabel. Polishing off her toast.

"And here I'd thought the deal was you go where *I* go," says Jo.

"Because *you* end up going where *I* want to go." Another bright smile. "See how easily it all works out?"

"Well," says Jo. "You damn well better want to go to work with me now."

"Indeed," says Ysabel. Sighing.

A boy in a brown bomber jacket sprints through the front doors of the former Masonic temple and takes the stairs to the second floor two at a time. His brown hair pops in a matted pompadour. He carries a brown paper bag. At the top he cuts around a humming bright Coke machine and comes up short before a white door hidden on the other side. He knocks a rollicking tattoo with one hand. There's a rustle behind the door and a deep voice booms, "Duncan will be one man."

"And Farquahr will be two, motherfucker," says the boy. "Open up."

The door opens with a burst of bright music and a bark of laughter that doesn't come from the man holding the door-knob. He's short and powerfully built. His eyes are big and wet. His long black hair gleams. The boy in the bomber jacket pushes past him and down the dark hallway into the bright room at its end. The music has a rolling bassline and a hard flat sliding pop, someone chanting I gotta pay respects to my posse from the West, and the laugh's from the young man in the gold silk shirt leaning back in the airy mesh-backed office chair. He wears a gold bracelet and monk's sandals. "Sweetloaf!" he cries. "What news on the Rialto?"

"I got your fucking beer," says the boy in the bomber jacket. "Your grace." The floor is covered in sunlight from two tall windows. He crosses it quickly brushing past the Stirrup in his linen suit to hand the brown paper bag to his grace, who sets aside a white takeout container with a couple of red chopsticks jutting out of it. He pulls a six-pack of dark bottles from the bag. Holds up a bottle for Sweetloaf, who shakes his head without looking away from the big flat television hanging on the wall. On the television two girls in school uniforms kiss in the rain.

"Brazilian beer," says his grace, flipping the bottle through the air to the Stirrup, who just manages to catch it. "Bhangra music. Russian videos." He works another bottle free and holds it out to the short man with the long lank hair. "Thai noodles on a whim." He works a third bottle loose and holds it up, his thumbnail under the lip of the cap. "Cell phones and cable modems. Japanese porn. German cars. Italian shirts." The cap pops loose spinning into the air. "The world keeps getting bet-ter, every day and in every way. And it all shows up on my doorstep with a phone call. So tell me," and he tosses back a swig, "why I should fuck it all for your dumbass idea."

"Because it will bring you the one thing you do not have, your grace," says the Stirrup.

"The Bride," says his grace.

"The Bride," says the Stirrup. "She and the Queen have had a falling out. This is indisputable. The *only* person watching the Bride these past few days has been the girl."

"*Mortal* girl," says the short man with the long lank hair.

"Who can't fight," says the Stirrup. "And I do not think your own knights will have cause to strike one another?" His swigs some beer. "The Bride left the Queen's demesne Sunday afternoon, your grace. Since then she's crossed neither river nor highway. You won't step on anyone's toes."

"So how does this work?" says his grace. "I walk up to her, hey, baby, how you doing, you wanna come back to my hideout?" He leans forward in the chair his elbows on his knees. "I don't think so."

"Let us presume," says the figure leaning there, in the shadows between the light that spills from the two tall windows. He has a long thin nose and the edges of his face are sharp. His eyes are pale blue and his long black hair is gathered in a single thick braid. He wears a blue and black sarong and a loose white shirt half-unbuttoned. "Perhaps the Bride is threatened? A gang of ruffians, shall we say, sets upon her as they leave this building tonight. A not uncommon threat, in any area of this city not held tightly by a strong lord." He inclines his narrow head toward his grace. His voice is highly pitched, rich and gentle and smooth. "Luckily, some knights happen to be passing by. They quickly put paid to these ruffians, but a problem presents itself: her current guardian obviously cannot keep the Bride safe. Whatever is a responsible knight to do?"

"Of course," says his grace. "So you think it's worth the risk."

"Risk?" The man in the blue and black sarong spreads his hands in a magnanimous shrug and smiles. "Who could fault you for taking her under your protection?"

"How about you, Tommy?" says his grace.

"I mislike it, m'lord," says the short man with the long lank hair with his deep, growling voice.

"I *pay* you to mislike it."

"It's too neat, m'lord. Too easy. Her majesty is no fool."

"True enough," says his grace, and then for a moment no one says anything. The stereo pops with tablas and rumbles with bass. Then he stands. "Sweetloaf," he says, "crack some petty cash and roust us some hounds. The usual places: under bridges, shelters. Enough to make Orlando's gang of ruffians."

"Fuckin' A," says Sweetloaf.

"M'lord, you shouldn't," says Tommy.

"They've already got a mortal on the field," says his grace. "Won't change the balance. Gaveston."

"Your grace," says the Stirrup.

"You work with Orlando here, and take Tommy with you. Just make *damn* sure the hounds don't fuck this up. They are *not* to touch her. Got it?" He claps his hands together. "Make me proud, boys. Tonight you're going to bag me a Bride."

"Actually, Jo," says Becker from his desk at the front of the phone room, "can I talk to you for a minute?"

"Sure," says Jo, her hand on the back of her chair.

"Let's use Tartt's office," says Becker.

Tartt's office is the same indecisive cream as the phone room. It's just big enough for a desk and a couple of chairs. Tacked to the bulletin board above the desk along with Post-it notes and phone messages is a big blue card that says Of course I don't look busy, I did it right the first time. Becker in his big plaid flannel shirt half-sits on the edge of a desk piled high with stacks of paper. Jo folds her arms and leans back against the closed door. The poster over her shoulder is a big picture of the full moon and says Shoot for the moon... Even if you miss, you'll land among the stars.

"It's not that I have a problem," says Becker.

"So why are we here?"

"Jo, is she going to be hanging out here every night?"

"Who, Ysabel?" Jo is looking directly at Becker, who's looking down at one of the piles of paper on Tartt's desk. "I told you. She has evil ex-boyfriend issues. She just doesn't feel safe by herself right now."

"Doesn't she have someplace else she could go and, uh, not be by herself?"

"It's just until we get stuff sorted. What's the deal, Becker? I mean, it's not like you have a problem with it or anything."

Becker looks up. Nets his fingers together in his lap. "She's a distraction."

"She stays in the kitchen reading a goddamn book!"

"People ask questions. Tartt is asking questions."

"So that's Tartt's problem."

"Jo – "

"Dammit, Becker, you said it would be okay!"

"I said it was okay on Monday. It's Wednesday. Jo, it's great you want to help her and all, but – "

"Shut up, Becker, okay? Just don't."

"Jo." Becker looks down at his hands. Up again. "I know it's only been a couple of days, but *try* to remember that I'm your boss now?"

"I'm sorry," snaps Jo, "was I not respectful enough?"

"Jo, dammit, just – "

"Sorry," says Jo. Looking down. "Sorry."

Becker takes a deep breath and blows it out in a sigh.

"If you're kicking her out tonight I have to go with her," says Jo, still looking down and away. "I don't have anything set up to take care of her tonight."

"Yeah, well, your numbers, it might not be such a bad thing."

Jo looks up, startled. "I got you five completes per hour last night – "

"Four point eight. And five's the expected. Some people, Guthrie, Lee, are hitting sixes and sevens. You're slipping, Jo."

"So I'm slipping – "

"She can stay here tonight," says Becker, standing up from his lean on Tartt's desk. "But tomorrow I want her gone and you here. A hundred percent." Jo's still leaning back against the door, her hands at her sides. "Jo," says Becker, "I have a job to do. Just like you. Okay?" Jo doesn't say anything. She doesn't nod. "I mean, it's great you want to help a friend and all. But," says Becker, and he lets it trail off.

"But what?" says Jo.

"Are you guys," says Becker, "I mean, is everything going to be okay?"

"It'll be fine, Becker," says Jo, opening the door. Not looking at him. "It'll be just fine."

Light from Fluorescent Ceiling Panels
A Dusty Hollow – Going Home – What is so Dangerous

Light from the fluorescent ceiling panels careens about the white kitchen. At the small table under a darkening window sits Ysabel in a white plastic chair. Tortoiseshell sunglasses, a can of Diet Coke, and a small plastic baggie lie next to the small thick book she isn't reading. Her eyes are closed. One corner of the baggie holds a pinch of something golden.

A thin man whose dark-nailed hands glitter with silver rings pushes open the door, letting in the mutter of an active phone room. She doesn't look up. His black T-shirt says Elegant Casualty. He yanks open the refrigerator, takes in a deep breath, blows it out half-heartedly. "You smoke?" he says.

"Who," she says, looking up at him. "Me?"

"Do you?" he says, closing the refrigerator. "Because the idea of warmed-over tempeh goulash is *not* revving my motor."

"Sometimes," says Ysabel. "Did you want a cigarette?"

"No," he says, looking down at his hands, over at the coffeemaker. "*I* don't smoke. I just thought you'd maybe like to have something to do. When we go outside to talk."

Ysabel looks at the closed door leading to the phone room. Uncrosses her legs. She's wearing tight blue jeans that flare at the ankles. "We're going outside," she says.

"Yeah," he says.

"What are we going to talk about?"

"How's Jo?" he asks. He brushes something from his black jeans.

"Jo's, ah," says Ysabel. She sits up a little, uncrossing her legs. "Jo's fine." She looks at the door to the phone room. "Is something wrong?"

He's looking over at the employee posters spelling out overtime rules, state-mandated lunch breaks, a busy spot of color on the blank wall. "It's all working out for you? Crashing at her place?"

"Her apartment is much too small. And it's wretched." Ysabel's smile is small and wry. "I take it we're *not* going outside?"

But he's brushing at his jeans again. "How's your boyfriend?"

"What?"

"Your boyfriend," he says, looking down at her book, at the little baggie beside it. "That's what Jo said. You're staying with her because your boyfriend is a mean sonofabitch."

"Then I'd say," says Ysabel, sitting back in her chair, "he's still mean." She crosses one leg over the other again. She's wearing leather thong sandals. Her toenails are painted gold. "You're Guthrie, aren't you?"

"Yeah," he says, his head canted to one side, still peering at her book. "What's that you're reading?"

Ysabel pulls the book into her lap and flips through to a page toward the beginning. "She turning back with ruefull countenance," she reads, "cride, Mercy mercy Sir vouchsafe to show on silly Dame, subiect to hard mischaunce, and to your mighty will. Her humblesse low in so ritch weedes and seeming glorious show, did much emmoue his stout heroïcke heart, and said, Deare dame, your suddein ouerthrow much rueth me." She closes her book and smiles at Guthrie, who's frowning at a corner of the table. "Spenser," she says.

"And see," says Guthrie, "that's the thing. That seeming glorious show. That was some party Saturday night."

"Yes," says Ysabel. "It was."

"Do you," says Guthrie, taking a deep breath, looking up at the bright ceiling, "have them often?"

"When we," Ysabel starts to say.

"Because," says Guthrie, looking down, looking at her, squinting a little, "I think I remember more than you think."

Ysabel's face is still for a moment. Then she says, "I don't know what you're on about. But if you're trying to secure an invitation to the next one – "

"I don't want an invitation to the next one," says Guthrie.

"What *do* you want?" asks Ysabel.

Guthrie reaches up and runs a hand through his thin hair. Bites his lip. Topples forward suddenly, hingeing at the waist, looming over Ysabel, catching himself on the back of her chair, the edge of the table. "I want to make sure," he says, in her ear. "That you get it. Jo's not alone in this. Okay? Whatever it is."

There's another burst of phone-room chatter as the door's pushed open. A blond girl with a coffee cup squeezes past Guthrie, headed for the coffeemaker. Guthrie straightens. "I should get back to the phones," he mumbles, reaching for the door.

"Guthrie," says Ysabel.

He stops, halfway through the open door.

"I do appreciate everything she's doing for me," she says.

"Good," he says, with a little shrug. The door swings shut behind him.

"Do you have any idea where the creamer's got to?" says the blond girl.

From the sidewalk the ground slopes steeply to an old cyclone fence. Beyond that a retaining wall drops twenty feet to the four-lane highway full of sixty-mile-an-hour traffic. Sweetloaf in his brown bomber jacket picks his way past a neatly trimmed shrub toward a dusty hollow tramped down in the weeds where the fence meets the concrete buttress of the bridge over the highway. On a flattened cardboard box squats a man wearing a grimy check sports jacket and a brown wispy beard. Next to him a filthy girl, grease smeared on her cheeks, her blackened hands wrapped in rags. An old mohawk sprawls across her stubbled scalp. The man standing by the bridge holds an empty bottle like a club. The others stare at Sweetloaf stepping carefully in his moccasin boots. The man by the fence doesn't look up from the traffic.

"Got a proposition," says Sweetloaf, his hands held out and away. "Fuckin' simplicity itself."

"Everything goes by the co," says the bearded man in a rusty monotone. "You know that."

"Of course I know that," says Sweetloaf, smiling. "And your co said whatever, fuck it. Run it by the jefes, do it fucking ad hoc, he doesn't give a fuck. So now I'm running it past the jefes. So." He hunkers down next to the bearded man. "Jefe. You want to make some fucking money?"

"Sure," says the bearded man. There's a long roll of industrial felt, grey, flecked with dark colors, wadded up against the concrete buttress. Twitching. It rolls over. There's a wild-eyed face poking out near one end. "Shut up shut up shut up," it says.

"These two girls," says Sweetloaf. "One of them has blond hair with these little fucking black bits in it. Can't miss her. She's wearing a black T-shirt with a devil on it and combat boots. They're going to come out of that building – " he leans back and points up at a modest skyscraper looming over them – "at a little after nine o'clock. That gives you a couple of hours."

The roll of industrial felt sits up and whoever's inside it wriggles half out of it, a torso and a couple of arms in a puffy, dirty, pink ski jack, that face tucked in under its hood. "Shut up I'm trying to sleep goddammit." Sweetloaf looks over at it and back at the bearded man. "Yours?"

"No," says the bearded man.

"Okay," says Sweetloaf. He looks at the girl with the mohawk, who's still staring at him. "You getting all this?" Sweetloaf snaps at her.

"The other one," says the girl with the mohawk.

"Yeah," says the man by the fence, who's more of a boy. His cheekbones hunch like shoulders under his squinting eyes. "The other girl."

"You said there was another girl," says the girl with the mohawk.

"I did," says Sweetloaf, looking down at the dust. "Shut up shut up shut up," says whoever's in the pink ski jacket. "You might be familiar with her," says Sweetloaf.

"Yeah?" says the girl with the mohawk.

"The Bride," says Sweetloaf.

"Fuck that," says the boy, pushing off the fence. "Fuck it. No way the CO signed off on this shit."

"You're just fucking hounds on this," says Sweetloaf, jerking to his feet. "You scare them. That's it." The boy isn't looking at him. "You don't get your hands dirty because you don't even fucking *think* of touching them. Just put on a show so his grace's men can rescue them. And *only* his grace's men. Nobody else. You have my word."

"Shyeah," says the boy.

"Shut up shut up!" shrieks whoever's in the pink ski jacket. It might be a woman, standing up, kicking loose from the heavy felt. "No peace no goddamn peace! Fucking niggers! Fucking goddamn slope niggers sand niggers spic niggers slit niggers fucking goddamn trying to fucking sleep!" The bearded man doesn't look away from Sweetloaf. The girl with the mohawk is looking up at the building. The boy is looking back out over the highway with his arms folded.

"None of your Queen's men?" says the bearded man.

"Fucking goddamn pixie niggers!" she yells, kicking the felt.

Sweetloaf grabs the woman pinning her back against the concrete with one hand. "Boo!" She flinches. "You know what I just did?" says Sweetloaf. "You know what the fuck I just did to you?" She's looking down, holding up a hand as a shield. "I just took a fucking year of your life, that's what I did!" he yells. "I took a filthy fucking year of your worthless miserable life!" She's panting, shallow, whooping breaths of air. "You want to try for more? You want to say it again?"

She says nothing. Coughs.

"Well?" snarls Sweetloaf.

Her hand still up as a shield.

"*None* of your Queen's men?" says the bearded man. "We're not getting caught in the middle of another skirmish."

Sweetloaf lets go, steps back. "No," he says. The woman in the pink ski jacket slumps down to sit with her back against the concrete. "You have my fucking word."

"And?" says the girl with the mohawk.

"Twenty dollars." Turning, Sweetloaf fishes three crisp new bills from his shirt pocket. "Each."

The bearded man smiles. "You have your hounds."

The door to the phone room swings open. Jo ducks her head around. "You ready?"

Ysabel looks up from her book.

"Let's go," says Jo.

"Where to now?"

"Home," says Jo. And as Ysabel opens her mouth to respond, "Don't even," says Jo.

"Just for a drink," says Ysabel. "One song."

"You can go wherever you want," says Jo. *"I'm* going home." She ducks back into the phone room. Ysabel slaps her book shut and stands.

In the hall, Jo punches the down button for the elevator. "It doesn't have to be a bar," says Ysabel. "Or a club." Jo doesn't say anything. "It," says Ysabel, "we could go – "

"Where?" says Jo.

"I don't know."

"Where, Ysabel? Where's the free drinks? With no cover? Huh?"

Ysabel looks back at Jo. "We don't," she starts to say.

"You blew the last of our cash on lunch." Jo kicks the elevator doors. "Slowest goddamn elevator in town, I swear."

"Second-slowest," says Ysabel.

The elevator dings. The doors jerk open. As Jo steps on, Guthrie and a short, older woman come out of the office down the hall. "Hey," says Guthrie, "could you hold..?"

"Oops," says Ysabel, pressing the close door button. The doors close. The elevator judders into motion.

"What did you," Jo starts to say.

"Is he," says Ysabel, "a friend of yours?"

"What does that have to do with – "

"Does he talk to you? Did you talk? Tonight?"

Jo leans back. Dozens of dim Jo reflections lean back with her in the tarnished mirrors lining the elevator. "We're on the phone all the time," she says. "We don't exactly hang out and chat."

"You're tired, aren't you," says Ysabel. "You don't actually do any *work* at this job, but – "

"People telling you to fuck off gets a little draining after a while," says Jo.

"So just," says Ysabel, lifting a finger, *"one* drink – "

"We can't!" snaps Jo. "Christ. Just take off by yourself." She's looking Ysabel up and down, her hip-hugging jeans, her peach tank top. "You wouldn't have to pay for a goddamn thing." The elevator grinds to a halt.

"If I go anywhere," says Ysabel quietly as the doors jerk open, "you have to go with me. You *know* that."

"Well," says Jo, stepping out, "I'm going home. There's your options."

"It's your *duty,*" snaps Ysabel, following her.

"Fuck that," says Jo, storming across the brightly lit lobby.

"You said yes!" calls Ysabel, click-clacking after her. "You *agreed!*"

"Wish to hell I hadn't," says Jo, rearing back, aiming a big black boot at the crashbar of the glass outer door, kicking it open. Outside, sunset smolders behind the western hills. The sky is a deep blue shading into indigos and blacks in the east, where only a few of the brightest stars can be seen. There is still more light in the air than what's put out by the streetlights and the bright hotel sign on the corner. Jo catches the closing door and holds it open for Ysabel. "Look," says Jo, who takes a deep breath, and then in a rush says "You can't come here tomorrow."

"What," says Ysabel flatly, stopping there in the doorway.

"You can't come here tomorrow," says Jo, looking down. "Becker said." She's still holding the door open for Ysabel. "You have to stay at my place."

"And you," says Ysabel, still standing in the doorway.

"Will go to work. Just like today."

Ysabel takes a deep breath. The street is empty. The only real sound is the susurrus of traffic on the highway two blocks away, hidden in its great gully. "You still don't understand," she says.

"*You* don't understand," snaps Jo. "I don't know what it was like, hanging out with Roland. Maybe he had some magic credit card, I don't know. I don't have that. Okay? We don't get to do that. I have a job. I *have* to have a job. And my boss is giving me shit because of you and I am *not* going to get fired."

"None of that matters," mutters Ysabel. She starts walking down the street, away from the highway behind them.

"So you can stay home tomorrow," Jo says as she lets the door close. She heads after Ysabel. "Or go wherever the fuck you want. I officially do not care."

"None of that *matters,*" says Ysabel. Jo leans out, catches her arm. Jerks her to a halt. "The fuck?" she says, as Ysabel's saying, "I am your *responsibility.* You have the keeping of me." Her eyes are wide, her mouth in a frown. She's trying not to breathe heavily. "You can't just leave me in that *pigsty.* Alone. You must keep me safe. No matter what."

Jo blinks. "Can you stop with the pigsty cracks?" she says.

"Dammit, Jo!" Ysabel jerks free. There's a weirdly distorted, glassy clink, somewhere away behind Jo.

"What?" says Jo. "What am I keeping you safe from?" There's a clank, and another.

"Jo," says Ysabel.

"What is so dangerous?" Another clink. "That you need a freaking bodyguard, twenty-four seven." Clonk.

Ysabel points. Jo turns.

Down the street from the bridge over the highway come four people: a girl with a limp mohawk, her hands wrapped in rags. A man in grimy grey and black camouflage, his shoes a pair of disintegrating Nikes. A tall boy in tight black jeans. A boy in an old grey sweatshirt, his face twisted in a scowl. He's got three empty glass bottles in his right hand, his fingers and his thumb jammed in their necks, and he lifts them and clinks them together, and again. "Chickie chickies," he says. "Boo," says the tall boy. They're a block away and spreading out, into the street, and the girl with the mohawk is holding her hands wide, grinning. "Chickie chickie," says the boy with the bottles. Clink. Clonk.

"We'd better," Ysabel starts to say, as Jo, frowning, takes a step towards them. "Christian?" says Jo.

"We'd better *go*," says Ysabel.

"Aw, shit," says the boy, dropping the hand that holds the bottles. The girl with the mohawk says "Come on!"

"Christian?" says Jo again. "What's going on?"

"Shit," says the boy. "The fuck *you* doing here, Jo?"

"CHICKIE *CHICKIE?*" – SCATTERING THE HOUNDS
UNEXPECTED VIOLENCE – SANCTUARY

"CHICKIE *CHICKIE?*" says Jo, laughing.

"Shut up," mutters Christian, tugging a bottle off his thumb. He tosses it up the sidewalk, spinning sideways. It smashes against the doorstop of a diner. "Would have worked. Would have scared the fuck out of you, you didn't know me."

"Christian, man," says the girl with the mohawk, digging her toe into the groove of a trolley track.

"Shut up, Mel," says Christian.

"You *know* these people?" says Ysabel. She's looking up toward the bridge over the highway, back down the street toward the unseen river.

"I know Chris," says Jo.

"*Christian*," he says, throwing the last bottle down the street to pop against the curb.

"Jo," says Ysabel.

"How long's it been?" says Jo. "Almost a year?"

"What are we doing here? Huh?" says the tall boy in tight black jeans.

"More than a year," says Christian. "Not since the trip to Sauvie's Island. Last August. How you been?"

"About," Jo starts to say.

"Come *on*, Christian," says the girl with the mohawk.

"Shut *up*, Mel," he says.

"About the same," Jo's saying. "Still working. Christian? What the *hell* are you doing?"

"Scaring you," says Christian. "Boo!"

"This ain't right," says the man in grey and black camo. "I ain't letting your friend put me wrong with the neighbors."

"Yeah," says the tall boy. He chops the air with one hand.

"*Fuck* that," snarls Christian. "The neighbors want to go at each other, trust me. Twenty bucks ain't enough to stand in the middle of that."

"Twenty?" says the tall boy.

"We said we'd do something," says the man in camo. "We got to make that right."

"Jo," says Ysabel, tugging at her arm. "We really – "

"Boo!" yells Christian, throwing his arms wide. Ysabel flinches. "We said we'd scare them," says Christian to the man in camo. "We tried. We failed. Fuck it."

"*I* didn't get twenty," says the tall boy.

"Jo," says Ysabel, grabbing Jo's arm. Tugging her back up the street toward the bridge over the highway. "We really should go."

"But," says Jo.

"*Now,*" says Ysabel.

"The apartment," Jo starts to say, pulling back against Ysabel.

"We're not going back there," says Ysabel. "Over the bridge. We're going back to my mother's house."

"Ysabel?" says Jo. Frowning. Taking another step after her up toward the bridge. "These guys, they don't – "

"These guys aren't the only ones *here,*" says Ysabel.

"Hounds!"

The word bells out around them in a loud clear voice. The man in camo throws up his hands. The tall boy yelps and runs away down the street. "Shit!" says the girl with the mohawk. Ysabel turns. On the bridge over the highway stands a slim figure in the shadows between the pinkish orange streetlights. Dressed in a blue black skirt, a white shirt, holding to one side a Japanese sword pointed lazily at the street.

"Too late," says Ysabel. "Too late."

"Run, hounds!" cries the figure. Walking toward them, slowly, raising the sword. "Flee! And pray we do not find you when our business here is done!"

"Fuck you!" yells Christian, stumbling after the man in camo.

"He's got a sword," says Jo.

"I see that," says Ysabel.

"He's got a fucking *sword.*"

"I *see* that. Jo." Ysabel tugs on Jo's arm.

"Right," says Jo. They're back away together, turning, walking quickly, breaking into a jog, Jo's boots thumping, Ysabel's sandals flip-flapping. Ysabel pulls them out across the street toward the corner under the big Danmoore Hotel neon sign. "If we get across Burnside," Ysabel's saying.

"Hold, my lady!"

This voice is deeper, though not so loud. In the middle of the street before them as they turn the corner is a man in a pale linen suit. A long black portfolio tube is slung from one shoulder. "There is no need to run," he says. "We will keep you safe." Three blocks behind him, traffic rolls quietly up and down the cross street.

"I was in no danger," says Ysabel. There under the buzzing hotel sign she takes Jo's hand. "I have my guardian. Go now, with my thanks." Jo's looking back and forth, up Morrison, along 12th, the man in the linen suit before them, the figure in the blue-black skirt still stalking towards them, the sword now held in both hands. *"Ysabel,"* she hisses.

"It would seem your guardian, my lady, is not up to the task," says the man in the linen suit. He unshoulders his portfolio tube and rests the butt end on the pavement. "There's no telling what else might beset you."

"Like you, perhaps?" says Ysabel, loudly. "You think you will lay hands on your Princess? Call off the Mooncalfe, Stirrup." The figure in the blue-black skirt has made it to the sidewalk on their side of the street. He crouches and takes long slow steps so that his head and shoulders and arms and sword remain smooth and steady. His feet are bare.

"Where the hell *is* everybody?" says Jo.

"My lady," the man in the linen suit is saying, "it need not come to that – "

"Call him *off*, Gaveston!" snaps Ysabel.

The Stirrup flinches. "Hold a moment, Orlando." He lifts his chin, scowling, so that he can loosen his red tie. "You're frightening our Princess." He unbuttons the top button of his shirt, then blots his brow with his forearm. The Mooncalfe glides to a stop, still in his crouch, his sword angling to point directly at them. A couple of blocks away, unseen, a trolley hoots.

"*They're* here," Ysabel murmurs to Jo.

"What?" says Jo.

"They're here. So we aren't exactly *there*, anymore."

Jo frowns. "I, um," she says.

"All we ask is that you come with us a moment, my lady." The Stirrup unzips the top of his portfolio. "Our master would have words with you."

"Do you have any ideas?" says Ysabel quietly to Jo. "At all?"

Jo, looking at the Stirrup, at the Mooncalfe, at the two empty streets, shrugs. "Scream," she says, out of the corner of her mouth.

"Scream?" says Ysabel.

"Hope it rattles them? Gives us a head start?" She glares at Ysabel. "Jesus. *I* don't know."

"Well?" says the Stirrup. "My lady?"

Ysabel squeezes Jo's hand. "What if," she says, and she swallows, "I didn't *want* to have words with your master?"

"I would be sorry to hear that, lady," says the Stirrup. He leans against the portfolio. "Truly sorry."

"In that case," says Ysabel, and she screams.

"Oh, fuck," says Jo, turning and starting to run, dragging Ysabel after her. The Stirrup flips back the unzipped top of the portfolio and frees the pommel and hilt of a sword. There's a scrape of metal as he draws it. The portfolio and the scabbard hidden inside drop with a clatter. "Orlando!" he bellows. "Tommy!"

Along 12th, crossing Morrison, Jo's boots clomping, Ysabel gasping, hand in hand. The Mooncalfe leans into a run at them, his feet slapping, but they're past him, across the street, hitting the sidewalk, running past the long blank wall of windows, posters advertising gold bank cards and low mortgage rates. He curls into their wake. The Stirrup huffing and puffing follows after. Barreling around the corner ahead of them a short thick man with long hair roaring, long arms spread to catch them up in a crushing hug, his face broken by a hideous snarling grin. *"Gotcha!"* He howls, throwing his hands into the air. Ysabel lets go of Jo's hand and staggering with her momentum turns head jerking to look behind at the Mooncalfe half a block away bowed low at a dead run sword swept up and back, at the Stirrup behind him, his sword like a baseball bat up over his head. Ysabel calls, "Jo, we – "

But Jo put her head down when Ysabel let go of her hand and arms pumping boots stomping ran straight at the short thick man with the eyes suddenly going wide as he tries to sidestep. Jo's shoulder her arm up slams into his chest sending the air whoofing out of him and he takes a stumbling step backwards and then another, those long arms waving for balance as Jo headlong running loses her footing and tumbles to the ground rolling. The short thick man sits down heavily, gasping. Retches up a cough. Jo sits up hands scraped tights ruined ripped around one bloody knee. Ysabel hands up over her mouth her eyes wide stands still in the middle of the sidewalk. The Mooncalfe stands upright waiting his sword held out away from his body, head cocked, alert. The Stirrup slowing lets his arms relax, his sword point drop. Tony leans back on one elbow, holding his chest, noisily sucking air.

"Ysabel!" says Jo, reaching out.

And Ysabel takes a step and then another, past Tony, faster, as Jo kicks herself to her feet catching Ysabel's hand. They're running. They're at the end of the block. They're pelting across the next street. The Mooncalfe patters after them, crouching low again, his sword up and back again, past Tony without looking back. The Stirrup, his sword on his shoulder, jogs up to Tony. Bends over. Slaps his shoulder, chuckling. "You okay?"

"Bitch," says Tony, gasping. "Bitch knocked the breath. Out of me."

"Well," says the Stirrup. "You're getting it back. Come on!"

Tony glares. The Stirrup helps him to his feet.

"The parking lot!" says Jo, pointing, and halfway across the street she jags left tugging Ysabel after her. Past a shuttered Indian food cart the parking attendant's booth is lit up, empty, a small chunk of bright indoor light trapped behind glass. They run past the far side of it. Jo winces as she slows, peering down the long dark rows of cars anonymous in the dim pink and orange streetlights. "Damn," she says. They have just come through the only entrance to the lot, which stays level as the street rises past it. Its far end is a wall chest-high with a railing above it. Behind them the rapid fluttering shuffle of the Mooncalfe's feet, the loudly hollow tocking of the Stirrup's shoes. Tony, growling, huffing and puffing behind them.

The Mooncalfe stops suddenly beside the empty attendant's booth, struck by the spill of white fluorescent light. He closes his eyes and the city around him grows quiet. The rolling surf of tires on pavement fades. No horns honk. No alarms shrill. No puling compact engines accelerating away from stop lights, no deep-throated rumbles of idling trucks, the brakes of the busses blocks away don't hiss and sigh as they stop. No one shouts. No music leaks from open windows. The white noise of rooftop ventilation fans washes away, and the wind doesn't toss the leaves of the trees before the church across the street. His sword dips and points slowly toward one aisle of parked cars. He takes a deep breath, and turns, slowly, pointing now toward the next aisle of cars.

"Well?" says the Stirrup, standing behind him.

Sighing, the Mooncalfe lifts his sword. "Be quiet," he says.

"We should," Tony starts to say.

"Be *quiet,*" says the Mooncalfe.

"It fell apart," says Tony. "We should cut and run."

"It has gotten a little out of hand," says the Stirrup.

"We told the Duke we'd deliver a Bride," says the Mooncalfe. "We will do just that." He closes his eyes again, and levels his sword. "Now shut. Up."

Tony glares at the Stirrup, who shrugs. He holds his sword lightly in one hand, resting on his shoulder, where the blade rumples the collar of his jacket. There's a scrape of gravel as someone deep within the parking lot shifts weight, and the Mooncalfe leaps suddenly onto the hood of the hatchback parked in front of them, his blade sweeping back, his bare feet slapping as he takes two steps and then over to the sedan and then to the Jeep, from hood to roof and hood again. Aggrieved car alarms whoop to life. A third of the way from the far end of the lot Jo's running out from behind a minivan, Ysabel ahead of her. "Go!" yells Jo, looking back over her shoulder at the Mooncalfe leaping lightly toward them, the cars left rocking and wailing in his wake.

The wall at the end is too high. Ysabel jumps up her blue-jeaned legs kicking to grab the railing, but she can't pull herself up and she loses her grip and falls back to her feet. She's calling out to Jo shaking her head as Jo runs up to her and hoists herself with both hands onto the back of a parked pickup truck and from there bounces once and catches the railing of the sidewalk above. She kicks the wall with her boots as she worms her way under the lowest rail.

"The church," Ysabel says, gasping.

"Come on!" says Jo, still on her belly, reaching back under the railing for Ysabel's hand. Ysabel shakes her head, saying somewhere under the yowling alarms, "I'm just in the way. Go on. Get out," as Jo's yelling over that "Come on, goddammit! Get up here!" Jo catches Ysabel's hand. "Step up on the bumper!" The Mooncalfe leaps from the curved roof of an Audi to delicately step along the top of a convertible's windshield once, twice, and from there up to the roof of the minivan. Ysabel's wincing her feet kicking as the bare skin between her sleeveless silk top and her hip-hugging jeans scrapes against the top of the wall. Jo squirms around and plants a boot against the railing pulling. Rolling over on her back Ysabel hunches over the edge of the wall and Jo pulls her through onto the sidewalk. A leather thong sandal kicked loose falls from Ysabel's foot as the Mooncalfe's blade strikes sparks from the concrete behind them.

"The church!" Ysabel says again, pointing.

Across the street is the bulk of an old stone church. The side door is tucked into a neat little porch blocked off by a metal gate.

Jo helps Ysabel to her feet. Tony's rounding the corner coming at them at a run. The Stirrup's pounding down the aisle of parked cars headed for the wall. The Mooncalfe steps lightly from the roof of the pickup truck. On the ground he takes four quick steps back away from the wall as leaning on each other Jo and Ysabel limp quickly across the street to the steps of the church. As Tony slows to a walk looking up and down the empty street, as the Stirrup runs up behind him, as Jo grabs the bars of the side-door gate, rattling the sign that says No Loitering Church Business Only Police Enforced, the Mooncalfe squats.

Then he jumps.

Jo turns in time to see him floating in the air, arms holding his sword up above his head, his blue-black skirt flapping, his half-opened white shirt billowing as one foot brushes the top of the metal railing. He lands crouching at the edge of the street.

"Don't let go of the gate," says Ysabel. Who has not climbed the steps after Jo. Who stands at their bottom, hugging herself tightly. "Leave her alone!" she cries.

"Ysabel?" says Jo.

"Leave her out of this," says Ysabel. "If you let her go unharmed, I will go with you wherever you wish."

"My lady," says the Stirrup, still in the parking lot. "We have no intention of harming either of you." He drops his sword ringing on top of the wall and pulls himself laboriously up after it.

"I want your word," says Ysabel. "As knights. As *gentry.*" The Mooncalfe putting a foot forward stops at that, and does not take his step.

"Ysabel!" says Jo.

"Don't," says Ysabel, turning to look up at Jo. There at the top of the stairs, holding onto the gate, one knee an angry red behind the sagging tatters of her ripped tights, her black T-shirt leering its red devil's grin. "Don't let go of the gate," says Ysabel, quietly.

"My lady," says the Stirrup. Bowing his head. "As gentry, we cannot but honor your request." He holds out his hand.

"*Halt!*" someone cries, and they all turn.

A man in a green track suit with silver stripes is running up the street. His yellow jagged sunglasses shine weirdly in the dim light, and in one hand he holds a long sword with a heavy golden pommel.

"Roland," says Ysabel, and she closes her eyes and sags in on herself. She smiles, just a little, as she takes a deep breath.

"The Chariot!" yells the Stirrup, and he scrambles for his sword.

"Oh, *shit,*" says Jo.

THE MUSIC'S LOUD – AS GENTLEMEN SETTLE
THE SECOND THRUST
THE NIGHTTIME CITY, FILLED WITH LIGHT

THE MUSIC'S LOUD. Jo in her leering devil T-shirt slumps in the dark red booth, laying her head back against the pillowy vinyl. Ysabel slides in next to her, her heavy black hair swinging as she leans over the table. Roland leans his sword against the table and slides into the booth across from them, ripping open the velcro of his fingerless gloves. A woman's voice is singing about how you can make dew into diamonds, and pacify the lions, but you know you can never love me more. Roland tugs his gloves off and lays them flat on the table. Looks up at Ysabel. Lifts his eyebrows, tries on a smile. Her expression doesn't change. "My lady," he starts to say.

"You really killed him, didn't you," says Jo, her head still lying back against the booth.

Roland looks down at his gloves on the table and tries again. "My lady. I am sorry I have not been with you directly these past few days."

"It's no longer your office," says Ysabel. She holds one of her hands in the other, her thumb absently stroking a wet red patch, rubbed raw, on her palm.

"It is no longer my office," says Roland. He looks directly at her again. "*And,* I am sorry I was not with you sooner tonight."

"We got by," says Ysabel.

"You really did kill that guy," says Jo, glaring at Roland. "He's *dead.*"

"You should not be forced to 'get by'," Roland's saying. "My only defense is that it should have been inconceivable for the Duke to act so openly, so quickly." He looks down at his gloves again. "A sad excuse, I know."

"What will you guys be having?" says the waitress.

"Vanilla Stoli and Diet Coke," says Ysabel crisply, putting her hands in her lap.

"Water for me," says Roland. "Thank you."

"And you?" says the waitress, turning to look at Jo and knocking Roland's sword over. "Oh," she says. "I'm sorry!" bending down to pick it up.

"That's a real sword, you know," says Jo.

"I'm, um," says the waitress, propping the sword back up against the table. "What?"

"That's a real sword. That's why it's so heavy. If you pull it out there's blood on it. *He* just *killed* somebody with that sword."

The waitress looks over at Roland, who's looking down at his gloves on the table. "You know," she says to Jo, "state law won't let us serve anybody who's visibly intoxicated."

"I'm not drunk," mutters Jo. "Yet."

"Well?" says the waitress.

"You buying?" says Jo to Roland.

"I suppose," he says.

"Then bring me one of those fishbowl drinks," says Jo. "Whichever one has a lot of rum in it. And umbrellas. And those little plastic mermaids."

"Okay," says the waitress.

Let the rain pour down, the woman's singing, let the valleys drown, still, you know you can never make me love you more.

"Look," says Jo suddenly. "I want out."

"You want out," says Roland. Ysabel's looking away, over at the bar, a dim confusion of shadowy people and light-struck glass.

"Yeah," says Jo.

"You were warned," says Roland. His eyes are a pale blue that washes away to nothing in the dim light.

"I don't *care*," says Jo. She covers her face with her hands and digs at her eyes with her fingertips. "I don't care," she says, her hands falling in on themselves to rest on the table. "I'll just, challenge you to a duel or something. I'll lose, I'll let you win. You can have her back. Take her back. I'm sorry," she says to Ysabel. "But." Ysabel doesn't say anything.

"It doesn't work like that," says Roland, looking up. The zipper on his jacket flashes, pulled up to his chin.

"Why not?" says Jo. "It's how I got into this mess."

"The Queen would never – "

"*Fuck* the Queen," snaps Jo.

Roland's hands curl into tight fists on the table. Ysabel blinks and turns her gaze slowly on Jo.

"Okay?" says Jo. "I mean, what's going to happen to us? To me?"

"Happen?" says Roland.

"With the cops!" says Jo. "And," she frowns, "and the cops!"

"It's none of their concern," says Ysabel.

"None of their," says Jo. "He *killed* that guy!"

"No, Jo," says Roland. His voice is gentle. He looks down at his fists, pursing his lips. Looks up at Jo. "I didn't," he says. "*You* did."

"What?" says Jo.

The Mooncalfe runs to meet the Chariot's charge as car alarms wail and yowl around them. The Stirrup scrabbles for the sword he'd left under the railing. The Mooncalfe swings his Japanese sword with two hands, hunkering low, his hips twisting this way, that. The Chariot takes his stand sideways, head leaning back and away, his off-hand tucked against his chest. Every now and then a straightforward cut is blocked by a solid parry ringing like a great bell cracked and sinking out of tune. More tentative ripostes and probing thrusts swatted aside sound like someone banging to clear the pipes of a steam radiator. "Roland!" cries the Stirrup, hefting his sword. "Roland! Surely we can settle this as gentlemen?"

"We *are*," snarls the Chariot, his blade scraping against the Mooncalfe's as they push and shove.

"Ysabel," hisses Jo from her perch at the top of the steps leading to the church's side door. Still clinging to the gate there she leans out, calling to Ysabel at the foot of the stairs. "Get up here!"

Ysabel looks up at Jo and shakes her head. At the corner on their side of the street stands Tommy, arms folded, his eyes on the fight. The Mooncalfe stumbles against the curb behind him. Ducking under the Chariot's slash sends him almost to his knees. "No quarter!" roars the Chariot. "Come at me as you like!"

"*Surely* we deserve to hear the nature of our crimes?" says the Stirrup, shifting his weight so one leg leads, his sword held low at his waist, away from the Chariot. "We only sought to protect the Princess!"

"*Liar!*" bellows the Chariot, backing away from the Mooncalfe. "I call you a liar, sir. And I *will* make good that claim upon your person." And as the Chariot lifts his blade and takes his first running step toward the Stirrup, as the Stirrup crouches, his sword still down, waiting, as Tommy stands there on the sidewalk, halfway between the corner and the church steps, his arms folded, watching the fight, the Mooncalfe steps up on the fender of a little round compact car and launches himself twisting into the air, his sword up above his head for a final blow. The Chariot's second step buckles as he ducks, rolling onto his back, his sword up.

"Hurk," says the Mooncalfe.

He crouches over the Chariot. Stuck on the blade passed clean through his body. His Japanese sword clatters dully as it falls to the pavement.

"Are these the Nazis, Walter?" says the nervous little guy on the big flat television hanging on the wall.

"They're nihilists, Donny," says the big guy. "Nothing to be afraid of."

His grace on the brown leather couch in his paisleyed dressing gown chuckles. The blond woman at the other end of the couch sits under the only light in the room. She's wearing black stockings and a black teddy, and she's reading a thick yellow paperback book. There's a muffled shout outside. Footsteps pounding up the stairs. "Baby?" says his grace, scooping up a remote. The television freezes on the image of a man doubling over, clutching his crotch, his face a cartoon mask of pain. The blond woman doesn't look up from her book. "You might want to," says his grace, and then down the hall the door bursts open. His grace leaps to his feet. The blond woman rolls her eyes and fiercely turns the page.

"Gaveston?" calls his grace.

It's the Mooncalfe who's first into the room. The Stirrup, his tie loosened, his shirt open, is next.

"Well?" says his grace. "Is she here?" He looks from one to the other and back again. "Well?" He frowns. "Where's Tommy?"

The Stirrup looks over at the Mooncalfe, who isn't really looking at anyone.

"Where the fuck is Tommy Rawhead?" says his grace.

The Stirrup reaches into his rumpled linen jacket and pulls out a bone. It's a good-sized bone, thick and long, the tibia of a short man. It glitters.

"Oh," says the blond woman, peering over the back of the couch. "Oh, no."

As his grace takes the bone in a trembling hand, gold dust shivers into the air, sparkling. He lifts the bone in both hands and rests his forehead against the knobbed flange at one end, his eyes closed. The Stirrup looks away. The Mooncalfe is still looking at no one in particular. Then with one hand his grace brushes up some of the gold dust still clinging to the bone. His eyes still closed he touches his fingers to his lips and murmurs. Then he opens them.

"Who did this?" he says.

"Hurk," says the Mooncalfe.

The Chariot reaches up to plant one hand on his chest and pushes him up as he pulls the blade down and out of his body. The Stirrup's running up, lifting his blade –

"Hey!" yells Jo.

– and the Chariot rolls to one side as Ysabel looks up startled at Jo at the top of the church steps and Tommy standing beside Ysabel reaches up to grab her arm and the Stirrup's blade swings down in a mighty blow to clang against the pavement where the Chariot had been lying. The Chariot on his feet blade up backs away. The Mooncalfe clutching his belly stomps angrily over to the curb. "Fuck!" he yells up into the pink-hazed night sky over the piercing car alarms.

"Let me go," Ysabel's saying. "Let me go!"

"Hey," says Tommy, easily holding her arm in his big hands. "Roland."

The Stirrup and the Chariot circle each other, blades wary between them.

"Hey," says Tommy.

The Chariot suddenly breaks for the church steps as Jo lets go of the gate. Startled, the Stirrup starts after him, as Jo runs down the steps toward Ysabel. Tommy hauls Ysabel over to one side away from the Chariot's wild lunge, throwing up one long arm to protect himself, as Jo scrambles on the steps to turn, reaching out for Ysabel's hand. Tommy knocks the first thrust aside letting the Chariot's blade slide along his forearm as Ysabel takes Jo's hand and then looks up to see her there and then cries out, "Oh, oh no. Jo – Roland!"

The Chariot's second thrust hits home, and everything is suddenly quiet.

Tommy looks down at the metal that's stuck in his chest. Opens his mouth. Something dark and wet falls out of it to spatter onto the sidewalk.

"Gallowglas!" bellows the Stirrup.

"I didn't," says the Chariot. He pulls his sword out of Tommy's body, and Tommy sinks softly to his knees. The front of his black turtleneck is stained with something that glitters in the streetlight. "I didn't know," says Roland.

"Gallowglas!" The Stirrup is marching toward the sidewalk, toward Tommy, falling onto his side, toward Jo, holding Ysabel's hand. The Mooncalfe on the other side of the street is climbing to his feet.

"Ysabel?" says Jo. "What's – "

"Run," says Ysabel.

"Gaveston," calls the Chariot. The Stirrup doesn't hear him. Doesn't look down at Tommy as he marches past, headed after Ysabel, and Jo, running now for the corner. The Chariot swings his sword and knocks the point of the Stirrup's sword down. "It's over!" He grabs the Stirrup's shoulder slamming him back against the church wall. The Stirrup gasps. "It's over," says Roland. An suv jerks to a stop in the intersection, honking as Jo and Ysabel hand-in-hand run across the street in front of it. "Take him with you and get out of here," says Roland.

"You will pay," says Gaveston.

"Go," says Roland.

"I'm a gallowglas," says Jo. With fumbling fingers she manages to get the miniskirt unzipped but working it down her legs she stumbles and falls onto her futon. She rolls over on her back. "I'm *the* Gallowglas. Hey. Hey. How come the other guy didn't die?"

Ysabel sits on the edge of the futon with a glass of water in one hand. "You should drink some," she says, holding it out for Jo.

"Need a towel." Jo tries to sit up and rolls over on her side. "Just in case. How come?"

"You weren't on the field of battle then," says Ysabel. She sets the glass of water down and picks up the Spongebob Squarepants towel. She smoothes it out on the futon by Jo's head. "It's only when you're actually fighting that, well."

"I make them. I can kill them. They can be killed," says Jo. "Makes no sense."

"It's not supposed to make sense," says Ysabel.

"It makes perfect sense," says Jo. "I fuck everything up." She pulls her knees up to her chest. Worrying at the ripped knee of her tights. "I fucked up the fight. I fucked up that guy. I'm fucking up my job. I fucked up my life. I fucked up high school.

I could have, I would have gone to Harvard. Did you know that?" She reaches out for Ysabel's hand. "If I had the money. I would have gone to Harvard. Or maybe Berkeley."

Ysabel strokes Jo's hair. Smiles, a little. "You should drink some water and get some sleep," she says.

"But I fucked that up," says Jo. Closing her eyes. "And I'm fucking you up," she says. She opens them, looking up at Ysabel. "I'm fucking up your life," she says. "I'm fucking up your life, and I'm really sorry about it." She closes her eyes again.

"Shh," says Ysabel. Setting the glass down on the floor by the futon she stands up and steps carefully around the piles of dirty laundry and shoes, past the sink full of dirty dishes, to the front door of the apartment. Out in the hallway stands Roland, his hands in the pockets of his green and silver track suit, looking down at his spotless white shoes.

"Do you need anything, my lady?" he asks, quietly.

"Well," she says.

"Anything I can bring you?"

"No," she says.

"My lady," he starts to say.

"Answer me this, Roland," she says. "Did my mother set you to watching me?"

"Well," he says. "I mean, well – "

"Did she?" says Ysabel.

Roland shrugs. "Yes," he says.

"In that case," says Ysabel, stepping back into the apartment, "I'll be seeing you around."

"My lady," says Roland, "I – "

She shuts the door.

Inside, on the futon, Jo snores.

Ysabel stands there in the middle of the cluttered apartment, in her hip-hugging jeans, her peach tank top, the nails on her bare feet glittering with gold paint. She swallows. She closes her eyes and bites her lip and briefly, just for an instant, shudders.

Then she reaches out and snaps off the light.

She makes it to the windowsill without stumbling. Jo mumbles at the stiff croak of the window as Ysabel cranks it open. She sits on the sill, working one long leg out onto the faux balcony. Plucks a cigarette out of a crumpled pack and lights it with a match. Jo starts snoring again in great bubbling snorts. Blowing smoke out the window, Ysabel looks out over the nighttime city, filled with light: the pink and orange haze of the streetlights, white-hot spots of arc light at a construction site, here and there rectangles of yellow still burning in buildings all around, neon squiggles in primary colors hanging in dark shop windows, billboards lit up like giant television screens. The stoplight below changes from red to green and with the change in color the whole world subtly shifts. Engines rumble and growl. Headlights and taillights start to move. A thumping bassline slides past. Ysabel leans back against the sill and closes her eyes.

FARELESS

"FARELESS," says Christian to the bus driver. His hands are jammed in the pockets of his old grey sweatshirt, tugging it low. He doesn't flash a transfer or a pass. He doesn't drop quarters in the fare box. The driver shrugs. "Lloyd Center?" she says.

"Yeah," says Christian. "Whatever."

The bus is nearly empty. He swings himself into the seat just behind the back door. His reflection glowers at him in the black window-glass.

"Running to Northeast," says one of the men sitting in the very back seat to the other one. "Now that seems pretty smart, first time you look at it."

The other man, the big one, doesn't say anything.

"Nobody's going to look for you up that way, at least not right off the proverbial bat," says the first guy, the little one. "Certainly not the people you pissed off. And not the people *they* pissed off, neither. You're out of the middle of them, and yay team for that. Plus, you're crossing water." The bus changes gears, surging up and around an on-ramp onto a bridge. "Always good to get some running water between you and your troubles.

Not that it necessarily has any practical effect, mind you. Come to think of it, it doesn't have much of any effect at all, does it? But it's what everybody does, they hit a patch of trouble too big for their britches. Makes you feel a little better to be doing it. It's *something*. You know?"

The big guy doesn't say anything.

"And see," says the little guy, "you start looking at this plan, this whole running to Northeast plan, with that attention to detail, well. It all starts to look less like a home run and more like a bunt, and maybe not even a base hit, you know? I mean, hell. Northeast. Here there be monsters. You don't know the signs and signals, the ways and means, you're gonna end up as lunch, make no mistake."

"What you need," says the big guy, "is a friend."

"And that is pre*cise*ly what I was about to say, Mr. Keightlinger. Hot damn. Hot damn indeed. Who *wouldn't* want a friend in times like these? The other fellow has somebody to back his play, what do *you* need? Somebody to back yours. But not just a friend, no. Not any old friend will do. You need a friend with britches big enough to stand up to your troubles. You need a friend with deep pockets to back your play. What you need, Mr. Keightlinger – "

"Dude likes the sound of his voice," says Christian, loudly.

"What you *need*, Mr. Keightlinger," says the little guy, "*especially* if you're a loud-mouthed pushy little sonofabitch like Christian Beaumont here, what you need is a goddamn *patron*."

"Make no mistake," says the big guy, who has a thick beard the color of mahogany furniture, bushy enough to bury the knot of his skinny black tie.

"The fuck are you?" says Christian, who's spun around on his seat to look at them.

"Me?" says the little guy, who's wearing a black suit just like the big guy's. "I'm Mr. Charlock. My associate is the aforementioned Mr. Keightlinger. And I'm assuming that you are in actual fact Mr. Christian Beaumont. If you aren't, what I'm saying probably makes no sense whatsoever. But if you *are*, my friend, well, you just stood yourself up between two houses of the gentry who are determined to butt heads and none too particular about what happens to the little folks stuck in the middle. Hell, you've got one or two of 'em ready to see to it *personally* you end up flatter than not. The kind of trouble you're in doesn't come any bigger. You *need* a patron. And we can fulfill that role, my associate and myself."

"And what if I told you to go fuck yourself?" says Christian.

"Well," says Mr. Charlock. "You have a couple of options, all of which involve running out of town. But! That costs money, doesn't it?"

"Quite a bit of money," says Mr. Keightlinger.

"More than Mr. Beaumont has, anyway."

"Fuck you," says Christian.

"He could hitchhike, I suppose," says Mr. Charlock, "or hobo his way south or east. Or he could sign up to fight forest fires! 'Tis the season, after all, and the commercial outfits aren't too picky about who they sign up. He could be out at the Three Sisters burn in a matter of days."

"He doesn't have days," says Mr. Keightlinger.

Christian rolls his eyes.

"Oh, you're right there," says Mr. Charlock. "That Mooncalfe is a *vicious* bastard. Murderous. What was it again he did to that obnoxious cowboy in the parking lot of the Red Lion?"

"Bet he didn't talk his motherfuckin' ears off," says Christian.

"No," says Mr. Charlock, his voice suddenly flat and quiet as the bus pulls into a stop. "No, he didn't."

"Lloyd Center," calls the bus driver. "End of Fareless Square."

Christian hauls himself up out of his seat. "So what do you want from me?" he says.

Standing, Mr. Charlock says, "You see, Mr. Keightlinger?" They follow Christian out the back door and onto the sidewalk in front of a dimly lit park. "The street is a harsh mistress, but her lessons are taken to heart. The invisible hand of the marketplace is hard at work, ensuring that services are rendered for value received. A patron is no mere friend, after all, to flee when the fair weather turns; a patron, after all, is a *mutual* obligation.

So let's by all means cut to the chase: we will, Mr. Beaumont, keep you safe from the Mooncalfe and the Stirrup and anyone they might send to effect their revenge. In return for which, you will educate us in the ways of one Jo Maguire."

"Jo?" says Christian.

"You *do* know Miss Maguire, don't you? Mr. Beaumont? Otherwise, I'm afraid this has been a dreadful waste of everyone's time."

Christian jams his hands into the pockets of his sweatshirt. He looks away from the two men in their black suits up the sidewalk toward the parking lot of a movie theater, filled with a slowly churning traffic jam of people and cars working their ways home after the last show. A number eight bus pulls up to the stop, opens its doors expectantly. He waves it off. "Buy me a burger," he says. "Let's talk about it."

"By all means, Mr. Beaumont," says Mr. Charlock. "By all means."

In this sad plight, friendlesse, vnfortunate,
  Now miserable I Fidessa dwell,
  Crauing of you in pitty of my state,
  To do none ill, if please ye not do well.
  He in great passion all this while did dwell,
  More busying his quicke eyes, her face to view,
  Then his dull eares, to heare what she did tell;
  And said, Faire Lady hart of flint would rew
The vndeserued woes and sorrowes, which ye shew.

—*Edmund Spenser*

NO. 3

ZOOBOMBING

One of the Club's Private Dining Rooms – Getting Cute
"You don't have to be any good at it" – This is Not a Sales Call
Hopeless Paperwork – Ysabel Triumphantly
the Changing of the Guard – Now and Here
a Mound of Bicycles – "Le Trash Blanc?" – Not her man
Something, Anything, It – Very simple questions
Whipped Cream – Like most people – Zoobombing
This Ray guy – Marfisa in the Hall – What he wants to Hear

IN ONE OF THE CLUB'S PRIVATE DINING ROOMS, long tables have been laid with dazzling white cloths and arranged in a blocky U. Two places have been set, on either side of one of the corners: bread plates and soup plates, fish forks and salad forks, butter knives and steak knives, wine glasses and tea cups. Dressed all in black the Queen sits before one of the settings, facing the door, her back to a window overlooking a parking garage. Her head nods. Her eyes close. Her chin brushes her chest. Behind her stands a woman wearing narrow black-rimmed glasses and a black sweater over a white shirt with an enormous stiff collar shading her shoulders. At some unseen signal she bends down to whisper in the Queen's ear. The Queen sits up, blinking. Smiles uncomfortably.

There is a bustle at the door.

The first to enter is a young man backing carefully, both hands held out with some concern, murmuring encouragement to an old man tottering slowly on two grey orthopædic canes. Ivory hair makes a wild crown about a pink head bobbing loosely, a delicately balanced counterweight to every hesitant step. His arms and legs are quite thin, lost in the copious folds of a soft blue suit, but his belly strains its buttons as raises up a little and croaks, "You're losing it, Duenna."

"Grandfather Count is honored as ever to join you for brunch, your majesty," says the young man over his shoulder, "and he offers his every felicitation to your illustrious reign. May it last forever."

"And we are delighted, as ever, by his company," says the Queen.

"That girl of yours is like honey," says the Count, making his slow, torturous way outside the tables toward the Queen, each shaky step braced by a cane in the opposite hand. "Leave a pot of it outside your tent," and he lifts a cane, poking its rubber tip in the general direction of the Queen, "and the bears get *frisky!*" He almost falls from the force of his rhetorical point. The young man catches an elbow. He, too, wears a soft blue suit, and his shirt is a blushing pink. His hair is also white, just touched with hints of pale gold, and it hangs in tangled dreadlocks down past his shoulders. "There are, of course," he's saying, as he helps the Count into his chair, "some matters Grandfather wishes to discuss," and the young man favors the Queen with a quick nod. "But none so pressing, ma'am, that they cannot wait until after we have eaten."

"If I might recommend," says the waiter, who in his white apron and black tie has appeared quite silently on the other side of the tables, "today's omelet is delicious – wild chanterelle mushrooms, leeks, walnuts – "

"Boca!" blares the Count.

"I also have black bean chili," says the waiter, brushing his walrusy black mustache.

"I want my Boca!"

"With," says the waiter, "semi-sweet chocolate base. And a delicious risotto with lemon and pomegranate – "

"I want my blasted Boca burger!" The Count bangs a fist on the table and the silverware chatters. "On sourdough! Made from the ever-lovin' Yukon Gold Rush culture!" Bang! "I want a slab of Irish cheddar steeped in whiskey on it! None of your skinflint skimping on that – I said a slab and I want a veritable slab! I want mango chutney and I want my jo-jos fried in certi-fied peanut oil and I want fresh cilantro, *fresh,* you hear me, cut this very morning, and I want the last tomato of summer!" Bang! "And gimme a bottle of Dr. Brown's Cel-Ray, you hear me?" Bang!

The waiter clears his throat. "I also have many surprises for dessert, but will tempt you with them later." He bows slightly and stiffly.

"Grandfather will have his usual," says the young man.

"The omelet," says the woman in the black-rimmed glasses standing behind the Queen's chair. "A light salad, oil and vinegar on the side. A cup of coffee. And please make sure we have some Splenda on the table?"

"Of course," says the waiter.

"Nothing but a jumped-up khokhol in a stuffed shirt," mutters the Count.

The waiter's mouth tightens at that, and his steps as he leaves are crisp.

"We should probably begin," says the Queen, "by discussing our plans for the upcoming year's end festivities." The woman in the black-rimmed glasses plucks a manila folder from the leather case at her feet and walks it over to the young man.

"Not while people are dying, we don't," says the Count. The young man pauses in the act of taking the folder. "Grandfather," he says, "is gravely concerned about a recent, incident? Involving the Princess, and some of the Duke's men – "

"We fail to see how that concerns the Count," says the Queen.

"Gallowglas," says the Count. "*That's* how it concerns me, blast it." He coughs. "All of us. Wretched outsider, threatening everything. Your girl got cute, Duenna. Whether she meant to or not."

"*Meant* to?" says the Queen, arching one thin black eyebrow.

The young man says "What Grandfather is trying to say" as the woman in the black-rimmed glasses says "The Queen must insist that this matter be kept – "

"Bullshit!" blares the Count. Bang! "She! Got! Cute!" Bang! "And you're trying to teach her a lesson." The Count waves this off. "But it's getting out of hand." He leans back from the table with a slow push. "*You* have to call it *off.*"

"Frederic," says the Queen, quietly. "You would do well to remember who I am. And that no one – not you, not the Duke, *certainly* not my daughter – dictates my actions."

"The Count is invited to note," says the woman in the black-rimmed glasses, "that the Princess and her guardian are effectively isolated from the court."

"Grandfather doesn't feel they're isolated *enough*," says the young man, eyeing the Count closely.

"If the Duke hadn't tried to kidnap the Princess," says the woman in the black-rimmed glasses, "none of this – "

"That's enough, Anna," says the Queen.

"Well?" says the Count.

"We have no intention of accepting the Gallowglas at court," says the Queen. "We have no intention of rescuing our daughter from the consequences of her actions. We will not insult one of our knights by making any more of his recent – indiscretion, and we have no intention of allowing the *Duke's* complaints to determine how and by whom the Princess is guarded. We trust this is clear?"

"Nothing will change," says the young man. The waiter has reappeared. He sets a small plate of dark little pancakes and a bowl of yogurt before the Count.

"Unless I change my mind," says the Queen. The waiter sets an omelet and a small salad before the Queen, and then he holds up a couple of small creamy envelopes. "These were delivered to front desk," he says, laying one before the Queen and one before the Count.

Anna lifts the envelope and rips it open with a finger. She tips out the card inside and scans it quickly as she hands it to the Queen.

"An invitation," she says. "From the Duke."

"To the court," says the young man, looking at the other card. "A hunt, in honor of the Princess." He looks up. His face is carefully blank. "This would seem to work *against* their isolation," he says.

The Count snorts as he scoops up a small spoonful of yogurt.

"You don't have to be any good at it"
This is Not a Sales Call – Hopeless Paperwork

"You don't have to be any good at it," says Jo, punching the fourth floor button. A dusting of powdered sugar is left behind. "Hell, you don't even have to *try*. You just have to make do for a week or so." She stoops and plucks another donut from one of the plastic sacks of groceries at her feet.

"You want me," says Ysabel, "to *work*. For *money*." One hand hangs by a thumb from a beltloop on her plum jeans. The other holds a bottle of peach tea.

"You said yourself it wasn't work. It's just talking to people on the phone."

"You want *me*. To exchange my time – hours out of my day – for money."

The elevator dings. The doors slide open. "Well, yeah," says Jo, hauling up a sack of groceries in either fist. "If it's not too much trouble."

Ysabel rolls her eyes.

"Look," says Jo, leading the way down the generic beige and burnt-orange hall. "See these groceries? That tea? If I don't go in and get my paycheck so I can cover the check I wrote for this shit, well, that's the sort of thing they take away your bank account for. If you don't have a bank account, you don't get to keep the apartment." At the end of the hall, Jo sets the groceries on the floor by a door and fishes in the cavernous pocket of her workpants for her keys. "And I tend to get cranky when I don't have an apartment. So. Since I have to go in *any-way*, and you have to go with me, well, Becker can't exactly kick you out if you *work* there."

"Why don't you call out sick again?" says Ysabel.

"You didn't listen to a thing I just said, did you," says Jo, unlocking the door.

"As little as possible," says Ysabel.

Jo blinks. *"What the fuck?"*

The window on the far wall of the apartment is framed by floor-length burgundy drapes. A gauzy shade filters the sunlight into something soft and cool. By the futon, neatly made and piled with a crazy quilt of patterned pillows, a glass-topped café table stands between two spindly wrought-iron chairs. A bulky blond wood armoire takes up the corner behind it, and a contraption of thin metal tubing hanging from one side racks a couple dozen pairs of shoes. The sink in the little hallway kitchen gleams mirror-bright, with only a single glass in it. A bit of milk rings the bottom.

"What the," says Jo. Looking at the number on the door. Looking into the apartment again.

"You like it?" says Ysabel, sliding past her. "I had someone in to clean the place while we were out."

"You had someone," says Jo, hefting the groceries up onto the spotless kitchen counter. "You," she says again, stepping into the main space of the apartment. "I," she says, looking at the expansively shaggy bouquet spreading across the table, the thick, stubby candles burning before it. "You," she says. Shakes her head. "Where the *fuck* is my stuff?"

"Black cumin," murmurs Ysabel, stroking some ghostly blue flowers frothing the top of the bouquet. "I'm sorry?" She turns, looks about the room. Points. At the foot of the futon are three or four blond wood crates filled with neatly folded clothing.

"You," Jo's saying. "I mean. I. You."

"You don't mind, do you?" says Ysabel, opening the armoire, running one hand along the shirts and tops and dresses and jackets and skirts hung within. "It's just while I'm staying here. Do you think you could make do? For a week or so?"

Jo's wrinkling her nose. "Smells like fucking Pine-Sol," she mutters.

It's a small, windowless room, not much bigger than the round table in the middle of it. Ysabel sits in one corner, staring up at a white board that says WinBank 4.3 an hour How to Improve? A small stack of typescript stapled in one corner sits on the table before her. Her hair's pulled back in a thick ponytail high on the back of her head. She's wearing a light turtleneck sweater in some nameless natural color.

The door pops open and a head peers around the frame. "Um, hey," it says from behind a curtain of black hair. "Becker said I should come in here and, uh, run you through the script – "

"Hello, Guthrie," says Ysabel.

"Um," says Guthrie, looking up at her. His eyes are ringed with black mascara. "Hi." He's wearing a black T-shirt that says Snarky Kite. "So I'm supposed to run you through the WinBank script," he says, stepping into the room, closing the door. "Um. They call this the Little Conference Room, which I think is some kind of joke, since the other conference room isn't any bigger."

"That isn't part of the script," says Ysabel.

"Um, no. It isn't. I guess you've already read the background memo?" Guthrie pulls out a chair and sits down.

"When you said that you might remember more than I'd thought, what did you mean?" Ysabel leans her elbows on the table.

"That, uh, isn't in the script, either," says Guthrie.

"Humor me."

He smiles, his eyes jerking away from her. "Um," he says. "I just mean, well. Becker doesn't remember how that guy fought Jo with a sword. And, uh. I do."

"And you think you weren't *supposed* to remember this?"

"I don't know," says Guthrie.

"Guthrie," says Ysabel. "Look at me." His smile has tensed into a grimace that's crawled up under his nose. "I don't have any secrets here, all right?" His eyes slide away from her. "I'm not hiding anything. I know Jo said there was an evil boyfriend, and there isn't, but that was her idea. Okay? I don't know why she said it. Okay? I'm a lousy liar, Guthrie. Guthrie. Look at me." He does, now, unsmiling. "It really doesn't matter if you remember the duel of not, okay? Got that?"

Guthrie nods. "Can we just, you know. Do the script?"

Ysabel shrugs. "Sure."

"I'll be the respondent," says Guthrie, "and you do the survey, okay? Just start from the top."

Ysabel holds her hands out in front of herself there on the table and traces a vague box shape in the air. She mimes plucking something and lifts it, an imaginary telephone handset, to her ear. She stabs the air with her finger where she's shaped out the vague box, six, seven times.

"What are you," says Guthrie. "What are you doing?"

"Calling you," says Ysabel. "I need to call you on the phone, right?"

"Yes," says Guthrie, "but, I mean, there's no need to, to *pretend* all this, we could just – "

"Your phone's ringing," says Ysabel, pointing to the space on the table before him.

Blinking, frowning a little, Guthrie mimes picking up a telephone handset. Silvery rings glitter on his fingers. "Hello?" he says.

"Good evening, sir," says Ysabel. "My name is Ysabel Perry, and I'm calling on behalf of Barshefsky Associates. This isn't a sales call. We're an independent market research firm located in Portland, Oregon, and we're conducting a brief survey. Am I speaking with the person who makes most of the financial decisions for your household?"

"Ah, yes," says Guthrie.

"Would you say that you make all of the financial decisions, at least half of the financial decisions, less than half of the financial decisions, or none of the financial decisions for your household? That's redundant," says Ysabel.

"I, what?"

"That's redundant. You already said you made *most* of those whatever decisions. So I shouldn't ask if you make less than half, or none."

"That's, ah," says Guthrie, holding up his hand, then pointing to the script, "that's how it's written."

"It's written badly," says Ysabel. "I shouldn't ask you a question you've already answered. It makes me look stupid."

"Yeah, but," says Guthrie, pointing to the script again. "Look, you have to ask each question as it's written. It has to be the *same*, every time you do the survey or anybody else does.

Otherwise, I mean, you're going to get different answers than somebody who's sticking to the script like you're supposed to."

"Isn't that the point?"

"I'm sorry?"

"I mean, if you wanted to get the *same* answers every time, you could just figure out what those are supposed to be and write them down and save the rest of us a lot of time and trouble."

Guthrie closes his eyes. "Just read the script. The way it's written. Okay?"

"The whole thing," says Ysabel.

"Yes," says Guthrie.

"Because there's some grammatical errors in here, you know."

"Just," says Guthrie. "Read it. What's the next question?"

Ysabel flips over the first page of the script. "I'm going to read you a list of financial products and services. For each one, please tell me whether you or someone in your household has that product or service. And I have a question here."

"What," says Guthrie, who hasn't opened his eyes.

"What on earth is a financial product?"

"I, uh," says Guthrie. The door pops open and Becker sticks his head in. "How's it going in here? You going through the script?"

"Ah," says Guthrie. "Yes," says Ysabel.

"Good," says Becker. "Ten more minutes, and then you'll go live, okay, Ysabel?"

"Okay," she says.

"Um," says Guthrie.

Becker pulls the door closed and heads down the narrow hall and around a corner into the phone room, full of chatter and grey late-afternoon light. He's got a new manila folder in one hand and he's wearing a bulky plaid flannel shirt. Jo's sitting midway down one side of the U of carrels. The black tufts in her hair stick up around the band of her telephone headset. She leans into her carrel, one hand up holding the mike closer to her mouth. "Well, sir," she's saying, "I don't – Well. We made the appointment with your wife – Yessir – Well, she said – Sir, I don't believe you. Just what I said, I don't believe you. Nobody makes *all* of the financial decisions in this day and age. Well, your wife seemed to think – Sir, you shouldn't say – Well, *fuck you too."* She yanks the headset off and drops it by her computer monitor.

Becker kneels down by her chair. "Hey," he says.

Jo jumps. "Jesus," she says. "Hey. He already hung up before I started swearing. Okay?"

"I figured," says Becker. "Actually, I wanted to talk to you about something else."

In Tartt's little office, with its poster on the door exhorting them to shoot for the moon, Becker holds up the manila folder. "I shouldn't be showing this to you, but I'm thinking you can help me with Ysabel."

"Yeah?" says Jo.

"Well, the paperwork for her I-9 is hopeless." He spreads the folder open on top of a couple of relatively level stacks of paper on Tartt's desk.

"Hopeless?" says Jo.

"She doesn't *have* any of it," says Becker. "No driver's license. No passport. No Social Security card. No birth certificate. No voter's registration card or school ID. She says she was born in the US, but she's got nothing to prove it. She wanted to know why her *word* wasn't good enough."

Jo chuckles.

"Look, it's not *that* funny. If we can't get this filled out, we can't pay her. Okay? And if we could, well," he flips over the larger form and pulls out a small half-sheet, "I'm not sure *what* the hell to make of what she put on her W-4."

Jo leans forward to peer at the form and says, "Oh, God." She claps her hand to her mouth.

"What?" says Becker.

"I had *no idea,"* says Jo, stifling a giggle, "that *that's* how she spells Ysabel."

It's a round room on the third floor of a tower, and it's empty except for a big three-way mirror and several cardboard boxes of clothes and more clothing strewn across the floor here and there and the woman who's standing in the middle of it all, wearing a pair of white boyshorts and lifting her mass of pale gold curls up into a pile the color of clotted cream on top of her head. The radio at her feet is muttering something sprightly and bossa–nova-ish. To be all she wants, it's singing, I cannot do. All the things it would take, just to pull it through.

She stoops and pulls a soft, baby-blue hooded jacket out of one of the boxes. She wrestles one arm and then the other into the long tight sleeves, lined with red piping, that flare suddenly at the cuffs, swallowing the heels of her hands. She has far too high expectations, sings the radio, she thinks she deserves all she can get. What she wants from me is something I cannot be. The hem of the jacket hits just above her navel. She works the one end of the zipper into the other and tugs it up to her throat, then pulls it down, to just about halfway between her breasts. Tilts her head, swings herself to one side, then the other, examining herself in the mirror. Pouts thoughtfully. Tugs the zipper down a little more.

"Hot date?" says the man leaning in the doorway.

She jumps a little. "Don't *scare* me like that," she says to him in the mirror. He's wearing a blushing salmon shirt, and his pale, pale hair hangs in tangled dreadlocks down past his shoulders. She squats by the cardboard box and rummages through it. "And no, brother dear. I'm just doing a favor for a friend." She pulls out a long athletic skirt in matching baby blue and red. Sitting on the floor, she pulls the skirt over her feet, then her knees, then works herself back up off the floor to yank it up her thighs and over her hips.

"Hey," says the man leaning in the doorway. "Let me help you with that." He steps behind her, helping her settle the skirt into place, low on her hips. Tugs the zipper up in back. "And would this friend be Roland?" he murmurs, in her ear. "And is this favor what I *think* it is?"

She reaches up and taps his nose lightly with a fingertip. "I told you," she says. "It isn't a hot date."

"Well," he says, stepping back. "You look fantastic."

"Naturally," she says, sitting by another cardboard box.

"Be sure to tell your cool date that your brother's jealous," he says, stepping back out of the room.

"Oh, I'll be sure to," she says, absently. Pulling out a pair of rose-colored running shoes. Frowning. Reaching back in for a pair of light blue jellied sandals.

YSABEL TRIUMPHANTLY – THE CHANGING OF THE GUARD –
NOW AND HERE – A MOUND OF BICYCLES

YSABEL TRIUMPHANTLY lifts her hand, her middle finger poised, circling the phone's disconnect button. "Why, no," she says into her telephone headset. "Thank *you*. I can only apologize for how badly the questions were written, and how boring it must have been for you. Not at all. And you have a good evening yourself. Goodbye." She punches the button. Sighs. Peers at the computer keyboard that takes up most what little desk space is left by the monitor and taps a couple of keys with index fingers poking out of loose fists. She peers at the screen, then punches a couple more keys. Becker kneels down next to her chair as she reaches for the phone again. "Hey," he says. "It's after nine. You're done."

"Oh," says Ysabel, leaning back in her chair.

"You've been on the phone about five hours. You logged 42 complete surveys. That's, ah, pretty much a record."

"Oh," says Ysabel. Jo comes up behind Becker, her arms folded, her mouth wryly turned. Behind her, other dialers are scooping up bags, books, empty water bottles, candy wrappers, gathering their things and heading for the door.

"Yeah," Becker's saying. "Seth monitored several of your calls – you did a fantastic job. We could maybe do with a little less, you know, insulting the survey, but – "

"Good," says Ysabel, pushing back, standing up, brushing off her khaki skirt. "So is that enough?" she asks Jo. "Are we done?"

"Sure," says Jo.

"Good job, Ysabel," says Becker, standing.

"Thanks," says Ysabel, bending over to tug one of her heathery wool socks back up over her knee. "Can we do something else tomorrow night?" she says to Jo. "This was *really* dull."

"Um," says Becker.

Roland in his green and silver track suit is standing on the sidewalk in the pink and orange light, under the multi-colored Tonic banner that whuffles in the evening air. With him is a woman a couple of fingers taller, whose hair the color of clotted cream is piled even higher that that. She's wearing a soft blue hoody and a matching full-length skirt. "What," says Jo, arms akimbo, looking them up and down. "We get an escort now?"

"This is Marfisa, the Axe," says Roland. "She will take the keeping of the Princess tonight. You and I have something we must do." He bows his head slightly. "With your permission, of course, my lady."

Ysabel nods. "Something we must do?" says Jo. "That's *great*. What if I already have something to do?"

"What would that be?" says Roland.

"Well," says Jo, looking away, "nothing, really." She jams her hands into the pockets of her workpants. "I just, don't like the way you guys haul off with the orders, you know? You will do this, you will go with me, you will hand over the Princess or get stabbed. It's rude, you know?"

"She's not very grateful, is she?" says Marfisa to Ysabel. Her voice is low and round and full.

Ysabel shrugs. *"Grateful?"* says Jo. "Listen, Glamazon. I'm out a hundred and thirty bucks thanks to your Princess. Hell, that's just the missed days of work – that doesn't count brunches and peach teas!"

"You were warned," says Roland.

"Yeah, I know." Jo shrugs herself more deeply into her bulky flannel shirt. "I was warned. I was told to walk away and I didn't and it's all my fault. You could have just *asked*, is all I'm saying. The principle of the thing, you know?"

"Jo Maguire," says Roland, looking down at the sidewalk, spreading his hands. "Though the Queen cannot recognize you as a member of the court, there are, nonetheless, certain events which will require you, as guardian of our Princess, to take a more public role. After some consideration, the Queen in her wisdom has decided you might benefit from some instruction, in how to carry yourself, what to say and do, how to handle a blade. And I, it seems, am to see to that instruction."

"There, see?" says Jo, after a moment. "That wasn't so hard. You even made me feel like a shithead. Added bonus."

"Will you come with me, then?" says Roland.

"Yes, yes, I'm coming. Christ." As Roland starts across the street toward the corner under the Danmoore Hotel sign, Jo, stepping off the curb, stops. Turns to look back. "Hey," she says to Ysabel. "You gonna..?"

"She'll be fine," says Marfisa.

"It's all right, Jo," says Ysabel. "Go on."

"Okay," says Jo. "I'll, ah. See you later." She sighs, steps off the curb, then trots after Roland.

"An odd girl," says Marfisa. Ysabel is looking sidelong at her, pursing her lips against a bemused smile. "What?" says Marfisa, looking down at her.

"Glamazon," says Ysabel.

Marfisa rolls her eyes, folding her arms, exasperated. Then she smiles, just a little. "Yeah," she says, "okay. *You* look good."

"Oh?" says Ysabel, in her oxblood boots, her knee socks, her khaki skirt, her turtleneck sweater in some nameless natural color, cropped an inch or above her hips. Her long high ponytail swings as she tilts her head. "I haven't been ruined by my exile?"

"Well, tonight's your night," says Marfisa, stepping down the sidewalk, swinging around. Offering up the city. "What are you in the mood for? Saucebox? Le Happy? Madame Damnable's? Panorama?"

"Actually," says Ysabel, standing still under the Tonic banner, "I was thinking – what with the recent incident and all – that it might be best if we headed back to Jo's apartment and holed up there. For safekeeping." She looks away, out into the streetlit night. "What do you think? As my guardian, for the evening."

"Well," says Marfisa. "I think. Given the recent incident, we should probably head back to her apartment. Hole up there. Till they get back. For safekeeping." The corner of her mouth quirks up. "Sounds like a plan."

Jo and Roland climb a narrow flight of stairs into the heart of an old commercial building. The second floor has white walls and a black floor painted so many times that they still look slick and wet. Corners are soft and round. There at the head of the staircase is a set of double doors with a frosted glass fanlight. Roland raps at the right-hand door with the back of his fist. "Come!" a man somewhere on the other side bellows.

Roland opens the door. The room beyond is wide and deep, the far end lost in shadows. Floor-to-ceiling mirrors line one wall. The dark floor is marked in a dozen spots with xes of blue masking tape. In the splash of light from a lone fluorescent ceiling panel stands a wiry man. His greying, balding hair is closely cropped, his soured mouth framed by a salt-and-pepper Van Dyke. His eyes are large and flash. "This is *it?*" he says. He's wearing drawstring pants and a T-shirt stretched across his broad chest and simple canvas shoes. One hand holds a bundle of swords tied together with a bit of rope. "This is what I'm supposed to work with?" His other hand is a metal hook at the end of a beige prosthetic, attached just below his left elbow.

"Jo Maguire," says Roland, "Vincent Erne. Vincent, Jo."

"She's scrawny," says Vincent. He walks across the room, laying the swords down on a rolled-up mat. "Terrible posture. An attitude thick enough to have already gotten on my nerves." He moves quickly, the balls of his feet wisping silently in those shoes on that floor as he circles Jo. "And, of course, she's a girl."

"That doesn't matter," says Roland.

"To you, yes. I know. *I'm* the one who has to make something viable of her by Wednesday of next week. Her hair will have to be cut – this is ri*dic*ulous."

"I thought this guy was supposed to teach me how to use a sword," says Jo, who's following Vincent with her glare.

"Ha!" says Vincent. "Ha! I'm going to teach you not to embarrass yourself, girl. In our pursuit of this goal, we shall endeavor to avoid *anything* involving the actual *use* of a sword. You," he says, turning and jabbing a finger at Roland, "leave. Come back in a couple of hours. You," he says jabbing a finger at Jo, "take off that bulky jacket so I can see you move. Then walk down to the end of the hall and back, and I will tell you everything you are doing wrong."

Jo, shucking out of her flannel shirt, glares at Roland, who shrugs.

"Chop chop!" says Vincent, clicking his prosthetic hook for emphasis. "We don't have all night!"

As Jo sets off down the dark wood floor, as Vincent says "Shoulders, for God's sake, shoulders back, don't slouch," Roland opens the big black door and steps out into the hall. Yawning, stretching, he sits on the top step. "Chin up! Up!" comes Vincent's voice faintly from the training hall. Roland smiles.

Ysabel's fingertip sparkles with gold dust. She holds it above her face, drawing a squiggle in the air, a floral pattern that lingers shimmering like the patterns made by sparklers on a dark night. She smiles at it, her eyes shining. Laughs, just a little. Closes her eyes and takes a deep breath. Opens them, and lets it out. The flower dissolves into glittering swirls, lost in a dim apartment lit only by flickering, guttering candles.

"Oh, how I miss you," says Marfisa, lying naked on her belly on the futon next to Ysabel.

"I miss all of you," says Ysabel, her hair undone, its dark weight pooled on the pillow, spilling over her bare shoulders. She still wears her wool socks. A small plastic baggie swollen with gold dust lies on her stomach.

"You know," says Marfisa, "I wanted to make you jealous tonight."

"Don't think like that," says Ysabel.

"I did. I did. I was going to hang on Roland when you came out with that girl and I was going to, I don't know. It was foolish."

"It was."

"Roland thought I was chilly. He offered me his jacket."

"Roland can be a bit – dense." Ysabel kisses her fingertip lightly, and dips it into the baggie for another smudge of gold dust.

"You were such a *bitch* at Robin's party," says Marfisa, rolling on her side, looking at Ysabel. "Dancing with that girl while I played your song. And then – "

"*Don't,*" says Ysabel. Her finger slashes through the air, sketching an angry shape. "Don't think like that. Don't think you can make me jealous, Marfisa. There's nothing to be jealous *for.*" The shape hangs glittering above them, ghosting slowly into the air. Ysabel turns to look at Marfisa, whose pale, pale hair is tangled across the pillows, her shoulder, tangled up with ghostly blue flowers about her wide face falling, her thin-lipped mouth turning down, her blue eyes shining wet and rimmed with red. "I know," says Marfisa. "I know. Some day the King will come and sit the Throne again. And you will – marry him. But until then – "

"No," says Ysabel. "No. There's no then. There's no until. There's no could be or maybe or can be."

Closing her eyes against threatening tears Marfisa turns her face to the pillow. "I *know,*" she says, muffled. "Lady, I *know.*"

"Shh." Ysabel dips her finger and thumb into the baggie, pulling out a pinch of dust and setting the baggie to one side. She rolls on her side to lie against Marfisa, kissing the thick round blue-tinged shoulder before her. "There's now," she says. "There's here." She sprinkles the pinch of dust floating glittering down through the air to land on Marfisa's back. "Oh," says Marfisa. Shivering. "There's now," says Ysabel, lightly stroking the dust into Marfisa's skin, "and here."

"Oh," says Marfisa.

Jo clomps down the narrow flight of stairs and kicks open the door at the bottom, fishing in her shirt pocket for a pack of cigarettes. The door's swinging shut as she lights one and sucks down a chestful of smoke.

"I liked it better when the brewery was here," says Roland, who's sitting on the sidewalk by the door. "I *liked* the smell. Some people didn't, but I did. It was rich. Sour, but – rich. Full of life. You knew something was growing here. Being made." He smiles. "I also liked the way the bottles would clink on the conveyor belt above the street. Like little glass bells." He looks up at Jo. "How'd it go?"

"He says I should quit smoking," says Jo, taking another drag. "Among other things. I'm supposed to come back Sunday for a *test.*" She looks back up at the long, two-storey building. "*Freak.*" One last drag, and then she flicks the cigarette sparking up at the blank black windows above them. "So what did you stick around for?"

"I thought I might walk you home," says Roland.

"Oh," says Jo. Shrugging, she holds out a hand. He takes it. She pulls him to his feet. "You going to tell me more about brewing?"

"It's good, honest work, brewing," says Roland.

"Actually," says Jo, as they set off down the sidewalk toward 10th. "I wanted to ask you something. About, about this thing I do, being a gallowglas."

"Go ahead," says Roland, frowning down at his shoes.

"When you challenged me. At that party. If I'd actually hit you – "

"You wouldn't have hit me," says Roland, walking more quickly.

"Yeah, but if I'd managed to – " says Jo, catching up.

"You couldn't manage to – "

"*If,* I'm saying. *If.* If I had. Would I have, well, I mean – "

"There's no way you could have. But. If you had – yes," says Roland, stopping at a corner. The stoplight over the intersection is blinking red in all four directions. "Yes," he says again.

"Because of who I am," says Jo.

"*What* you are. Yes."

"I could have killed you. Just like that guy the other night."

"You wouldn't have – "

"And you challenged me anyway."

"There wasn't any danger!" says Roland. Jo throws up her hands and starts across the street. "There shouldn't have been any danger," says Roland, following after.

"Oh, no," says Jo. "None at all. *I* just woke up in Ysabel's house with a hole in my back and no idea what the *fuck* had happened."

"Jo," says Roland. "Jo!" He runs and catches her arm. The two of them swing to a stop, facing each other, before the darkened windows of a bookstore. "I am sorry for that," says Roland. "And I promise you: I will make amends."

"You," says Jo. "Will make amends. To me."

Roland smiles. Laughs a little. "You are rude, Jo. You're impatient and disrespectful. You don't listen and you don't care and you laugh at things you don't understand. But the night before last you proved yourself."

Jo starts to say something, and stops, and then throws up her hands. "Night before last I *ran*. I got some guy *killed*, boiled away into *nothing*, because I didn't know where to put my *feet.*"

"You fought," says Roland, "to keep the Princess safe with everything you had. That's all that matters to me."

Jo shakes her head. "I am never going to understand you people."

"Why should you?" says Roland. He gestures toward the next intersection with his hand, and shrugging, Jo sets off. He follows.

There at the corner of 10th and Burnside, waiting for the light to change, Jo points across the intersection. "What the hell is *that?*"

On a wedge of sidewalk piercing the five-way intersection, across from a pizza place, is a mound of bicycles: kid-sized bikes in candy colors, mirror-bright dirt bikes, banana-seat choppers sparkling with glitter, white rimmed wheels glowing pink in the streetlight, plastic handlebars feathered with tassels, all piled up in a heap about as tall as Roland. "I have no idea," he says.

"It just seems like something you people would do."

"My people?" says Roland.

"Well, it seems like it." Jo frowns.

"I have no idea, Jo," says Roland. "The light's changed."

"Yeah, yeah," says Jo.

"Le Trash Blanc?" – Not her man – Something, Anything, It – Very simple questions

"Le Trash Blanc?" says Jo.

"Go on," says Ysabel. "For another fifty cents you get a can of beer."

Jo shrugs. "Why not."

"Demi-vegan," says Ysabel, handing their menus up to the waitress. "And a glass of the Bordelet sydre doux."

The room is dimly lit and red. Jo and Ysabel sit side-by-side on a low couch under the front window. Over a ringing cocktail-hour piano and a lonely trumpet an unearthly chorus is singing Dare no harienu, daiya no kokoro tsumetai watashi no. Past the closely packed tables toward the back there's an open kitchen, where a goatee'd man pours batter on a hot griddle, swirling it in a circle with a wide flat paddle. "Ah," says Ysabel. She's wearing black jeans and a tight white T-shirt. A black leather jacket rustling with fringe slumps on the couch next to her. "This is nice."

"Yeah," says Jo. "We're under twenty bucks, with booze." She's wearing baggy brown cords and a blue and orange rugby shirt, her mismatched Chuck Taylors perched on the edge of the coffee table in front of them. One black, one white, the toe swaddled in grubby duct tape.

"What I *meant* was," Ysabel's saying, "it's just about been a week since you challenged Roland. And in all that time, we haven't really had much of a chance to sit down and – "

"Eat out?" says Jo.

"Don't," says Ysabel, quietly. Jo looks down at her hands in her lap, reaches for the glass of water on the table between her feet. Sips. "You think you can spring for dessert?" says Ysabel.

"We'll see," says Jo.

"We could split one," says Ysabel. "The lemon-ginger. And a cup of coffee. That's it. I swear."

"We'll see," says Jo.

Donna tenshi mo akogare sasayaki mo, the chorus is singing. Otoko no ainado todoki wa shinai, todoki wa shinai.

"So what's your life like when I'm not interrupting it?" says Ysabel. The waitress in her periwinkle dress sets a glass of cider and a can of Pabst Blue Ribbon on the low table.

"You've pretty much seen it," says Jo. "Work. Home. Sleep. Every now and then I order a pizza."

"Yes, but," says Ysabel. "I mean, friends. You were out with some last Saturday – Becker, and, well, that funny little goth – "

"Guthrie," says Jo, shrugging, leaning forward, popping the top on the can of beer. "And Becker, yeah. Friends from work. I've known Becker maybe, what, eight months? He's kinda turning into an asshole, now that he's been promoted." She grins as she pours the beer into an empty glass. "Which is what we were celebrating last week, his promotion, I mean. Not his assholishness."

Ysabel lays one thin arm along the back of the sofa. "And what about anybody else?"

"What about them?" says Jo.

"*You* know," says Ysabel. "Is there? Anyone in particular?"

"Well," says Jo, the glass of pale beer in her hand. "There used to be."

Her hand up by her temple, toying with her thick dark tangled curls, Ysabel smiles. "Does this anyone have a name?"

"Frankie," says Jo. "And, I mean, it's over. It's definitely over. It ended badly." She takes a long drink of beer. "So," she says, setting the glass down.

"So?" says Ysabel.

"So," says Jo, shrugging. "It's over. So I guess the answer is there isn't."

"And Christian?" says Ysabel.

"*Christian?*" says Jo. "No. I mean, what? We just – "

"How did you get to know him?" says Ysabel.

"He was one of the first people I met when I moved here," says Jo, looking sidelong at Ysabel. "About four years ago."

Ysabel sips her cider. "He just," she says, "doesn't seem like the sort of person you'd, well. Know."

"Yeah, well," says Jo, "he was. Okay? For a while there – I did some stupid stuff, and some stupid stuff happened. And Christian is a wild guy, you know? But, if you're a friend, he's *there*. Period." She smiles. "It was cool, seeing him again."

"Stupid stuff?" says Ysabel, an eyebrow raised.

"Yeah," says Jo. "Which is why these days I go to work, and I come home, to my apartment, and every now and then I order a pizza."

Ysabel nods a little at that.

"Of course," says Jo, "your man Vincent doesn't think that'll do me a bit of good."

"Vincent?" says Ysabel.

"He says no matter what, I'm always going to be looking for trouble. Looking for a fight." She grins a little at herself. "I guess I proved that last week."

"He's not my man," says Ysabel.

"He isn't?" says Jo.

"I've never actually met Vincent Erne," says Ysabel. "What's he like?"

"He talks too much," says Jo.

"Chin up! Up!" snaps Vincent.

Jo at the other end of the mirror-walled room spins around. "What the fuck?" she says. "I'm *walking*. Like you said."

"You're walking, all right," he says. The metal hook at the end of his left arm clacks in a dismissive snap. "You're walking like a goddamn *kid*. Like you're going to *detention*. Like your *mother* just called you home for supper and you want the whole world to know you hate collard greens." He's gliding down the dark, tape-marked floor, jabbing at her with his thin, knobby forefinger. "Boo. Fucking. Hoo." Jo's spreading her arms, staring at him, her mouth open in dismay, in anger. "What?" he says, circling her. "What? Come on. Let me have it." Jo's mouth tightens.

"Whaddaya got? Come on." Her hand squeezes into a fist and opens up again. "Well? What are you gonna do about it, huh? Come *on!*" Leaning back to one side Jo throws the heel of her hand at his face.

He catches it easily.

"You have nothing," he says.

She tries to jerk her hand free. He holds it there in the air between them, his fingers tightening about her wrist.

"You have nothing," he says again, "and everybody knows it. So you curl up tightly about it and when somebody tries to poke you to see what's what, all you can do is take that someone's head off. So go on. Take my head off."

Jo jerks her arm again, trying to throw her hips into it, and when he hauls her hand back up between them she shoves the motion into her shoulder, lunging at him. He blocks her with his beige prosthetic arm. Then he lets go, stepping back.

"You walk into a roomful of gentry like that," he says, shaking his head.

"What the fuck *is* this?" snarls Jo.

"These are people who would as soon gut you and leave you for dead as take your lunch money," says Vincent. "You walk into a room, full of nothing, like *that,* you won't walk out." Turning away he walks back down the long room toward the lit end. "Now walk like you *have* something," he calls over his shoulder. "Walk like you mean it."

"I killed one of them," she says.

"*No,*" he says, standing there under the light at the other end of the room. "No, you did *not.* The *Chariot* did. And he wasn't gentry. He was just Tommy Rawhead. Mothers used his name to scare their kids. Get up to bed, or Rawhead and Bloody Bones will eat! You! Up!" Vincent shakes his head. "And then some idiot got it into his head he's going after the Bride, and Tommy got in the middle of it, and *you* stuck your foot in when you were told to stay put, and *this* is what you thought you were bringing to the table?"

Jo's looking down at her boots.

"Luckily, it's all about appearance," he says. "If you *look* like you have it, then you *have* it. That is the secret, my dear. Plain and simple. If you walk into a room with the Bride on your arm and you *look* like you have it, no one is going to poke you to find out otherwise."

"So," says Jo, "what do I – "

"Walk towards me," says Vincent. "By the time you get here, I want to believe you *have* something. Anything. *It.*"

Jo takes a deep breath. Squares her shoulders. Looks him straight in the eye. The light's shining off his forehead, the tip of his nose. His hand held loosely at his side, waiting.

She starts walking, striding down the dark floor toward him. He sighs. Looks away, at the floor-to-ceiling mirror running down the wall. Heads toward her suddenly. She falters as he circles behind her, takes her shoulders in his hand, the butt of his prosthesis, turning her to face the mirror. "Look," he says, leaning over her shoulder. "Look at yourself. *Look.* What do you have? What do you have to be proud of?"

Jo's face in the mirror is slack. The line of her nose is the only sharp thing about it. Shadows pool in her cheeks and smudge the skin under her eyes. Her lips parted, just. Taking a breath. "What is it?" he says. "At the end of the day, what can you look back on and say, I *did* that? Find that thing. Find it and let it fill you up so you can walk with your shoulders back and your chin up and your head high. Find it so you can look them in the eye and they will *see* that you are a person to be reckoned with. Find it, Jo, and *show* it to them, and you won't have to prove it." Jo closes her eyes. Swallows. "But you have to *find* it, Jo."

She opens her eyes, looking down at his hand. "Please," she says. "Get your hand off my shoulder."

Vincent backs away a couple of steps. "Walk," he says. "Go on. Down to the end of the room and back again. Go."

"So what about you?" says Jo, leaning forward to fork up a mouthful of crêpe.

"Me?" says Ysabel, polishing off her cider. It's too much me, a woman's singing breathily over a weepy steel guitar, and not enough of the people I wanna be.

"Yeah," says Jo. "Do you have a particular anyone?"

Nine ninety-nine, sings the woman, pretty good wine, a beautiful time. Ysabel smiles. "No," she says. "I never have."

"Never," says Jo.

"I can't," says Ysabel. She leans back, toying with the fringe of the jacket beside her. "I'm the Princess," she says. "The Bride. I can't."

"So this Bride business is, I mean, it's literal?" says Jo. "You're going to get married?"

"To the King," says Ysabel. "When he returns. So I suppose there *is* a particular anyone, after all." She leans forward, picking up her fork to chase a last bit of black bean paste.

"What's he like?" says Jo.

"I don't know," says Ysabel. "No one knows who the King will be, or when he will come." She looks back at Jo. "Which might be why someone was trying so very hard to talk to me Wednesday. Perhaps he thinks it works the same backwards as forwards – if he were to marry me," and she licks the last bite from her fork.

"He'd become King," says Jo.

"And it might very well work that way," says Ysabel. "But until then," she shrugs. "I can't."

"Now," says Jo, "when you say never, do you mean – "

"I think I mean it's none of your business."

"Yeah, but. Never?"

"Did you want to split a crêpe for dessert?" says Ysabel.

The phone rings, so he picks it up. "Hello," he says, tucking it between his ear and his shoulder, picking up the knife. "I, uh," he says, crunching a garlic clove under the flat of the blade. "Look," he says. "It's a Sunday, for God's sake. You people shouldn't be."

"Oh, I understand," says Ysabel into her telephone headset. "But this isn't a sales call. It's just a survey, sir. We only want to ask you how satisfied you are with various financial products and services. It'll only take five or six minutes of your time, tops, and you'll be helping a bank do a better job of giving its customers what they want. Perhaps *your* bank. Look at it as a good deed for the day."

"Yeah, well," he says, peeling the paper from the clove, "I don't think."

"And you should understand, sir, that we don't know who you are. Your phone number was randomly generated. I wouldn't know you from Adam, sir, if I were to bump into you on the street. So." She swivels in her chair, looking out of her carrel along the length of the narrow office with its indecisive cream walls. A couple of spaces down, Jo is hunched over her phone, making some emphatic point with her hands. Guthrie's hanging up his phone. The woman with the wattle under her chin is headed for the kitchen, on a break. Becker at his desk, holding a handset to his ear, monitoring someone's call. "With that in mind," says Ysabel, "do you think you might want me?"

"I, uh." His brown hair is shaggy, and has enough grey in it to look dusty as well as unkempt. He holds the knife in one hand, looking down at a jumble of unpeeled garlic cloves. "What?" he says.

"Would you want to answer my questions?"

"I," he says.

"Keep in mind, they're very simple. It'll only take five or six minutes of your time. For instance: do you find me desirable?"

"I'm *married*," he says. Putting the knife down on the counter.

"Doesn't matter for the purposes of this survey," says Ysabel. She's looking at her gold-painted nails. At his desk Becker's looking up, at her, frowning. "How would you rate me, on a scale of one to ten, one being lowest, and ten being highest?"

"A ten," he says. "I thought you said this was about financial – "

"It's about how *satisfied* you are," says Ysabel. Becker's making slashing gestures across his throat at her. "How satisfied do you think you'd be with me?" Becker's getting up from behind his desk. "Would you say very satisfied, somewhat satisfied, somewhat dissatisfied, or very dissatisfied?"

"Oh," he says, looking across the kitchen at a woman typing on a laptop on a little desk in an alcove under a crowded bookshelf. "Very satisfied. But – Hello? Hello?"

Ysabel stands as Becker takes his finger off the disconnect button. "What the hell was that?" he says.

"I was," says Ysabel, "flirting. Trying to keep him interested in doing the survey."

"That wasn't *flirting,*" says Becker. "That was – weird."

Ysabel shrugs.

"Don't *do* that," says Becker. "You do that again, I'll have to pull you off the phones. Okay? There's just an hour left in the shift – " Ysabel's hanging her headset up in the carrel, squatting to pick up a little purse from the floor under her desk. "What are you," says Becker.

"Leaving," says Ysabel. "I'm bored, and I'd almost certainly do it again. I'm saving you the trouble."

"What's up?" says Jo, standing there behind Becker.

"Get back on the phone," says Becker.

"Shut the fuck up," says Jo. "Ysabel?"

"Don't," says Becker.

"I'm going," says Ysabel. "I'm done."

"Don't talk," says Becker.

"Let me get my jacket," says Jo.

"Don't *talk* to me like that," says Becker. People are looking up from their phones. "Jo, sit down. Ysabel, just head over to the Little Conference Room. I'll meet you there in a minute."

"I think," says Ysabel, "I would be very dissatisfied with that."

"That doesn't matter," says Becker. quietly. Not looking at either of them.

"Back the fuck off," says Jo, yanking her jacket off the back of her chair. Shutting off her computer.

"Don't you leave," says Becker.

"If you're throwing her out," says Jo, "I have to go with her. You *know* that."

"I'm not – " says Becker. "Sit the fuck *down,* Jo. Ysabel – "

"Or what?" says Jo. "You'll *fire* me?" She pulls on her jacket. "Come on."

"What the hell," says Becker, there in the middle of the aisle of kelly green carrels.

WHIPPED CREAM – LIKE MOST PEOPLE – ZOOBOMBING
THIS RAY GUY

THE WHIPPED CREAM melts into an oily sludge. Fluffy curds calve off, bobbing up and down as Ysabel pokes them with a plastic stirrer.

"We could sell the stuff," says Jo.

"The stuff," says Ysabel, not looking up.

"The furniture," says Jo, leaning forward, her elbows on the table. "The chest-thing. That whoever it was brought, who came in and cleaned up the place."

"We can't sell that."

"We can't," says Jo.

"We can't sell it, Jo," snaps Ysabel, throwing the plastic stirrer down by her coffee. "Honestly. Do you really think somebody hauled all that up the elevator and set it up in your apartment while we were out shopping for a half an hour?" She slumps back in her chair, looking up at the yellowing ceiling tiles. "It's not mine to sell," she says.

"What were you doing on the phone?" says Jo.

"I was *flirting*," says Ysabel.

"For *flirting*," says Jo, "Becker cuts you off? For flirting, he wants to talk to you in the conference room?"

"Yes," says Ysabel simply.

"Whatever," says Jo.

"So," says Ysabel, picking the stirrer back up. "Do you think you're," and she sinks a large, unwieldy blob of whipped cream, "fired?"

"For *that*?" Jo snorts. "I'd have to go postal or something to get fired there. It's you I'm worried about."

"You think I'm fired?"

"I think you quit."

Ysabel shrugs. Dunks another shred of whipped cream.

"Are you going to drink that?"

"Probably not," says Ysabel.

"Fine," says Jo, pushing back her chair. "It's about time to go meet Roland and whatshername, anyway. You know," she says, as Ysabel plucks her jacket from the back of the chair, "we could get *her* to guard you while I'm working – "

"No," says Ysabel, heading for the door.

"No?" says Jo.

"*No,*" Ysabel calls over her shoulder.

"Okay, fine, whatever," mutters Jo, following after.

After a moment, she's back, snagging the cup of coffee, taking it with her.

"She surprises me," says Roland, standing once again under the multi-colored Tonic banner. He's wearing a silvery track suit with green piping. His shoes are puffy and white and spotless, and blue and white headphones cling to his neck. "I keep expecting her to give up, and she doesn't."

"Her nose is too big," says Marfisa. Her hands are tucked into the pockets of a baby blue fleece pullover.

"The Princess?" says Roland.

"No," says Marfisa. "I thought you were talking about the girl. Jo."

"I meant the Princess."

"The Princess's nose is fine."

"I know."

"I thought you meant *Jo* was refusing to give up."

"I know."

Marfisa reaches up to tuck a curl of hair behind her ear. "And Jo *is* surprising."

"Jo," says Roland, "is surprising in precisely the way you'd expect."

Marfisa frowns.

"Hey," calls Jo from the corner, Ysabel behind her, a dark shape in her dark suit. Roland looks over at the front door of the building, back to the two of them coming up the street. "Change in plans," says Jo. "I mean, we're still going to Vincent's. Right? We just, um. Left work a little early."

"Oh," says Roland.

Hall light spills onto crinkled posters for plays long since over, with titles like The Maid's Tragedy and The Courier's Tragedy, The Insatiate Countess and The Knight of the Burning Pestle. "You weren't in the studio," says Roland.

"I'm not," says Vincent Erne, as the ceiling lights flicker to life, "am I." He's sitting cross-legged in an office chair, his back to a long table lost under haphazard stacks of books and piles of paper. He holds a coffee mug loosely, his finger through the ring. On the desk a bottle with a finger's worth of sooty whiskey.

"You're drinking," says Roland.

"Why yes," says Vincent. "I *am*. Did you bring your protégée? Jo?"

She's leaning in the doorway, her head against the jamb. "She'll be ready for Wednesday?" says Roland.

"What will you *do* to her, Wednesday?"

Jo's eyes flick from Vincent to Roland and back again. "Vincent Erne," Roland's saying, "you have incurred certain obligations – "

"*You* don't need to remind me, boy," snaps Vincent. "Why don't you run along, and allow me to discharge them. *As,*" he says, climbing slowly out of his chair, "I see fit."

"Should we go over to the," says Jo, pointing down the hall after Roland.

"I'm not in the mood for running around and yelling at you," says Vincent. A long axe, hung with ribbons and limp felt banners, leans in the corner. On the floor a large white kite-shaped shield with a gold and black bee. Vincent squats there, clattering something. "Are you in the mood to run around and be yelled at?"

"No," says Jo.

"Then we shan't go over to the studio," says Vincent. He stands up, holding a sword. "Here." He tosses it hilt down at Jo who just barely catches it above the saucer-shaped guard.

"It's a sword," she says.

"And *this* is a sheath." He holds it up, a limp leather sock dangling from the hook at the end of his left arm. "Take off your jacket."

"Why?" says Jo.

"So I can tie it to your *belt,*" he says, kneeling heavily before her, catching himself with his hand on the floor.

"You're not," says Jo, arms raised awkwardly out of his way. "You're not one of them. Are you." The scabbard hangs from a fold of black satiny fabric with a couple of long ties that he works under Jo's belt. "I mean," she says, "I knew you weren't a *knight*. But I didn't realize you weren't a, well, a..."

"Go on," says Vincent.

"You're not – you're like me. You're like most people."

"I highly doubt that," he says, leaning back. "Then, *no* one is like most people. Sheathe the sword."

"I thought," says Jo, looking down, aiming the wavering tip at the sheath's mouth, "I wasn't going anywhere near a sword, or something. All of a sudden I'm worthy?"

Vincent climbs to his feet. "It's a piece-of-shit épée that would set you back maybe a hundred bucks." He grins. "I get them wholesale. Now. Let me show you everything you need to know."

He takes her left hand in his and places it on the hilt. "The most common mistake a newcomer makes with a sword is to hold it here, by the hilt. Go on. Grab it." Jo does. The sword swings a little on her hip, the end of it sticking out behind her clunking into the door. "See?" says Vincent. "It's a long piece of metal. You want to keep it under control, but if you grab it like that, the tip sticks out. If you were to bow before the Queen, you'd put out the eye of whomever's standing behind you. Let go. Rest your wrist against the hilt. Push the hilt *out,"* and she does. From its black satiny baldric the hilt pushed out swings the blade in its sheath to tuck up against the backs of her thighs. "Under control," says Vincent. "If you bow, just remember to keep pushing the hilt out like that. It will become second nature."

"Okay," says Jo. "Now. What if I get into a fight?"

"If you get in a fight, Jo," he says, "you will *lose."* He heads over to his desk and pours the last finger of whiskey into his mug. "So don't get in a fight. Don't curl up. Don't snap."

"Vincent," says Jo.

"Mr. Erne," he says, sipping.

"Mr. Erne," says Jo. "What's going to happen on Wednesday?"

Swallowing, Vincent lowers his mug. "A hunt," he says.

"It's a stupid way to run things, if you ask me," says Ysabel. She's sitting on the edge of the counter in the bathroom, next to the sink.

"Hold still," says Marfisa. "Close your eyes." She's standing between Ysabel's knees, leaning in close, a brush in one hand to smooth a pale and creamy beige across Ysabel's eyelid.

"She wakes up," says Ysabel, closing her eyes. "She spends six hours a day telephoning people and asking them how much they like their things. She does this for just enough money so she can come back to her apartment. Sometimes she orders a pizza." Marfisa picks up a skinny brush and dips it into a pot of bright pink in a jumbled muddle of colors and brushes in a My Little Pony lunchbox. "She doesn't even *have* half the things she asks about. Money markets. Mutual funds." Ysabel's hands rest idly on Marfisa's hips. "An annuity. She doesn't even know what those *are."*

"Something that happens once a year," mutters Marfisa, carefully drawing a thin pink line along the edge of Ysabel's eyelid.

"I don't think what she *does* matters. Whether she's calling people or making donuts or delivering pizzas. What she's *really* doing is shoveling money. From the company that pays people to ask questions to the people who own this apartment building and make the pizzas who probably put it into mutual funds which they aren't all that satisfied with. It's like a tide," says Ysabel, "constantly rushing out, and she has to help it along, and she can't ever stop and take any for herself."

"Her loss," says Marfisa, leaning back a little, looking at Ysabel's closed eyes. "How's that?"

Ysabel looks over her shoulder at herself in the mirror. Blinks. "Looks good," she says, turning to look up at Marfisa. Smiling. "Let's go."

"The Bear?" says Roland, as they pass the white brick wall of the old armory. "The Stag? The Boar? *None* of these?"

"All he talked about was how I walked," says Jo.

"The *Fox?*"

"Look," says Jo, "I didn't even know there was going to *be* this hunt until tonight. You haven't exactly been upfront yourself."

"I thought *he* was telling you," mutters Roland. "He didn't even talk about the Hare?"

"He gave me *this,*" snaps Jo, holding up the épée she's been carrying at her side, still in its black leather sheath, her hand an awkwardly tight fist under the bell guard. "What the hell am I supposed to do with it?"

"Don't go waving it around," says Roland, reaching out, pushing her hand down.

"It doesn't even have a *point,*" says Jo.

"Roland!" calls someone up ahead. "Roland, is that you?"

"What the hell is he up to?" says Roland, looking back the way they've come.

"Who, him?" says Jo, pointing with the hilt of her sword at a man with a shock of pinkish orange hair, up ahead at the corner of the intersection with Burnside. He's wearing a black leather jacket and black jeans and he's slouching over the handlebars of a little pink bicycle. His knees jackknife up to either side like some spindly frog. White streamers on the handlebars flutter in the breeze.

"Roland!" he calls. "It *is* you!"

"*I* was talking about Vincent," mutters Roland. "Just hold onto the sword for now, and," but Jo's stepped past him.

"It's one of those bicycles," she says. She looks back, frowning. "I thought you said you guys didn't do the bicycles."

"He's *not* one of my guys. Just ignore him, and he'll – *Jo* – "

"Hey!" Jo's calling to the guy on the bike. "What the hell are you guys doing?"

His face cracks open in an enormous grin. He slings his arms out to either side and yells up into the light-stained nighttime sky, *"Zoobombing!"*

At the underground station a dozen of them get off the train. They wear sweaters and hooded sweatshirts, jeans and hacked-off khakis. There's a woman in a green and yellow cheerleader outfit. Somebody's wearing a rabbit head with a metallic, skull-like face. Some of them carry little kids' bikes, like the pink one on the shoulder of the guy with the pinkish orange hair. Some of them carry silvery dirt bikes. The cheerleader has a big blue bicycle with fat tires and a flowery white basket hooked to the front. One guy has a rickety looking homebuilt machine with a yellow banana seat and a tiny back wheel and a long fork for the front wheel, like a chopped penny-farthing.

They head for the elevators at either end of the platform. Roland frowning hefts a battered red dirt bike. Jo after him sets a purple kids' bike on its back wheel. "Hey," says the guy with pinkish orange hair, last to push his way in. "Roland. If you don't think this is going to be a blast – "

"I said I'd do it, Ray," mutters Roland. "So I'll do it."

"Going up," says whoever's wearing the rabbit head, punching the top button. The digital readout starts counting down from 260 feet to the surface.

"Young and tall and tan and slender," sings someone else, giggling.

"You guys do this every week?" says Jo.

"Just about," says a woman in a white tank top, her muscled arms ringed with tattoos and elbow pads. "First time?"

"Yeah," says Jo.

"You know, Roland," says Ray, "You don't have to – "

"I *said*," snaps Roland, as the elevator doors slide open, "I'd do it."

"Heads up!" yells somebody outside, and something comes winging in at them. Ray puts out his hand and catches it, thwock! A can of Pabst Blue Ribbon. "Oh *ho,*" says Ray. A couple of people in the milling crowd outside break into a run, and violently shaking up the can of beer he takes off after them.

Out of the elevator a sidewalk overlooks a cluster of dimly lit parking lots sloping generally down toward the dark gate of the Oregon Zoo. There's a swarm of people on bikes, people walking bikes, people sitting by bikes drinking beer and bottle water, snapping photos of each other posing on bikes. "I told you," says Roland. A big guy walks past, wearing only an army helmet and a pair of white underpants. "Not us."

"Yeah," says Jo. "But Ray is. Right?"

"Ray is an asshole," says Roland, after a moment.

"So what are you doing up here?"

"First," says Roland, "I have to make sure you get back to the Princess."

"You don't have to worry about that," says Jo. "She's in my apartment."

"And I will *not* allow anyone to say I backed down from a challenge," he says.

"It's not that bad," says the tattooed woman. "It's all downhill from here into town. We get up to thirty, forty miles an hour, but the worst we've seen is a busted collarbone." She grins. "You *will* wipe out. You *will* scrape stuff up. But it's a hell of a run."

Someone's chanting something – the words lost in a thick fake Cockney accent. Somebody else takes it up: "We are the Self-Preservation, Society! We are the Self-Preservation, Society!"

"Zoobombing," says Jo, shaking her head.

The swarm sorts itself out into a line snaking up out from under the parking lot lights along the switchbacking length of Kingston.

The sky to either side glows with the lights of downtown, the suburbs on the other side of the hills. The only other lights shine from the fronts of the bicycles, bob on helmets, flicker and flash from cameras and cell phones, wink unexpectedly from reflectors in spokes. Kingston dead-ends suddenly at the top of the ridge into Fairview. The line of bicyclists starts clumping up here in ragged groups on either side of the road. There's Ray, waddling out into the middle on his little pink bike. "Hey!" he yells. "Hey!" He sits there a moment as whistles and claps waft around him, and then throwing back his head he bellows, "Get a bloomin' move on!" He lifts his feet, jackknifing his legs to get them onto the pedals. The bike wobbling rolls slowly downhill. Picking up speed as he leans into the curve and out of sight.

And everyone starts to follow him. Wheeling and pedaling out into the street and kicking off down the hill, dirt bikes and kids' bikes and a ten-speed like an old greyhound, a red folding bicycle with little wheels, the homebuilt chopped penny farthing. Whoops and cries ring out. Jo follows the tattooed woman out onto the street, and Roland follows her. "Watch out," says the tattooed woman, "for cops," and then she's off.

"Cops," says Jo.

"This was your idea," says Roland.

"*You* were the one who said yeah, whatever, we'll do it."

"You were the one who wouldn't ignore him in the first place."

"You know," says Jo, as the guy in the army hat and the white underpants pedals past, giggling, "there's a story there. If we make it to the bottom in one piece, you're gonna have to tell me what the hell it is with you and this Ray guy."

"Do not think to *bargain* with me, Jo Maguire," snaps Roland, and he kicks off, pedaling jerkily down the hill on his red dirt bike.

Jo sits there a moment, looking after him. And then she shrugs, pushes off, finds the little pedals with her feet. "Ho. Ly. *Fuck!*" she yells, picking up speed.

Marfisa in the hall sits back against Jo's door, long legs in blue and brown striped socks stretched across the orange carpet. She wears blue shorts and a tight grey T-shirt that says Property of s.h.i.e.l.d. Her arms folded over the blue fleece pullover wadded up in her lap. When the elevator down the hall dings, she opens her eyes.

"No, seriously," Jo's saying.

"I do not," says Roland.

"That was one hell of a spill."

"I do *not* need *help.*"

"I'm not," says Jo, as Roland pushes past her, out of the elevator. "Helping," she says. Following him, the épée still in its black leather sheath balanced on one shoulder, her hand up holding it lightly. "It's just, you're limping – "

"Jo," says Roland.

The blue fleece pullover wadded about her left hand held up before them Marfisa elbow crooked up high in her right hand holds a sword, fluorescent light stretched thin glaring from the tip at Jo. She opens her mouth to say something.

"Don't," says Roland.

"I *will,*" says Marfisa. "Jo Maguire – "

"Do not do this," says Roland.

"Jo Maguire," says Marfisa, "I challenge – "

"What has she *done* to you?" says Roland. "What harm?"

"For *her,*" says Marfisa. "It's for her. The way she – "

"No," Roland's saying, "it isn't. Put up your blade. Put up – *Jo* – "

Jo her blunted épée still resting on one shoulder is stepping past him. Marfisa lowers her swaddled hand a little, sword hand still held high. "Stop," says Roland. Marfisa's sword is bright, two fingers wide without a curve until its sudden tip, quivering, scraping nervous squiggles in the air. "You know what?" says Jo. Marfisa sucks a quick breath, sword twisting at the jump in her wrist as Jo lifts the épée and her hand drooping lets the black leather tip of it swing down to thump against the carpet. "I'm tired," says Jo. "I'm really fucking tired. I'm going to walk past you, go into my apartment, I'm going to crawl into bed, and go to sleep." Jo looks down at the épée in her hand almost swallowed by the cuff of her army jacket. The bell is dull and dented. The hilt under her fingers is wrapped with grubby red tape. She lets go, catching it about the leather sheath. Hefts it, tucking it under her arm. Lifts her head. Marfisa's looking away, working at the pullover wrapped about her left hand.

"I will not," Roland's saying, "mention this to your brother."

"Thank you," says Marfisa, and then, reaching out suddenly, her hand on Jo's shoulder, "Wait."

Jo eyes wide looks at that hand.

"If you *hurt* her," says Marfisa.

Jo frowns. "I won't," she says. "Let go."

"I will kill you if anything happens to her."

"Marfisa," says Roland. "Let her go. Leave her to guard the Princess. Let her go, or I will call you out myself."

Marfisa lifts her hand. Jo awkwardly clamping the épée under her arm fishes for her keys. Marfisa shaking out her pullover watches as Jo unlocks the door. "Well," says Jo. "Goodnight."

The door closed, there in the dark, Jo sags back against it, shivering. The épée falls to the floor with a muffled clank.

"So," says the little guy in the dark suit.

"So?" says Mr. Lier, washing his hands at a stained plastic sink on spindly legs.

"What do you think?"

Mr. Lier, smiling, holds up one finger. His white shirt open at the collar, the cuffs unbuttoned and rolled back. A rust-colored smudge still on one wrist that he worries with his thumb, walking back across the dusty floor to the harsh white glare of the arc light hanging from a hook. "Well, Mr. Kerr?" he says.

"I, um," says the man in the blue striped shirt. The wooden floor under that bright light has been swept clear of dust. It's marred with a smattering of black charred spots. "He was – magnificent."

"And?" says Mr. Lier, smiling.

"It's like I was saying," says Kerr. His tie is much the same blue as the stripes on his shirt, and the watch on his wrist is heavy and gold. "The EPA rules coming down, security, with the terrorism thing – like it's ever going to happen here, but still. People are scared."

"Which isn't what I want to hear," says Mr. Lier, still smiling. "What I want to hear is those reservoirs are an important part of the fabric of this city. I want to hear you say you have no intention of burying them in tanks under the hillside, that's what I want." One of the charred spots still smolders, putting up a thready stream of pale quick smoke. "And for now, *he* listens to *me*." Mr. Lier smothers it neatly with his white and ivory saddle shoe.

"Well," says Kerr. He is clean-shaven, his dark hair carefully swept back. "I could talk to the commissioner. Arrange another study. It's not like we can just turn around and say no."

"But you will," says Mr. Lier. "Eventually."

"Um," says Kerr. He nods. "Thanks," he says. "Thank you. Very much."

When Kerr has left, Mr. Lier walks over to the sink, where the little guy waits next to the big guy in the dark suit. "Mr. Keightlinger," says Mr. Lier, unrolling his sleeves, "tell Mr. Charlock what today's date is."

"What I'm saying," says the little guy, "we can get this girl six ways from Sunday the minute you say the word."

"Three," says Mr. Lier, pulling cufflinks from his pocket. "Only one of which is likely to work. Mr. Keightlinger?"

"It's an expression," mumbles the little guy, looking down at his shoes.

"The nineteenth of September," says Mr. Keightlinger.

"It's the fucking eighteenth," says Mr. Charlock, elbowing him.

"Ten past," says Mr. Keightlinger. "Midnight."

"Not even the equinox," says Mr. Lier. "Months to go, and what would we do with her? Where would we put her?"

"The suite at the Lucia?" says Mr. Charlock.

"We wait until the solstice," says Mr. Lier, "and *then* we deal with the one who has her keeping. Not whoever's the most un-usual. Vulnerable." He smoothes his cuffs, brushes something from one sleeve. "Don't get me wrong, Mr. Charlock. This was good work. I don't think it'll be this girl, but if it is, we're ready. Meanwhile, you keep up your observations and investigations. Whoever it is, we'll be ready."

"Yessir," says Mr. Charlock. Mr. Keightlinger nods, once.

And then Mr. Lier says, "The boy?"

"Who," says Mr. Charlock. "Beaumont?"

"He won't mess this up?"

"Nah," says Mr. Charlock. "We took care of him."

"Good," says Mr. Lier.

"Jo?" says Ysabel.

"Go back to sleep," says Jo, smoking a cigarette in the dark. The épée lies on the glass-topped café table before her, between the ash-tray and the vase full of tea roses unearthly pale in the streetlight.

"Did you pass?" says Ysabel, rolling over, up on one elbow.

"I have no idea," says Jo. "I got a sword. I rode somebody's bike down the west hills from the zoo in the dark. Roland wiped out on this corner up by the rose gardens, I helped him get up. Fucked up his knee, you know?" She takes a drag. "What's the deal with Marfisa?"

"Did she say something?"

"She nearly," says Jo, and then she says, "Never mind. Forget it."

"There's no deal," says Ysabel, rubbing her eye with the heel of one hand. "She's a knight. Like Roland. The Axe. What were you doing tonight?"

"Zoobombing," says Jo, and then she shakes her head. "I have no fucking idea." She stubs out the cigarette.

i encourage you and your friend to come bomb,
but yeah, there is name calling and trash
talking, nobody ever said zoobomb was for the
fragile

—cupcake

NO. 4

A-Hunting

Five hundred bucks – The Thing in the Shadows
a Half-dozen T-shirts, most of them black – Formal dress
Some qualities of Vengeance – Every felicitation
the Lights above – Leaning green – Glad Wide Jars
What happened, What didn't – "Puertas a mi izquierda"
We Revellers – the Duke's ecstatic – Her choice
Down by the Ice Rink – a Side-bet – a Roomful of Gentry
Her honor – the Very Air – They march – the Conquering Hero

"Five hundred bucks," says Frankie, shoveling the hair out of his face, looking up at the red-headed man. "It's only fair," he says. He frowns. "I mean, we're not gonna *hurt* her. Right?"

"He says it's only fair," says the red-headed man into a slim red phone. He's standing in the apartment's open doorway, dark against the soft grey light outside, leaning lightly on a long portfolio tube. "Did you catch that?"

"What?" says the man in the dark gold shirt. Lit by a single bulb he's standing in a basement at the foot of a sagging flight of stairs. "What's fair," he says, half stooping, swinging his head back and forth, craning to tilt the antenna of his purple phone. "Reception's fucking wretched down here." Somewhere in the dark something large clip-clops back and forth, grunting. A woman in a black vinyl miniskirt sits at the top of the stairs. She's eyeing the shadows nervously.

"Five hundred," says the red-headed man. "He wants five hundred, your grace. Half a thousand." Frankie biting his lip says, "You're not gonna hurt her," to the thin man perched on the arm of the couch. "Right?" The thin man's looking at the handle of his Japanese sword. His feet are bare.

"Five hundred dollars," says his grace. He turns to look up at the woman in the black vinyl miniskirt. She shrugs. "This is the ex," he says.

119

"Yes, your grace," says the red-headed man.

"Fuck him," says his grace. From somewhere in the darkness a lugubrious voice says, "Sir." His grace lifts a hand, finger up, admonishing. "We don't need him. Not five hundred dollars' worth of him."

"Sir," says the red-headed man. He takes a step out onto the balcony. "I'm sorry, sir, I – "

"Blast and rot, Gaveston, you know this. We could pull anybody off the street for this, anybody in the city, and you call me to ask if I want to pay out five hundred dollars for an ex-boyfriend. Stop bothering me with this shit."

"Yes, your grace," says Gaveston. He snaps his red phone shut and stands there a moment, one hand on the wrought-iron railing of the balcony, looking down at the little parking lot. A woman cuts across it, trailing cigarette smoke, a heavy white garbage bag held in one hand out away from her body.

"Well?" says Frankie. "What's up?"

"We have the pleasure," says Gaveston, tucking his phone into the pocket of his brown cardigan, "of refusing your offer."

"What?" says Frankie. The thin man pushes off from the couch, headed for the door. He bats an empty Diet Coke bottle away across the carpet with the scabbarded tip of his sword.

"There will be no counter-offer," says Gaveston, lifting his portfolio tube. "Do have a good afternoon."

"But," says Frankie, as they close the door behind them.

The steps down the outside of the yellow apartment building are quite narrow. They go down single-file, footsteps clanging. The thin man lifts his sword and rests it on his shoulder. "Vengeance," he says, "should never be done on a budget."

"The Duke has spoken, Orlando," says Gaveston. He sighs. "And we cannot but obey."

In the basement the Duke holds a finger uncertainly over his purple phone. "The middle button," says the woman in the black miniskirt. "The one that says End."

"Your grace," says the lugubrious voice from somewhere in the darkness. The clip-clopping has stopped. There's a wheezing grunt, and then that voice says, "He has decided. He will hear your petition."

The Duke turns there in the circle of harsh light under the bulb and facing the shadows squats in the dust. One hand on his knee he closes his eyes and bows his head. "Erymathos," he says, his voice ragged. He clears his throat. "You do me unspeakable honor." He looks up, into those shadows. "My offer is this: two days of safety, and dreamless sleep, and all the meat and cereal, wine and water your belly can hold. In return, come the Equinox, we'll hunt you with a gallowglas." Looking down, he brushes something unseen from his knee. "You will taste the mettle of knights," he says, "and have a chance at oblivion." The Duke looks up into the shadows again. "That is my offer."

After a long moment – clip-clop, clip-clop. The shadows gather themselves into a thing that hulks just outside the light. A suggestion of an arc, old yellow in this light, glistening. A black wet eye shines above it. The Duke catches his breath. At the top of the stairs the woman in the black miniskirt covers her mouth with her hand. The thing in the shadows nods, that tooth, that eye ducking once and coming up again.

"It," says that lugubrious voice, "is acceptable."

His grace sighs and looks away, rolling his eyes. "I can *see* that," he snaps.

A Half-dozen T-shirts, most of them black
Formal dress – Some qualities of Vengeance
Every felicitation

A half-dozen T-shirts, most of them black, are scattered across the unmade futon. There's a red one that says Farmers & Mechanics Bank in peeling brown letters. The empty legs of tights unrolled, unfolded lying across them, black again, red, dull green, blue jeans, grey jeans that once were black, a couple pairs of workpants, plumber's navy, package delivery brown, frayed cuffs and the greasy sheen of nylon. Soft flannel shirts, arms tangled, dark green, a plaid of faded berry colors, a short black denim skirt, a longer Catholic tartan. Ysabel in an over-sized blue sweatshirt that says Brigadoon! squats at the foot of the futon, looking over it all. The droning spatter of the shower cuts off, and there's Jo's voice, "Somewhere like New York City sounds oh so pretty, but let's leave the timing to fate – !" Ysabel leans over and scoops a double handful of underwear and socks from one of the blond wood crates against the wall.

"I'll be the one in tears," sings Jo, coming out of the bathroom in a pair of boxer shorts, towelling her hair, "I'll be the one who's trying to make up for the what the fuck?"

Ysabel's holding up a pair of washed-out pink underwear with a finger crooked through the split side seam. "Do these have some sort of sentimental value?" she says, frowning theatrically.

"What are you doing?" says Jo.

"You have nothing to wear," says Ysabel, wadding up the underwear and tossing it onto the tangle of clothes.

"What?" says Jo. "Oh, fuck it. Just give me a goddamn T-shirt."

"I'm perfectly serious," says Ysabel. "The hunt is Wednesday night, and you have absolutely *nothing* to wear." She leans back on one elbow, her mouth trying not to smile.

"Would you toss me a clean shirt," says Jo. "Please."

"We must go shopping," says Ysabel.

Jo throws back her head and lets out a guttural sigh. She stalks past Ysabel and kneels by the futon, pulling a black T-shirt from the tangle.

"Why did you get that tattoo?" says Ysabel. She's looking at Jo's belly. Black lines claw up from the waistband of her boxers. Two dots that might be eyes peer out from under her navel.

"Don't change the subject," says Jo. She hauls the T-shirt over her head and tugs it down. A red devil leers across the front of it, lined and pocked by silkscreen craquelure. "What the hell is wrong with the clothes I've got?"

"You need a dress," says Ysabel. "Something light, that you can move in, but with a good full skirt – What?"

Jo's shaking her head. "I'm supposed to wear a dress to go hunting."

Ysabel sits up, leans forward, her elbows on her knees. "This hunt is being called in my honor. Even though you aren't of the court, you will be *very* noticeable. It's important you dress well."

"In a dress," says Jo. She looks over at the glass-topped café table under the window. "For a hunt." A sword in its black sheath is lying on top of the table, next to a blue vase full of tiny wild roses.

"It's expected," says Ysabel.

"You wear jeans," says Jo. "And pants. All the time."

"Not at court."

"So this is a thing?" says Jo. "Like, for your people, all the women have to wear dresses?"

Ysabel's eyes are dark, and sharp. Her lips purse themselves before she parts them to say, "Yes, Jo. My people like to dress formally for formal occasions." Her bare feet have burrowed under some socks that once were white. She kicks them free. "Don't yours?"

Jo leans over, grabs a pair of blue jeans, bundles them into a small, irregular wad, tosses them past Ysabel into one of the blond wood crates. She grabs a couple of T-shirts.

"I need to get something myself," says Ysabel. "I can't wear any of *those.*" She's pointing at the bulky blond armoire looming in the corner, doors ajar, a mad welter of fabrics and colors stuffed within, trains spilling out at the bottom, a froth of lace dangling from a half-open drawer.

Jo reaches past Ysabel, snags her tartan skirt, shakes it out. "You going to sell some of them, or something?" She folds it in half and starts rolling it up.

"I couldn't," says Ysabel. "I can't."

"Then what are we going shopping with?" Jo tosses the skirt into a crate, followed in quick succession by three more T-shirts.

"You mean money," says Ysabel.

"Of *course* I mean money."

"What I have in mind won't cost us anything."

"I'm listening," says Jo.

Over the two leather armchairs large copper letters say Barshefsky Associates: Quality Assured. Orlando's in one of the armchairs, absently rolling the tip of his black braid between his fingers and his thumb. Gaveston stands, his knuckles rapping a martial tattoo on the top of his portfolio tube. Behind him a door swings open and his impromptu drumbeat's lost in a sudden wash of questioning voices and clacking keys. A big guy in a faded red sweatshirt steps through, a pen behind each of his ears. Gaveston smiling offers up a hand. "Arnold Becker?"

"Can I help you?" says Becker. A lick of brown hair sticks straight up from the back of his head. He keeps his clipboard folded up against his chest with both arms.

"I certainly hope so," says Gaveston, pulling back his hand, still smiling. "You're a friend of Jo Maguire's?"

"She's off today. What can I – "

"We asked," says Orlando, not looking up from his braid, "if you were her friend."

"I'm her boss," says Becker, looking from Gaveston to Orlando and back again. "Who are you guys?"

"It's a delicate matter, Mr. Becker," says Gaveston. "Is there perhaps somewhere we could – "

"Here's fine," says Becker.

"I see. Well." Gaveston sighs. "The girl? Ysabel? Jo has been seeing a lot of her lately – "

"She's off today, too," says Becker.

Gaveston looks sidelong at Orlando. "She works here?"

"She *works?*" mutters Orlando.

"Her family," says Gaveston quickly, loudly, "*Ysabel's* family, is concerned. It's – " He takes a deep breath. "As I said, it's a delicate matter, one that requires a certain degree of, of *tact,* and circumspection."

"Help me out here, guys," says Becker. He looks over his shoulder at the door behind them. "I have no idea what this has to do with me."

His hands together fingers interlaced on top of the portfolio tube, Gaveston leans forward. Something in the pocket of his cardigan sways pendulously. "We'd like to offer you some money," he says, quietly.

"Money," says Becker.

"Wednesday night," says Gaveston. "The day after tomorrow, to be precise. Ysabel intends to attend a – shall we say, *gathering*, at the Lloyd Center, with your friend, Jo. We would pay you to attend as well, if you were to report back to us your impressions." Becker's frowning, his mouth shaping a question. "As it *would* be late at night," says Gaveston, "we are more than willing to compensate you accordingly. With half the agreed-upon sum right away." He thumps the top of his portfolio tube. "On the barrelhead, as it were. All you need do is say yes."

"This," says Becker. Still frowning. "Is really strange. Look, you guys – "

"It isn't working," says Orlando from his chair.

"I," says Becker. "What?"

"You're quite right," says Gaveston. He sighs. "It isn't."

"It wasn't working when we came through that door." Pulling himself to his feet Orlando flips his braid back over his shoulder. "It wasn't working when we walked into this building."

"What do you propose, friend Mooncalfe?" says Gaveston.

"Vengeance," says Orlando, "has no budget." Smoothing the front of his loose white shirt. "It is not polite. It does not ask." He looks up at Gaveston. His eyes are pale and blue on either side of his sharp long nose. "It takes what it needs, or it isn't vengeance."

"Hey," says Becker. "You – "

"Don't," says Orlando. "Do not."

Gaveston's nodding. "I think I take your meaning, friend. What's more," and he hauls up his portfolio tube, slinging it from one shoulder, "I concur."

And together they walk across the little lobby toward the glass doors.

"What the," says Becker, and then, as Gaveston's stepping out into the hall, Becker shakes his head, raises his voice, "What the hell are you doing?"

The glass door closes with a click. Becker wide-eyed lets out a little half-laugh.

"I, um. Hey."

Becker turns so sharply a pen tumbles from behind one of his ears and he nearly drops the clipboard trying to catch it. "Jesus," he says. Guthrie's standing there, black jeans, a black T-shirt that says Gutshot Goose. "How the hell long have you been behind me?"

"Well," says Guthrie. He looks over at the glass doors a moment, then looks back at Becker. "We really ought to talk," he says.

The woman in the broad straw hat kneels and reaches out to ruffle the grass with her fingers. "Benjamin," she says. "Come on, Benjamin. What on earth do you think you're going to do with that?" A yard or so away a little brindle cat squats suspiciously over a mouthful of dull blue feathers and bright black eyes, a beak wide open, white throat beneath it jerking for air. The cat hunkering down stretches a paw out, eyes looking this way, now that. "Benjamin," says the woman in the straw hat, slapping the grass. She's wearing dirty white gardening gloves with yellow cuffs. Looking down, the cat opens its mouth tentatively. The bird freezes, its beak still hanging open, its throat now still. Tilting his head the cat finds a new hold about the bird's shoulders. The bird starts panting again. "You have no idea," says the woman. "Do you." Her hair is heavy and long and dark, glossy chains of curls gathered by a simple yellow scrunchie.

"Majesty?" says a tall man in a black suit, leaning over her from behind.

The cat looks up and that's when the bird kicks loose, its wing-flaps an explosion in the tiny yard, darting and bobbing low over the grass as it looks for a way out, the house to one side, red brick wall close on the other, trees all about, the cat bounding after. The bird arcs up sharply, threading the gap between gate and ivy-draggled arch, banks over the street beyond under lowering trees, back toward the house and up, headed for open sky. Below, the tall man in the black suit bows slightly, his collar a shining ring of white. The Queen one hand on her hat climbs to her feet. The tall man leads the way to the house. Behind them, the cat has circled back from the foot of the gate. Stopping suddenly, he falls to one side, scrubbing his cheek against the grass. He assiduously begins to lick a paw.

The wide-mouthed jar is half full of gold dust. Lines hashed in white ink down the side denote ounces, gills, mutchkins, a thirdendeal. The woman wearing narrow black-rimmed glasses scoops up a spoonful and taps it into a plastic baggie on one plate of a small balancing scale. A man in a soft blue suit watches over her shoulder, his white hair matted in long dreadlocks. When the French doors behind them open with a creak, he turns. "Majesty," he says, ducking his head in a brief bow.

"We are always pleased to see the grandson of Count Pinabel," says the Queen, tugging the gloves from her hands.

He smiles. "You've heard the venue's been announced for Duke Barganax' hunt?" Behind him, the woman in the black-rimmed glasses plucks the filled baggie from the scale, twisting it closed.

"Of course," says the Queen. "I'd like a glass of water," she says, settling herself on the long white sofa.

"Grandfather wonders what is to be done." He glances down at the baggie held up for his approval and nods crisply. The woman in the black-rimmed glasses tosses the baggie to the other man standing by her table, who catches it in the armload of little baggies crinkling against his chest. His dark blue suit is tight across his shoulders.

"Done?" says the Queen. She leans forward, plucking up a slice of lemon, twisting it into a tall glass of ice water. "What would you have us do, Sir Axehandle? It is our sister's demesne. It is the Duke's hunt. We trust he has seen to the necessary precautions. What shall we do, Agravante?" She takes a sip of water. "We shall arrive promptly and enjoy his hospitality. We hope to see you there."

"Of course," says Agravante. "Pyrocles will stand for Pinabel in the hunt."

"Pyrocles," says the Queen.

The big man nods. "Ma'am." His long mustaches lend his face a somber air above those crinkling baggies.

"And for yourself and your daughter, ma'am?" says Agravante. "I must say, everyone is eager to see what this gallowglas you've found can do."

"Indeed," says the Queen. She sets her water on the table. "This interview has been delightful, Axehandle, but I'm afraid our Chariot has arrived." There in the doorway by the Majordomo stands Roland, a yellow tie knotted tightly beneath his chin.

"No more need be said, ma'am," says Agravante. "Pyrocles?" The big man in the dark blue suit leads the way. "Every felicitation, ma'am."

"Our best to the Count. Anna, if you would also – ?"

The woman in the black-rimmed glasses screws the lid back on the wide-mouthed jar and follows them out. The Majordomo closes the doors as he leaves.

"How *is* our Gallowglas?" asks the Queen.

"Majesty," says Roland, stepping forward, leaning against the back of the long white sofa, "she means well. I would never doubt her heart."

"But," says the Queen.

"She does not understand, ma'am. What must be done, and how. She cannot take the field."

"So that *you* might take her place?"

Roland draws back. "You wound me, ma'am," he says, quietly. "If there is the chance she might embarrass us by her presence, then she must embarrass us with her absence."

"You heard Pinabel," says the Queen. "They all expect to hunt with a gallowglas. They'll be disappointed if they can't."

"Erne says there is nothing he can teach to someone who won't learn, ma'am,"

"Really?" says the Queen. She looks at him, then, her eyes dark, her face expressionless. "It's you they'll blame, Chariot. Say you're jealous of a girl who beat you by turning her back. You're afraid to take the field with a gallowglas." She holds up a hand as he opens his mouth to speak. "You wear your pride so openly. Out where anyone might strike it. I can't have you wounding yourself on every pointed remark."

"That will not happen, ma'am," says Roland. "Your pride and honor I place before my own."

The Queen stands. "See that you do," she says.

the Lights above – Leaning green – Glad Wide Jars What happened, What didn't

The lights above the escalator are set in metal cups, the ceiling about them sooty from years of incandescent heat. At the top behind a low glass wall shine three glossy mannequins, smooth white shells with hair and lips and eyelids painted in bright thin colors. One wears a T-shirt that says Virgo! Are you absolutely positive? Another wears a T-shirt with Albert Einstein on it, that says INTP in big block letters. The center of attention! says the poster hanging above them. None of them wears shoes. Jo turns as her step nears the top, looking down at Ysabel behind her. "What?" says Ysabel.

"I don't know," says Jo, stepping off. "I figured you as more a Nordstrom's girl."

"Nordstrom," says Ysabel.

"What?"

"Never mind." Silvery letters on the wall say Petites. Designer Dresses, say signs atop racks hung with deep greens, reds and browns like wet earth, like wines, all the toasted colors, umbras and siennas, ochres, butters. "Shall we?" says Ysabel.

Arms outstretched Jo presses her hands firmly against the beige walls to either side and regards her reflection. Lips pursed. Eyebrow crooked. Her short hair, blond at the tips, is dark about the scalp. Longer black shocks spike out halfheartedly, already wilting, lying back against the blond. She lifts her chin.

Frowns. The dress is long and soft, a heathery grey. Yellow and white stripes pipe down either side. She tucks a black bra strap under. When she lowers her arms, it slips back out. "You know," she says, "I like the capris better."

"No," says Ysabel. A rustle and a thump and her hands appear at the top of the wall, her head peeking over. "I told you. A dress. How's the skirt? For moving?"

Jo squats, stands up. Rolls her eyes. Plants her feet wide spreading her knees and slapping her hands on them, hunkering over like a sumo wrestler. The skirt stretches taut. She sticks her tongue out at her reflection, googles her eyes. "Well?" says Ysabel. Jo's knocking her knees together, hands shuffling back and forth in a Charleston. She snorts. "It's fine," she says, standing up. "Stretchy." Half-turning. Her bra clearly visible in the mirror, there where the wide straps of the dress join in the back.

"We can get you one of those bandeau bras," says Ysabel. She looks down, her head disappearing. There's another thump.

"I don't like those bras," mutters Jo. She hikes up the dress, bending over, peeling it up and off. "And the colors," Ysabel's saying. "The colors are perfect. I definitely say that's the one."

"So this hunt," says Jo, standing there in her boxer shorts and bra. "What is it we're, uh, hunting?"

"I don't know," says Ysabel. "Ow."

"Ow?" Jo looks at the wall, up, her hands pausing, the dress half-clipped to its hanger.

"Ripped a nail. Blasted jeans."

"So," says Jo. She hangs the dress from the hook on the door. "We don't know what we're hunting. And it's being thrown by the Duke, right?" She picks up her black T-shirt and still bent over rubs the scab on her knee with her thumb.

"Yes," says Ysabel. "Duke, umf, Duke Barganax." There's another thump.

"The same guy who sent those guys after us."

"Yes, Jo."

"So I don't get it." Jo sits on the narrow bench by the mirror, turning her T-shirt right-side out. "What do we get by going right up to him? What's he gonna pull?"

"He's not going to 'pull' anything, Jo. He's called a hunt, in my honor." Jo starts to wrestle her way into her T-shirt. "He may even mean this as an apology. Whatever else he's done, he's a Duke. I'm leaning toward the green one."

"Yeah?"

"Tell me what you think."

Jo pops open the flimsy louvered door of her fitting room and steps around to the next, rattling its door until it unsticks with a jerk. Ysabel's smiling, arms akimbo. The green in her dress is rich and deep like old glass bottles. The skirt is cut above the knee to one side, below it to the other. Thin straps leave her shoulders bare beneath her dark curls. "Well?"

"Works," says Jo.

Ysabel drops one hand, exasperated. "That's it?"

"It gets the job done," says Jo. "That's, which, the two hundred and fifty dollar one? What?"

"I'm sorry," says Ysabel, sputtering with laughter. "I'm sorry. It's the, it's the boxer shorts. Really."

"Whatever," says Jo, rolling her eyes, leaning against the jamb.

"We must get you some new underwear while we're at it. Along with the bra. A thong, considering the cut of that dress."

"Hell no," snaps Jo, straightening up away from the door.

"They're really much more comfortable than you think," says Ysabel.

"*Hell* no."

"Frankie?" says Gaveston. He knocks. "Mr. Reichart?"

Orlando pushes himself up from the wrought-iron railing he's been leaning against. "Allow me," he says.

"Just a moment," says Gaveston. "Perhaps he's – "

Orlando hikes up his leg and kicks. There's a crunch and a twang. Around the deadbolt plate the door buckles. Biting his lip Orlando swings his leg back, taps the ball of his foot against the concrete, swings forward and up, knee to his chest, drives his foot into the door. It pops open, bouncing off the wall inside, swinging shut. He catches it as he steps through. Gaveston shakes his head and is about to follow when somebody says, "Hey!"

At the bottom of the stairs down the outside of the apartment building there's Frankie, looking up, one hand shading his eyes, a six-pack of hard lemonade dangling from the other. "Orlando!" calls Gaveston, swinging his portfolio tube up onto his shoulder, coming down the stairs quickly, carefully, one hand on the railing. "Who the," Frankie's saying, "what are you, hey!" as Orlando pops out of the doorway. The bottle ring and clank but none of them breaks. Hands free, Frankie's taking a couple of hasty steps backwards, arms windmilling for balance as he turns, leans, starts to run. Orlando crouches there on the balcony and leaps, legs gathered under himself, half-unbuttoned shirt whipping, long slim curve of his Japanese sword up over his head, shining.

Green flocking flakes from the fake topiary to reveal a dark wicker frame. Buckets filled with dusty silk flowers line the bottom of the glass case. A fountain to be mounted on a wall leans against the base of one of the bushes, its lion's mouth dry, a black tube dangling unattached from its back. On a plinth above a gaggle of grey plastic ducks sits a young girl, her butterfly wings rendered in thick grey plaster. "Jo?" says Ysabel.

Jo looks away from the glass case, the only thing to be seen on this small landing. Ysabel's standing at the base of the escalator up, one hand on her hip. "Up to housewares?" says Jo.

Ysabel points to a blank door, the same dull white as the walls. "Oh," says Jo.

"Offices are on this floor," says Ysabel. "Go through there and down to the last one on the left. There aren't any doors. Don't look at anything, don't say anything, don't have anything to do with anything but the last one on the left." She's reaching into the front pocket of her jeans. "When you get there, knock four times on the wall outside. Do exactly as you are told." She's worming a clear plastic baggie from her pocket.

A spoonful of gold dust snakes along the bottom. "Answer every question truthfully. You'll do fine."

"And then what?" Jo frowns as Ysabel pinches some gold dust and sprinkles it on the doorknob. "Close your eyes," says Ysabel.

Jo takes a step closer. Shrugs, and closes her eyes. Ysabel pauses, her gold-dusted finger poised by Jo's face. Looks at her, standing there in her old black jeans and her black T-shirt. The dresses slumped over one arm, soft grey, slippery silky green. Black underwear dangling from a little plastic hanger in her other hand, a packet of stockings. Ysabel smiles. She brushes Jo's eyelids lightly one and then the other with her fingertip, glittering them. "You'll be fine," she says, in Jo's ear.

Jo opens her eyes. "Whoa," she says.

The offices are dim. The cubicle walls are chin-high, a dingy, nappy brown. Jo doesn't look at the plaques by each opening. Warm light glows from the cubicle to the right. "No," someone's saying. "Shadow-time's orthogonal to pseudo-time. Plates? They're gonna be glad wide jars again. Yeah. The car under the stale light is a familiar answer, but don't run to the stranger's benison – there is nothing in the end but now, and now – " Jo hurries past, dresses rustling like underbrush. Her knocks against the wall outside the last cubicle on the left are muffled. "Come in," a woman says.

She's sitting in a black leatherette chair, flipping through an enormous stack of green-and-white fanfold printout next to an old computer terminal, black screen glowing with amber characters. She wears a white blouse and a big soft grey bow knotted under her collar. There's nowhere to sit. Jo stands in the cubicle entrance, the load awkward in her arms. The woman pauses her rapid flipping, holds a chunk of printout in the air while selecting a clear plastic ruler, which she lays along the blurry lines of data. "Jo Maguire," she says.

"Yes," says Jo.

"That wasn't a question," she says. "The first question is: do you miss him?"

Jo frowns. "Do I miss him? Who?"

The woman's peering at the printout. "Do you miss him."

Jo blinks. Her lips part as the frown slips from her face. She closes her eyes. "Oh," she says. Opens them. "Yes. I do."

The clear plastic ruler jerks down a line. "Do you love him?"

"Of course," says Jo. Her voice rough, far away. She clears her throat.

The ruler jerks down once more. "If you could say one thing to him, what would it be?"

"I'm sorry," says Jo. "I'm very sorry."

The woman neatens up her pile of printout. "That will do," she says, standing. Bending in front of Jo she pats down the dresses, finds a security tag, pops it off with an orange plastic grip. She pulls a shopping bag from the shelf above her terminal, unfurls it with a shake. Jo drops the dresses in, the stockings, the underwear. "Thank you so much for shopping with us," says the woman.

Becker leans back, rubbing one eye with the heel of his hand. A piano rings softly through the speakers to either side of his computer monitor. Samson went back to bed, a woman's singing, not much hair left on his head. Ate a slice of Wonderbread and went right back to bed. The office is dark, lit only by the lamp on his desk and the bright white glaring from the door to the kitchen, where Guthrie's standing, arms folded. "Hey," he says.

"Jesus," says Becker, starting. "I thought everybody was gone."

"I was waiting," says Guthrie. "We were going to talk."

"Yeah, well," says Becker, "perks of being promoted." He turns down the music. "First in, last out. So."

"So?"

"What are we talking about?"

Guthrie's pulling a chair up to Becker's desk. "The two guys," he says. He straddles the back of the chair, frowning.

"Two guys," says Becker, shifting his mouse, clicking, tapping a number on the keyboard. "Help me out here. What two guys?"

"The," says Guthrie, "the two guys." He points to the door to the lobby. "Wanted to talk to you about Jo, and Ysabel."

"Oh," says Becker. "Those two guys. What about them?"

"They didn't seem weird to you?"

"Just about everything with that girl is weird."

Guthrie's fiddling with a fat binder clip, opening and closing the little metal arms. It clinks against the rings on his fingers. "You remember how we met her?"

"Jo brought her in," says Becker.

Guthrie drops the clip into a wire basket full of them. "That's not when we met her."

"There was the thing," says Becker. "When I got bumped up. At the VC. She was there, wasn't she? And then Jo went off with her to some party up in Northwest, and – what?"

Guthrie's shaking his head. "That's not it," he says. "You don't remember." His hands float over Becker's desk as if he's unsure what shape to make with them. "We were there. It was a big old house on Everett."

"No, see, I remember the party," says Becker. "It was a little, I had a lot of beer. It's a little fuzzy."

"I had way too much beer," says Guthrie. He taps his head. "Still clear as a bell. You remember the girl who tried to steal your watch?"

"Yeah, but," says Becker.

"Or the one who said she'd been herself in a former life?"

"I don't – "

"You remember the band, right?" Guthrie looks up at Becker now, and Becker looks right back at him, eyes a little wide, frowning just. "They were pretty good," says Guthrie. "You remember Ysabel's boyfriend picking a fight? With a sword?"

"Now wait a," says Becker.

"How he stabbed Jo in the back?"

"Guthrie." Becker pushes back, hands up, as if he expects Guthrie to leap over the desk at him. Guthrie doesn't move, doesn't look away. He says, "That's when you – "

"I never," says Becker.

" – when you went for him. He was still holding that damn sword, but you went roaring at him. Took three of them to hold you back. And he never even looked at you, he just, he put up his sword, and he walked away."

"You are so full of shit," says Becker.

At that Guthrie looks down. His pale hands curl in on themselves, fingernails coated in chipped black polish. "I didn't do anything," he says. "I just watched them haul you outside. Watched them bundle her up in a blanket. They told me they were taking her across the street and I said okay. They told me not to worry about it. She was going to be fine. And I said whatever, okay. They told me to take you home." Guthrie flattens his hands on Becker's desk and looks up at him. "You were standing there on the porch. Staring off at nothing. I said, let's get you home. You said sure. You'd already forgotten everything."

"That's because it never happened," says Becker, gently.

"Ask Jo," says Guthrie. "Ask Ysabel." He pushes back from Becker's desk. "Anyway. That's what I wanted to talk to you about." He stands up, bumping the chair back towards the line of phone carrels. "Which is why I think we should go to this thing tomorrow night. You know. That those two guys were telling you about?" He shrugs. "Or maybe that never happened, either."

"Puertas a mi izquierda," says the recording. "Lloyd Center, Northeast Eleventh Avenue. Doors to my left." Jo starts awake, nearly dropping the long bundle wrapped in red. Ysabel's shaking her shoulder. "Our stop," she says. Her reflection hangs in the dark window like a ghost, the green of her new dress shining over a dimly lit office lobby across the street.

Outside, Jo in her army jacket and her new grey dress, red bundle under one arm, walks to the end of the platform, looking out over the parking lot. It's almost empty, drowned in a dulling haze of streetlight. Past it a long barn of a movie theater lit up with neon. Across the street another empty lot spreads before the anonymous prow of a shopping mall. A bell rings. With a rising, grinding hum the train pulls away, clank-chunking over a rail junction. "Where is everybody?" says Jo.

"Inside," says Ysabel.

"Inside." Jo points across the street. "In the mall." She shakes her head. "Of course they're in the mall."

"Give me your sword," says Ysabel.

"It's really fucking late," says Jo, holding out the bundle.

"The witching hour," says Ysabel. She's unwinding the long red scarf from the short épée in its black sheath. "Hold still." She stoops on one knee there before Jo, shaking the belt loose. Reaches up, wrapping it around Jo's hips. "Hold still," she says, buckling it. "We should have gotten you some shoes."

Jo peers down at her mismatched Chuck Taylors, the white one held together with duct tape. "They're comfortable."

"They're appalling," says Ysabel, working the sheath's ties under the belt. "A nice pair of Nikes, maybe, cream and yellow – "

"Yeah," snaps Jo, "and I woulda had to," and then she looks away, across the street, toward the mall. Behind her the theater marquee suddenly goes dark. "You look good," she says. "In that dress."

"Thank you," says Ysabel, sitting back on her heels.

Jo looks down, at Ysabel's bare shoulders, the green skirt falling away from one knee. "You chilly at all?"

"If I were," says Ysabel, reaching up, "would you give me your jacket?"

"That part of the job description?" says Jo, taking her hand.

Ysabel shrugs, and pulls herself to her feet.

The restroom's dark. Becker crouches over a toilet, feet on either side of the seat, hands braced on either side of the stall. "This is nuts," he says.

"What?" says Guthrie, one stall over.

"This is *nuts.*"

"They'll *hear* you."

"Nobody's gonna hear us." Becker lifts a foot, stretches his leg out and down. Puts his weight on it. Steps off the toilet, shaking out his other leg. "Oh," he says. "Whoa, yeah."

"*What* are you *doing?* We have to wait till it's all clear – "

"You know what they're gonna do when they get here, Guthrie? The people you think will hear us?"

"Becker, they'll see your feet!"

"They're gonna clean the toilets, is what." Becker stretches his arms up, arches his back. "They aren't gonna come in and crouch down and look under the damn doors to see if anyone's hiding in here and say it's all clear. They're gonna straight off *clean* the *toilets*. With a mop and a sponge and a bucket." He works his head from side to side. "We'll be hard to miss." He unlatches the stall door. "I can't believe I let you talk me into coming here."

"Would you just," says Guthrie, and then the lights come on, cold and bright. Orlando in a long grey skirt steps into the restroom head up, one hand lifting, a warning.

"Trouble, friend Mooncalfe?" says Gaveston, in a rumpled, rust-colored suit, one hand on Frankie's shoulder. "God damn," Frankie's saying, taking in the glossy white tile, the long stainless steel mirror over the sinks. "Hell of a bathroom."

"Keep him *quiet,*" snaps Orlando, kneeling.

"Hey," says Gaveston. Orlando, black braid brushing the floor, peers under the stalls. "I mean," Frankie's saying, "the mirrors! They're so." Eyes squeezed shut Becker's hunkering feet on either side of the toilet seat hands braced against the stall. "*Damn* shiny," says Frankie.

"Hey," says Gaveston again, laying two fingers against Frankie's lips. "Orlando. Nobody's here."

Standing and turning in one smooth movement Orlando draws his sword like a curl of light in the air between them. "I can smell him," he says.

Becker opens his eyes.

"Fine," says Gaveston. "They missed a janitor, he's cowering in the stalls, fearful of your majesty. Who cares? *You* have an appointment to keep."

Snarling Orlando swings the sword to one side up and back. "Do not think to mock me," he says, quietly.

"There's *no one here,*" says Gaveston, and then he flinches as a toilet flushes. Orlando spins. Becker's opening his stall door and stepping out to see Orlando in a crouch, his sword up over his head. Becker stops mid-step, face blanching.

"What are you doing here?" says Orlando.

"Uh," says Becker. "What are *you* doing here?"

Orlando rears back, sword lowering, eyebrow climbing. "Waiting," says Gaveston, quickly, smoothly.

Becker blinks, then shrugs. "Oh," he says. "Well. We're done." He knocks on the door to Guthrie's stall. "Hey. We done?"

There's a thump.

"You, ah, you might want to flush," says Becker. He looks from Gaveston, one hand on Frankie's shoulder, to Frankie, staring at himself in the watery steel mirror. To Orlando in his grey skirt, sword-tip twitching just above the glossy tile. "So," says Becker, and he swallows. "All yours." Guthrie's door is slowly opening.

Pop and twang from the little brown speaker by the boy's tapping foot. "The oaten pipes blow wondrous shrill," he croons, and someone laughs, "the hemlock small blow clear, and louder notes from hemlock large and bog-reed strike the ear." He's curled around his big-bellied guitar, leaning against a store-front grate under a darkened sign that says Meier & Frank. "For solemn sounds, and sober thoughts, we revelers can't bear!" Cheers and applause as he starts a thunderous strumming. Men and woman crowd the footbridge before him, the railings that line the broad open atrium, dark glossy suits in browns and blacks, there a burgundy over a velvet vest, gowns in reds and golds that sway like bells, old ivory, slim black skirts, a shimmer like metaled water. The mall about them is dim, grates lowered over store fronts, signs all gone dark. Lanterns bob on poles above the crowd, keeping time. The ice rink on the floor below glimmers uncertainly. Candles in paper bags light the steps of stalled escalators up to the third floor balconies, where banners have been hung: a blue hound standing primly on a rose-colored ground, a red hawk glaring, its wings slashing across brown, and between them a great bee picked out in black and yellow on a creamy field.

Jo's leaning over the bee, elbows on the railing, watching the crowd below. An old man in a porkpie hat shuffles up by the boy with the guitar and bends over carefully, finding a microphone there on the floor. Blows into it. More cheers as the boy's strumming tumbles to a chug-a-lug beat and the old man starts to croak, oh, some ride a black one some ride a brown one mine's as red as the blood in your veins. Laughter and applause.

"You should be armed, miss. And armored."

Jo turns, jerking as the sword at her hip bangs the bars of the railing. A big guy's standing there, blue jeans and a tight white T-shirt, a smile somewhere under his long grey mustaches. Next to him a green and purple table laden with worn brown leather, plate the color of old keys, shapeless puddles of slippery mail. "I'm Pyrocles, miss," he says. Spears lean against the table, and there by his feet a pile of shields like round-bottomed sleds, like big kites. "I'll hunt with you this night, under the Count's banner."

"Jo Maguire," she says. I'm a babe in arms and a snake in the grass, comes the old man's growl from below. I'm a star in the sky up over your head.

"The Gallowglas," says Pyrocles.

She looks away. "I guess," she says. "I'm here for the Princess." The wrist of her left hand leaning against the grubby red tape wrapping the hilt of her épée, pushing it out a little, back. Tucking the scabbard against her legs. "We are all here for the Princess," Pyrocles is saying.

"I didn't mean you weren't," says Jo, and it's the heel of her hand on the hilt now. "It's only she's not here. She's off, with her mother or something. Getting her hair done. Besides, I already have a sword."

"You'll want a spear." Pyrocles hefts one, shifting it in both hands, eyeing its rule. "A strong straight haft of oak or ash. A shield would only get in your way, but you'll want a cuirass.

Perhaps some greaves." He's shaking his head. "Find one with a good boar-stop, miss."

Jo lets go of the spear she'd picked up. "Boar-stop?" she says.

The Duke lurching hikes a knee up on a green and purple table and pulls himself after it. "Give," he says, swaying upright in his cream-colored suit, his yellow tie, "give praise, my brethren," lifting his glass in the air, "for what you are about to receive – Old John Barleycorn, nicotine, and the temptations of the rock 'n' roll chord E." Draining the glass as someone across the food court whoops, a man in a powder-blue tux, leaning on the counter of a darkened Chick-fil-A. Down by the Sbarro a fiddle scrapes to life, a red-headed guy jigging with it by a woman smiling as she lifts her voice, window shopping, finger popping, hanging in our favorite shopping mall. "You'll fall, your grace," says the woman in the short black dress, peering up at him through narrow black-rimmed glasses.

"You say that," says the Duke, squatting, bracing himself with his free hand, "like it's a bad thing." He hops off the table. "At least I'm not squirreling myself away in the bathroom."

"It's your party," she says, reaching into her slim black purse.

"In *her* honor," says the Duke. He lifts his glass, frowns. She's holding out a plastic baggie with a palmful of gold dust inside. "Here," she says, when he doesn't take it.

"Garçon!" roars the Duke. She flinches. "Garçon! *There* he is." Gaveston in his rumpled, rust-colored suit, making his way toward them through the crowd. "More John Barleycorn!" calls the Duke, waving his glass. He giggles.

"Your grace," says Gaveston. He nods to the woman in the black-rimmed glasses and reaches for the plastic baggie in her hand. The Duke has turned to set his empty glass on the green and purple table. "Come," he says, and he throws an arm over Gaveston's shoulder. "Walk about with me." Gaveston's tucking the baggie in his jacket pocket. "He's ready?" says the Duke, leaning close, speaking softly.

"Your grace, her friends are here. One of the men we interviewed. And another."

The Duke is shaking his head. "Is he ready?"

Gaveston nods. "Sweetloaf's dressing him."

"It's five hundred dollars, you call me." The Duke's smiling. "You decide to *snatch* the sonofabitch, broad daylight, suddenly you don't want to bother me? You just, *fft?*"

"Your grace?" says Gaveston. "I'm sorry, I – "

"Don't apologize," says the Duke, jerking Gaveston to a halt. "We needed him, we got him. I'm ecstatic. I wasn't, believe me, you'd know. You play these games." The Duke leans even closer, pressing a hand to Gaveston's chest. "It's counterproductive. The call's made? Orlando's in place?"

"They're still *here,*" says Gaveston, looking down at the Duke's hand. "Her friends. Somewhere in the crowd."

"The call," says the Duke. "It was made?"

Gaveston looks up. "I got the machine," he says. "I left a message."

"You *always* get the machine," says the Duke. "We're set!" He claps Gaveston on the back. Gaveston winces. The Duke heads up a couple of steps onto the broad balcony littered with green and purple tables. "Your grace?" says Gaveston, not moving. "Sir?"

The Duke stops, turns, spreads his hands. "I'm going to take her measure," he says, heading back down the steps. "This girl who got Tommy Rawhead killed."

"Her *friends,* your grace," says Gaveston.

The Duke smiles. "Two of them? You interviewed one, and there's this other guy?" Gaveston's nodding. The Duke leans in. "I think we outnumber them, Stirrup."

He's back up the steps. Gaveston sighs, and follows.

"It fits," says Pyrocles, tightening a belt at Jo's hip.

"I look like an idiot," says Jo.

"A mail shirt would be too dangerous," says Pyrocles. He steps back, tugs one of her shoulder straps. "A blow from a tusk or hoof would shatter links and drive them into your flesh. A mortification for you, miss, if I'm not mistaken."

"It's just so," says Jo, turning. Her breastplate, painted with milky enamel, edged with gold, shaped to suggest round hips, sleek muscles, well-formed breasts, wide nipples ringed with gold filigree. A navel hammered into the pale stiff belly rayed with gold leaf. "Anatomical."

"You'll be glad of it when the hunt begins," says Pyrocles.

"I like your hair," says the Duke.

He stands behind Pyrocles, one hand on the knot of his yellow tie. His smirk uncoiling into a smile as he looks her in the eye.

"Thanks," says Jo flatly, after a moment. "I'm thinking of shaving my head."

"Won't you get cold?" says the Duke.

She shrugs. "I'll wear a hat." Pyrocles tugs at her backplate, checking the fit. She shrugs again.

"It is a pleasure to meet you, Jo Gallowglas, who has caused me so much trouble. You'll remember the Stirrup," jerking a thumb over his shoulder at Gaveston behind him. Jo's eyes widen and she opens her mouth to say something. "I'm Southeast," he says, "the Duke – "

"Excuse me," Jo's saying, pushing past him, past Gaveston who reaches after her. "Ap," says the Duke, and Gaveston checks. "Your grace," he says. "Orlando – "

"A moment, Stirrup," says the Duke.

Jo leaps down the couple of steps from the balcony and past a man in a blue sailor suit dodging a woman in a burgundy skirt turning her sword bouncing off Orlando's shins as she grabs the arm of a woman in a short black dress. "What are you," says Jo, and then, "I'm sorry," and then, "Why do you have that?"

The woman looks at Jo through narrow black-rimmed glasses. There's a dress draped over her arm, a green dress, a green as rich and deep as old glass bottles. "Miss Maguire," she starts to say, but Jo's let go, pushing through the crowd. "Hey!" says someone, and "Watch it!" says someone else. Orlando cranes his head to watch her go, his hand on the hilt of his Japanese sword.

"Mooncalfe!" calls the Duke. Orlando whips around. The Duke nods once, slowly, lifting a finger to tap alongside his nose. Orlando glares.

There's a hallway off the food court, there beside the Sbarro, lit by more candles in paper bags and the fluorescent light from a couple of doorways at the end, one lined in dull blue tile, the other in dusty pink. Roland stands by the pink doorway, a spear against his shoulder. He shakes his head, the pale fuzz of his hair struck by the harsh light. "They're not to be disturbed," he says, quietly.

"I need to see her," says Jo. "Dammit, Roland – "

"Oh, let her in," sighs someone inside.

An old woman with long, glossy white hair and a mouthful of pins kneels on the tile floor by Ysabel's feet. Ysabel's standing on something, a low stool, there between the toilet stalls and the row of sinks, looking at herself in the long dim mirror. Her gown is the color of worn ivory, high-waisted, a full skirt waterfalling past the stool to the floor, covered all about with a fantastic garden of beadwork, outlines of great flowers flashing like fireworks. Her black hair piled in artful disarray upon her head. A woman wearing a pince-nez stretching up to tuck in a gold chopstick.

"Jo," says Ysabel, "I didn't – "

"Yes, Jo," says the Queen. "Thank you for all your efforts on our behalf." She sits in a long black dress on a yellow folding canvas chair in the corner. "But the situation is, as I'm sure you'll credit, both subtle and dangerous. Roland will hunt for us tonight." She stands as Jo opens her mouth to say something. "We wished the secret to be closely kept as long as possible, or we'd have told you sooner. You may stand with us, of course, and be honored as my daughter's guardian. Or," as Jo's turning, throwing up her hands, "Swear to fucking *God*," she's muttering, stalking out of the bathroom, "or," says the Queen, "you may storm off somewhere and sulk."

Jo's gone. Ysabel turns back to her reflection in the mirror.

"Your choice is out of my hands," says the Queen.

Down by the Ice Rink – a Side-bet
a Roomful of Gentry – Her honor – the Very Air

Down by the ice rink it's quiet. Differing songs float down through the big central atrium, a guitar, the fiddle, a flute off away somewhere, the slap of a drum not keeping time with any of them. Guthrie's looking up one wing of the mall and down the other but potted trees and dead escalators and kiosks muffled under dust covers make it hard to see very far. "It was supposed to be a city within the city," someone says, and he jumps.

There's this woman next to him, swaddled in three or four skirts in muddy colors and a couple of sweaters under a grubby orange rain shell. "I'm just waiting," Guthrie says. "Looking for a friend of mine. They're both – just a minute ago. They were here. He was. No *idea* it was so late. I." She's laughing. Guthrie's starting to grin. "What?"

"It's fun, sneaking in," she says. Her eyes are bright and blue and her hair is lost under a confetti-colored cap. "Like they don't know."

"It's not what we were," says Guthrie, looking up at the food court. Someone's yelling. The fiddle's stopped. "Not what he was expecting, anyway. I'm, uh. Kinda looking forward."

"It should have been twenty-one storeys," she's saying, "just like the Waldorf-Astoria. What's the Midnight Disease?" She's pointing at his T-shirt. Her fingerless glove is yellow and spotted with red unravelling stars.

"A band," he says. "Waldorf-Astoria?"

But she's looking up at the food court. "We should get up there before they let it out." There's another shout, and a crash, metal against metal. "Your friends are probably up there already." Clangs, now, up there, one after another.

"I hope not," says Guthrie, and then, "Let *what* out?"

Orlando leans forward, feet braced, his Japanese sword in one hand down and back. Pyrocles facing him holds his greatsword one hand on the long pommel below the hilt, the other gripping the blade above, where it's wrapped in ruddy leather. He steps back, then forth, boots squeaking. "What *possible* reason?" says Pyrocles.

"You presume I might confront you without one," says Orlando. "That alone is reason enough." Pyrocles swings once, twice, great looping cuts. Orlando ducks the first and parries the second, his sword scraping into a slice that forces Pyrocles back, back toward the balcony railing, knocking a chair out of the way.

"Shall I get him?" says Gaveston in the Duke's ear.

"Get who?" says the Duke, and then, "No. Fuck."

"Do not play with me, boy!" roars Pyrocles, kicking another chair at Orlando who runs back, away, jumping up on a table as Pyrocles follows the chair with a sword thrust at Orlando leaping up and over, skirt flapping, sword slashing Pyrocles' back.

"Without Jo," says Gaveston.

"Enough," says the Duke. "There's enough in play already. No need to spoil our surprise for a side bet."

Pryocles twisting catches the next slash with his greatsword like a bar in both hands shoving Orlando over and back off his feet, rolling as Pyrocles shatters a line of tile with a blow.

"Call off your man," says Agravante. He's there behind the Duke in his pale pink suit, his long white scarf, his pale, pale dreadlocks gathered in a stiff sheaf at the back of his head.

"The Mooncalfe is no one's man," says the Duke without turning.

Another great booming blow and another, tumbling tables in a flurry of dust and chips of tile.

"Call him *off,* dammit. I'll not have our huntsman compromised by your silly games."

"Call him off yourself," says the Duke. "He'll be done in but a moment."

Pyrocles lifting his greatsword for another blow eyes widening as Orlando isn't rolling but lunging forward not back, up from the floor his sword in both hands curling in a flash through Pyrocles' chest to burst from his back.

"There," says the Duke. "All yours, Axehandle." He leans toward Gaveston. "Make sure," he says, quietly, "we get someone to fix the floor before we go."

Pyrocles, wincing, sees Agravante as Orlando yanks free his blade. "Sorry, milord," he says.

Roland jerks upright as with a rustle of black skirts the Queen steps from the bathroom into the long dim hall. He touches his knuckles to his forehead. She nods once, and heads past him down the hall toward the food court.

Ysabel steps out. Candles in paper bags along the floor light up a flurry of sparks from the beads coiling about her belled ivory skirts, along the trailing points of her sleeves. She stands there a moment, her eyes shadowed, her face still. A trumpet's sounding out in the atrium.

"I said what I did," says Roland, "to keep her safe. I – " But she's shaking her head. "You should know," she says, heading past him, down the hall, "I would never give you another chance."

He shoulders his spear and then he follows her, down the hall, toward the food court.

"Friends and neighbors, gentles all!" booms a voice out there. "Your Queen! Your Princess!"

Pyrocles sits on a spindly plastic chair on the far side of the food court, leaning forward on his knees, head down, grey mustaches drooping from his grey and haggard face. He's shirtless. The wound in his back is ragged, wet and red. He holds a red plastic cup to the wound in his chest, a puckered maw oozing something white and thick. "Christ," says Jo, and he starts. "This is somehow my fault, isn't it."

"He drew the sword," says Pyrocles. "I lost my temper. I see no part for your apology to play."

She kneels beside him. "Let me hold that."

"That's for a page to do," he says, and she says, "You think I give a good goddamn?" and he doesn't stop her hand from taking the cup. With her other hand she starts to worry at a shoulder-buckle holding breastplate to backplate. "Even if this is the stupidest fucking piece of armor ever."

He's smiling, somewhere beneath his mustaches. "So Roland will hunt in your stead, and Marfisa in mine." Away off in the middle of the food court, the Duke addresses the crowd, arms wide, Roland to one side, his left arm sheathed in a great steel gauntlet, Marfisa to the other in a shimmering minidress like metaled water, greaves of pink bronze strapped to her thighs and calves, a glaive held loosely in one hand.

"Throw Orlando in the mix," says Jo, "and I'm definitely rooting for the boar." She's staring at the stuff seeping from his wound like spun honey, glimmers of gold in milky drops that fall, slowly, into the cup.

"He wouldn't hunt," says Pyrocles. "Not even for the Duke. I wonder," he says, closing his eyes. He touches two fingers to the wound on his chest. "I wonder who."

The Duke smiles. "I must say I *am* disappointed," he says for all to hear, looking from Roland to the Queen. "At this last-minute substitution. Can it be you do not trust me, ma'am?"

"Do not flatter yourself, Southeast," says the Queen. Ysabel beside her, looking at the floor. "Introduce your huntsman. Let's get started."

Pyrocles shakes his head slowly, mustaches wagging. "His grace's usual henchmen aren't about." He opens his eyes. "The Dagger, the Helm. The Mason."

"Becker?" says Jo, eyes wide.

"Well," bellows the Duke, "I know we all hoped to see a hunt with a real gallowglas on the field. And you all know how I *hate* to let you down." The crowd cheers.

Pyrocles, frowning, looks over his shoulder. There's Becker in his red and green plaid shirt. "I've been looking all over for you," he says. "Did you know he's here?"

"What the hell are *you* doing here?' says Jo. And then she looks over at the center of the court, where the Duke with a flourish bellows, "I give you, friends and neighbors, the huntsman for Southeast – my very own gallowglas!"

A clatter, a squeak of metal. Titters, rippling through the crowd. A scuffle, and Frankie's pushed out stiff-legged before them all by a boy in a tight brown suit. Frankie grins as laughter blooms all around him. Stovepipes clamped about his legs. His cuirass a plastic garbage lid in back, a great stainless-steel pot lid before. A colander for a helm. In one hand an iron poker, wobbling in time with his bobbing head.

"Hold this," says Jo. After a moment, Becker reaches out to take the cup. She stands, her shoulder-strap loose, her cuirass cracked open, breastplate sagging. Her hand on the hilt of her épée.

"Jo," says Pyrocles. "He means to mock. He wants you angry."

"And now! cries the Duke. "If you will follow me to the railings and direct your attention to the ground floor so very far below!" The crowd rushes all across the court, up the stairs, roiling about Frankie turning dizzily in place to be taken in hand by the boy in the brown suit. He drags Frankie with him toward the dead escalators, after Marfisa, after Roland.

"You walk into a roomful of gentry," Jo says to herself. "Full of nothing. Like that." Looks back at them. "Becker. Can you stay here, with him?"

"What are you going to do?" says Becker.

"I don't know," she says, walking away. "Nothing stupid."

"You don't need to stay with me," says Pyrocles.

"It's okay," says Becker, looking at the cup he's holding. "You're hurt." Blinking, then, at the wound above it. "Good Lord!" he says. "What happened?"

"I'm a knight," says Pyrocles. "The Anvil. My name is Pyrocles."

"Becker," says Becker. "I manage a phone bank."

"I give you, friends and neighbors, our quarry!" The Duke, leaning out over the empty atrium, pointing to the floor below as lights thunk to life down there. "The boar, Erymathos!"

"How many heads?" says Roland, stepping slowly down the dead escalator to the second floor. Cheers ring out from the balconies around the atrium. From the first floor below, a grunting roar, a hurried clip-clop-clip-clop-clip.

"One," says Marfisa, just ahead of him.

"Venom?" says Roland. "Ichor? Flame?"

"Just a foul temper," says Marfisa. "His bristled back like a forest of spears. And really big tusks." The crowd on the second floor has left a corridor clear between the escalator up and the escalator down. Marfisa steps out into it, spinning her glaive above her head, kneeling into a swooping lunge and cut. Sets the glaive to one side, adjusting the buckle of a greave. From below, a tremendous crash, a squeal of triumph.

"You won't take a cuirass?" says Roland.

She looks sidelong up at him with a wry smile. "Nor you, neither?"

He shrugs, the massive steel gauntlet settling with a clank. "I'll rush him first, drive him back, then work around and run him up to you for the finish."

"Simple," she says, grabbing her glaive. "Direct." Standing up.

"And no quibbling over who gets the kill."

"Oh, it's a joint effort, to be sure."

"The Anvil is a fool," says Roland.

She shakes her head. "The Mooncalfe is provocative. What's your excuse?"

He looks away. "A promise." He points back up the escalator. "And him?"

"Hope he stays the hell out of the way," says Marfisa.

Frankie's clattering down the escalator, led by the boy in the brown suit as laughter washes away the claps and cheers. "Hell of a," says Frankie, a big smile smeared across his face. "An escalator," he says, as he follows the boy off the last step. "Never seen one that couldn't move. Wow."

"Don't even fucking *think* about it," says the boy, leaning in close to Marfisa and Roland. "Don't fucking *think* about offering me fucking fiat paper or valuta or fee fucking simple to keep this fucker off the field."

"Wouldn't dream of it," says Roland, quietly.

"How dare you suggest otherwise," says Marfisa, smiling.

"I, um," says the boy. "I mean. Fuck."

"What's that?" says Frankie, grinning.

"Besides," says Roland, "I think they'd notice, up there. If he weren't on the field."

"That clomping noise?" says Frankie. "Like boots? What is that?"

"Fine," says the boy, scowling. "Fuck it." He gives Frankie a shove toward the escalator down to the first floor. "Wait," says Roland. "I'm first."

Cheers erupt again as Roland spear in hand marches past Frankie to the top of the second escalator. He lifts the spear over his head and the crowd begins to roar, and he throws back his head and roars with them, a deep-throated booming call that swamps the crowd-noise, echoing throughout the atrium. An answering squeal from below, the clip-clop becoming a sudden hailstorm of hoofbeats. Roland lowers his spear and runs down the escalator, taking the stalled steps two at a time.

"Let go," says Jo.

"No," says Ysabel.

They're at the back of the food court crowd, near the first escalator. No one's looking at them; they're all leaning over the railings to see what can be seen below.

"You said," says Jo. "You said he wouldn't pull anything. That this was just going to be what it was. A hunt in your – "

"*Stop* it," says Ysabel. "Your honor," says Jo. "Stop it," says Ysabel. She's holding Jo's right hand in both of hers and she pulls Jo stumbling close. Their hands trapped between Jo's white cuirass, Ysabel's beaded gown. "Do not throw *his* lies and *his* deception in my face." She leans her forehead against Jo's. "This is *all* the Duke's doing, and none of mine."

"I didn't," says Jo. From below a growl and another crash, monumental, metal twanging, glass cascading, Roland yelling something, the crowd about them taking in one deep murmuring breath.

"And there is nothing you can do," says Ysabel.

"Then tell me," says Jo, leaning back, leaning away. "Tell me he can't get hurt. Tell me it's against the rules. Tell me it's only a game."

"You," says Ysabel, and then she stops, and then she starts again. "You are impossible, Jo Maguire."

Jo doesn't say anything.

"What *is* he to you?" says Ysabel.

The lights go out. All of them: faint lights deep inside locked stores, safety lights under soffits, the dim sparks left glowing in the big lamps hanging from the rafters far above. Candles snuffed and torches guttered as if they'd never been lit. The crowd shuffling, crying out in a dozen voices, a hundred of shock and alarm and fear. More glass breaks below. Hoofbeats falter and stop. A flash of light, blue-white, everything lit up for an instant and plunged away, and more screams and cries and yells for everyone else to remain calm.

"Her eyes like stars," says Ysabel. "Her hands of iron. The hair of her head hanging down to the ground." Another flash of light, flickering now, solidifying into something cold and pale, far below, throwing outrageous shadows up along the walls and storefronts, the rafters and bridges, great black shifting bodiless things with monstrous heads and grasping hands around and above them all.

"What?" says Jo. There's a piercing wail from below, as thin and pale as the light. "Who?" says Jo.

"She has nineteen names," says Ysabel.

"Erymathos!" cries the woman standing in the middle of the ice rink. She is wrapped in a long black cloak that she holds shut at her throat. Its folds and tatters are caught along with her snarled black hair in the winds that whirl about her. In her other hand she holds a gnarled grey stick, smooth and dull as driftwood, its tip a spark of blue-white light too bright to look upon. A shriek of grinding metal as clip-clop from the darkness beyond the ice rink comes the boar, up to the low wall about the ice rink. A bent and ragged store-front grate hangs from one great tusk. Glass glitters in the ruff behind the blocky wedge of his head. He lays his snout on the wall, and black blood drips to the ice and smokes there.

"Who has done this?" cries the woman on the ice in that harsh, scraping voice, and the shadows above them all leap and shiver. "Who called you out of sleep and left you stranded in this place?"

"He came of his own choice," calls the Duke, from above.

"You!" cries the woman on the ice, pointing her stick at him, lighting him up as he leans over the balcony, the shadows suddenly thick behind him. "He is a simple beast, Barganax. Much as yourself. I smell my sister, here."

"We are guests of the Duke," calls down the Queen, over across the atrium from the Duke. "This hunt is of his devising. If he truly did not seek your approval of field and quarry, in this your demesne, we offer our sympathies, and gladly take your part in the quarrel." Out of the darkness away across from the boar comes Roland without his spear, the length of his steel gauntlet stained a bluish black. Marfisa follows him, limping, dragging her glaive along the floor.

"It is true, ma'am, that I am simple," says the Duke. "I plead simplicity. Of course we shall call off the hunt, and my man on the field stands forfeit."

"Which is your man," cries the woman on the ice, as the crowd all about mutters and gasps. "Which is your man?"

"Why," calls down the Duke, "my Gallowglas."

Wailing the woman spins on the ice, thrusting her stick at the darkness all about her. "Where? Where? You would use a *mortal man* to hunt my splendid Erymathos, and send him down to dust? *Show him to me!*" And the light finds Frankie, cowering against the side of the escalator, his colandered head in his hands. "You!" cries the woman on the ice. "*You!* Stand up! I would crack open your ribs and set the very air free from your lungs!"

"The hell you will," says Jo Maguire.

She's stepping down the dead escalator to the first floor, her épée in her right hand high and pointed at the woman on the ice. "Frankie's under my protection," she says.

"Is he," says the woman on the ice.

"Him," says Jo, crossing the floor to the low wall about the ice rink, "and her." She points the sword up and behind her, then levels it at the woman on the ice. "The Princess. Ysabel. Anybody else in here you want, you're welcome to them. But you so much as give either of *them* a fucking *goosebump,* I'll stick you with this."

The woman on the ice says nothing, stands stock still, her stick and its bright light pointed at Jo.

"I'm the other gallowglas," says Jo. "From what I've seen, that's about all it takes. Right?"

The mall is silent, still. Even the shadows hung on the walls about them hold still for two long breaths, then three. The woman on the ice lowers her stick. From somewhere a quiet sound grows louder, a creak, a crackling groan. She's smiling. She's lifting her head. Not looking away from Jo, she's started to laugh.

They march – the Conquering Hero

THEY MARCH past clots of cars and trucks haphazardly parked under the buzzing lights, many of them heading on foot up the curve of the ramp and out to the surface and the night above. The boy with the big-bellied guitar slung across his back is helping a red-headed man load a large white drum into the back of a van adorned with a candy-colored pin-up girl, holding a massive snake above her body with both hands. The side door's open. Marfisa in a soft blue robe sits slumped, a cloth to her face, her greaves stacked on the pavement by her bare feet, her hair the color of clotted cream hanging like a curtain before her face. Agravante kneels before her, reaching up to brush the hair out of her eyes. "He's loose," she says, her voice slurred. One side of her face is puffy, mottled red and white and yellow, the eye swollen shut. "He's out there, somewhere."

"The Duke's problem," says Agravante, gently. "Not ours."

Across the garage, halfway up the ramp, Pyrocles pauses to look back at them. His blue jacket draped across his shoulders, his bare chest wrapped in a white bandage. His expression masked by those long grey mustaches. Becker, unlocking the door of a little red hatchback, looks up to see Pyrocles trudging away up the ramp. "I don't," he says, looking about the parking garage, at the people marching past, a pickup truck with wood-framed plastic wings stashed in the back, a sedan topped by a monkey-faced stone idol strewn with ivy, spitting water on the windshield. "I don't want to forget this," says Becker, but Guthrie over on the other side of the car is looking down at his thin hands wrapped around each other. "Do you," he says, "need a ride? Anywhere?"

"Anywhere," says the woman swaddled in those skirts and sweaters. "Anywhere that isn't." She's pointing at a black car parked a couple of spaces over from them, a powerful black thing standing empty. Meticulous lines of hand-painted white letters whorl up and over the sides and hood and roof.

"Give me a minute," says Becker, closing his door, heading back across the garage.

"Ow!" says Frankie, a hand to his cheek, down by a concrete pillar.

"You with us now?" says Gaveston. "You need another one?"

"No, no," says Frankie. "No, I'm good. I'm hey! Watch it!" Gaveston's bent over, tugging at the pot lid strapped to Frankie's chest. He glowers up at the boy in the tight brown suit. "What on earth did you use, Sweetloaf?"

"Fuckin' duct tape," says Sweetloaf, opening a butterfly knife with a practiced whipcrack flourish.

"The conquering hero approaches," says Orlando.

Jo's walking quickly over to them, holding her sword in its sheath in one hand at her side. "Miss Maguire," says Gaveston, straightening up. "A delight to see you again. Congratulations on your – "

"You hurt?" she says to Frankie, brushing past Gaveston.

"Hey, Jo," he mumbles.

"Are you *hurt?*" she says. "Did that thing touch you?"

"No," says Frankie, "I'm – " Jo shoves him back, and back again, into the pillar. "The *fuck?*" she's yelling. "What the fucking *hell* were you thinking?"

"I missed you," says Frankie.

"Well *stop!*" says Jo. "Jesus. Just stay the fuck away from me." He's about to say something and she shoves him once more. "It's for your own *good,* you goddamn idiot."

"Gallowglas," calls the Duke, walking over to them in his cream-colored suit, his immaculate yellow tie.

"*Not* now," says Jo.

"Forgive me, Miss Maguire, but I meant Frankie, here. Frankie Gallowglas." Smiling, the Duke holds out a stuffed brown leather wallet. "Five hundred bucks, sir," he says, handing it to Frankie. "As agreed."

"But I thought you said," says Frankie, as Gaveston, sidelong eyeing the Duke, says, "Come, Mr. Reichart. Don't be chary. You've served us well."

Frankie takes the wallet and stuffs it in his pocket, the stovepipes about his shins clanking. "Son of a bitch," says Jo.

"And *now,* Miss Maguire," says the Duke, "for you. Your bravery saved more than Frankie here from the, ah, *consequences* of my folly." He puts a hand on her shoulder and she does not shrug it off. "I would grant you a boon, Miss Maguire. Name your heart's desire. If I can grant it or do it or steal it, it's yours."

"Leave my friends alone," she says.

"What," says the Duke, "*all* of them? You'll have to give me a list." He steps back. "Very well. It's done. Nevermore bothered by me or mine! Come, gentlemen." He turns to go.

"What about the boar?" says Jo, and the Duke stops.

"Erymathos," he says, "has been taking care of himself for longer than you can remember. The boar," he says, turning to look back at her, "will be fine."

Gaveston hurries after the Duke, followed by Sweetloaf.

"I'll be curious to see what happens next," says Orlando. "She took a liking to you in there, but you've caught her attention." He smiles. "That's never wise." He saunters off after the others.

"Jo," says Frankie. "Can I –"

"Shut up," says Jo, and she walks away. A dark blue car floats between them, the pavement beneath glowing an unearthly blue-white, the hubcaps spinning pinwheels of colored lights.

Frankie sits in a clatter of makeshift armor and starts wrestling with the pot lid taped to his chest.

Becker catches up with Jo in the middle of the parking garage. "Hey," he says. "You need a ride, or something?"

"No," says Jo, pointing down to the other end of the garage, a long white limousine there, a white suv by it with gold trim. "The Queen's giving us a lift. Thanks, though. Maybe Frankie? If you're feeling generous."

"Look," is what Becker says then, "I'm going to forget all of this."

"I, uh," says Jo.

"And what I wanted to say is if I've been an asshole, I mean, I *have* been an asshole, to you and her, and I'm sorry, okay?" A sudden blare of a car horn. A grimy white bus is bulling its way down the ramp through the last of the crowd on its way up and out. There's a man in green coveralls leaning out the front door, yelling and shaking a mop. "It's all so goddamn," says Becker.

"Yeah," says Jo.

"Hey, tomorrow," says Becker. "Don't worry about coming in, okay? I'll square it with Tartt."

Jo laughs. "Jesus. I hadn't even. Thanks, Becker, but I really need the money." She slings her sheathed sword over her shoulder, holding the ties in one hand. "Hell, I'll bring *her* along, too. After tonight, she owes me. Big time."

Becker snorts. "So, what is she, a Princess? What's that about?"

"You're going to forget all this tomorrow," says Jo. "Remember?"

Becker smiles, a little. "Guthrie won't let me."

"It's for the best," says Jo. "I mean, I appreciate it, really. Thank you. *And* Guthrie. But forget it. Okay? You don't want to get mixed up in this. Believe me. I'll, uh, I'll see you tomorrow."

"Yeah," says Becker. "Tomorrow." He watches her walk away, down toward the white suv. Ysabel's waiting by it in her long ivory gown, Jo's army jacket draped over her shoulders.

Up the airy mountain
Down the rushy glen,
We dare n't go a-hunting,
For fear of little men;

—*William Allingham*

NO. 5

FREEWAY

THE PRINTER SPITS – IT'S COVERED – A SCALE OF ONE TO TEN
the HALF-FULL GLASS – DOG-CATCHERS – HANGING UP
"COULD YOU MAYBE DESCRIBE" – the whole FIVE HUNDRED
ROOM TO CLAP – NO DUTY BOUND – LIGHTING A CIGARETTE
LIFE AND LIMB – AN EVEN HALF DOZEN – THOSE TEETH
"ELELEU!" – BACKLASH – before the END – CLIP-CLOP-CLIP
"LEO, HONEY"

THE PRINTER SPITS out a photo of Ysabel, head and shoulders before an empty blue background, her dark hair swept back, pinned up out of her vaguely smiling face. "See?" says the fat man, leaning over the foot of the rumpled double bed to pluck up the photo. He settles back by the laptop near the pillows, handing the photo to Jo. "No red eye. Light's too bright. Focus off just enough. That's some quality DMV shit." His T-shirt has a grainy picture of a graveyard on it. We have found a new home for the rich, it says. It's hard to tell where his thin beard ends and his scraggly hair begins.

"It's supposed to say Oregon," says Jo.

"It will," says the fat man with the scraggly hair. "It'll be smaller, too, and printed on a card." He pats the laptop, scratched silver and snarled in cables dangling off the sides and the end of the bed. "I've got a killer template set up for this. That's a six-jet printer. Not four colors - *six*. Won't pass a UV scanner, but it'll fool any pair of naked eyeballs in the state. All I have to do is plug in the pretty." He leans back against the pillows, smiling. "Which I do when you show me the cheddar." He tilts his head, looks past Jo. "We're done with the camera, baby. Come over here, make yourself comfortable. Or there." He's pointing to the other double bed. The coverlet's been pulled off. It's hanging over the window at the front of the room. A tall guy's lying on his belly on the white

159

sheets, his bare feet sticking off the edge of the bed. "Don't mind Abe," says the fat man with the scraggly hair. "He's only sleeping."

"I'm fine," says Ysabel, undoing her hair. She's sitting on a low stool over in the corner, lit up by a harsh light on a tripod. A big piece of blue paper tacked to the door behind her.

"Suit yourself," says the fat man with the scraggly hair. "That ain't a wallet," he says to Jo. She's handing him the photo. "I don't need to fool any pair of eyeballs in the state," she says. "I told you. I just need a cheap-ass license and a social that can fool a crappy copy machine."

"I get it," he says. "An I-9." He tilts his head to smile at Ysabel again. "You illegal, baby? Where you from, Canada?"

"It's neighbor shit," says the girl with the floppy mohawk.

She's sitting on the counter at the back of the room, between the two sinks. Her hooded sweatshirt's grey, the sleeves hacked off at the shoulders. She's playing with an empty orange prescription bottle. The sink to her right is full of them, all empty. "Shut up, Mel," says the fat man.

Mel shrugs. "It's that shit a couple weeks ago. She's the one we's supposed to watch out for, with the hair." Pointing at Jo. "And she's the, I don't know." Pointing at Ysabel. "Queen of all a them that's in it, or whatever."

"Do not start that neighbor bullshit with me," says the fat man.

"Okay," says Mel. "But Hib wakes up screaming ever since, and nobody's seen Christian." She's not looking up from the pre-scription bottle turning over in her hands. "Not since. And you *know* what they did to Popgun, just up back of the Denny's."

"Christian?" says Jo, but the fat man's saying, "No, Mel, nobody knows who did what the fuck to Popgun, and I *do* not want to hear this gutterpunk neighbors and vampires and angel-fucking aliens from out of my hairy ass bullshit. Okay?" He's smiling up at Jo again. "Now. We gonna do business? 'Cause I have other obligations."

"Business," says Jo, running a hand through her hair, short and blond and brown at the roots, black tufts lying against it here and there. "Yeah. Like you said, Timmo, it's an I-9. So she can get paid." Ysabel's frowning at her nails. "See, we need the paycheck for the money, and the I-9 for the paycheck, and the license for the I-9…"

"Not my problem," he's saying, shaking his head.

"End of the month, you get paid."

"Then that's when you get the ID."

"Timmo, please, I – "

"Credit? Dead it." He leans back on the pillows, hands behind his head. *"Especially* not for former clientele."

"I," says Jo. "We really need this. Please."

"I tell you what," he says, tilting his head, looking past Jo. "Baby." Ysabel on the stool in her tight denim shorts, her white blouse knotted over a yellow tank top. "Sweetheart." She looks up at that. "How about we clear the room," he says. "Just you and me. Strictly photography. Whatever you're comfortable with, but I bet you can convince me to bend the sixth commandment just this once."

"Oh, hell no," says Jo.

"What are you, her mouth?" says Timmo. An orange prescription bottle bounces off his head. "Hey!" He bats another one out of the air. "Goddammit, Mel!"

"You," she's saying, laughing, "you are such a fucking skeeveball," scooping up bottle after bottle from the sink. "Mel, you goddamn tweak," Timmo's saying as he scoots down to the end of the bed. A bottle hits the coverlet hanging over the window with a soft thump. Jo ducks one. Another one hits the mirror over the dresser and Abe jerks at the clack, drawing in one long bubbling snore. Mel freezes, arm cocked. Timmo sits there at the end of the bed, glaring. Ysabel stands up.

Jo, straightening, watches Ysabel work a hand into her front pocket. "I think," says Ysabel, pulling out a couple of bills folded between her index and middle fingers, Jo opening her mouth to say something and closing it again, "this should cover it?" Holding the money out to Timmo, his bare feet dangling over the printer.

He sighs. Takes the money. "You got it, beautiful," he says. Rolling over. Grabbing the laptop.

"Be sure you spend it all in one place," says Ysabel. "On something terribly impractical."

The little man walks right into the closed door of the pickup truck and bounces back, arms waving, head wobbling. Grimacing. His teeth are very long and snag the dim streetlight, the blue-white shine from the sign on the corner: Shilo Inn. Affordable excellence. Roland catches him by his collar and his arm. "Well?" he says, leaning in close to the little man's ear. It twitches. "Bedamned if *I* know," says the little man.

Roland shoves, and the little man bounces off the pickup truck again. As he staggers back, Roland grabs him by his shirt and lifts him off the ground with one hand. The other's holding his sword. The sleeve of his silver tracksuit rent to ribbons. "Tell her, Cearb," says Roland, and he sets the tip of his sword against the little man's belly. "Tell your loathly lady the Chariot still guards the Bride." Leaning into a thrust, he pulls the little man choking down the blade. Across the lot in the crook of the motel's elbow the door to room 109 opens. Jo steps out, followed by Ysabel. Cearb reaches out a hand his mouth working and Roland hauls him down behind the big beige box that hides the motel's dumpster, kneeling there, his blade still deep in Cearb's belly. Roland's sunglasses are broken, one yellow lens missing. The headphones around his neck askew, an earpiece broken loose.

"How much?" Jo's saying, working a pack of cigarettes out of the pocket of her workpants.

"How much?" says Ysabel.

Jo stops short. "You know what the fuck I'm talking about and you knew I was going to ask you the fucking question the minute you pulled it out so I wish to God you would for once just give me a straight fucking answer."

"Nothing, Jo."

"Nothing what?"

"I have no money. As you well know. I told you the very first day."

Jo looks away. "So you just." She frowns.

"I gave him – "

"Shut up," says Jo. She grabs Ysabel's arm, the pack of cigarettes forgotten in her other hand. Starts walking along the motel's portico, lighted doors to the left, dark lot to the right. "Just shut up. Don't say a word."

There's a crunch out there behind the big wood box that hides the motel's dumpster. "What?" says Jo. Stopping. "What was that?"

"It's *quiet,*" says Ysabel. The red light of the sign across the street. Red Lion Hotel. Welcome Boomers.

"I just heard," says Jo.

"It's quiet," says Ysabel. "It's all gone quiet. There's someone here."

"Someone."

"We shouldn't have come," says Ysabel. "Not up here. Not this soon."

"Timmo doesn't exactly have an office downtown," says Jo. "He ever finds out," she's looking back at the motel room, "you're the one that stiffed him." She shakes her head. "He's a fuck of a lot more dangerous than anything *you're* worried about."

Behind the dumpster box, Roland's working his sword free, slowly. "Gallowglas," wheezes the little man. Roland nods. "Be glad, Cearb," he whispers, and the he catches the hand that's grabbed his wrist and pries it open. "Fair and square," he says, "you're out of it. *Fair* and *square.*" With a sigh and a slump, Cearb lets his hand fall. "Be glad," says Roland, "I didn't call her over to join the fray."

Cearb smiles around those teeth.

A Scale of One to Ten – the Half-full Glass
Dog-catchers – Hanging up

"On a scale of one to ten," says Ysabel, "where one is – "

"Yeah, I know," says the man over the phone.

"Where one is – "

"Not at all satisfied, yeah, I know, you said it already."

"Please," says Ysabel. "I need to read the whole question to you as it's written." One leg crossed over the other she sits sideways at her narrow carrel, idly plucking at the hem of her skirt there above her knee. "Besides, we might have changed the scale. Just to see if you're paying attention."

"So read the question," says the man.

"On a scale of one to ten, where one is very dissatisfied and ten is very satisfied, how would you rate your most recent visit, overall, to Pet Depot?"

"See?" says the man. "It's the same one. You didn't change anything."

"You're paying attention," says Ysabel. She's pushed her skirt a little higher, fingertips resting on her knee, her thumb drawing loops on the skin of her thigh.

"Can't you just average up all the numbers I've already given you?"

"It wouldn't be as meaningful as what you say when I ask the question." Ysabel taps the number seven on her keyboard.

"Well, I'd say seven, but I'll give 'em a ten if I never get another survey call like this," says the man.

"I have to ask you to pick just one," says Ysabel. She's already hit enter and brought up the next question on her screen.

"I *know* you heard that one," she's whispering. Sits up there on the low bed in the middle of the big dark room, pushing the bare shoulder next to her. Her blond hair ruddied by the light leaking through the tall narrow windows. "Your *grace*," she hisses. *"Leo."*

"Cats," he says, suddenly. "The building's settled. What?" Grimacing, his head still on the pillow, digging at the corners of his eyes.

"You heard that," she says.

"Doll," he says, "there's a restaurant downstairs. They're washing up."

"At *three* in the *morning?*" she says, and there's a clattering crash.

Lights flicker to life in the wide white stairwell as the Duke descends, belting up a dressing gown of purples and golds. "Fucking Tommy," he's muttering. "Goes and gets himself killed. Fucking useless Stirrup." In the foyer, the doors to the right stand open, the room beyond dark. The Duke stands in the doorway a moment. A confusion of chairs upended, resting on tables, legs in the air. A squeak of wood shifting. "Up horse, motherfucker," says the Duke, feeling for the light switch. "Up with the hattock."

One of the chairs has been set upright on the floor. The man sitting in it is bent over, picking up a platter from the floor. His pants the color of gravel. His shirt the color of ash. He holds the platter up – a lid, from the steam table beside him. "Your eloquence compels me, your grace," he says. His voice slow and lugubrious. His face like old oatmeal. The Duke, there in the doorway, says nothing. The grey man sets the lid on the steam table. "You aren't happy to see me?"

The Duke swallows. "I did all I said I would do," he says.

"No," says the grey man, standing up. "Not for Erymathos."

"A *chance,*" says the Duke. "A *chance* at oblivion." But the grey man's walking toward him, shaking his head. "The boar is loose," he says. "I held him apart, and gave him up to you, and now he's loose. That's on your head."

"Hell," says the Duke, "she let him walk – " The grey man puts a hand on his shoulder. The Duke licks his lips, still open around the next word. Closes his eyes.

"You will see me once more yet," says the grey man.

"Honestly," says the Duke, "you don't have to go to all this trouble." But there's no one there.

"Hello, people who don't live here," says the woman on the television screen.

"Hi, hello!" say the people on the couch.

"I gave you a key for *emergencies!*" she says. Laughter.

"Why do we go to work so late?" says Ysabel, opening the fridge. "Aren't you people supposed to work from nine to five?"

Jo's on her side on the futon, tapping a cigarette into a coffee cup. "Nobody's worked nine to five in *years,*" she says. "Third wife sold separately," says the man on the television screen. More laughter.

"All right," says Ysabel. "But why do we wait until three in the afternoon?" She's pinching open a carton of milk.

"We're calling people at home," says Jo. She takes a drag. "Better to wait till they're home from work." Blows the smoke out. "Life-sized Imperial Stormtroopers from Sharper Image?" says the man on the television screen. "Two," says the woman.

"So," says Ysabel, setting a glass on the counter of the narrow kitchenette, "most people just work till three now?"

Jo hitches up on one elbow. "No, Pet Depot's a national survey. We're calling the East Coast at three. What are you doing?"

"Pouring milk," says Ysabel, tilting her head, pouring slowly, watching the level of the milk rise by the four fingers she's set against the glass. "So it's people on the East Coast who only work till three?"

"No," says Jo, "we're only allowed to make residential calls between six and nine. So we start out there."

"Right," says the woman on the television set. "At the end, you choked on a cookie." The man says, "That was real." Jo leans up and snaps it off.

"So the time's different out there?" says Ysabel, opening the fridge again, returning the carton.

"Time zones," says Jo. "It's across the country." Stubbing out her cigarette in the coffee cup. "The sun *moves,* you know?"

"Oh," says Ysabel. "I thought they'd figured it was the other way round. Whichever." She steps over to the blond armoire in the corner. "It's twenty of three now." She pulls out a thin burgundy cardigan. Slips it on. "Or twenty of six. Time for another day on the phones."

"Are you," says Jo, and then she looks down and away, smiling, shaking her head. "Are you going to drink the milk?" The glass half-full sits there on the counter by the sink.

"Are you going to take your sword?"

Jo gets up off the futon. "No, Ysabel, I'm not taking the sword with us to work."

"And I'm not drinking the milk," says Ysabel.

"Okay then," says Jo.

"Yes," he says. And again, "Yes." He's behind the scant cover of a payphone, handset tucked between ear and hunched shoulder. His suit's black. His tie skinny and black, the knot of it lost somewhere under a thick beard the color of mahogany furniture. "I understand," he says. He's pulling a black notebook from his jacket, big as the palm of his hand, thumbing the elastic band off the cover. Opens it to a page that says THURS 29 SEPT at the top. "No. No." He scribbles G-K under that, shoots his cuff, checks the time. "Probably not." 2.48, he writes. He's wearing a pair of black sunglasses. Something is written on one lens, in white, spidery letters.

Across the street Jo steps out of the apartment building, laughing, turning to say something to Ysabel behind her. JEANS, he writes, then OVERSHIRT PLAID BERRY, then WHITE SKIRT. "Tonight? This afternoon." SWEATER = WINE. He crosses out WINE. "As soon as we're done here." RED WINE. He closes the notebook, hangs up the phone.

The payphone's at the edge of a small corner parking lot, by the yellow Pay Here box. He waits behind the phone as they walk past, Jo saying, "that *it* moves, what I was saying, what I meant was that's how it," and then he heads down the line of parked cars toward the black one in the middle, a powerful-looking thing with dark windows. Spidery lines of white paint whorl over the fenders, across the hood and roof. There's a little guy sitting padmasana on the hood, there in the middle of the concentric rings of cramped white letters. His suit is black. His tie is skinny and black. His eyes behind black sunglasses, the feather tied to one side stirring by the lank grey curls crowding his ear.

"Mr. Charlock," says the big guy with the thick beard.

The little guy dips his head, rolls it from one side to the other. Takes a deep breath his shoulders opening and tipping back, his chest lifting up and out.

"Mr. Charlock," says the big guy again.

"Could you shut up for maybe one more goddamn minute?" says the little guy. The big guy shrugs and reaches up for his sunglasses and the little guy says "Wssht!" Roland's coming up the side street, pale yellow track suit, spotless white shoes, black headphones over his ears, headband stark against his closecut silvery hair. Hands in his pockets. Nodding to himself as he turns the corner after Jo and Ysabel.

"Where they go, he goes," says Mr. Charlock. He spits in the palm of his hand and dabs a finger in it, then smears a dark wet line right through the circles of letters. Unfolding his legs, he scoots off the hood. "You oughta remember that by now, Mr. Keightlinger." He yanks off his sunglasses, glaring at the apartment building across the street. "And every fucking thing else. It's all guns under pillows and leashes on pews up there – I could be at it all night and still get fucking bupkes."

Mr. Keightlinger opens the door on the driver's side with a sharp popping squonk. "Time to put it away," he says. He tucks his sunglasses into a jacket pocket.

"What *did* our master's voice whisper in your tremendous ear?" says Mr. Charlock, opening his door. "What errand slipped his mind on the way to the office this morning? Milk to be soured? Thumbs to prick? His dry cleaning?"

Mr. Keightlinger shakes his head. "Something won't go back where it came from," he says. "Sullivan's Gulch." Jerks a thumb over his shoulder. "Across the river."

"Some *thing,*" says Mr. Charlock. He takes in a breath and blows it out, an overdone sigh. "We're playing *dog-catcher?*"

"It will be noticed," says Mr. Keightlinger, climbing into the car. "We keep it out of sight. Favor for a friend." A jingle of keys. The engine rumbles to life.

"I swear to any fucking god you care to name," mutters Mr. Charlock, shaking his head, climbing into the car, "if this weren't the only game in town."

"On a scale of one to ten," Guthrie's saying, as Jo walks by down the narrow aisle of kelly green carrels. "Where one is very dissatisfied and ten is very satisfied." His T-shirt is black and says Not The Bullet But The Hole. He doesn't look up. "How would you rate the service provided by the receptionist at Pet Depot?"

Becker's sitting behind the desk at the front of the office, peering at his computer screen, one hand on his mouse, the other on the phone. Jo snags a chair from an empty carrel and pulls it over by the desk, straddling the back of it. "Hey."

"You should be dialing," says Becker. "I just opened up Central. Fresh new numbers, ready and waiting."

"State law," says Jo. "Fifteen minutes paid break every two hours of work."

"You've been here an hour and a half."

She shrugs, elbows propped on the back of the chair. "Wanted to catch you before Tartt left. Tomorrow's payday. Everything cool?"

Becker takes his hand off the mouse and his hand off the phone and folds them in his lap, sitting back, head tilted. He's wearing a floppy white T-shirt and his hair's sticking up in a number of different directions. There's a pen behind each ear. "Yes, Jo. Everything's cool. Ysabel will get a check cut tomorrow."

Jo lets out a breath, dips her head to rest a moment on her forearms. Lifts it grinning. "Great," she says, getting up. "Thanks, Becker."

"You're going to have to tell me," he says, "one of these days, I mean, how you ended up doing all this stuff for her. It's nice, it's great, but." He looks down, then over at his computer screeen. Grabs his mouse. "I mean, it's your business. Obviously." Down at the end of the narrow aisle Ysabel's laughing into the mike of her headset. Nodding, she's saying something, smiling. Sees Jo and shakes her head, rolls her eyes, leans forward in her carrel, never losing that smile.

"Yeah," says Jo. "There's a story there. Look, I should get back on the phones."

"Thought you were on break," says Becker.

"Did I say that? I'm talking to my supervisor. We still do that on the clock, right?" Becker scowls over the top of his monitor. "Anyway," says Jo, "breaks are every two hours. I've got another twenty-five minutes to go. At least." She leans over the desk. "I'm beating rate," she says.

"You were," says Becker. "You got nine on the board. You need two more by five to beat rate."

"Oh ye of little faith," says Jo, heading back to her carrel.

"Ten minutes, tops," says Jo into her headset. "And you'll be helping Pet Depot learn how better to serve their customers." She frowns.

"I just," says the woman, into her phone. She's kneeling, scooping up a clump from the litter box. Sifting loose bits of litter from the clump. "I only ever went the one time."

"Doesn't matter," says Jo. "They still want to know what you think."

"But we normally go to Pet Samaritan," says the woman, dumping the clump into a plastic shopping bag that says Thank You! Have a nice day. "I don't really like those big-box places." Her sleeve riding up exposes arabesques of blue–black ink circling her forearm. More ink like ivy curls up past the collar of her T-shirt.

"So you're here in Portland?" says Jo. "I really don't think," says the woman, as Jo's saying, "I mean, Pet Samaritan, right?" Ysabel's standing by her carrel, her sweater draped over one arm. Jo points to her headset. A short, older woman pushes past, shouldering a gym bag.

"I really don't think that's necessary," says the woman, standing, picking up the shopping bag.

Jo leans forward, elbows on her carrel's desk, crowding her keyboard. "Everything you say, ma'am, is held in the strictest confidence. It's why Pet Depot hired Barshefsky Associates. They don't want to see who's answering the questions, they just want to see what people are saying. We strip out your contact information when we're done."

"I still," says the woman. "I just don't think." She backs through a swinging door into a bright kitchen, yellow walls, an avocado refrigerator. Bag still hanging from one hand. "We only went that one time, for the flea emergency."

Jo's bent over, forehead on fingertips, eyes closed. "For the survey to mean anything we have to talk to as many people as possible, whether they like it or not, whether they go all the time or not."

"Well," says the woman, opening the back door out of the kitchen. "You could tell them I saw a flea on Colin on a Sunday and he was due for more Advantage anyway, but it was a Sunday – " From around the corner there's a clatter, a snorting grunt.

"Well," says Jo, "there's a set of questions I need to ask of everybody who does the survey. Like I said, it takes about ten minutes – "

"Colin?" says the woman, heading down the back stairs, phone still to her ear.

"Ma'am?" says Jo.

"Colin," says the woman. There's a clopping sound. The side of the house suddenly lit up, empty yellow recycling tub, green garbage can on its side, clutter everywhere, paper towels, eggshells, a takeout carton ripped open. The shopping bag that says Thank You! Have a nice day plops to the ground. The boar looks up, harsh light catching the grey-white fringe of the ruff behind the blocky wedge of his head. Tusks curling up and up and around, one smeared with peanut sauce. Dark eyes glittering. The phone drops to the ground. The woman lifts a hand to her mouth.

"Ma'am?" says Jo. She frowns. Shakes her head. Lifts her headset off, blowing out a sigh. "She hung up," she says.

"Whatever," says Ysabel. "Let's go."

"Let me do my timesheet," says Jo.

"Could you maybe describe what you saw?" says Mr. Charlock.

"Well," says the woman. She's sitting on one end of the spavined couch. Mr. Charlock's sitting on the tile-topped coffee table before her, hands on her knees leaning forward, looking up into her eyes. "Would you really use the word huge?" he says. An owl's feather dangles from the sunglasses tucked into his jacket pocket.

"Well," she says, "I, um."

"Monster?" says Mr. Charlock. "Is that really the right word?"

"Monstrous," says Mr. Keightlinger, fingering the gauzy curtains hanging in the big front window.

"I wouldn't use that word either," says Mr. Charlock. "Step it back. Last night. What did you do? What did you see?"

"Well," she says.

"You come out of the house, back door. It's dark. Hypocrisy in your hands. Light on the side of the house goes on, garbage can, recycling tub, then what? What's knocked it over? What's rooting around in the coffee grounds? Just this? All this? All this fuss over a little possum?"

"Coyote," says Mr. Keightlinger.

"A little coyote?" says Mr. Charlock, lifting his hands from her knees. "Well?"

"I guess it was," says the woman, blinking. A shiver rippling through her. Reaching out to lean on the arm of the couch. "Was just, a, just a."

"A coyote."

"Coyote."

Mr. Charlock's standing up. "Makes more sense now, doesn't it?" She's nodding vaguely, with a wisp of a frown. Mr. Charlock's smile slips and twists into a grimace, and he lets his head droop, chin on chest, pressing fingertips into the corners of his eyes. "I wouldn't," he says, looking up, smiling again, "I wouldn't bother with the posters."

"Posters?" she says.

"Lost cat," says Mr. Charlock. "Trying would only make it hurt more. Hope, you know?" He shakes his head. "We can show ourselves out."

"I like your tattoos," says Mr. Keightlinger, following him.

She sits there on the couch, mouth half open, still faintly frowning.

Jo's in the corner of the white office kitchen, under the window filled with sunlight, sitting knees up on the white floor, black jeans and a red shirt unbuttoned over a black tank top, mismatched Chuck Taylors, white phone against her ear. "What," Frankie's saying. "You think I was gonna have the cops up in here or something?"

"So you just said you did it."

"I said Austin did it. Had a party, you know, got rowdy, he kicked the door." Frankie sniffs.

"And they bought it."

"I paid 'em to buy it. Funny thing. Your friends give me five hundred bucks, but first they break down my fuckin' door."

"Serves you right," says Jo.

"You didn't need to say that," says Frankie.

Jo looks up at the windowsill. "So it took the whole five hundred?"

"No, it didn't take the whole five hundred. Why do you care?"

"I just, I wanted to check to see if there was anything funny about it. The money."

"Funny," says Frankie.

Jo takes a deep breath. "Did you spend it all?"

"What do you think?'

"That's great, Frankie," says Jo. She lets the phone droop in her hand. "That's just great." He's saying something, a tinny squawk from the earpiece. She looks up to see Ysabel standing by the phone on the wall, her hand on the plunger. She presses it. The handset in Jo's hand goes silent.

"We've been punished enough," says Ysabel. She holds up two white envelopes. "Becker just gave me these. I understand you have some occult means of turning them into cash?"

Jo shrugs.

"So I want to go out," says Ysabel. "I want to hear music. I want to dance. And I will not take no for an answer."

Jo pulls herself to her feet. "Okay," she says. She hangs up the phone.

The man in the black leather jacket stand on the corner looking up at a big, blocky brick building. The cornerstone is marked with a Masonic compass and square. Signs advertising an Indian restaurant and a head shop hang over the front doors between green-topped white columns. "Hey," says a burly man, poking his head around the edge of the bus shelter. "Hey, buddy." He comes over, flip-flops, khaki shorts, a dirty T-shirt that says America the Beautiful over a soaring eagle. "Got something for you." He's digging in a side pocket of those shorts, comes up with a clear plastic bottle, label torn, some Snapple tea, something milky sloshing inside. "Yeah?" says the burly man.

"It's diseased," says the man in the black leather jacket.

"Naw, bro, no," says the burly man, shaking the bottle at him. "You got to take it. Kettle's due."

"I'm not your brother," says the man in the black leather jacket. His hair is dark and flops about his eyes and ears, his lean face roughened by a half-grown beard. He shrugs. "Take better care of yourself." He ducks under the laundry lines of prayer flags, reduced, and steps into the hemp and bead and world crafts shop.

"Dagger," says the man behind the counter. His hair is richly red and he wears a blue-striped shirt with white French cuffs. The top two buttons undone.

"Stirrup," says the man in the leather jacket. "You're the Duke's man, now?"

"Kills the time," says the Stirrup.

"And how are you doing?" says the Dagger, leaning on the counter. "With the sword."

"He's expecting you," says the Stirrup, pointing upstairs.

"Sidney!" cries the Duke, opening the white door to his rooms.

"M'lord," says the Dagger.

"Come in, come in." The Duke's wearing brown corduroy pants and a brown sweater vest over a white T-shirt. He leads the Dagger down a dark hall into a room filled with sunlight from tall, narrow windows. "It's not," a woman's saying, "as if I don't understand. You had your thing with the kitchen knight. Fine. But we should have been there. We would have kept you from embarrassment." She's standing by the big brown desk, holding a glass of wine. Her hair short and gunmetal grey. She wears brown tights and a long red shirt. The Duke stops in the middle of the room, spreads his hand, looks from her to the Dagger and back. "What are you," he says, "my mother?"

"No, m'lord," says the grey-haired woman. She sips her wine.

"Two things," says the Duke. "First, should me no would haves. That buck has sailed. Two: I could give a shit about embarrassment. Tonight we're going up into Northeast to kill that fucking boar."

"Just the three of us?" says the grey-haired woman.

"Boar?" says the Dagger.

"Uh, Duke?" says the blond woman sitting behind the desk. She's wearing a satiny pink camisole and holding out a phone. "I got his machine again."

"Okay," says the Duke. "Okay." He sighs. "The three of us, plus two more," he says to the grey-haired woman. "Catch Sidney up while I make this call." He steps over, takes the phone. "In the, in the other room. I'll be right back."

The blond woman's smiling at the Dagger. "Want something to drink?"

"But I can't I-do it if I don't believe it," she sings, there in the dark-paneled corner, as the guitars loop around for another chiming pass. "So I sit here alone like a sword in a stone and I wait for a man to come by," her fingers bouncing from the strings of her bass to lay a floor for them all, "who's stuck equally fast with the wit to at last pull us free!" The drummer's ruddy head shines under an errant light behind the whirling blurry fence of his sticks. Red hair bobbing one guitarist's bouncing behind her, the other not more than a kid curled about his big-bellied acoustic, flocks of bright chords beating about his head canted to find the mike and harmonize with her, "Just a plain and artless Art with a warm spot in his heart for the girl inside the Guinevere clothes – for me!"

Plaid shirts, a green hoodie, corduroy and a wallet chain, tank tops, a leather cowboy hat, glasses and bottles held high cheering and clapping packed between a long L-shaped padded bench and the band there in the corner, blue jeans and striped T-shirts, stubbled head and hornrims, kilts and shorts and a snap-front Western shirt, a trucker's cap that says Trans-Alaska Pipeline System shouting and whistling, standing on chairs and tables against the back wall. There by the bench Jo has to lift her hands above her head to find room to clap. Ysabel beside her, baggy cargo pants and a ringer belly shirt, holding her hair back out of her upturned face eyes closed, laughing under all the applause. "Thanks," says the singer, ducking as she hauls the bass off her shoulder. "Thanks for indulging. An oldie, a goodie, ought to be more of a standard than it is." A waitress carefully navigates the gap between crowd and bench, tray up, empty bottles, a glass full of something light and fizzy. "We're Stone and Salt," says the singer. "I think that's what we decided on." Laughter, more applause, jumping, jostled, the waitress lowers her tray curling over it braced one hand against the back of the bench.

"We got some whiskey," says the red-headed man, who's put down his guitar and picked up a fiddle.

"Is that Willamette Week?" says the singer. "Mark from the Willamette Week, ladies and gentlemen, slaking our thirst. Port-land Mercury, y'all gonna put out?" The waitress pushes past Jo who stumbles leaning into a guy in a grey hoodie leaning back. "Is the Mercury in the house?" The waitress puts her hand on Ysabel's shoulder, Ysabel turning, puzzled, shaking her head, "What?" she says. The waitress trying to give her the glass.

"Portland Monthly?" says the red-headed man.

"Oregonian?" says the kid, not looking up from the capo he's strapping to his guitar.

"Two Louies, gonna buy us a round?"

Ysabel's saying something to the waitress, "I don't want this." The guy in the grey hoodie lifts his phone up eyeing the blue-lit screen, angling for a shot of the singer, handing up shot glasses from the tray on the floor. "We have a," she's saying.

"Anodyne? Anodyne Magazine, in the house?"

"Daily Vanguard?"

"We didn't order anything," says Jo.

"We have a problem," the singer says, standing up.

"I told you," says the drummer. "I'm not doing jokes."

"Oregon Business? Street Roots?"

The waitress points back, toward the bar. Jo's looking, Ysabel craning up on her toes. A man in a black turtleneck looking right back at her, smiling. Waving. "We're a five-piece," says the singer. "These days. Not a quartet. I guess Mark couldn't see our organist, off to the side. We couldn't fit her on stage!" The drummer rattles off a sudden riff, thumping down the toms to crash against a cymbal. Marfisa's standing up from behind a couple of keyboards, tangled hair pale like clotted cream shining under the lights. The man in the black turtleneck at the bar shrugging, looking only at Ysabel. Ysabel's shaking her head. The waitress rolls her eyes.

Marfisa's tucking a leather bag under her arm, drone pipes clattering. "She's piping for us this next song," says the singer, "and that is thirsty work. Can anybody," and Ysabel's reaching out to pluck the glass from the tray, the waitress already turned to go, tray wobbling from the shift in weight. "Can anybody spare a glass or a swallow?" says the singer.

Ysabel hands the glass to the guy in the grey hoodie. "Pass it up!" she says. He grins. Takes the glass. "Hey!" he bellows. "Pass it up!"

Hand to hand above the crowd the glass makes its way up to the singer, smiling, who takes it, hands it to Marfisa. "Thanks," she says, "Yeah," says Marfisa, leaning into the drummer's mike. "Thank you, anonymous benefactor," says the singer. The man in the black turtleneck turning away, lost in the press by the bar. "Okay," says the singer. A low keening seeps into the room, stilling the crowd. Marfisa's started blowing. Ysabel takes Jo's hand. "This one's gonna be on the album," says the singer. Jo looks down at her hand, looks up at Ysabel, Ysabel's eyes on the stage, shining, smiling. "Here it comes," she says.

"Words," the singer wails, "what use are words?" An echo, a ghost of a melody laid over the droning pipes. "I'm leaving, like the first morning. I'm held like the wind in your hand." The fiddle groans, a rotting chord. "I ate my toast with butter and I drank my coffee with cream," the guitar spieling under it all, "I wore your mask for a year and a day," and with a crash of cymbals everything drops away but the drone and her voice. "But I'm not gonna scream," she sings, simply, quietly, the drums fluttering up behind her, building, the red-headed man his fiddle high holding his bow ready, Marfisa hands on her pipes eyes closed blowing and ready, the kid's hands shivering over the strings shedding notes as she opens her mouth and cries, "I'm leaving – "

A desk lamp on the floor, plugged into an orange extension cord snaking off into the shadows. By the lamp a rotary phone and an answering machine. A bare foot steps into the light. Above it crisp folds of a dark blue skirt. He kneels there, by the light. Reaches out to press the rewind button on the answering machine. A scribble of voice in the air. Stop.

He sits back on his heels, face in shadow. His long black hair loose, spilling over the shoulders of his white shirt.

He leans forward. Presses play. Stands.

"Orlando, you sonofabitch, I know you're there. Pick up." He stands, steps away from the light. Unbuttons his shirt. "Listen, I'm calling on you. You owe me. You know it." The shirt drops to the floor. A rustle, the darkness of his skirt falling away. The dark windows high in the wall before him, blank with dust weakly catching the lamplight. "I told you to find me a gallowglas. You did." Naked, he folds his hands together and bows his head. "You were going to cut her down right there in front of everybody until I told you not to. And you didn't." He lifts his head. Turns around. A thin dark line of hair dropping from his navel interrupted by something pale, dead skin tight and shining, a ripple, a knot, scars hunched across his belly from hip to hip.

"Orlando. Dammit, pick up."

He steps back into the circle of lamplight and kneels. One hand holding a long knife, a slight curl to it, a simple Japanese hilt. "Don't give me that shit about no oath sworn and no duty bound. *You did it.*" His other hand floats under the blade shining suddenly harsh. "For me." Wraps his fingers about it, there below the hand on the hilt. "You need me. Admit it." He closes his eyes. Squeezes them shut as he tightens his grip. "Tonight we're going after Erymathos. The Dagger, the Helm, the Stirrup, and Jo fucking Gallowglas. I need you there, to watch my back. You hear me?" A drop of something colorless slides down the blade. Hangs a moment at the tip, an inch from the scar above his right hip. "You hear me? Orlando. Pick up."

He yanks the knife into himself. Sits there a moment. His breath quick and shallow.

"You owe me. Seven ways, you owe me."

Forearms tensed fists bunched tight one above the other he draws them straight upright along the frozen ripple of that scar, opening something wet and yellow in the light.

"*Dammit.*" A rattle, a click. Dial tone. He leans forward, reaches out with a hand shaking to press the stop button. Sits back. Swallows. Pulls the knife from his body.

After a moment he lays it to one side. His other arm cradling the wound, wet and shining, glittering, golden.

He leans forward. Presses rewind. The voice scribbles. Stop. Play.

Lighting a cigarette Jo tips her head back, lets a curl of smoke escape the corner of her mouth. "So you're like a real band now and everything, huh?"

"This whole side of town is dangerous," says Marfisa, head down, hands tight on the straps of her small purple backpack. Ysabel whoops spinning arms outstretched under the blinking red stoplights ahead of them, streets empty of traffic all around her.

"You got a CD coming out? You giving it away on the internet?" says Jo, heading down the sidewalk after Ysabel. "This isn't a joke," says Marfisa, following her. Wingtips clocking past an open lot full of idle Coke machines. "You should damn well know to stay downtown by now." Argyle socks up over her knees and a tweed coat longer than her short checked skirt.

"We're two fucking blocks from the bridge," says Jo.

"You shouldn't have crossed the water," says Marfisa.

"Stop fighting!" calls Ysabel back over her shoulder.

"She wanted to see a band tonight," says Jo, and Marfisa says "It doesn't matter" as Jo's saying, "Apparently, she wanted to see *you.* "

"It doesn't *matter,* " says Marfisa, stopping at the corner, and then she lifts her head and calls, "Princess!"

Ysabel walking backwards down the street says, "Sing for me."

"Lady, come back to the sidewalk."

"Sing!" says Ysabel. "Your lady commands it." Laughing.

"Lady, it's Southeast's street. The Hawthorne. Runs right through the heart of his demesne."

"The Duke?" says Jo. "Don't worry about the Duke."

"How did it go?" says Ysabel, in the crosswalk now, as Jo says "He promised." Ysabel's singing, "I'm wearing Heidi braids, and aviator shades, my sailor suit is blue."

"He *promised?*" Marfisa slowly turns her head to look at Jo. "You witless fool." The next stoplight down the street turns red, and an engine snarls. Headlights appear, turn right, coming at them. Ysabel's singing, "And if it weren't for you, I'd take it off and leave it in a heap," her voice faltering, turning to watch the car approach. "Right here in the street." Marfisa's small purple backpack falls to the sidewalk.

The car's a reddish brown, a black stripe down the side. The driver's hair is blond. She wears a grey chauffeur's cap. The engine settles into a slow deep idle. A face appears up over the top of the car, a big smile, floppy brown hair, the Duke, pulling himself up out the window on the passenger's side, resting his elbows on the roof of the car. "Put it away, Axe," he says, sweetly. "The Princess is a friend of Jo's, and I'm a man of my word."

"Told you," says Jo to herself. Marfisa holding the hilt of her sword down by her hip point up edges out into the street between Ysabel and the car.

"The Princess is a friend of Jo's," says the Duke, a little louder, "but you, Axe, are not – unless?" He looks to Jo, spreading his hands.

"Yeah," says Jo, quickly. "She's a friend of mine."

"Damn," says the Duke, slapping the roof of his car. "I hope you won't be *too* profligate with that particular honor." Looks down, into the car. "Babe, remind me, at some point I really need to get a copy of that list from her." Marfisa looking sidelong at Jo, her arm relaxing. The tip of her sword swinging slowly down toward the pavement.

"You've interrupted my first night out in over a week," says Ysabel.

"I know, lady," says the Duke, "and I am sorry. Direst need compels me."

"But you can't mess with her," says Jo. "And you can't mess with Marfisa."

The Duke cocks a finger at her. "Thing is," he says, "I'm sure, a little work, you could devise a cunning sophistry around how one must first love oneself before loving others, but the spirit of my boon is as clear as the letter: I'm only to leave your friends alone."

Jo sighs. "But me you're gonna fuck with however you want."

"*Fuck* with?" The Duke shakes his head, sadly. "I need your *help*, Gallowglas." And then he smiles, his eyes lighting up. "You ever ridden a horse?"

Pop pop pop a string of firecrackers tossed from the back of the pickup truck slithers along the metal grating of the bridge. The Stirrup in his linen suit jumps, dropping a handful of paper-wrapped packets, bright red and gold under the fluorescent lights, bouncing on the bridge. "Fucking hell," yells the boy in the brown leather jacket, "not fucking yet!" He reaches up into the truck, slapping at the people crammed in the back, seven or eight of them, hands in ripped leather gloves, a dirty blue gore-tex shoulder, a black T-shirt snarled with a face in cracked white ink.

"Cut it out!" bellows the Duke, brown boots ringing on the bridge, hands in the pockets of his long red coat. "Now listen up." The Stirrup handing up the last of his firecrackers, the boy in the brown leather jacket tossing cheap lighters up into the pickup, purple and orange, green and yellow and blue. "My boys, Gaveston and Sweetloaf, they're gonna in a minute here drive you out by the Lloyd Center. Start dropping you off every couple of blocks." Pacing back and forth by the back of the truck. "You're looking for a pig," he says. "Biggest fucking monster pig there ever was." The people in the back of the truck watching him, faces still, glasses blank in the streetlight, leaning over to spit something, cheeks pitted with old acne, picking at teeth with a grimy thumbnail. "You find him, you set him off running south. Down onto I-84. Kick up a ruckus, holler, spook him with those fireworks." Nobody says anything. Maybe a shrug. "Everybody got their money?" Nods now, smiles, "Oh, yass," says someone, the scarred face. "Okay," says the Duke. "End of the night, you meet us on the freeway. Job's done right, and we've got our boar, you'll get double what's in your pockets now." Sweetloaf and the Stirrup climbing into the cab of the truck. "Keep in mind," says the Duke, "there's no life or limb on the table here. Nobody's asking you to *fight* the damn thing. Just run him south, to us. But you don't do a good job of *that...*" He slaps the side of the truck as it rumbles to life. "Go get him!"

"How will you stop me?" says Ysabel, sitting in the cramped back seat of the Duke's car. City of tiny lites, murmurs the radio. Don't you wanna go?

Marfisa beside her knees jackknifed takes Ysabel's hand in hers. "I'll say please." She lifts Ysabel's hand to her lips. "Don't."

"You can do better than that," says Ysabel. Tiny lightning, in the storm. Tiny blankets keep you warm.

The Duke's car is parked down the bridge where grate meets pavement, by the towering red-and-white striped crossing gates. Behind it a dark wall of trees along the riverfront and then up climbs the city, windows lit, spotlights and streetlights, billboards shining jostling building against building, depth lost in the darkness hazed by all that light. Shoulders hunched, hands jammed in the pockets of his red coat, the Duke walks up to the blond woman in the grey chauffeur's cap, grey uniform jacket buttoned up to her throat, leaning against the fender, her back to the city. She stands as he steps close to her, hands on her hips. "When we're gone," he says, "take those two wherever they want to go. If I'm not back in the morning."

"Leo," she says. He leans up on his toes, reaching for the back of her head, pulling her mouth down to his. "Don't," he says, after the kiss, "don't call me that. Not here. If I'm not back in the morning, there's good cash money in the upper left drawer of the desk. Whoever's next can't keep it from you."

"I can never find your fucking desk," she says.

He kisses her again. "It'll be there." Steps back from her. Touches his fingers to his lips. "So where the fuck are these horses?" says Jo, loudly.

The Duke sighs. "Problem, Gallowglas?"

Jo's on the sidewalk, flicking a cigarette-spark off into the dark past the bridge, out toward the great cranes away south sleeping by half-built bulks of glass-wrapped towers, red guide lights winking. "The Dagger and the Helm are fetching the horses," says the Duke. "But you're not pissed about the horses." He leans on the bridge railing beside her. "And it can't be Erymathos. You yourself told me off for letting him go, and here I am doing something about it."

"What did you do with Christian Beaumont?"

"And just like that," says the Duke, "you make demands of me."

"Yeah," says Jo.

"Who the fuck is Christian Beaumont?"

"Someone I used to know," says Jo. "You picked him up the last time you got one of these posses together."

"*Another* friend?" says the Duke. "If you mean the ruffians who set upon yourself and the Princess – "

"Please."

His smile is small and tight. " – then I've got to remind you that occurred a couple weeks ago. Well before any words passed directly between us."

"No one's seen him since," she says. "Your grace."

A pattering rainfall of hoofbeats, off in the distance. "I'm touched," says the Duke, turning away, walking across the bridge. "You think I ever even knew their names in the first place." He looks down the bridge toward the ramp curving up from the dark trees below. The hoofbeats drumming closer, quickly. "Trust me, Jo Gallowglas," he calls over his shoulder. "When you got Tommy Rawhead killed, the only name I had in mind was yours."

Up the bridge at a quick trot come the horses, heads tossing, six of them, the Dagger riding at the lead, all in black under his red coat. The grey-haired woman bringing up the rear, stepping her horse back and forth as the horses slow to a walk and stop, blowing, there where the pavement meets metal, there before the Duke, who reaches slowly up, carefully, the horse before him all rust red and black points saddled and bridled, reins tucked away, stands still, shivers, blinks. The Duke's hand settles on the horse's neck, and nothing happens. His shoulders drop. His head tilts to the side. Smiling, he closes his eyes, strokes the horse's neck. "So warm," he says.

Jo pats the horse next to his, dark with a wide white blaze, gold glittering about the eyes. Fingers the saddle blanket, blue with gold trim. The seal in the corner. "Portland Police?" she says.

"They have horses," says the Duke, opening his eyes. "We put them back when we're done."

"The hounds are away?" says the Helm, her voice rough.

"And so should we be," says the Duke, lifting his foot into the stirrup, hauling himself up and up into the saddle, his horse stepping back and forth for balance. "Coming, Gallowglas?"

"Who else are we expecting, m'lord?" says the Dagger. Jo reaches up for the saddle of her horse. "We fetched six, but there's only four of us."

"I'd thought the Princess would ride one," says the Duke, "to keep up with her guardian. But the Axe happened along, just in time to – "

"Whoop," says Jo as her horse wheels, herself half in the saddle. "Whoa," she says. "Whoa. Like riding a bicycle." Teeth gritted, setting her feet in the stirrups, untangling the reins. "A really fucking *big* bicycle. With feet."

The Duke laughs. The Dagger's smiling. The Helm walks her horse over by Jo's, looks her over, shrugs, nodding at the Duke. "I *said*," says Ysabel, reaching up eyes closed to stroke the neck of a grey horse pale among the others, "that I'm going with you." She opens her eyes. "So it's just as well you brought them."

"Lady," says the Duke, after a moment. "I hadn't seen you leave the car." She swings herself into the saddle, leans forward to lay her cheek against the grey's mane. "You'll be cold," he says.

"I don't care," she says, straightening.

"I can't risk it," he says. "With a gallowglas on the field. If something were to happen."

"No one's asking you to risk it," she says. "And you were willing enough when you thought you had no one worthy of seeing me home."

"I thought I'd have no choice," he says.

"You don't," she says.

"And you, Axe?" says the Duke. Jo's glaring at Ysabel. Ysabel's shooting Jo a dark fierce look. "You'll make it an even half dozen?"

Marfisa's already hauling herself up onto the pinto, kicking one long leg over, settling her skirt, the skirts of her coat. "I would have words with Erymathos," she says, "before the end."

"Fine," says the Duke. "Marvelous. Okay. Head north, for I-5, and take the I-84 exit." He leans forward and whispers in his horse's ear. "Soft loam under hoof, and clear sharp air in your lungs, and sweet grass and cold water when it's done." He straightens, looks about at the others. "Last one under the Grand Avenue bridge buys the bourbon!" he shouts. "Heeyup!"

The horses gallop away down the bridge, striking sparks, flying under the green sign that says Seattle, The Dalles, climbing the curving off-ramp leaning up and off to the left, into the empty, quiet confusion of freeway lanes. Roland jogs to a stop, bent over panting at the other end of the bridge, sweat-dark T-shirt, sunglasses shining in the streetlight, headphones over his ears. He straightens, claps his hands together, takes a deep breath in through his nose, blown out through his mouth. And again, hunching over, shaking out one leg then the other. And again, clapping his hands together once more, and then again, as one step after another after another and another the Chariot begins to run.

THOSE TEETH – "ELELEU!" – BACKLASH
BEFORE THE END – CLIP-CLOP-CLIP

Those teeth shining Cearb clings to the green fence railing the bridge above the welter of freeway ramps. A horn blats from the traffic trundling behind him. He's staring down, humming, one arm hooked through the wire mesh, face pressed against it. Tires whining red lights chase white lights down the freeway under the bridge beneath him. He purses thin lips about those teeth and thunder welling up under the sounds of engines and wheels he closes his eyes.

He opens them. The freeway below is empty. He turns his head. The bridge behind him quiet and still. "Yes," whispers Cearb. The thunder spills over as one two six horses race around the curl of the ramp down the eastbound lanes, riders in red coats dark in the dim pink light. "Yes!" cries Cearb, letting go, falling back to the sidewalk and tumble scuttling across the empty bridge through a wailing ghost of a horn, clambering up the green fence railing the other side. He perches there panting, hands and sneakered feet wrapped around the green rail. Horses galloping below slow and faltering lean one way and another double back. Laughter and whoops. "Catch me," says Cearb, "judge me, beat me," the words like handclaps, "write what I've done in your big black book!" His voice a rasp snagging on labored breaths. "But where will you write down all *I've* suffered?" Cearb rears up hands in the air and roars, "Who will rage for *me*? Gallowglas! *Gallowglas!*"

Clang the spear shivering head caught in the mesh below his sneakers thrumming arms whirling for balance as below the Duke yells *"Dagger!"* The laughter's gone. A horse screams. The spear caught still reaching for the top of its arc, spear-haft a lever, spear-head wrenching the mesh, as Cearb grabs for the railing with one wild hand, hanging there for one long moment, spear-butt floating, drooping, falling, spear-head pulling free with a squawk tumbling butt catching the edge of the bridge with a clunk spinning out over them below, the Duke's horse rearing, the Dagger's wallowing sideways hooves churning on the pavement as the spear-haft clatters bouncing end-to-end on the freeway. "The fuck are you trying to do?" The Duke, hauling his reins half-standing in the saddle, glaring at the Dagger. "Strike him? With a mortal on the field, you moron?"

"Eleleu!" cries Cearb, slapping the railing. "Eleleu!"

"Ignore him!" says the Duke, big bay stepping sideways, back again. "Bad enough we're hunting the boar. Kill *that* little fuck, you'll bring her down on our heads for sure. Helm!"

"Lord!" she calls from behind him.

"Take the moron east to the Thiry-third Avenue bridge and hold there." He looks back over his shoulder at her. "Wind if you see the fucker. Pin him but damn well do *not* finish him until I show, got me?"

"M'lord," says the Helm. In one hand she's holding a coiled horn the color of old piano keys.

"Not so fast, moron," says the Duke. The Dagger about to kick one foot free of the stirrup settles back mouth pinched. "You leave that thing right the hell where it lays. Gallowglas." Jo's looking back and forth, Ysabel to the Duke, the spear on the pavement,

Ysabel again, her horse stepping nervously in place. "Eleleu!" cries Cearb above them. "Pick it up, Gallowglas," says the Duke.

"M'lord!" says the Dagger.

"Go!" bellows the Duke. The Helm kicks her horse into a run down the freeway. "Get the hell down to the Thirty-third bridge!" The Dagger, scowling, gallops after. "Gallowglas, pick up the damn spear."

"I'm here, uh, to do what I do," says Jo. "Be on the field of battle. Whatever. I – "

"I'll be sure to tell him when he's running us down," says the Duke. "Pick it up, don't pick it up. I were you, I had nothing in my pocket, I'd take whatever I could get." He's not looking away from her. Shivering, Jo shakes a foot loose and over her horse's back, sliding to the ground. "Strike, Gallowglas!" cries Cearb, metal clanging furiously. "Eleleu! Strike!"

"Shut the fuck *up!*" yells Jo, stock still, fists balled, glaring up into the pink-hazed darkness, and then the only sound is the wind tugging at trees to either side of the freeway. Ysabel's horse, clopping, one step and another. "Who *is* that guy?" says Jo.

"You're holding this end," the Duke is saying to Marfisa. "You got a horn?"

"If we see him, you'll hear me," says Marfisa.

"You see him, I want you hauling ass back over the river," says the Duke. "I got no fucking clue in this world why I'm not telling you to do that right this minute."

"I'll keep her safe, your grace," says Marfisa.

"Yes," says the Duke. "You will."

Jo stands, the spear in both hands, looking up and down its length. The head like a mirrored leaf long as her forearm butted by round black quillions almost as long. The haft-wood dark and smooth and straight, swelling at the end to a ringed black ferrule that chimes gently as she shifts it. "Good boar-stop," she says, and then, "He *threw* this?"

"You ready?" says the Duke.

"A minute," says Jo, looking up at her horse. She shifts the spear to her left hand, reaches up for the reins with her right, starts to lift her left foot for the stirrup and stops. "Shit," she says.

Lets go of the reins, takes the spear in her right hand, reaches up with her left for the reins, then the pommel. Takes a deep breath. "Let me," says Ysabel. She's behind Jo, reaching down for the spear. "Climb up, I'll hand it back to you," she says.

"Avaunt already," says the Duke. "Ain't got all night."

"How was the ride?" says Ysabel.

"I don't," says Jo, both hands on the saddle and reins, grunting as she hauls herself up, "I don't like leaving you alone."

"I'm not alone."

Jo looks over her shoulder as the Duke canters away to the east, hoofbeats thudding on the dark freeway. "This is getting out of hand."

"Was it ever in hand?" says Ysabel, handing her the spear, butt-first. "Don't think about the traffic."

"Traffic?" says Jo.

"Don't think about it," says Ysabel.

"You mean to strike Erymathos with that?" says the Helm.

White lights shine deep in the blade of the Dagger's sword. Long and slender, wrapped in brown leather above the quillions, corded hilt ending in a pommel like a great joint. He holds it out to the side in one hand up at the top of the hilt, fingers curled about those quillions. "Bertilak dismounted," he says, lifting his arm, slowly, "brandished his bright blade, and boldy stepped forward," lifting that sword up over his head, passing the hilt to his other hand, lowering, slowly, out to the other side. "Strode through the ford to where his foe waited." Red lights shine, deep in the blade of his sword.

"You're no Bertilak," says the Helm. Her horse whickers. Up past the bridge behind her red letters on the wall of a big blank building say Gordon's Fireplace Shop. "He dismounted. A sword's hardly the thing to strike a boar from horseback."

"You still think we're going to strike the boar."

"Well," says the Helm. "There's but one relay of hounds. If you can call it a relay. It's to flush him out, not run him down. His grace posted us here on the off-chance Erymathos misses him, standing in the middle of the damn," she's looking up the freeway, turns, looks down it, squinting into the shadows. "Ford," she adds. "No," she says. "I don't think we will. This is a duel, not a hunt."

"How long has it been since we've had a proper hunt?" says the Dagger.

"You're not angry about losing your spear," says the Helm.

"The blood, at the unmaking, bright on the snow," says the Dagger. He laughs, a short flat bark. "How long has it been since we've seen a proper snow?"

"Sidney," says the Helm.

"You saw her," says the Dagger. "What she's doing to our lady. Out cavorting all night with her like that."

"What business is that of ours," says the Helm, looking at him, the sword in his hand.

"She's the bride of the King Come Back!" says the Dagger.

"Don't tell me what you would do," says the Helm. "And I won't tell you not to do it."

"Listen!" says the Dagger, sitting up in his saddle. Off in the dark, the sound of firecrackers, pop pop pop.

One hand beating the steering wheel Mr. Charlock writhes on the front seat blindly kicking the door. Head in Mr. Keightlinger's lap, face lost somewhere under Mr. Keightlinger's palm. A wrench and he's suddenly still, taut, his voice slicing through the car, pitched high, scoured. His back arches, heels dug into the seat, then sagging, drooping, quiet. Mr. Keightlinger lifts his hand. Mr. Charlock takes a deep breath and rolls over in a sudden coughing fit. "Fucking *backlash*," he says, when he can sit up, feather dangling from his sunglasses. He straightens his collar, the knot of his tie. Smooths wayward curls by his ears.

"They coming?" says Mr. Keightlinger.

"They're *here*," says Mr. Charlock, pointing out the front window toward the darkness at the end of the street. "Right down the freeway. Whole big chunk of it decoupled."

Mr. Keightlinger grunts. He pulls off his sunglasses, wipes them on his tie.

"She's right there with 'em," says Mr. Charlock, and then pop pop pop pop pop.

Mr. Keightlinger jerks open his door, steps out on the sidewalk. Mr. Charlock's already running down the street toward the great mass of darkness shouldering treebranches aside, starting into streetlight as another string of firecrackers pops at its feet. Grey and white and yellow hair like quills about its ruff. Tusks swinging through the air as it screams. A man in a dirty blue raincoat yelling something worthless as he lights another string, pop pop. The boar hunching leaning into a run down the street. Mr. Charlock watches as it locomotives past, pop pop pop. "Run you magnificent sonofabitch! *Run!*" Past Mr. Keightlinger, past the black car whorled with spidery white letters, down the street toward the house at the end, the high fence behind it, the darkness beyond.

The walls of the gulch rise to either side of the freeway, dark and close and lined with shapeless trees, crowned with a row of houses to the north. The Duke's horse trotting through dappled pools of thin dirty light down the eastbound lanes, Jo behind, leaning in the saddle, the long black spear under one arm. "Come on," calls the Duke back over his shoulder.

"I'm, uh," says Jo, reins in one hand out to the side, trying to haul back the spear swinging wide, "a bit distracted – "

"Well," says the Duke, looking away, "don't worry about me, Gallowglas."

"What?" says Jo, horse leaning one way after the reins, herself the other, after the spear.

"I have an appointment yet to keep," says the Duke, not looking back. "You won't be the death of *me.*"

"Why do," says Jo, and then "hey, whoa -- " Her horse kicks forward as she lurches back spear tipping out of her hand dropping spear-head striking the pavement with a bright clang. Yanking the reins her horse stomping to a stop. "The fuck," the Duke's saying, hauling his horse around. "I thought you could ride."

"Why do you keep blaming me for that?" says Jo, slumped in her saddle. Looking up. "It was *Roland* who killed him – "

"A sword thrust?" sneers the Duke. "A sword thrust is nothing. You hadn't been there, he'd've laughed and bought the Chariot a drink. If you hadn't been there, Tommy'd be telling me right now what an ass I am, out here in the middle of the night like this."

"So instead you'd be what, in bed with your blonde?" says Jo, looking him in the eye. "Leave that monster out here to run amok doing God knows what?"

"Hark! The screams!" The Duke lifts a hand to his ear. "The people, fleeing from a monster run amok!" He drops his hand, arches an eyebrow. "Two things, okay, and leave her the hell out of this. She's a nice girl. First. The boar wants one thing and one thing only and I'm right here and don't you dare, don't you dare even *suggest* I would not keep my word. And anyway, you're so fucking worried about this monster, why didn't you come do something about it? Why wait for me?"

"What can I do?" says Jo. Throwing her hands out. "What the *fuck* can I do? I can't even hold a goddamn spear!"

"You don't have to do anything!" roars the Duke. "Just standing there you could kill us all!"

Jo's horse kicks the pavement, shifting. She doesn't look away. The Duke's horse stands still and the Duke is holding a spear now, the spear-haft dark and red, the head a broad flat ugly blade, and he doesn't look away.

"I don't," says Jo, as the Duke says "Pick up your spear." Above them, away behind the line of houses, the sudden pop pop pop of firecrackers. "Pick up the damn spear!" says the Duke.

A crack and something, boards, flying into the air, a squealing roar, dark trees shaking undergrowth ripping a rattling crash and then the sound of debris, settling. There on the roof of a long low building squatting above the freeway a great dark shape, bristling ruff high above the snout lowered over them, curls of old yellow glistening in the dim light. "The tracks," says Jo. "He can't – " Below the building a sharp drop in the gulch wall down to railroad tracks, a high wall back up to the freeway, ten or fifteen feet up, the great dark shape hunkering low, a growl, Jo's horse snorting, head tossing. The boar springs from the roof, over those tracks, clearing the wall, a scream and a thunderclap, the horses staggering, "Oh, shit," says Jo, and there he stands in a cloud of pink-lit dust on the freeway, chunks of pavement pattering down like rain.

"They'll be fine," says Ysabel, eyes closed, standing there under the bridge, her cheek against the throat of her pale grey horse. "Or did you really want words with Erymathos, before the end?"

Marfisa stands with her back to Ysabel out on the freeway, watching away down the eastbound lanes.

"He hurt you so badly," says Ysabel, opening her eyes. "Your poor face. You could have died. Gone down to dust. You still could."

"My lady seems almost upset at the idea," says Marfisa.

Ysabel walks away from the horses, out from under the bridge. Puts her arms around Marfisa, leans against her back, her head on Marfisa's shoulder, cheek against the tweed. Marfisa puts her hand on Ysabel's hands, her head tilting back, hair the color of clotted cream tangling with loose black curls.

"You're not very good at this game," says Ysabel, smiling.

Stiffening Marfisa tries to step away. "I don't want to play games," she says, pulling at Ysabel's hands.

"Then don't," says Ysabel, letting her go, pulling her back. Face to face now, Marfisa turning away, looking down, Ysabel's hands clasped at the small of Marfisa's back, Marfisa's hanging useless at her side. Smiling Ysabel leans up, kisses the tip of Marfisa's nose. "The boar," says Marfisa, her voice thick.

"Let it," says Ysabel. Light grows around them, bright, yellow-white.

"We should be – "

"We should be doing what we're doing."

"Lady," says Marfisa, squinting against the light.

"Shut up," says Ysabel, pulling her into a kiss as the light splits in two, a sudden blare of engine overwhelming white snout of a truck headlights passing either side buffeted by spinning wheels, the trailer over and around them dark as they kiss clinging to each other red taillights whipping past and gone. The horses watch as laughing Ysabel spinning stumbling tugs Marfisa after her to the barricade in the middle of the freeway another rush of engine dopplering past them slashing ghosts of white and red light through the air. Ysabel half-sitting on the barricade one hand under Marfisa's skirt the other buried in pale curls stained a dirty peach in the weak light, Marfisa kissing her mouth, her throat, Marfisa's hands jerking buttons loose, tugging Ysabel's baggy pants over her hips, Marfisa stooping, those pale curls eclipsing the light winking from Ysabel's belly. Ysabel one arm around the squat green pillar set in the barricade throws her head back as half-heard half-seen cars and trucks billow past east and west, before and behind her, stitching the darkness with light.

"Oh shit," says Jo on her hands and knees, "oh God." Sobbing for breath. "It's not," the Duke is saying, strained, over away somewhere, "it's not *dead*." A grunt, the scrape of hair like quills against broken concrete, muscles creaking, something else, metal, something groaning, out of it all a single hoofbeat: clip. Another, clop. Jo scrabbling, Chuck Taylors kicking into almost a run, hands brushing the freeway, head down, "Oh *shit*." A blustering, querulous snort. "It's not," says the Duke again. "You sonofabitch. You *lied*." Clip. "*Fuck* me, it hurts. It's not dead."

Clop.

The boar Erymathos stands in the middle of the eastbound lanes swaying from side to side. From his left shoulder juts a dark red spear-haft. The pale cracked concrete beneath him smeared black. He blows, head ducking, tusks dipping, takes another couple of steps, clip-clop-clip. Spear-haft quivering. Head turning this way and that. Behind him the Duke's horse jerks its head up and legs kicking the air rolls upright. The

Duke screams. The boar turns to glare at him, head canted, spear drooping. "Stupid! Fucking! Horse!"

There by the barricade the black spear. Jo reaches for it when the boar looks away. The Duke's horse staggers past, empty brown boot flopping from one stirrup. Clop-clip, the boar unsteadily steps toward the Duke. "Hey," says Jo, standing, black spear braced in both hands. "Hey!"

"Gallowglas?" cries the Duke. "The horn! The fucking horn!" Trying to push himself up on one elbow. "Don't be a moron. Blow!"

"*Hey!*" yells Jo. Clop-clip, clop. That great head grey and yellow and white hair like quills in its ruff turning like a sail, those old yellow tusks, those little black eyes casting back and forth. "Over here!" Clip-clop, and two more steps, clop-clop. "The horn!" says the Duke again.

Jo swallows. Redoubles her grip on the spear-haft. The boar looming over her. "It's on your fucking horse," she says, squeezing her eyes shut.

The boar Erymathos takes one last step and with a sigh crumples to the ground.

Jo opens her eyes. She's on her knees, the black spear laid beside her. Someone's hand on her shoulder. "The tongue," says the Helm, grey hair dull in this thin light. "Fix the tongue." Jo lifts a hand. Drifts of glittering dust spill from her arm to her lap, sparkle across the freeway about her. "Fix the tongue before it all blows away."

The boar's head still looms before her. Dust sloughs from the tusks, whips into the air in a sudden gout that suddenly subsides. One of the tusks sags avalanching down the boar's hollow cheek, dust shining in the ruff itself dissolving into dust. Beyond the head nothing but dust and more dust, empty pavement, thin dirty light. The Helm reaches past Jo for the slack jaw, working it open, the tongue purple and black in her fist. She stabs it with a slender knife, striking the concrete with a tinny clink. Rocks back on her heels, a hand on Jo's shoulder again. Jo blinking against the glittering dust thick in the air about them. "My leg," says the Duke, over away somewhere. "Really fucking hurts."

"Whatsisname," says Jo, brushing dust from her arms, then reaching for the black spear. "The Dagger. Where – "

"He won't want it back," says the Helm, standing.

"I didn't," says Jo, but the Helm's headed over to the Duke. "I mean," says Jo. The back of the boar's head collapses then in swirls of dust. The remaining tusk wobbles, dust unskeining as it settles but doesn't fall. Hoofbeats. Jo climbs to her feet, the spear left there on the freeway. "Hey," she says, looking about. "Dagger?"

Marfisa's riding toward them, leading the Duke's horse by the reins, Ysabel on her pale grey horse behind. "Jo!" Ysabel calls. Kicking one leg over her horse's back even as it slows.

"Yeah," Jo's saying, looking about. "I've got to, um." She leans down, reaching for the spear.

Marfisa comes up behind the Helm, kneeling over the Duke still flat on his back. "Your leg's broken," she says.

"Bullshit," says the Duke, his face pale, slick.

"I've seen one before," says Marfisa, kneeling beside the Helm. The Helm stands.

"Jo," Ysabel's saying, and Jo says "I'm okay. I'm okay," and "What the hell are you doing here?" as Ysabel says "Are you okay?"

"You were supposed to get the hell out of here," says Jo.

"We heard the horn," says Ysabel. "Marfisa wouldn't. Are you okay?"

"The Dagger," Jo's saying. She coughs. "I need to give it back to him. Where the fuck is he?"

The Dagger kicking drifts of dust stalks among the horses. In one hand his slender sword, wrapped in brown leather just above the quillions. In the other a coiled horn the color of old keys.

"Don't," Ysabel's saying. "Put it down. Put the spear down."

"The Duke," says Jo. "Killed it. Why is there so much *dust*."

"Jo," says Ysabel, and then her eyes go wide. "Ysabel?" says Jo, and she turns to look as the Dagger swings his sword up and back behind his head.

"My DDR game's pretty much fucked, isn't it," gasps the Duke, eyes closed. Marfisa nods, her fingers gently probing his misshapen leg. The Dagger's boot crunching beside her. She looks up to see that sword swinging around from behind his head in a flat arc at her neck. She has time to say "What?"

Clang.

Blade tip braced against pavement sword hilt clutched in his gloved fist a fencepost stopping the Dagger's cut the Chariot, stretched forward in a lunge, chest heaving, T-shirt dark with sweat, sunglasses shining in the streetlight. Straightening as the Dagger steps back. Swinging his sword around to point at the Dagger, leaning back a little, off-hand tucked against his chest. The Dagger taking another step back, and another. "I," he says.

"Oh, no," says the Chariot. "Don't run."

"LEO, HONEY"

"LEO, HONEY," she's whispering. Down the hallway a booming knock. She sits up there on the low bed in the middle of the big dark room, the Duke beside her on his back, right leg lying on top of the blanket, splinted with thin sticks, wrapped in purple cloth. "I don't," he murmurs, eyes closed. Shirt buttons undone. His chest and forehead gleaming, his hair slick with sweat. "Don't." Again the pounding at the door.

Belting a short silk robe of whites and pale blues she walks down the dark hall to the white door rattling from another flurry of knocks. "Go away," she says.

The pounding stops. "I would have words with his grace," says someone on the other side, his voice highly pitched, rich and gentle and smooth.

"He doesn't want to see anyone," she says. "Or have words."

"I'm afraid I'll have to hear that from his lips. Not yours."

"Go away," she says. "Come back tomorrow."

"Is he hurt?"

She opens her mouth to say something, stops. "No," she says. "Why would you – " The door shivers at a mighty blow, and another. "The password!" he cries, his voice no longer gentle.

Another blow. She steps away, hands up, head down. "Duncan," she says, "Duncan will be one man."

"And Farquahr will be two!" The door bursts open. Stepping backward she stumbles and falls, clutching at her robe falling open slipping off one shoulder. His bare feet stride past, dark blue skirt rustling. His long black hair unbound. Past the pitted yellow tusk on the floor still shining with gold dust to kneel by the bed. She sits up against the wall, head in her hand, still clutching her robe.

He's taken the Duke's hand in his own. Raised it to his lips. His black hair slipping from his shoulder slithering down, obscuring the kiss. "Mooncalfe," says the Duke.

Orlando murmurs something, not looking up from the Duke's hand. "I don't," says the Duke, pulling his hand back. Orlando stands. Stoops over the Duke, black hair falling like a curtain again, but the Duke puts up his hand over his face, turning away. Orlando hangs there a moment, then straightens. Brushes his fingertips against his lips, presses them to the Duke's bare chest. Turns and walks away.

"Whatever will you do?" he says, in the doorway, bathed in the ruddy light of the Coke machine.

"What?" she says.

"Wherever will you go? What was that place called? Devil's Point? Would they still take you back, I wonder..."

"What are you talking about? What's wrong with him?"

"Isn't it obvious?" He turns then, to look at her, his face lost in shadow. "He no longer wants you, either."

"Where were you?" she says. "Tonight." She climbs to her feet, steps toward him. "He needed you and you weren't there for him. Where were you?"

He lifts a hand, curls it in a loose fist and tilts the knuckles toward her. "You *are* brave," he says, tightening his fist. Her eyes widen, her mouth opens, jaw working, curling into herself, shivering violently. He drops his hand and she lets out the breath she's been holding, takes in a great shuddering drag of air, leaning against the wall. "What did you do to me?" she asks. "*What* did you *do* to me?" He closes the door gently between them.

Jo still in her black jeans, her black tank top, her mismatched Chuck Taylors lies on her side, facing the wall. It's dark, the only light leaking up from the street below. Her eyes are not closed.

Ysabel snoring lightly lies on her belly, dark hair pillowed on one arm curled atop the pillows, one bare leg kicked out from under the blankets trailing off the futon on the floor. There beside her foot by her shucked baggy pants the black spear-haft stretching off to the head like a mirrored leaf under a spindly, wrought-iron chair. On the glass-topped table by a low glass bowl full of sunflower heads and little light-colored roses a plate, something long and dark on it in a puddle of something dark and thick, pierced through by a slender knife.

"I don't know if I can keep doing this," says Jo, to no one at all.

No, he can't sleep on the floor.
What do you think I'm yelling for?
I'll drop him near the freeway.
Doesn't he have a home?

—Steely Dan

NO. 6

ANVIL

JUST A LITTLE SHE SMILES and opens her eyes. "All right then," says Ysabel. Standing by the window in her yellow underwear. The daylight soft and grey, dappled by raindrops on glass. She looks down at the cigarette burning between her fingers. Black blood thick on her fingertips and palm. Blood smeared around her mouth, her chin. "Pfeh," she says, cocking her hand, wiping her lips with the back of her wrist. Blood's splashed between her breasts, a trickle of it black and shining oozes down her belly trembling a fat drop of it falling to plop on her bare foot. She takes in a sharp breath through her nose and lets it out in a sudden shivery laugh. "All right," she says.

A rustle from the futon across the room.

"Jo?" says Ysabel.

"The hell you will," says Jo, muffled. Kicking her mismatched Chuck Taylors in the sheets.

Ysabel stubs out the cigarette in a plate puddled with black blood, a slender bloodstained knife on the table beside it. Scrubs at her chest with her fingers, knocking loose a sparkling fall of dust. She crosses the room to kneel by the futon. "Jo," she says again. Jo moans, her face buried in the blue-and-white striped pillow. Ysabel brushes Jo's cheek with the back of her hand. "Wake up, Jo," she says. "It's October." Jo jerks her head away, one arm fighting free of the blanket.

Pushing herself up breathing sharply, blinking. "I can't," she says, "what?" Staring unseeing at the wall.

Jo spits toothpaste into the sink and rinses her toothbrush under the tap. Runs the brush around her teeth and spits again.

"What did she tell you?" says Ysabel, leaning on the open door of the refrigerator. She's pulled on a white tank top. Something glitters at the corner of her mouth.

"She didn't," says Jo, running her fingers through her hair, pushing back the blond fuzz to reveal dark roots. Tugging at one of the longer black locks. "Not for real. For real, she just laughed that goddamn laugh and walked away across the ice." Out in the little hallway kitchen Ysabel pulls a carton of milk from the fridge. "But in the dream it was like she'd been saying something all along and, it's not like I couldn't hear her or it was in another language or something. I could understand her. I just wasn't paying attention." Ysabel takes a glass down from the cabinet and pinches open the carton. "I was looking at something else, I don't know, but by the time I figured out she was saying something important and started paying attention she was laughing and turning and walking away." Ysabel sets one hand on edge by the glass, four fingers curled around it. She pours the milk slowly, watching the level rise finger by finger. "And whatever it was was so *important,*" says Jo, "and I'd *missed* it, and I knew I was never going to get another chance." Ysabel puts the carton back in the fridge. "Which just. *Hurt.*" In the bathroom, Jo's still looking at herself in the mirror. "Nineteen goddamn names and I don't know a one of them," she says, quietly. She runs some water, catches it in her hands, splashes her face. Shuts the water off. Something's trickling. Jo frowns. Looks out, into the little hallway kitchen. Ysabel's holding up the glass tipped over, pouring milk over the counter, down to the floor. "The fuck?" says Jo.

"You shouldn't be having dreams like that," says Ysabel. She shakes the last drops of milk from the glass and sets it down on the counter.

"So you make a fucking mess?"

"It's a punishment," says Ysabel.

"Oh," says Jo, pushing past her, out into the main room, "the milk, the blood, that fucking *tongue,* it's a punishment all right." She stops, staring down at the plate on the glass-topped table, the cigarette butt in the blood, the slender bloodstained knife. "Ysabel?" she says, turning around. "Where's the tongue?"

Ysabel's dipping a finger in the milk.

"The tongue. That was ripped from the head of that – *thing.* And dropped on this plate right here last night. That tongue?"

Ysabel turns, opening her mouth to say something. The phone rings. "I'll get it," she says.

"No!" says Jo. "Let it ring."

"It could be – "

"Spam," snaps Jo. "Fucking telemarketers selling a fucking timeshare or something. Look. Don't tell me about the tongue. Okay? Fine. I don't trip over it or find it in the freezer or something, it's gone, I'm good. Okay? Just put on some pants or something so we can go to work."

"Or we could not go to work," says Ysabel. "Go see a movie or something."

"*God*ammit."

"We had a long night," says Ysabel. "I'm tired. You're exhausted. And you're already paid rent, right? So – "

"Yeah, but now I have to buy more fucking milk!" The phone's stopped ringing. "We've been over this," says Jo. "I *have* to go to work. And I have to keep an eye on you. So *you* have to come to *work* with *me.* Dead fucking simple. And it's gonna be like that until, I don't know. Something happens."

"Like what?"

"Maybe one of your bully-boys challenges me to a duel and I lose and you get to be his problem instead."

"That's not going to happen," says Ysabel, smiling.

"Oh yeah? Maybe I'll just pick a fight with Roland the next time he swings by. I bet he'd like that. Are you going to clean that up?"

Ysabel looks back at the puddle of milk. "No," she says.

"*I'm* not touching it."

"Of course not."

Jo throws her hands in the air. "Just, just get dressed. Okay? Let's go."

"WHO ARE THE THREE LIONS?"
A MILD AND TEMPERATE KNIGHT – HER HAIR
EXALTATION – WHAT HE SAID

"WHO ARE THE THREE LIONS?" says Marfisa.

"What?" says Roland, headphones down around his neck. On the table a thick white mug half-filled with coffee, a scatter of gel caps, a little toy car, silver and green.

"The three lions," says Marfisa, pointing back to the words painted on the window by the door. "I was just wondering who they were."

"Haile Selassie," says the woman sitting across from Roland. "Richard Nixon. Luke Skywalker." She's hunched in a sweater the color of flour, a floppy brown hat pulled low over her yellow hair. Roland snorts. Marfisa looks about, the gleaming barista station, the long glass case full of brightly lit pastries, the blackboard clouded with palimpsests of old menus. "What?" says the woman. "Was it a rhetorical question?" Her face tics sourly, her eyes darting under the brim of her hat.

"Here," says Roland, scooping up the caps. "Hold out your hand." She does. The fingers tremble, just a little. He sets the pills in her palm, one by one, picks up the toy car, folds her fingers over it. Marfisa pulls a spindly chair over from an empty table. "I was wondering how you were keeping up your rounds," she says. She drapes her blue rainshell over the back of the chair.

"Thank you, Miss Cheney," Roland's saying. The woman in the floppy brown hat stands, stuffing her hand in the pocket of her corduroy skirt. "Thank *you,* Chariot," she says. "May you be fierce and proud, precise and steady, proper, unified, vigorous, nimble-handed, swift, ardent-coursing, very dextrous, and un-hesitating." She takes up the red-tipped cane leaning against the table and tapping it before her makes her way out of the café.

"I didn't ask you here to speak about my business, Axe," says Roland as Marfisa sits.

"Of course not, Chariot," says Marfisa, looking back from Miss Cheney's exit to Roland's frown. His track suit crisp and white with green and yellow stripes down the sleeves. "The four fifths know I'd've died last night if you hadn't happened by. I owe you," and she tilts her head back a little, jaw working, "my life." Curls the color of clotted cream unsprung from her tightly bunched ponytail. "So I guess you want to tell me what I must do to see that debt discharged."

Roland's picking at the velcro on his bicycle gloves. "We hunted the boar together with a gallowglas. A joint effort. Either of us could have died then. I'm not," and then he looks up and says, "You must do it because it's right. Not because of a debt."

"What," says Marfisa, after a moment.

Roland's laid his gloved hands flat on the table. "Stop seeing her," he says.

"Who?" says Marfisa.

"You know," says Roland, and then he stops himself and says, "the Princess."

"How can I not *see* her?" says Marfisa. "Should I put out my eyes?"

"She's the Bride." Roland's glaring, leaning over the table. "Promised to the King Come Back. You'll do nothing to jeopardize that promise." His voice low, the words bitten short.

"Jeopardize?" says Marfisa. "How could I do that? Tell me, Chariot. Spell it out for me."

Roland sits back. "The Dagger," he says. "As mild and temperate a knight as you could ask, for all that he was the Duke's man. This knight would have struck your head from your shoulders last night. Would have wiped you from this world."

"So we're back to the debt," says Marfisa.

"*Why?*" says Roland, his eyes burning. "Why would he try to do something like that?"

"I don't know," says Marfisa, but she looks away from him, down at her hands, curled in her lap. Roland drinks his coffee. "You must stop," he says. "Now. I won't be able to allow it when she's under my protection once more."

Marfisa looks up. "You must worry," she says, "about facing a gallowglas, to win her back. Jo's a friend of yours, isn't she?"

Roland finishes his coffee and sets the mug on the table. "The Queen will tire of indulging her daughter's whims soon enough."

"Without a fight, huh?" says Marfisa, standing. "Is that what Miss Cheney told you is going to happen?"

"Stop," says Roland. "It's the right thing to do."

"Yeah," says Marfisa, putting on her rainshell, "try telling *her* that."

Night falls. They come around the corner of the building and duck out of the rain, three of them, under a dull burgundy awning that says Fada Salon. Already fishing for cigarettes. Jo's lit, she flicks the match away into the rain and shakes open a newspaper. Ysabel, unlit cigarette in her fingers, turns to the short older woman with a loose wattle under her chin. "Do you know," says the older woman, thumbing open a lighter, "a young man insists I am from India." Her voice rough with old smoke. Ysabel leans over her small flame. "I asked him, how is it so, and he said, you have an accent. Of course. I am from France. He says no one in France must call people for money." The older woman shrugs. "So now I am Indian."

"Fuck," says Jo, rattling her paper shut. The window behind them dark. Rows of shampoo bottles catch what little light. She steps under the next awning down, dark grey over a glass door lit up inside, a beige hall, a row of dented mailboxes. Holds the paper up in the light, turns it inside out. "You know, Crecy," says Ysabel, "Jo says there's a difference. Between spam, and what we do."

"Of course, darling," says the older woman. "Spam is on the internet."

"*Phone* spam," says Ysabel. "Sales calls," says Jo, scowling at her paper.

"We don't do sales," says Crecy.

"But it *is* a transaction," says Ysabel. "It's not a *sales call*," growls Jo.

"We don't ask for money," says Crecy.

"We ask for their time," says Ysabel. "A piece of their life. And isn't time money? Why does this make you so angry?" she says, turning to Jo.

"What do we sell?" says Crecy. "If we are selling."

"Your answers," says Ysabel brightly, "will help Pet Depot better determine where and how to improve their service to ensure our clients and their people will have the *best possible* Pet Depot experience. What was it we said for Winthrop Bank? Your answers will enable WinBank to *better assess* the service they provide? It's a good deed," she says. "A chance to help. *Attention*. That's the transaction. Time, for attention."

"Sales," says Crecy. "No, sales we go to do when we can't do *this*. Out to Market Solutions in Beaverton, hour and a half by bus, and we *sell*. Or worse, to a customer service farm." She lets her cigarette fall to the sidewalk and mashes it with her heel. "No one trusts a phone anymore. All the sales and the robots, and the Indians. So many surveys done on the internet now."

"Like spam," says Ysabel.

"You are being difficult," says Crecy.

"Not a goddamn thing," says Jo, dropping the newspaper. She flicks her cigarette-spark into the rain. "Get your things."

"There's an hour left in the shift," says Ysabel.

"I don't care," says Jo. "There's something I need to see."

"What?" says Ysabel, as Crecy shaking her head says "With Guthrie out *again*, and Dorfman – what will you tell Becker?"

"That I feel like shit," says Jo. "What else?"

Leaning against the dingy fridge, head down, long black hair to one side like a curtain drawn back. Rings glitter on his fingers, an ankh, a skull, dice. "Wow," he says, hauling himself upright, scratching his ribs. Black drawstring pants hang from his narrow hips, cuffs lapping his bare feet. He pulls a clear plastic pitcher from the fridge and pours water into his mouth.

"Guthrie," she says. The hall behind her's dark. Hard rattle of rain outside the half-closed window. Her black T-shirt tight says A Mysterious Chunk of Space Debris. Her hair lost under a confetti-colored patchwork cap.

"You never take that off," he says. "Do you. The hat."

"I have my reasons," she says.

"I, see, have no idea how you pulled that shirt on over it."

"Same way you took it off, except." Her hands spin about each other. "In reverse."

"That's one of *my* shirts," he says. "*Your* shirt buttoned up the front. *Un*buttoned." He runs his fingers up the T-shirt to brush her chin. She bites at them. "Like your sweater. And your other sweater. And your jacket unzipped. So."

"My skirt," she says, "and my *other* skirt," and she kisses him.

"And your bicycle shorts," he says, "and those goddamn granny panties," and he kisses her chin. "But not the hat. Is it a thing? If I take off your hat, do you leave and I never see you again?"

"Such questions," she says, kissing his throat. Her hand in his pants. He spins her around bare feet shuffling and lifts her shrieking with laughter to sit on the edge of the sink. The hem of her shirt rucked up past her hips, the hair crowning her thighs dull brown and glossy auburn, fiery red licking the edges, coiled springs of gold here and there, white glistening, thin black shading a ghostly line up her belly under the shirt. "If you're supposed to make me forget," he says, as she leans forward, reaching for his pants, "I remember everything." He helps her push them down. "The window and the boar and the swords and." She stops his mouth with a fingertip. "Do you want to forget?" she says.

Guthrie shakes his head.

"Am I safe here?" she says.

He shrugs, his face torn between a frown and a smile. "As houses," he says.

"I have your word?" she says, and his face falls. He kisses her, a long rolling lick of a kiss, and closes his eyes, and lays his forehead against her chest. "Of course," he says.

"Guthrie," she says.

When he looks up she tugs the patchwork cap up and off and out spills her hair, tumbling over her shoulders, down her back, into the sink, across the counter, down, brushing his knees, coiling about his feet. "Wow," he says.

She shivers as he touches her hair, takes up a heavy hank of it in his hand, lets it run through his fingers like water. "Oh," she says as he sinks his fingers into her hair to either side of her face, his palms, his wrists. "Wow," he says, and she nods and says, "Like that," breathing quickly, her hair brushing his forearms, his elbows. "Wow," he says, and he kisses her. The rain long since gentled to a hush.

The weirdly slender doll tosses an arch salute in the harsh light of the desk lamp. Its uniform a tight orange jacket and a short flippy skirt, dark stockings stretched halfway up elongated thighs. Mr. Charlock touches its head carefully, as if it might burn. "Week ago Wednesday," he says. "The equinox. That's where I'm putting my money. So he was out and about a week before you called us in? Still." Mr. Charlock touches the doll again. "Seven confirmed sightings – five solos and a deuce. We cleared 'em all."

"Seven," says Mr. Leir. His eyes almost grey. His face unlined under all that white hair.

"Mr. Keightlinger's sources back us up," says Mr. Charlock.

"I don't doubt it," says Mr. Leir. "But seven is a rather... *notable* number."

"Yeah," says Mr. Charlock. "So's three and five and twelve and nine and four."

"And eight," says Mr. Keightlinger, in the shadows behind Mr. Charlock.

"But this is seven," says Mr. Leir.

Mr. Charlock shrugs. "Anyway, last night they run him out of the world and into a hunt. Being my understanding of your instructions was not to interfere, we didn't." Mr. Leir nods. "Bride was there," says Mr. Charlock. He picks up the doll, fingering a long brown plastic ponytail. "On the hunt." Tips the doll over, looking up its skirt. "Gallowglas, too."

"On a horse," says Mr. Keightlinger, leaning forward, his beard ruddied in the light. Mr. Charlock looks up at him, curl bobbing on his forehead. "Yeah," he says, "there were horses. Point being, they pull this girl any closer, they'd have to knight her or something."

Mr. Leir reaches across his desk, pale hand palm up.

"She'll be as hard to peel off as one of their own," says Mr. Charlock. "Harder, even."

Mr. Leir's fingers beckon once, twice. Mr. Charlock lays the doll in his hand. "What in hell are those things for, anyway?" says Mr. Charlock.

"Numquam sine phantasmate intelligit anima," says Mr. Leir, standing. He opens a glass cabinet behind his desk and sets the doll on a shelf lined with more dolls, a schoolgirl in a kilt, a swordswoman in a chainmail bikini, a girl in a maillot climbing onto a blocky scooter, a magician in a top hat and bustier. "You think," says Mr. Leir, and then, "I'm not certain what you think." He closes the cabinet. "That you're to help me by stealing the Bride from them?" He plants his fists on the desk, leaning over them. "You are to watch, and report, and that is all. You've watched. You've reported. I thank you."

"Sure," says Mr. Charlock, jerking his shoulder from beneath Mr. Keightlinger's hand, "but what's it all *for?*"

Mr. Leir smiles under those cold clear eyes. "She is exaltation," he says. "She will cross each sign at its zenith. She is the morning that climbs into the sky and the rose that arises from tears. Her throne is a high mountain and from there the sky of light is beneath her feet, and her diadem the stars." His smile leaves. "Would you like to ask another question, Mr. Charlock?"

"Not so much?" says Mr. Charlock, swallowing. He stands. "Maybe some other time."

A white tray laid on the low broad ottoman. Two glossy cards lie on it, one white, printed with a stylized bee in black and yellow.

The other brown, a hawk's head in red and black. A small stone cup overturned, salt spilled from it on the tray. A clear glass saucer dotted with bread crumbs. A small brass lamp, low flame smoking at its tip. The Duke looms over it, leaning heavily on a cane. He blows out the lamp. Picks up the silver-handled knife on the ottoman before the tray and pushes himself upright. Drops the knife in the pocket of his tweed jacket.

"Thank you," he says.

"There's no need to thank me," says the Queen. Dressed all in black, she sits at one end of the long white leather sofa. A little brindle cat beside her ducks its head to lick at its chest.

"Ah," says the Duke, "but I would ask another boon of you."

The Queen strokes the little cat's back. "No," she says.

"No?" says the Duke. "But you don't – "

"We will not ennoble Jo Maguire." The cat slumps against her, lifting a leg to worry at its haunch. "Unless you had something else in mind?"

"No," says the Duke, "no, that's what, ah, I – " He frowns. "Why not? You've a perfect excuse. She hadn't done what she did, I'd be dust blowing down the highway, instead of that fucking pig. I don't care what the Bodach said."

"So offer her a street yourself," says the Queen. "Sidney must have left something behind."

"But I take her in, I get your daughter as well," says the Duke. "That's crazy. *You* give her the knighthood. That brings the Bride back here, safe and sound, away from clutching grasps like mine – "

The Queen stands. The little cat freezes, then leaps from the sofa, scampering into the shadows. "You forget yourself, Southeast," she says. "We will *not* have a gallowglas in this house."

After a moment, the Duke ducks his head. "Can't say I didn't try." He turns to go, but stops, one foot on the shallow steps. "Duenna," he says. "I *will* sit the Throne one day. Whether you'd will it or no." He looks over his shoulder at her. She's sitting again, the white card in her hand. "But this has nothing to do with that. This is me, trying to do what's right. Remember that."

She smiles to herself. "We will always have been who we are," she says, laying the card back on the tray, next to the brown one.

She gets out of the car, a low-slung thing, and opens the passenger door as he lurches down the porch steps. She wears a short clear plastic raincoat over a grey chauffeur's jacket. The Duke leans on the roof of the car and levers his left leg in, lowering himself into the seat. Pulls his right leg in, wincing. Tosses the cane over into the narrow back seat. She lowers the hand she'd put out to help him. "You shouldn't be walking on that," she says, climbing into the driver's seat.

He runs a hand through his hair, shaking out the rain.

"You want to," she says, starting the engine, putting the car in gear. He snaps on the radio. Guitars and a clattering drumkit crash into a slow keening verse, cymbal ringing like a bell, in a town, deep in the dark wood, there were streets of colored lanterns, there were musicians and juggling troupes, sticky baked things and booths and booths. "Want to do anything tonight?" she says.

"Go home," he says.

"Because if you want, you know, to take it easy." She steals a glance at him. He's looking out the window. "You must be exhausted, so I was thinking, right? I could call a friend of mine. Penny? From the club?" She looks about, signals, eases over into the right lane. "We could put on a show, if you like."

"Yeah, okay," he says, still looking out the window.

"Yeah?" she says.

"You *should* go out. With whoever. See a show. I'll be okay." He smiles at her. "You went above and beyond last night, you know? Take the night off."

"Oh," she says. "Okay. Thanks."

And then she says, "How'd it go?"

"As well as you'd expect," he says. "Hey. Last night. Did the Mooncalfe finally show? Or was I dreaming?"

"Orlando?" she says. "Yeah, he showed."

"What did he have to say for himself?"

"Just," she says, "you know. Get well soon."

He snorts, looking down at his leg. "Fat chance of that," he says.

THE BLUE UMBRELLA – THE THREE ACORNS
ROLY-POLY GANG BANG – "JUST LET IT RING" – HER PROMISE

THE BLUE UMBRELLA'S smeared with whorls of starry light, a fiery painted circle of yellow moon. Ysabel eyes the rain dripping from its edges with moued lips and pinched brows. "I'm not dressed for this," she says.

"No one told you to wear heels," says Jo. Hatless, she's flipped up the collar of her army green jacket.

"I didn't know we'd be walking for miles tonight," says Ysabel.

"It's a couple of fucking blocks," says Jo, glaring at the ivy-choked fence that towers to the right.

"Thirteen," says Ysabel. "Since we got off the train."

"So it's a big couple," says Jo.

"You're not going to see anything," says Ysabel.

After a minute, Jo says "I think that" as Ysabel stops there in the middle of the street and snaps, "You're not going to *see* anything! Thirteen blocks in the rain and it's cold, my feet hurt and we're in Northeast again, *again,* and it's all a complete waste of time because you're not going to *see anything!*"

"I think," says Jo, slowly, pointing up the sidewalk, "that driveway there, that's a parking lot, it'll take us to the edge. Past this crap." She walks on, hands jammed in her pockets, shoulders hunched.

Ysabel spins the umbrella between her hands, flinging raindrops about. Tips her head, resting it against the umbrella's shaft. The other side of the street lined with parked cars. The house behind her porch lit up, strings of lights wound about the columns, draped from the eaves.

The ivy-choked fence ends at the driveway. The driveway opens into a parking lot for a rambling low apartment complex. Jo's there, under a sign that says American Property Management, No

Trespassing or Loitering, Violators Will Be Prosecuted. Her fingers laced in the chained links of a gate. Past the gate another lot dips down the edge of the gulch around a jumble of building, weather-beaten oblongs under a flat tarpaper roof. Below it the railroad tracks. Beyond them a wall ten or fifteen feet high and then the freeway, traffic shushing busily east and west through the rain.

"He must have come through that fence up there," says Jo, pointing back along the top of the gulch. "Down the slope and maybe he jumped from there to the roof. Where we saw him. That's." She thumbs a trickle of rain from her forehead. "He jumped," she says. "From there to the fucking freeway. The *freeway*. Landed so hard he broke the *road*. I was picking pieces of pavement out of my hair. He *broke* the fucking *road* and look." She rattles the fence. Rainwater splats the shoulders of her jacket. Traffic passing back and forth below, red lights and white lights and the yellow wink of a turn signal. "Nothing. No work crews. No orange cones. Not a goddamn crack. Like it never happened. Like he was never there."

"Jo," says Ysabel, "he was a monster." Jo looks at her over her shoulder, frowning, "I," she starts to say. "His name was Ery-mathos," says Ysabel, and "I *know* what his name," says Jo as Ys-abel's saying, "and a long time ago, as everyone knows, he winnowed the oak-mast of the forests above Eugea, there among the ankle-bones of the Dyfün Mountain, until he found and gobbled three certain acorns." She lifts her umbrella, hold-ing it over both of them. "The first swelled his shoulders like a mighty canopy of oak, sun-shield and thunder-trap. The second rooted the four great boles of him to the earth, and from then on he could never be overturned. But the third." She stands quite close to Jo now, her voice a soft murmur over the distracted rain. "The third acorn hardened his heart like knot-wood, shriveling it down to a nubbin no bigger than his eye, and as black." She reaches out to brush more rain from Jo's forehead. Jo shakes her head away. "There will never again be a forest above Eugea."

"I don't," says Jo, turning back to the fence, the ramshackle building, the trees along the wall of the gulch, the railroad tracks below, the freeway.

"Why are you so angry, Jo Maguire? Because he's gone? He was a *monster*. For all that cities terrified him, and concrete was like ice under his hooves." Ysabel's hand on Jo's shoulder, the umbrella brushing the fence above them. "A hundred hundred knights sought him out with sword and spear and hound and he laughed at them all and sent more than a few down to dust. Is it because the Duke picked you for his gallowglas? It could have been anyone. Any one of you, ten months from now, or ten years, by his side, or the Anvil's, or the Chariot's."

"It's, I just," says Jo. She hits the fence again. Rain splashes. "He should have stopped traffic. You know? After all that."

"Three weeks?" says Ysabel, sitting on the bench under the shelter, umbrella furled between her knees.

"It was a Saturday night," says Jo, leaning against the ticket machine. "Becker's little promotion shindig at the vc." She cranes her head, peering down the railroad tracks into the rainy darkness. Pulls a pack of cigarettes from her jacket pocket. "Three weeks ago."

"Twenty-one days," says Ysabel.

"Assuming math still works," says Jo, cigarette bouncing in the corner of her mouth. A pop and a match flares in her hands.

"Seems longer."

Jo blows a stream of smoke up and out past the dim lights of the shelter.

"You're still angry," says Ysabel.

"I'm not angry," says Jo.

"You *are,*" says Ysabel. There's a light down the tracks, getting brighter. Jo laughs. "Works every time," she says, taking one last long drag from the cigarette.

"What?" says Ysabel.

"That's why I haven't quit," says Jo. "You're waiting for a bus or a train? Light one up and boom. There it is." She drops the cigarette to the platform. "Like magic."

"Jo," says Ysabel, as the train pulls in. Jokes on us, says the ad running along the side of it, swarming with smiling television stars. Jo steps into the second car and climbs a couple of steps up from the floor to the raised rear seats. The car's otherwise empty. Ysabel's standing in the doorway. "Come on," says Jo, as a recorded voice says "This is a Red Line train to Portland City Center. Next stop is Northeast Seventh Avenue." Another voice says, "Este un tren de la línea roja a Portland City Center." The first voice says, "The doors are closing."

Ysabel steps into the car. The doors close. "What's wrong?" says Jo.

"I'm not sure," says Ysabel. She grabs for the handrail as the train lurches into motion. The lights flicker.

"What is it?" says Jo.

"I don't," says Ysabel. "Gabba gabba hey," says the boy lounging in the accordioned joint in the middle of the car. "Jo?" says Ysabel.

"Yeah, I see him," says Jo.

"And he," says Ysabel.

"He wasn't there when we got on," says Jo.

"Gowan," says the boy. "Smile!" His head's bald. He's wearing a grey denim jacket over a baggy grey hoodie.

"Why don't you," Jo's saying, as Ysabel says "I told you we shouldn't have." Jo's standing in the aisle. "Why don't you get up here."

"Lovely," says the man standing next to the boy, swaying with the motion of the train. Ysabel's quickly climbing the couple of steps and swinging into a seat. The man wears a tan trench coat and his pink and yellow tie is loose. An old brown briefcase on the floor between his feet. "Hubba hubba," says the boy in the hoodie. The lights flicker.

"What's going on?" says Jo.

"We're in Northeast," says Ysabel.

"Yeah? So?"

"A spitfire!" says the man in the grimy blue coveralls, pushing past the boy in the hoodie, out onto the floor between the doors. "Lose the jacket," says the boy in the hoode. "Hell yeah!" says the lanky guy in basketball shorts. He's back by the man in the trench coat. "Panties," says the man in the trench coat. He giggles. They're all laughing, barking, roaring, the lanky guy hooting, the man in the coveralls doubled over, hanging one-handed from the handrail, slapping his knee. "Jesus," says Jo to herself. "Where the fuck are they coming from?"

"Gimme a kiss," says the boy in the hoodie, laughing. "Let's see them legs!" says the man in the coveralls. "Sweet little things," says the man in the trench coat. "Northeast Seventh Avenue," says the recorded voice. "Doors to my right."

"Get up," says Jo. "Slowly. Get up. We're getting off." She heads down to the floor of the car one slow step at a time, eyes not leaving the men no longer laughing, swaying together with the train.

"It's not stopping," says Ysabel, standing up.

"It's not stopping," says Jo. The lights flicker. "It's not stopping!" A woman's face sweeps by outside, dismayed, framed in a yellow slicker hood. The man in the coveralls plants his feet against the wobble of the train, arms out, hands free, grinning. "You want some of this," he says.

"Of course she does," says the man in the trench coat. "Tag team," says the lanky guy. "Fuck yeah!" says the boy in the hoodie. "Swallow this!"

"Jo?" says Ysabel, eyes wide.

"I, ah," says Jo. "Are these your people?"

"What?" says Ysabel. The man in the trench coat snorts. "Gagging lolita," says the lanky guy.

"Are they, you know, like you?" says Jo.

"What kind of question is that?"

"Gang bang, gang bang," sing-songs the boy in the hoodie. "Roly-poly gang bang."

"Shut *up!*" yells Jo. The man in the coveralls frowning, smiling, chuckling deep in his throat like a growl. "Jesus whichever," says Jo, "it's self-defense anyway. Get ready."

"For what?" says Ysabel, but Jo's foot has already left the floor.

"Baby wants to pinch them," snarls the man in the coveralls, and then the crook of Jo's foot catches him right in the crotch, lifts him up on his toes. There's a smash like breaking crockery.

His arms curling in mouth rounding air blowing out of him in one big burst. Her foot dropping she reaches past him for the front of the boy's grey hoodie hauling as the man in the coveralls sags over the seat beside him. Hauls the boy past her and around squawking "Yah!" to fetch up clang his forehead into the handrail knocked back arms wheeling over and down. The man in the coveralls still moaning.

"Excuse me," says the man in the trench coat.

"Now!" yells Jo, throwing her elbow back, hurling a sharp-knuckled punch into the lanky guy's chest. "Hey," he says. "Now!" yells Jo, kicking at his knee and missing.

"Now *what?*" screams Ysabel standing, fingers white around the handrail. *"Jo!"*

The lanky guy's caught Jo's off-balanced fist in his big flat hand. He lifts, wrenching her wrist. "Now!" she yells, and hisses, eyes crumpled. "The *brake!* Pull it!" She kicks again. Her toe bounces off his shin with a tinny clank. The man in the coveralls growling on the floor hands slipping and pushing at nothing. The boy in the hoodie rearing back off him hands to his forehead wobbling upright, a deep dent dug in that bald head. The lanky guy grunts as Jo kicks him and kicks him again. "Pull it!"

"Pull *what?*"

"The brake! The brake! The motherfucking brake!" Jo throws herself at the lanky guy and back, yanking at her fist still locked in that hand. Ysabel's looking all about her eyes wild one hand up to her mouth. "On the wall!" cries Jo. The man in the trench coat steps gingerly around the lanky guy, wary of the rocking of the train. "Behind you! On the damn wall!"

"You little *bitch,*" says the man in the trench coat, and hunkering arm dropped swings his briefcase up at Jo's head. Ysabel screams. Jo dangles from the lanky guy's fist head back blood shining her cheekbone. Spun about the man in the trench coat swings back at Jo the briefcase into her gut. He pulls but doubled over she's caught it with her free hand. Roaring. The man in the trench coat stumbles as she yanks it from him. The lanky guy watches frowning as the man in the coveralls grabs his ankle. "Do you know who I am?" bellows Jo, her other hand still caught. "The fucking *Gallowglas!*" She slams the briefcase into the lanky guy's chest and again. "I will *end you!*" And again.

The lights flicker. *"Whore,"* grunts the man in the coveralls, crumbling the word, pushing himself to his knees clanking a weight dangling between his thighs. "Let *go* of me!" Jo's screaming. "Frigid little *cunt,"* spits the man in the trench coat, rubbing his wrist. "Jo, I can't," Ysabel's saying, "I don't," and Jo's face twists. "Fucking *dyke,"* says the man in the trench coat. His briefcase hits him squarely in the nose. Something crunches. His hands up shaking as Jo lowers the briefcase, his nose gone, sunk with his eyes, his brows and mouth and chin clenched around it all, he backs away, feeling for his face, yowling, muffled, choked. Jo looks up at the lanky guy, at her fist in his hand, his warm-up jacket fluttering, blowing out as he exhales, sucked flat against his chest as he inhales, rasping, ragged. He squeezes.

Jo yanks harder eyes frantic her fist not moving kicking his shin and his knee and it twangs bent by her shoe. He grunts. The man in the coveralls crotch clanking plants his foot grabbing her jacket yanking it to one side swaying with the train his other hand wrapping under Jo's chin fingers denting her cheek smearing blood thumb along her jaw pushing up and back. "You, you will," he says, fighting for breath, "Fuck. You." The lights flicker. *"Fuck* you." The lights go out and the train shakes a wallow ripples its length squealing monstrously and they all fall Jo suddenly free, briefcase tumbling away down the car as the train judders slowing, squalling, stopping.

"On the wall," says Ysabel, bent over clutching the handrail. She laughs, a little gasping burst. It's gone quiet.

"Jesus," says Jo, in the shadows.

"Jo?" says Ysabel. "Jo!"

On her shoulder and elbow and knees cheek to the floor in the accordioned joint in the middle of the car Jo says "Fucking hell."

"I found it," says Ysabel, "I did it. I found it."

"Yeah," says Jo, sitting back on her heels. Blood streaks her reddened face, a handprint smeared along her cheek. There's no one else in the car.

In the darkness by the sink a dishtowel's laid flat. On the towel a small plate, a slender knife, a glass set upside down. Out in the main room on the glass-topped café table a spill of smooth clean pebbles, a scatter of dead leaves. A key rattles in the lock. Jo limps in shrugging a shoulder out of her sodden jacket, flicking on the light in the little hallway kitchen. The knife gleams. She shimmies her other arm free and lets the jacket plop to the floor. Heads across the main room stumbling over the black spear-haft stretching away under the table and sinks to her knees by the futon. She falls forward, onto her face, arms flung wide.

"You're soaking," says Ysabel. She sets the furled umbrella by the armoire in the corner. Jo says something into the comforter. "You're on my side of the bed," says Ysabel. She opens the armoire, squats to tug at a drawer at the bottom. "You're still bleeding, Jo. Get up."

The phone rings.

"I should get that?" says Ysabel.

"No," says Jo. She's pushed herself up on her elbows, head hung.

"Just let it ring," says Ysabel.

"Telemarketers," says Jo. "Windshield repair. Timeshares in Bend." Her fingertips dotting the blood along the split skin of her swollen cheek. "Gonna leave a hella mark."

"No," says Ysabel. "It isn't. Roll over." Jo settles on her side. Ysabel sits on the floor beside her. In her hands a clear plastic baggie swollen with dust the color of old clay in this weak light.

"What *is* that stuff?" says Jo.

"Don't," says Ysabel, scooping up a pinch of dust glimmering faintly.

"Don't what?" says Jo. The phone's stopped ringing.

"Don't," says Ysabel. "Hold still."

"Don't hold still?"

"Jo," says Ysabel. She strokes Jo's cut cheek and again, the darkening bruise, the skin puffed under her eye, glittering her face with gold dust. "You could have been killed," says Ysabel.

Jo snorts. "Don't," says Ysabel. She taps dust from her finger-tips back into the baggie. Jo says "What are you," and then she says "Come on."

"They were going to kill you," says Ysabel, twisting the baggie shut.

"How?" says Jo. She sits up abruptly, swinging her feet off the futon. Ysabel leans out of her way, shifting to climb to her feet, but Jo grabs her wrist. "How the hell were they gonna do that?"

"Don't," says Ysabel.

"Huh?" says Jo. "I mean, with what? That briefcase?"

"That hurts," says Ysabel.

Jo lets go. "Roland had a goddamn sword," she says. "He shoved a goddamn *sword* through me. Right here." She taps her chest.

"We can't hurt you," says Ysabel. "People like me. Is that what you think?" She sets the baggie on the floor by her knee. "I," says Jo, but Ysabel's saying, "You were in Robin Goodfellow's house when Roland struck you with a borrowed blade. You were brought to my Gammer and her potions within the hour. If any of that had been otherwise, you'd never have come back."

"Come – back?" says Jo.

"People like me," says Ysabel. "You don't know *what* they were. *I* don't know. Monsters? Vengeful spirits? Men, like you, ensorcelled?"

"They weren't like," says Jo.

"You don't know!" snaps Ysabel.

"Well how the fuck am I supposed to find out if you blow me off every time I ask a question?"

"I don't," says Ysabel, and then she says, "You don't ask questions, Jo. You demand answers."

"Rah!" yells Jo, leaping to her feet. Stepping past Ysabel, over the spear-haft. Stopping in the little hallway kitchen. Head down, she touches her cheek unswollen, the bruise faded, the gash an angry red line. "What's it called?" she says, her voice low. "The powder stuff. The glitter."

"Owr," says Ysabel.

"Our what?" says Jo.

Ysabel stands. "*Owr.* Just owr."

Jo turns to face her, one hand squeezing into a fist, opening flat again. "And those guys. If I hadn't leaped in like that, what were they gonna do to us?"

"I don't know," says Ysabel.

"Yeah, you do," says Jo. "I'm supposed to protect you, right? Keep you safe? That's what I swore to do, three weeks ago."

"Jo, you've kept me, as you should, warm, and dry, and fed."

"So you're a cat now?" Jo reaches out for Ysabel's hand. "You don't have to," says Ysabel. "I said yes, and I mean it," says Jo. "I'm all in. I will not let you down."

"But you *mustn't die*," says Ysabel.

"Ain't planning on it," says Jo.

Ysabel closes her eyes at that. "All right then," she says. She opens her eyes. Smiles just a little. Tips her head to kiss Jo's cheek, lightly, where the cut had been.

BECKER RUNS HIS HAND – AN INVITATION – HER HAIRCUT
THAT MILD AND TEMPERATE KNIGHT

BECKER'S RUNNING HIS HAND through what little of his hair is left. "Hey," he says as Jo walks past his desk. "You talked to Guthrie."

"Not since, what, a couple days ago," says Jo. "Last time he was here. Why?"

"No, I mean, you talked to Guthrie," says Becker. "He said he wasn't feeling well. Right? Said that's why he hasn't been in."

"I, uh," says Jo. Ysabel, standing behind her, frowns. A bald man pushes past them, a crumb of lipstick at the corner of his mouth, his eyes raccooned by blurry eyeshadow.

"You see him again the next day or so," says Becker, "tell him we mailed his check."

"Okay," says Jo.

"That's it," says Becker, eyes on his computer monitor. "Best find yourself a phone." He's typing something.

"Yeah," says Jo. She moves past Becker's desk into the narrow office full of people taking seats before kelly green carrels, a couple dozen of them set up on long folding tables against the walls. She grabs a chair next to Crecy, who's stuffing a tapestry bag into the space between carrel wall and computer monitor, headset already cramping her curly coppery hair.

"What was that about?" says Ysabel, sitting in the chair next to Jo's.

"Three days," says Jo.

"What?"

"All right, listen up," says Becker. He's leaning back in his chair, looking around his monitor to take them all in. "Yes, we're almost done with our monthly round of Pet Depot. And no, we don't have anything in the pipeline to replace it. That doesn't mean you can take it slow and drag it out. Maybe we've got nothing today, but maybe they land something tomorrow, and I'll pick my team based on the numbers. So you want to keep your numbers up. I know Sales is working on some business-to-business possibilities, which means small crews and day shifts. Okay? And maybe there's a political thing." He shrugs. "Phones are live. Clock is ticking. Let's go."

Rattle of fingers on keys, clatter of handsets pulled from phones. "What's three days?" says Ysabel, adjusting the mike of her headset.

"Good evening, ma'am," says Crecy into her mike. "I'm calling from Barshefsky Associates, an independent market research firm. Is Sara Ryan available?"

"Since Guthrie's showed for a shift," says Jo, bringing up her survey database on the computer. "If he hasn't called in, on the third shift you're fired. Pretty much automatically." She flashes a grin at Ysabel. "He's covering for him."

"Actually," says Ysabel, looking up past Jo, "he's waving at us."

Jo leans back, looks past her carrel. Becker at his desk one hand holding a phone to his ear is pointing at them, two fingers waggling then crooked, beckoning.

"Huh," says Jo. "We haven't been here long enough to screw up."

He's standing between the two leather armchairs under the large copper letters on the wall that say Barshefsky Associates: Quality Assured. He's tall, his suit is black with shiny elbows. His face narrow and somber under extravagant gin blossoms that apple his nose and sunken cheeks. To one side of the lobby a door opens on a wash of questioning voices and clacking keys. He turns, nods. "Princess," he says.

"Oh," says Jo.

"Hello," says Ysabel.

"Your mother," he says, and he sniffs. Shudders suddenly. "The Queen has sent me to ask that you join her for dinner."

"Dinner," says Jo. Ysabel puts a hand on her arm. "Dinner?" she says.

"A car will be by for you at seven o'clock," he says. "Now. If you'll excuse me..." He nods, once, his chin dipping between the upright points of his stiff white collar, and turns to leave. He stops before the glass doors leading out of the lobby, looking them up and down before reaching out hesitantly to push the crash bar.

"The Queen," says Jo.

"Yes," says Ysabel. "We'd better go get ready."

"*Go?*" says Jo, rounding on Ysabel. "It's only just past three. We haven't even made a phone call yet."

"I know. It leaves us barely enough time to do something about your hair."

Jo scowls, jams her hands in her pockets. "The fuck are we gonna tell Becker?"

"What else?" says Ysabel brightly. "You feel like shit."

It's a dark cave of a garage, most of the bay doors closed against the rain. Fluorescent lights aren't doing much from the ceiling. Racked drawers of tools and parts stand here and there, a red metal stool, by a column a tall still fan, its cage long gone. A single radiator stands upright on a couple of bricks. By a workbench in the back a pilot light fitfully licks the air.

"Anvil!"

224

The Duke stands in the soft grey light falling through the open bay door. He's leaning on a wooden cane, his fingers clutching the stern, rough-hewn hawk at its head. He's looking down at the radiator standing upright on the bricks before him, a coil of wire looped carelessly about it on the stained floor. His coat is long and camel-colored, his hat a derby, reddish-brown.

"There's nobody here," says the woman in the tight blue jeans. She's standing to one side, out of the rain, arms crossed, shoulders hunched in her brown bomber jacket. The Duke looks up, toward the back of the garage. "Anvil!" he calls again. "Pyrocles! We have business!" He raps his cane against the floor.

At the back of the garage up and to one side there's windows in the concrete wall, a metal staircase bolted beneath them up to a blue metal door. Warm lights shine through the grime and stacks of binders and paper can just be made out through the glass. The door opens and a big man steps out onto the top step, leaning against the railing, head ducked up there under the rough concrete ceiling. "Your grace," he says. He has long grey mustaches and he wears blue coveralls over a faded pink T-shirt.

"Where is everybody?" says the Duke.

"It's Sunday," says Pyrocles.

"So?"

Pyrocles shrugs, coming down the stairs that creak with every deliberate step. "What do you need, your grace?"

"How's your, ah, how's your back? No hard feelings, I hope?"

"Why should there be, your grace? Orlando isn't your man."

"Of course not," says the Duke, smiling. "I need a sword, Anvil."

Pyrocles stops, there at the bottom of the stairs. Perched on his forehead a delicate pair of glasses, silvery, the lenses small half-moons. He pulls them down and cleans them with a rag from his pocket. "You should go to Hawthorne Cutlery," he says, settling the glasses on his face. "I can put an edge on one of the replicas for you." He pushes them up the bridge of his nose with his thumb. "It won't hold for very long, your grace, but it'll look nice enough." The Duke's shaking his head. "I need a *sword*," he says. "A new sword forged by hand with someone very particular in mind."

"Whom?" says Pyrocles.

"Jo Gallowglas," says the Duke. "I believe you've met her?"

Pyrocles looks down, his mustaches drooping about his pursed lips. "No one's ever given a sword to a gallowglas before."

"I know! I'll be the first. Ain't that a kick in the shorts?" The Duke takes a couple of limping steps toward Pyrocles. "I mean, technically I guess I'll be giving it to the *Queen,* and she'll whack Jo on either shoulder, bang bang, and then *she'll* be the first ever to give a sword to a gallowglas, but hey. I'll've done my part."

"The Queen means to knight a gallowglas?" says Pyrocles.

"Whether she will or no," says the Duke.

Pyrocles takes off his spectacles, rubs his nose with dirty fingers. "Your grace," he says, shaking his head, "I, ah, I don't think – "

"Oh, for fuck's sake!" bellows the Duke. "What does a fellow have to *do* in this town to be trusted?"

"Don't you see?" A lock of black hair falls to the white tile floor. "She's going to *recognize* you. Keep your eyes closed."

"Which is why you're cutting my hair," mutters Jo.

"You were starting to look bedraggled," says Ysabel.

"Stop trying to talk me into this," says Jo. "I'm here."

"And your roots are making everything look so *muddy.*"

"*Do* it already," says Jo. Scissors whick and flash, and another lock falls. "It's just dinner with your mother. I don't get what's – "

"There *is* no just dinner with my mother." Another lock, and another. "She hasn't let me set foot, she hasn't *seen* me in three weeks."

"I know," says Jo, quietly.

"Don't blame yourself." Whick-wick. "It's not your fault you are what you are. It isn't my mother's fault she's a hidebound reactionary prig." The scissors hang there a moment. "Go on," says Ysabel. "I didn't," says Jo. "Eyes *closed,*" says Ysabel. "She's asked me to come to her now, *knowing* you'll come with me, as you still have my keeping. She'll recognize you, she has to. You'll be there. I think this is about something more."

"Something more than her saying oh, hey, how's it going, Jo?"

"I think she's going to announce your knighthood. We're not done yet!"

"Knighthood," says Jo, eyes wide under her closed eyelids. "Like, knight in shining armor hood. Like I'm gonna be Sir Jo."

"You'll be the Gallowglas," says Ysabel.

"I thought that was already the problem."

"You'll be a knight in her service, a member of her house. *My* house. I can finally go home, Jo, because you'll finally be able to come with me. You'll never have to make a spam call ever again."

"This is," says Jo, "I don't, this is all coming out of nowhere."

"You saved me last night."

"Oh." Out in the main room of the apartment the phone rings. "But," says Jo. "I'll get it," says Ysabel, stepping out of the bathroom. "You wouldn't have been there in the first place if I hadn't," says Jo, and then, "Ysabel! Don't answer – "

Scissors whick. The last lock of black hair falls to the floor. Jo opens her eyes. There in the mirror over the sink a man standing behind her, short, peering over Jo's shoulder frozen, eyes black in sun-darkened cheeks blotted with black freckles. "Hello," says Ysabel, out in the apartment. Silver scissor rings cruelly jammed over a wide flat thumb and a thick index finger. "The phone," says Jo. The scissors fall to the floor. The mirror's empty.

"The fuck?" says Jo.

The sky above still filled with soft grey light that does not seep down here among the trees. Stalking up the path she's heedless of the buckled pavement, past a green-doored mausoleum, brick crumbling through cracked stucco wrapped in rickety chain-link fence. Her long brown coat unbelted hanging open. Reliable, says the rusted sign hanging from the corner post. Fence and Construction. Her short hair gunmetal grey. Up at the top of the hill he's sitting on a low stone wall, elbows on his knees, head in his hands. "Dagger," she says.

He looks up. "Not since last night," he says, lifting a hand from his pocket. "I swear I could *feel* it," spreading his fingers suddenly, a burst, "when they took salt and bread and fire from me." He puts his hand back in his pocket. "I would have thought the whole *city* could feel it."

"Sidney," she says. Looking away, one hand before her face.

"Just Sidney," he says. "Did you bring it? The fiat?" She doesn't say anything. "Like I asked?" he says. Across the path a grave lies buried under fallen flowers, legs of a tumbled tripod jutting up to one side, a banner that says Our Beloved trailing in the dirt. Past it another grave, headstone dark, a silvery photograph etched in the polished stone, a couple of mirrored balls purple and green, pinwheels stuck in the grass before them. An unopened bottle of orange soda. "I can't stay here," he says. "Just sitting here on this wall. I can't. I need a ticket. For a bus, a train, a plane, whatever, I need a ticket. I need fiat for the ticket. Did you bring it?"

She's lowered her hand. "How long," she says, still looking away, "have we known each other?"

"You're angry," he says, flatly.

"How long, Sidney?"

He says, "A night and a day."

"A night and a," she says. "All that, and you."

"I can't stay, Helm." He shifts, his feet crunching gravel at the edge of the path.

"No," she says, "you can't. Set one foot out of this cemetery in any of the days to come and the Count's men and the Duke's men will cut your belt and snap your spurs and break your sword. If you can find it. No," she says, reaching for something in the pocket of her long brown coat, "you can't stay. But you can't leave, Sidney." She tosses something to the ground before him. "You can't leave."

Sidney stands, looking down. "What is that," he says. A knife, unsheathed, hilt wrapped in brown leather, long blade with a single edge, there between his feet. "A joke?"

"Pick it up," says the Helm.

"It isn't funny," says Sidney.

"Pick it up," says the Helm. In her hand a sword, short and broad, a battered round guard rattling loosely above the hilt. "You're not getting on a bus, you're not getting on a train, you're not climbing into any tin can. You aren't sailing down the river to the sea. Pick it up, Sidney. You aren't leaving."

"Helm," he says.

"You didn't tell me," she says.

"You said not to tell you what I would do."

"You didn't tell me what you were *doing,* Sidney."

"And you said you wouldn't tell me not to do it."

"I didn't know what it was!"

"That isn't," says Sidney, and "I," and then he shuts his mouth. He kneels slowly. "You can't," he says, "you can't strike me here." He doesn't reach for the knife. "Cemeteries and churches. The Axe," he says, "broke her oath – "

"You tried to destroy her," says the Helm.

"So you'll destroy me?" he says. "I don't see a gallowglas."

"Who sleeps in the ground all about us?" She shifts, her sword held back, the skirts of her long brown coat wound about her left arm low before her. "Let's see what happens."

"The Axe," he says, his hand over the knife, "broke her oath – "

"It's not your place to judge," she says, and steps into a low-slung cut at his arm as he snatches the knife and springs back, blade up before his face. "To the King Come Back!" he says. "Her oath!"

"You don't make that call!"

"Someone has to!" He catches her blade with the knife a bang scraping as he pushes back both hands on the hilt. "Someone has to prove we're not all carpet knights and popinjays!"

"Then prove it." She cuts at his arms, his head, him scuttling back, ducking, swinging the knife in jagged chops she bats aside with her swaddled arm. She lunges thrusting just wide of him as he twists and lunges in turn. They stand still a moment held close, face almost to face. "Linesse," he says. She steps back, the knife jammed in her left shoulder. She lets her sword fall to the grass. Someone away down the path laughs. "What have you done?" says Sidney.

"It's what you've done," says the Helm. "Struck me, on her ground. She doesn't like that."

"You did this on *purpose,*" says Sidney. There's a flash of light, blue-white, everything about them lit up for an instant, limned by crisp black shadows.

"You aren't staying," says the Helm. "You aren't leaving. You aren't going to embarrass us." She yanks the knife free, grimacing. "Go on," she says, dropping it at his feet. "You're hers now." Sidney turns, and the woman standing behind him throws wide her arms. In one hand a gnarled grey stick, smooth and dull as driftwood, its tip a blue-white spark too bright to look upon. He steps back but his arm is caught, his hand already sunk in the tatters of her black cloak lofting in the sudden wind. She laughs again and his eyes go wide his mouth opens as she folds her arms about him and the wind dies. He is gone.

One hand to her shoulder the Helm kneels, grunting, peering about at the grass. "I," she says, "I can't – "

"It's not the shed I mind," says the woman. Holding her cloak shut with her free hand at her throat. The tip of her gnarled grey stick still lit up blue and bright. "Of blood nor honey. What's another spill?" She smiles. The Helm still on her knees. "Such a cruel trick to have played on that young man."

"Ma'am," says the Helm. "I mean no disrespect, but I can't find my sword."

"He was betrayed, little knight," says the woman, "and betrayal must needs have a traitor. It's *that* I mind."

"Lady," says the Helm, climbing slowly to her feet.

"Do not fret." The woman spreads her arms once more. "Such work I have for you! You'll both be kept quite busy."

"Of course I wasn't going to do it myself," says Ysabel. The taxi starts then lurches to a stop as a woman under a clear umbrella dashes across the street before them. "Farging pedestrians," mutters the driver.

"You could have said, is all," says Jo. "Before."

"You could have asked," says Ysabel. "Or haven't you noticed you haven't had to do laundry in weeks? You didn't *thank* him, did you?" She glares at Jo. "Or ask his name?"

"The mystery man in my mirror?" says Jo. "I was too busy being shocked. You have to tell me these things – "

"How about your *mother?* How about if you'd said something about *that?*"

"I told you not to answer the phone," says Jo.

"Because of *spam!*"

"Ladies," the driver's saying.

"Can we worry about *your* mother instead?" says Jo.

"Ladies, we're here," says the driver. The taxi's pulled up by a loading dock rising dark and green to a black metal railing, tables up there under grey umbrellas. Ysabel's opened her door. The driver's reaching over the seat as Jo opens hers. "Four seventy-five," he says. "Ladies?"

"Oh," says Jo, half out the door. "He said they'd send a car, I mean – "

"Four seventy-five, miss," says the driver.

"Here," says the tall man, coming around the front of the taxi. His suit is black, his face narrow and somber. "Here," he says. In one white-gloved hand he's holding out a folded five-dollar bill. Ysabel's headed up the steps of the loading dock. A round clock hangs there, blue hands lit up by white neon. Jo takes the bill and shaking her head reaches down to the top of her boot and plucks out a small wad of money clamped in a medium-sized binder clip. She tugs free a couple of ones and hands them with the crisp five to the driver. "Miss," he says. A boy in a blue and white rainshell at a valet stand by the steps, eyeing a yellow suv rolling up in the rain. Laughter from a knot of people around one of the tables, ruddy in the glow of heat lamps. None of them Ysabel. "Inside," says the tall man, gesturing with a hand now bare. The taxi's nosing around the suv into the street.

Inside candlelit tables with low brown chairs curtained here and there by gauzy grey-brown drapes hung from thick white beams. The floor well-worn, painted white. "Perry party?" says the woman by the hostess stand. "Your table's not quite ready, but if you'd like to wait in the bar?" Behind her a low dark room walled here and there by more drapes, lit by a wall of liquor bottles, white light shining through caramel and red, green and yellow, orange and cold clear nothing. A synthesizer chirps under a loop of boys chanting oh, oh ah oh. Ysabel there in her long-sleeved minidress shining silver and white, a drink already in her hand. A drumbeat perking under the music opens into a blare of guitar like a jet engine. Oh but we go out at night, chant the boys. Ysabel laughs. The man next to her smiling, saying something else. White dreadlocks brush the shoulders of his blue seersucker suit. Roland sits there, hunched over a table head in his hands headphones over his ears. Ignoring the man leaning over him, red hair bobbing. Marfisa by the bar, her coatdress pale and blue. "Take your coat?" says the Duke.

Jo shakes her head, hands in pockets pulling her army green jacket closed. "How's your leg?" she asks.

He lurches back, leaning heavily on his wooden cane. "Lends a certain gravitas, don't you think?"

"He said *dinner,*" says Jo. "I wasn't expecting a normal, you know, restaurant. A normal, fancy restaurant."

"The Queen may take you into her house," says the Duke, "but she'll never let you in her home. What's with the crest?" He's pointing at her shirt, bright yellow, a squirrel posed with an acorn as if stiff-arming through a defensive line. "Not hound, nor hawk, nor hive," he says, "Not hare, hind, or hollow. But squirrel."

"Ysabel said wear something yellow," says Jo, looking around. Marfisa's pushed away from the bar, headed toward the back of the restaurant. "Where'd she go? I should – "

"We're all friends here," says the Duke, his hand on her arm. "Let me buy you a drink. They make a Manhattan where they rinse the glass with port. It's," he kisses his fingertips. "What do you say?"

"It's not much," says Marfisa in Ysabel's ear.

"I still have so much left," says Ysabel. A faint lip print left on Marfisa's throat. In her palm by Marfisa's hip a small clear plastic bag, a thimbleful of gold dust sparkling. "You're too generous." Dark hair against curls the color of clotted cream. "You should leave something for yourself." Another kiss on her cheek, her mouth. Ysabel's other hand working a button loose on Marfisa's coatdress, and another. All those beautiful boys, flutes a voice over unseen speakers. Tattoos of ships and tattoos of tears.

"Lady," says Marfisa. Shaking her head away. "We can't." Stepping back against the corner of the bathroom stall. Ysabel's hand falling away. *"Can't?"* she says. "That word doesn't work. Not here. Not with me."

"They're *all* out there," says Marfisa. "My brother – "

"And they have no idea," says Ysabel, pulling Marfisa back. Kissing her and kissing her again. "My mother's," she says, "always late." Loosing another button above Marfisa's knees, and another.

"Roland," says Marfisa.

"Roland is a dolt," says Ysabel.

"Roland saw."

"Saw what?" says Ysabel, leaning back in Marfisa's arms, looking up at her.

"Us, lady. The night of the hunt, when we. Stopped playing games. He said as much. He told me – "

"What did he tell you," says Ysabel.

Marfisa takes one hand from the small of Ysabel's back to brush her fingertips along Ysabel's cheek. "I love you, Princess," she says. "Beyond all reason. But that's on me only. You are promised to the King – " Ysabel jerks free from her grasp. "Lady, listen, please, you are promised – " Ysabel's thrown the bolt on the stall door, shoved it open and out into the restroom. Aged eighty-seven, a woman's singing from the unseen speakers. Could justifiably be called the last to go up to Surrealist heaven.

"You've decided then," says Ysabel, her back to Marfisa. Baggie of dust in one clenched fist.

"I have no choice," says Marfisa.

"Yes, *you do,*" says Ysabel. "I'm giving it to you. Marfisa. Please."

"Roland will – "

"*Roland!*" Ysabel spins around, glaring. "Of *course!*"

"What do you – "

"I said *of course* he saw us! How else was I going to get you to *leave me alone?*" Ysabel steps over to the sinks. "Like some six-foot fucking puppy dog I swear." Sets the bagging on the counter and runs cold water over her hands. "Go box up your mouth and your hands and your heart in your room, Axe. You'll be perfectly safe. He's very discreet, he won't say a word. Watch it all from your window, Axe. I am going home." She splashes her face with water, yanks paper towels from the dispenser to blot it dry. "My mother will take Jo as a knight and she will come home with me and she will *never* tell me I am promised to *anyone.*" Marfisa isn't looking at her, hasn't moved. "I will have everything I need," says Ysabel. "You can *rot,* Marfisa. Rot *safely.* I won't need your *pathetic* hand-outs ever again." Leaning over the sink mashes the baggie against the mirror, mashing until it pops, gold dust clouding her hand, streaking the mirror, glass darkening, creaking, a crack chasing through it suddenly to the edge. Dust settling on the counter, blackening where it hits the water puddled about the sink. Ysabel turns to go. Marfisa's lifting her hands to her mouth. Deep in her throat a rough-edged keening, almost a growl.

Laughing Jo comes down the stairs, her boots, her kilt, her yellow T-shirt. Her jacket's gone. The Duke a few steps behind her. "Hand to heart," he says.

"And then he?" says Jo.

"Right over the edge," says the Duke. "I lost count after the fifth bounce." Jo's laughing harder, stumbling over the last step, one arm out liquor sloshing from her cocktail glass. "Whoa," says the

Duke, catching her other hand. "Oh," says Jo, looking about. It's a close room, long enough for the table running down the center of it draped in white cloth, lined with wineglasses licked by candlelight. Leather banquettes along one wall behind a row of shorter tables. The other's racked with wine bottles floor to ceiling, thousands of them, flickering black-green and honey-green and deep blood brown. Ysabel sits in a straight brown chair, elbows on the table, chin on her hands, one hand wrapped in a white napkin. Candlelight spangles the silver sewn into her dress. Her eyes are hidden behind her hair. Across the table an old man in a soft blue suit, ivory hair a wild crown about his pink head bobbing. There at the head a young man in blue seersucker, his white dreadlocks touched with gold, smiling and saying something to an older man in a crisp white shirt and a white apron brushing his shoe-tops. "Gallowglas," says Roland. His jacket checked with green and black. His hand on the back of the straight brown chair by Ysabel.

"Such an ugly word," says the Duke, letting go of Jo's hand.

"Truth is frequently ugly, your grace," says Roland.

"Truth is a process, boy," says the Duke, limping into the room. His high-buttoned vest of deep red suede with a pinstriped back. "Not our fault it turns to shit in your hands. You'll want to sit next to the Princess," he says to Jo.

"*Boy?*" says Roland.

"Privileges of rank," says the Duke airily. Jo's pulling out a chair next to Ysabel. "You okay?" she says, softly.

Ysabel looks up from the napkin wrapped about her fist. "I'm fine," she says. "Why would you ask?"

"I don't know," says Jo. "I just thought – "

"Roasted beets!" blares the old man. "Red and gold with arugula and spinach and the first blood oranges of the year. Virgin olive oil from a cold first press and cracked pepper – *not* ground – a sherry vinegar, and sea salt smoked over an alderwood fire. Alder!" He bangs the table with a fist surprisingly large for such a skinny arm. "I will know if it's not. And the risotto, with the heirloom squash and the wild mushrooms. They *were* picked this morning?" He's suddenly querulous, looking about at the rest of them. "With the shallots?"

"We ordering?" says the Duke, sitting a couple of places down from the old man.

The waiter in his apron carefully unsmiling inclines his head, a nod and a shrug at once. "We have a succotash," he starts to say.

"Surprise me," says the Duke. "Agravante! Have you met Jo Gallowglas, who saved our Princess from a fate most foul?"

"His usual, yes," the man in the blue seersucker's saying. "I'd quite like the risotto myself, and the twenty greens salad. I hadn't," he says as he heads toward Jo, hand outstretched, "had the honor, not in person, though of course I saw you at the Duke's Equinox hunt. Agravante." Jo half-stands, shakes his hand. "The Axehandle."

"Marfisa's brother," says Jo.

"The very same," says Agravante.

"The risotto," says Ysabel. "It's not an heirloom," the waiter starts to say, and she says, "That's fine." He turns to Jo.

"Are we it? Do you know what you want?" she says to Roland.

"The onion salad," he says.

"I mean, I thought there was more of us or something, I guess. More of you. The party, I mean."

"You would choose who sits at our table, Miss Maguire?" says the Queen, standing at the bottom of the stairs dressed all in black. The Duke smiles. Ysabel's unwinding the napkin from her fist. "No, ma'am," says Jo, "majesty, I, um. Ma'am. I've just never been to a dinner party in a fancy restaurant with a queen before. I don't know the protocol."

"One could never tell," says the Queen. She's come around to the head of the table. "Do you know what you'd like?" she says, sitting.

"The, um," says Jo, looking up at the waiter, "steak? The New York whatsis, with the, um." The waiter is not nodding. He isn't smiling. The Duke's looking at an empty wineglass at the end of the table. Ysabel's wrapped the napkin around the fingers of both her hands. The old man's glaring at Jo, one fat fist trembling over his plate, and the Queen's smiling to herself.

"The succotash, perhaps?" says the waiter.

"Sure," says Jo. "The succotash."

"I'd like that as well," says the Queen. Bang! Cutlery rattles and glasses chime. "You bring it with you wherever you go, girl," snarls the old man, and he bangs the table again with his fist. *"Blood,* and death – "

"Enough, Frederic," says the Queen. He lowers his fist, spreads it open on the table, fingers bent and trembling. "Unless a dinner's an affair of state, Miss Maguire, we prefer them to be small, and intimate. We'd asked our vassals each to bring but one guest, much as our daughter would, much as we have our Chariot. The Count, of course, has brought his grandson. The Duke, however..?"

"My Helm, it seems, is otherwise engaged," says the Duke.

"Perhaps she seeks your Dagger?" says the Queen. "No matter. But though this is a small and intimate dinner, there's still business to conduct before the bread. The Duke has sought through honesty what he could not accomplish through guile: he has openly asked you be knighted in honor of the service you did us last night."

"But not *formally* petitioned," says the Duke.

"Why so modest, Leo?" says the Queen. He shrugs. "Have you anything to say to this news, Miss Maguire?"

"What I did, ma'am," says Jo, "I didn't do for any reward, or honor. We were being *attacked.* I'm not just going to let that happen."

"Perhaps you'll listen, then, when told our sister's demesne is not to be trifled with? No matter. We have decided to grant the Duke's request. However informal."

Ysabel lets out a breath she'd been holding. The Count curls his hand into a fist again. The Duke sips from his cocktail. Agravante frowns. Roland sits quite still with his hands in his lap.

"We shall create you a knight banneret, Jo Maguire, at the Samani at the end of this month."

"Banneret?" says Jo.

"A great honor," says the Duke, frowning. Setting down his cocktail glass. "A *very* great honor," says Agravante. He isn't frowning. Ysabel's tightened her grip on the napkin.

"I'm sorry," says Jo, "but what's it mean?"

"You may fight under your own device," says Agravante. "The squirrel," says the Duke. The Count's sitting back in his chair, fist falling open. "Responsible to no one," says Agravante. "Like the Mooncalfe. But no one's responsible for you, either. Still: mortals have no need of owr, and three weeks without seem to have done the Princess little harm." Ysabel scrapes back her chair and drops her napkin on her plate. Jo puts her hand on Ysabel's. "Is something wrong?" she says.

"Of course not," says Ysabel.

"Isn't this what you said would happen?"

"I said – " says Ysabel. "I want to go – " She stands. "Wash my face. Let go. Please."

"I meant it. I'd take that chance."

"Jo."

"Have someone fight me. If that's what it takes to set this right. I'd – "

Agravante's laughing. Ysabel's yanked her hand free. She's walking away, down the length of the long white table.

"What *happened?*" says Jo.

"No one will challenge you," says Roland, quietly. "If there's a hint you'd lose deliberately."

"You said yes, Gallowglas," says the Queen.

"I cannot have her in my house," says the Queen, quietly. Ysabel does not turn to face her. Across the bar Jo's handing a ticket to the hostess. "Doing such an honor to a gallowglas when lackeys are *dying* and knights being run out of town is – unthinkable." The Queen puts her hand on Ysabel's shoulder. "Who was bringing the owr to you? The Axe?" Ysabel jerks at that. "Did you think I was blind, child?" says the Queen. "Did you think I *cared?*"

"I will be Queen, mother," says Ysabel.

"One day, yes," says the Queen.

"*Soon,*" says Ysabel. "I've seen it. And she will be at my side." The hostess is handing Jo her army green coat. "She's so much stronger than you know."

"Poor Erymathos," says the Queen, lifting her hand from Ysabel's shoulder. "I've seen things as well," she says. She leans close, and murmurs in Ysabel's ear. "You will not be the one to break her heart."

"Here," says Jo, holding her jacket out to Ysabel.

"Why?" says Ysabel.

"Unless you've got cash for a cab, we're walking. And you don't have a coat. And neither of us has an umbrella. But hey." She holds up a white paper bag. "At least we've got lots of risotto for lunch."

"You'll freeze," says Ysabel, taking the jacket.

"So let's hustle," says Jo. "It's maybe a mile. Come on." She turns to go.

"Happy birthday, Jo," says Ysabel, settling into the jacket.

"What?" says Jo, scowling.

"It's what your mother said. On the phone. Tell her happy birthday for me."

"I *told* you I didn't want to talk about it."

"Well, I didn't know, and I thought I should say something. When was it?"

"Yesterday," says Jo, still scowling. "The first."

"Happy birthday, then," says Ysabel.

"What happened?" says Jo. "I was supposed to be knighted, or whatever, and I'm gonna be, and that's suddenly like the worst thing in the world?"

"Nothing happened, Jo," says Ysabel. "Nothing changed. Nothing at all."

Sitting on the Banks of the Sea

Sitting on the banks of the sea, sings the radio. She had a forty-four strapped around her body, and a banjo on her knee. He shuts off the engine. The radio goes silent.

He's a big man, fussing about the back of the pickup truck. His raincoat blue, hood up, shining slick in the weird dim morning light. He comes up with a pair of grey workgloves and tugs them on. Rain trickles from his hood as he leans into the truck again. Long grey mustaches droop to either side of his flat mouth. He comes up with some brightly colored bungee cords and an armload of canvas sack.

The building over across the street is a long warehouse, a grey corrugated metal wall interrupted here and there by garage doors. Big letters in flaking paint say Bushnell Warehouse, Corp. over the doors. Down at the end there's a slice of parking lot, a flatbed trailer with a load of rebar. He stands there a moment by a telephone pole, looking over the trailer. The rebar's long and straight and black, piled neatly and wrapped in clear rain-beaded plastic. Raindrops splat on his hood. There's a piece of white card nailed up over his head. 5+ Acres, say the sloppy black letters. 55K Lg Down. Another sign nailed to the next pole down the line says the same thing. He heaves the load of sack and cord over one shoulder and walks past the trailer, around the back end. Over past it up against the back wall of the warehouse is a pile of rusting sheet metal, tangles of steel cable, bent and broken rebar jutting at odd angles, streaked with orange and red. He rubs his gloved hands together, his mustaches spread by a small smile.

"Hey," says a young guy in shapeless green coveralls, up on the concrete steps by the back door to the warehouse. "Hey! *What* the fuck are you doing?"

The big man straightens up, brushing his knees. "I'm the Anvil," he says, peering up from under his hood. "Pyrocles. Open Mike around?"

"Who?" says the young guy in green coveralls.

"You go and find Open Mike or Twice Tom. Tell them the Anvil is here."

"You know Tommy Tom?"

"Yes," says Pyrocles, squatting back down. "Okay," says the young guy, opening the back door. Pyrocles is reaching under a corner of the pile to pull at something. Bends down to get both hands under there, wrenching it loose.

The back door jerks open and a short, heavy man in shapeless green coveralls steps out into the rain. "You white-shoe motherfucker," he says, grinning. "What, come to fill your nose with an honest stink?" He's wearing a blue meshback cap that says Vanport 15.

"This, this is good. I like it. Can I have it?" Pyrocles doesn't look up from the long gently curved bar of metal in his lap. He's stroking it with his gloved hands, worrying at scales of rust, knocking some free with a slap.

"That's a leaf spring," says Twice Tom. "From Peabo's dead Buick, I think. No idea what the hell it's doing back here."

"Never went as fast as it wanted," says Pyrocles. "I'd need to cut it down, but the rust'll help with that. Also some cable." He points back over his shoulder, still looking down at the bar. "I can just take a coil instead of trying to cut it here."

"You got to tell me what you're doing with it, first," says Twice Tom, leaning on the metal railing.

"The cable's just warm-up," says Pyrocles. "Maybe a couple knives. But this?" He looks up from the bar, his hood falling back to settle on his shoulders. "This I'm making a sword."

Twice Tom whistles. "And how long has it been since you made one of those?"

"A while," says Pyrocles, looking down at the bar again. "Quite a while." Rain shining in his close-cropped grey hair. "But it's not like I *forgot.*"

Never mind the sooty faces
Tugging at the Forge!

—*Emily Dickinson*

NO. 7
GIN-SOAKED

SLOPPING TWO FINGERS OF BOURBON into a coffee cup he makes a face, eyes wide, head bobbing, "They *fight*," he says, his mouth within his salt-and-pepper Van Dyke twisting around the words. He sets the bottle on the edge of a long table lost under haphazard stacks of books and piles of paper, picks up the cork and jams it home, then picks up the coffee cup and throws back one long swallow. His other hand a metal hook at the end of a beige prosthetic attached just below his elbow. He sets the cup down, snaps off the light.

Past the double doors under a frosted fanlight a wide deep room the far end lost in shadows, one wall lined with floor-to-ceiling mirrors. She stands in the middle of it threadbare slipper-toe worrying at an x of blue masking tape stuck to the floor, her hair a great crown of tiny braids wound about with colored thread and beads all held up atop her head by a blue silk scarf. A half-dozen kids lined up roughly between her and the mirrors, sweatpants and yoga pants, gym shorts over longjohns, a brown sweater vest over a white T-shirt. She looks up at them, a hank of hair slipping from the scarf and slithering down her shoulder. *"They fight,"* she says quite loudly.

Over by the doors he snorts. He's tugging loose with his hook the twine about a bundle of swords.

"Shakespeare was never much of one for stage directions," she says, "but here we are, at the climax of our play, our Harry and our Hotspur have finally met on the field of battle, and how does the Bard frame the epic action of his climax? 'They. Fight.'" A murmur of chuckles, someone laughs. He's clutched the swords in his right arm, pulling the twine free. "So we will need," she says, "to write our own scene of *actions,* to complement the *words*. But." She holds the moment then, until all of them are still, are looking at her, even the laughing girl in the T-shirt that says Bard with Bite. "The blocking – the choreography – we devise; that's just as words on paper." She looks down then at the x, smiling. "Just. You all need to become as adept with a sword as you are with your voice: to *know,* Shaquina," to the laughing girl, "how to riposte as *surely* as you know how to tell him you'll no longer brook his vanities. To *know,* Jason," to the boy in the sweater vest, "not only that you must drive her up and stage left, but *how* Harry would do it." She turns then with a magnanimous sweep of her hand introducing him there by the doors. "Vincent Erne has been the fight director for every Serpents Tooth production that's needed one."

"*Almost* every," he mutters, walking toward the line of kids, swords rattling.

"He'll train you in stage combat, and work closely with me in blocking the fights, but most importantly he'll work with each of you to become comfortable with this admittedly strange way to move – with these *weapons,* on your hips and in your hands." He's offering the bouquet of swords still tucked under his arm to them, tapping the bundled hilts with his hook. "Go on," he says. "Until," she's saying, "you know, in your *bones,* how to move, how to strike, as Harry, as Hotspur, as Falstaff, or the King."

"Judith is too kind," he says. "I'll settle for none of you putting out an eye." And they laugh, swords in hand, fingering the blunted tips, whipping the swords about, striking poses in the mirrors. "It's been two hundred and sixty-seven days since our last workplace incident," he says, and there's chuckles now instead of laughs, and the swinging stops. "All right. It looks like you all know which end to hold, so we'll skip straight to lesson two – " One of the double doors creaks open. Judith turns her head sharply, beads clattering. "Excuse me," she says, "this is a closed rehearsal."

"I'm sorry," says Jo Maguire, one hand on the doorknob. "I didn't have the phone number." She limps into the room, her short brown hair sleek, her army-green jacket dark with rain. Under her left arm a bundle long and thin, wrapped in towels. "I could come back."

"Please do," snaps Judith, not yet turning back to her kids.

"We're done, you and I," says Vincent.

"Yeah," says Jo, "I just, I wanted to talk about – " but Vincent's started across the room toward her, the doors, the last sword in his hand, toward Ysabel stepping up beside her, pushing back the hood of her yellow slicker, coils of black hair glossy tumbling free, Vincent head ducked dropping to one knee at her feet, Ysabel's feet, the sword laid to the floor hilt first before her, his hook tucked up in the small of his back.

"Majesty," he says.

"*Highness,*" murmurs Ysabel, smiling just.

"Of course," says Vincent, sitting back on his heel. "Lady." Looking up at her, the ugly bruise swallowing her eye, the scrape along her cheekbone. "What," he says, and he swallows, "what happened?"

The sanctuary's dark. Pink-tinged streetlight leaks through high narrow windows, a false dawn staining white columns that loom over the aisles. Jo's sitting toward the front slumped down, her mismatched Chuck Taylors black and grubby white propped up on the back of the pew before her. A click of a door latch somewhere in back. A man steps out from the shadows under the white-railed balcony, his hair a shock of pinkish-orange bobbing as he comes down the aisle, his eyes bulging over an uncertain grin. "*There* you are," he's saying. His leather jacket creaks as he folds himself elbows and knees into the pew across from her.

"Just needed to, I don't know," says Jo. "I'm such a fucking idiot." Forehead in her hand, elbow braced on the knee before her. "You'd think I'd've figured it out by now. Never go any-where with her. Not without a fucking army."

"We could keep waiting," he says. He's looking down at the bottle in his hands, green glass dark in the dim light.

"For who, the Duke?" says Jo. "Roland? Anybody'd help us has to get through them out there, same as the Anvil. Might as well wait for *her* to show up herself, and her goddamn nineteen names."

"She wouldn't cross the river," he says, sloshing the bottle at her.

"What else has she got that would?" says Jo.

He shrugs, unscrews the cap. Swigs. "So *don't* wait," he says, looking up at the ceiling. "He's under the, the damn bridge." His eyes slide over in a smile at her. He points back over his shoulder. "Maybe ten blocks or so. You can't miss it."

"You're right," says Jo. "We won't."

"Jesus," he says. "Christ. It's not like I'm ducking out on you or anything. I'll take you there."

"Last week," she says, still looking not at him but up at the dark altar, "a two-ton boar took out the east-bound lanes of I-84. Smashed 'em to bits. Can you take me there, too?"

He frowns, looks down at the bottle. "I don't, I mean, sure, of course – "

"Because maybe he'll be there under the bridge, and maybe he won't, you know? I just don't trust anything where you people are involved."

"Me people? *My* people?" He laughs and takes another swig. "Jesus, Jo. Here I am, sitting in a church, drinking gin from the bottle..."

"Is that supposed to make you more like me, or them?" says Jo. "Because there's a roomful of them in the basement, and Ysabel drinks like a fucking fish."

"Sure," he says, "but they aren't up *here* in the, the, she does?"

"Yup. The Duke, too. I don't think I've ever seen him *un*-loaded."

"Huh." Eyes goggling, he grins around snaggled teeth. "Guess there's a difference between can't, and don't usually." He holds out the bottle. " You sure you don't want a taste? Before we take off?" Jo takes it from him. "I mean, if they are me people – if I *am* like them, and I go out there, you'd know soon enough. One touch from those spooky motherfuckers and I'd be toast."

"But you're like me, Ray," says Jo, "so it'll be nothing but kisses and love-taps." She sips, screws up her face. He laughs. "Fucking turpentine," says Jo.

"Clears the noggin," says Ray, tapping his temple.

"You're plenty clear," says Jo. She hands the bottle back to him. "Let's go."

"Okay, okay," says Ray, climbing wobbly to his feet.

Becker's waiting in the shadows under the white-railed balcony, arms folded, licks of hair sprung out by his ears, on top of his head. Jo says, "He ready?" as she comes up the aisle toward him. Ray behind her stumbles over a ruck in the carpet.

"Are you?" says Becker. Ray laughs and makes a show of shaking out his left foot, then his right.

"We'll be fine," says Jo. "We just have to run. You get downstairs with the Princess."

"Sure," says Becker. "She can help me keep Guthrie calm."

Off away through brick dimly a roar and shrieks, the belling scrape of metal. "There he goes," says Jo. She puts a hand on Becker's arm. "Whatever happens," she says, *"whatever* happens," squeezing his arm, "don't set foot out there. Not till it's over. He's gone for sure if you do."

Ray's kneeling by the double doors leading outside, one hand on the crash bar. He pushes gently, cracking the right door open. A swarm a flurry a half-dozen bicycles down on the street circling circling, bicycles all painted white, gleaming white smooth and patchy white uneven daubs and once-bright racing stripes and brand names lost under foggy coats of sprayed white paint, white-walled tires and grimy whitened treads, blank white cards tucked ratcheting in spokes, a fluttering train of xeroxed notices on white paper. Dried flowers the only washed-out colors, wired to a whippy pole clamped to the back of a white-taped banana seat, dead green and pale yellow flowers piled in a white-painted handlebar basket, flowers once red and blue draped about this rider's neck, that rider's wrists, riders in grey sweatshirts, a hood up here, a grey helmet, a brown helmet there, grey sneakers pumping white pedals as they swoop to peel away left and right, chains and cards clacking, flowers rustling, speeding away to the back of the church.

"It's working," says Ray. He stands, lets the door close, claps his hands and rubs them quickly together, tilting his head to one side and the other. Nods.

Jo kicks open the doors.

A Big Man straining – What she Owes
Four Simple Lessons

He's a big man straining the shoulders of a dark blue jacket, sitting back in one of the leather armchairs beneath the large copper letters that say Barshefsky Associates: Quality Assured. Long grey mustaches droop to either side of his mouth. He flips over and over in his hands a white business card. When the side door swings open with a sudden wash of questioning voices and clacking keys he climbs to his feet and those mustaches spread around a smile. Becker steps out into the lobby, a big striped shirt unbuttoned over a yellow T-shirt, thin brown hair licked up here and there at the top of his head.

"It's Becker!" says the big man. "You manage a phone bank."

"I'm, sorry," says Becker. "You're very – Do I know you?"

"Of course," says the big man. "Pyrocles."

"Pyrocles," says Becker. About to nod, he shakes his head slowly instead, his face settling toward a frown. "Is that, what, is that Greek?"

"No, I'm from Vergina, where the Argead ruled. But they have heard of me in Byzantium."

"Huh. I didn't know there was a Byzantium left."

"Goodness," says Pyrocles. "I certainly hope so."

"And you're here because…"

"Oh! Jo Maguire. I need to speak with her. Briefly, of course."

"Had to be one of those two," mutters Becker.

"You see, I must examine her hands."

"Her hands?"

"I'm making," says Pyrocles, and then he holds up the business card. "Forgive me, is this appropriate? As her sigil?"

"Her what?" The card's printed with a stylized B, rounded, with furled serifs. "That's the Barshefsky logo."

"This is her house, isn't it?" says Pyrocles, and one of Becker's frowning eyebrows goes up. "She does work here, doesn't she?"

"Sure, but she's not – "

"Oh but I should ask her myself," says Pyrocles. "Not waste your time like this, I'm sorry."

"Thing is," says Becker, "she's off. Today."

"Off?"

"Not working. Don't know where she is, in fact."

"Oh."

"Not that I could tell you if I did."

"I see," says Pyrocles.

"I mean, it's not. Regulations. Nothing personal."

"I wouldn't think to take it personally."

"If there's anything else?"

"No, no, I've taken up quite enough of your time – " says Pyrocles, as Becker says "I'll be sure to let her know, I'm sorry, you were here – "

"I guess I'll have to come back, then," says Pyrocles.

"All right," says Becker. "Whenever. Although – five's a good time. Weekdays. Usually taking their first break right around then."

"I'll keep that in mind."

Jo sits tailor-fashion midway along a line of bookshelves. By her side a stack of books, old, clothbound, titles written on the spines in white ink, a big flat paperback with a glossy photo cover, a figure in a white outfit anonymous behind a mesh mask foil held up *en garde,* the tip obscured behind a barcode sticker. A book splayed open in her lap. Her right arm stretched out to one side she looks down its length to her hand, relaxed, palm down. "Pronation," she says. She rolls her arm over her palm now facing up. "Supination," she says. Curls her fingers into a loose fist and rolls it back and over again.

"Wouldn't that be easier with the sword?" says Ysabel, her back to Jo. Idly running her fingers along book-spines.

"I'm sorry," says Jo. "Did you say something?"

Ysabel tips a book from its place on the shelf with a finger, tips it back. Jo's still eyeing her fist now moving in a little square, up here, up there, down there, down here. Palm up, palm down.

They come down the wide sweeping stairs into the lobby one after the other, Jo her books stacked in her arms, Ysabel's long patched denim skirt swaying like a bell, frayed hem brushing the dark stone steps. "You'll never learn a thing of value, reading those," she says.

"I know you can't be talking to *me,*" says Jo. "What with swearing a mighty oath just this morning never to speak to me again." She's headed past the self-serve kiosks to the high dark counter running down one side of the lobby, where she drops her books by a librarian's flat-screen monitor. "I need to take care of some fines," she says, pulling a wodge of cards and paper from the pocket of her army-surplus jacket, undoing the purple hair-tie holding it together. She peels a grubby white library card from the middle and hands it over. The librarian scans it and hands it back, not looking away from his screen. "Been awhile," he says. His hair is sandy, his eyes red-rimmed.

"How much," says Jo. She's counting through the bills clamped in a medium-sized binder clip.

"Y'know, you could always give us your email address," says the librarian.

"How *much,*" says Jo.

"Because that way we could send you email when your books are due. And you can renew online. Which – "

"Which would be great if I had a computer instead of having to come *here* to get online, which kinda defeats your whole point. How much. Do I. Owe."

"Twenty-seven seventy-five," says the librarian. He starts scanning Jo's stack of books.

"What," says Jo sidelong to Ysabel beside her. Hands in the pockets of her skirt leaning back against the counter Ysabel lifts her head a little, pointing with her chin. Jo turns. A short, heavy man in shapeless green coveralls stands by the self-serve kiosks. He isn't looking at them. He isn't looking anywhere else. Turning over and over in his hands a blue meshback cap. "Highness," he says.

"Shit," says Jo.

"Highness, we're meeting tonight, and we wonder, our Soames wonders, if you're willing and able to attend."

"Attend?" says Jo. "Who the hell are you?"

"Twice Thomas," he says, and he ducks his head. His thick black hair shines with grease.

"I'd love to," says Ysabel.

"You have any idea who this guy is?" says Jo.

"I know all my mother's subjects," says Ysabel. "And who are we, Twice Thomas?" He looks puzzled. "The we, who'll be meeting?"

"The Local Two Three Five, lady," he says.

"Ah," she says. "The Hare."

"No, lady, I'd never – "

"Please," says Ysabel.

"Just a fucking minute," says Jo.

"You know, Thomas," says Ysabel, "it would be so much easier if you'd challenge her to a duel." His laugh's more of a hiccup. "Ysabel," says Jo, sharply. Ysabel's smiling. "She can't fight, you know. Has to read about it in books. Defeat her, and all her offices are forfeit. There'd be no impediment to my attendance."

"This is *way* past being funny," says Jo.

"You are a glory to behold, lady," says Twice Thomas, "but my hand's not fit for the likes of yours."

"Oh, well said," says Ysabel. "You see, Jo, *he* knows his place."

"I should just let you go," says Jo. "Fart off where the fuck ever. Get kidnapped again. I'd be done with you."

"All right," says Ysabel, and she steps up to Twice Thomas and takes his arm.

"Oh, fuck me," says Jo.

"Um," says the librarian. "The, uh, they're due back the twenty-sixth."

"Right," says Jo. She scoops up the stack of books. "I'll write it down somewhere." Jo heads off after Ysabel marching away, Twice Thomas stumbling at her side, mouth slack eyes wide at the sight of her hands tucked in the crook of his elbow.

Jo leans back against the long table lost under haphazard stacks of books and piles of paper, wincing, rubbing her hip. "You should sit," says Ysabel, leaning forward in the office chair to put her hand on Jo's. Jo shakes her head. "If I'm gonna be a knight," says says, "I should get used to that whole chivalry thing, right?" The poster on the wall behind her says Gorboduc – Ferrex and Porrex.

"Don't be an ass," says Ysabel, squeezing Jo's hand, sitting back in the chair. The door to the office opens. Vincent's there in the doorway, the cable running along his prosthetic jerking, the hook snapping open and shut, open and shut. "Well?" he says.

"I need to learn how to fight with a sword," says Jo.

"Why come to me?"

"Because you know why I need to learn how to fight with a sword."

Vincent snorts.

"Mr. Erne," says Ysabel.

"Highness," he says, "I'd never question your judgment, but – "

"Good," says Ysabel.

His hook snaps one last time. "Where's the épée, girl. That piece of shit I gave you." Jo's stooping to pick up the long thin bundle, undoing the rubber bands, unwinding the towels. Careful with her left hand, the palm gone red and raw. "Were you trying to keep it dry?"

"Out of sight," says Jo. "Cops'd jack me for a butter knife in my back pocket."

Vincent snorts again. "What good is this gonna do you? I told you. You get in a fight with these people, you lose."

"I've done pretty well so far."

"Have you," says Vincent. "You lose with a sword in your hand, you die."

"I know." Jo balances the sheathed sword tip 2on the duct-taped toe of her shoe the loose hilt with its dull and battered bell lightly in one hand. The other, raw, distractedly rubs her chest, there where her jacket's parted over a T-shirt that says Farmers and Mechanics Bank. "But they're making me one."

"They are," says Vincent, flatly. His hand held open at his side, his thin sweater hanging loosely from his shoulders.

"Jo Maguire is to be made a knight," says Ysabel, leaning back and crossing her stockinged legs, primly careful of her short tweed skirt.

Vincent steps back, his hand on the doorknob. "Come with me," he says. He nods at the épée. "Bring that."

Lights flicker to life in the wide deep room, the far end still lost in shadows. Practice swords laid in a serried row on the floor. Vincent stoops to pick one up. "You arrive promptly at eleven o'clock in the morning for an hour or two of instruction, depending on my schedule. Monday through Friday." Jo, limping, pulls her jacket off, lets it drop to the floor. "You pay me two hundred dollars a month. In advance."

"Is *that* how to change your mind," says Jo, drawing her sword.

"That's less than ten dollars an hour for me," says Vincent. "For private instruction. Not exactly lining my wallet." He slashes the air once, twice, turns to face Jo. Ysabel's lowering herself to the floor, her back to the mirrors. "Has to cost you something, girl. So you aren't ever tempted to fuck off and not come in one fine eleven o'clock. Money spent tends to focus the attention."

"How long does it take?" says Jo. She's turned her right foot toward him, looking at him over her right shoulder. The tip of her sword touching an x of blue masking tape stuck to the floor.

"How long?"

"To learn how to fight with a sword. The Vincent Erne way. How many months do I have to focus my attention with two hundred bucks?"

"To learn?" He smiles, a sour twist in his salt-and-pepper Van Dyke. "I'll teach you everything you need to know tonight. Four simple lessons. The rest is practice. We'll know in six months how good you'll ever be."

"Okay," says Jo, lifting her blade, settling herself, knees bent a little. Her left arm hitched up and back, crooked over, her left hand dangling over her shoulder. "Four lessons. First is which end to hold it by, right?"

"No, girl," says Vincent. "That's a joke, for theatre students who aren't learning how to fight. First lesson's a question."

"A question?"

"A question. Where are you, girl?"

The basement room is brightly lit. A felt banner hangs on the back wall, an abstract blob of a dove, green leaves, a rainbow hanging over a folding table laden with a coffee urn, paper cups, corrugated paper jackets, packets of sugar and non-dairy creamer, a plate of crumbs and a couple of donuts. A baby grand piano on giant casters under a quilted brown cloth. A rack piled high with folded chairs, more chairs unfolded in a rough circle, men and women standing around them and beside them, coveralls in blue and green, overalls and dungarees, denim jackets, meshback caps in hands. Jo over by the coffee urn in army green, beside her pink-haired Ray in his black leather jacket. In the center of it all stands Ysabel next to a very small woman wearing a pink T-shirt that says Choose a Job. The very small woman holds a tarnished metal tray. On the tray a dozen or more small clear glasses. In each glass glimmering in the bright light a pinch of golden dust.

He stands at the head of the low flight of stairs leading into the room, a blue-black cloak thrown back from his shoulders, his arms and head bare, his dark hair shot through with white, flopping about his eyes and ears, his lean face roughened by a half-grown grey-black beard. His cuirass milky white and edged with silver, though it is shadowed with dents, and the edging pitted. His right hand rests on the hilt of a long knife stuck through a belt of greenish silver links. Shining around his neck a polished silver torc.

"I do not know you, knight," says the very small woman. Her face is worn, her cheeks round and ruddy. She wears small round spectacles with a thin chain that droops about her neck and her yellow-white hair's pulled back in a tight bun. "But you must know this is hallowed ground, made sacral by their long use and habit. There'll be no fighting here."

"And if I were to draw my blade?" He pulls the knife from its sheath. "The one you'd call, who'd see I keep the peace, it's *her* bidding I'm about. Take one more step, Gallowglas, and I let loose my arm. People *will* get cut."

Jo hasn't moved. Her fists are clenched.

"I know you," says Ysabel, stepping away from the very small woman, her long patched denim skirt sweeping the floor. "And I can tell you, Dagger, neither you nor her – "

He comes down in a rush then, a sudden squall of chairs scraping, men and women stepping back away as Jo steps up between Ysabel and the knight stopped still at the bottom of the stairs. His hand up knife reversed in his fist blade flat back against his forearm. "Not any more," he says, and he spits. "Just Sidney now, plain Sidney. Your mother's seen handily to *that.*"

A SHELL OF GLOSSY WHITE
A FRANK AND OPEN EXCHANGE – RABBITS IN THEIR DEN

A SHELL OF GLOSSY WHITE paint flecking from the doorframe Becker's leaning against. He picks at it crackling under his nails. The door opens slightly, Guthrie peering around the edge. Becker clears his throat. Guthrie jumps. "Sorry," says Becker.

"Fuck," says Guthrie, opening the door. His black T-shirt says Mai Pastede Hed in white letters. A guitar strums through cheap speakers from somewhere further in. I would like another way to breathe, sings a girl over the guitar. Keep my eyes wide open in my sleep. 'Cause when I'm underwater, you keep me under glass...

"You haven't showed up in almost a week," says Becker.

"To work," says Guthrie.

"Yeah."

"You're here about work."

"Yeah," says Becker.

"You getting paid for this? Come to my place and wake me up for, for uh, to what exactly?"

"You haven't showed up. You quit? Did you find something else?

"Because, I mean, you don't show up at Burger King, the manager doesn't come to your place and ask, you know, what's up, where you been." Becker says "Manager at Burger King isn't your friend," as Guthrie's saying "They just fire your ass. And Tartt never would have showed up here or anything."

"Tartt wasn't your friend either. You *want* me to fire you? *Did* you find something else? Because I'm seriously covering your ass on this."

"I didn't ask you to – "

"Dammit, Guthrie!" Becker runs a hand through what little of his hair is left. "Just shut up a minute, okay?"

"What is it," says Guthrie.

Becker's looking up at the flaking ceiling. "You remember those two guys. That you, that you wanted to talk to me about. That one time. And we never, I mean, the two guys," but Guthrie's shaking his head. "We did," he's saying. "You forgot."

"Forgot," says Becker. "Did one of them have a mustache? Long, and, uh, grey, and – "

"No," says Guthrie. A pale hand a sleeve the color of oatmeal snakes around his waist. "No mustache." A confetti-colored cap over two eyes bright and blue smiling as she stretches up bare feet tiptoed to lick at Guthrie's ear. "Come back," she says, and kisses his cheek. "Come back." Her legs bare beneath the ragged hem of her sweater. Over the cheap speakers a woman's singing I'm in a backless dress in a pastel ward that's shining, think I want you still, but it may be pills at work. She sees Becker then, and her blue eyes corner under pinched brows. Still pressed against Guthrie she lifts an arm across the doorway two fingers pointing to just so touch his nose. Becker jolts back.

"You shouldn't be here," she says.

"The hell?" says Becker, rubbing his nose.

"Didn't anyone tell you? You'll spoil it all!" She steps out into the hallway.

"Um," says Guthrie, "hey – "

"We have to get him where he's supposed to be," she says.

"I mean," says Guthrie, "um, *pants* – "

"No *time,*" she snaps, and she stomps a foot clomp ringing from the heel of a worn workboot, laces undone, tongue lolling, spinning about shimmying her hips hands smoothing a fall of orange pleats, a heavy corduroy skit. "And you're already *wearing* pants!" She stomps her other foot flatly flop a dirty green and yellow running shoe. "We have to go now." And turning again she clomp-flops down the hall.

"What," says Becker, staring after her, "just happened?"

The woman in the pink T-shirt beams up at them through her small round glasses. "I can't say, highness. A tremendous honor."

"Yes," says Ysabel. "And you are..?"

"Nell," she says, bowing her head slightly, "the Soames. Welcome, lady."

"And this is," says Ysabel, turning as Jo says, "Excuse me," and walks away across the basement toward the coffee urn, there on the table in the back.

"That was Jo," says Ysabel behind her. "My Gallowglas."

The man standing by the coffee urn straightens, lifting a paper cup. His hair's a shock of pink and orange. "Hey," says Jo. "It's Ray, right?" His paper cup stops halfway between the table and his quirked mouth under goggling blue eyes. "I'd like to think," he says, "I'd've noticed if I'd seen you here before."

"No, from the Zoobomb. Roland's friend."

"Friend?" he says, and his cup salutes her. "That's, that's good. About time he got one of those."

"He said *you* were a friend of his."

"Did he." Ray lifts the cup, lowers it again. His smile's gone apologetic. "I *know* him. Roland doesn't have any friends."

Jo picks up a cup of her own. "He also said you weren't like him."

"Well, I *do* have a couple of friends..." His cup floats back towards his lips again. "Hey, Sproat," he says.

"Hey," says the little man with the extraordinarily large nose, pouring himself a cup of coffee.

"I mean," says Jo, "you're not, you're not one of his people. You're not from wherever it is they're from."

"The West Hills?"

"Ha. You're like me, is what I mean."

He cocks an eyebrow over one of those bulging eyes. "I hope I'd've noticed *that,* too."

"I know why *I'm* here, is what I'm getting at," says Jo, twisting the spigot on the urn, filling her cup. "Because of *her.* Why're you here?"

"Her?" says Ray. Ysabel's stooped to listen to the Soames, who's ticking points on the palm of her hand. "Really? Huh." His cup makes it this time. He sips. One of those eyes screws shut and his lips pucker. He fishes in a pocket of his leather jacket, pulling out a green glass bottle with a silver cap. "Is that why you're being such a dick?"

"What?" says Jo.

"The coffee," says Ray, "not that it's any of your business." He pours a slug of something colorless into his coffee. "Was that too rough? 'Dick'? If that was too rough – no, that's weaselly. It *was* too rough. So I apologize. No ifs."

"The coffee?" says Jo. "I don't – "

"It's free," says Ray. "To answer your question. Shitty, but free. And *this* is free, this meeting, as in speech, as in beer. So again. I'm sorry. But you're the one who leaped in demanding answers."

"I didn't – "

"You did a lousy job of hiding how badly you wanted me to justify myself."

"Yeah?" says Jo, her voice gone low and fast and quiet. "Well I got dragged here on *her* whim with some guy I never met and I don't know what's going on and usually, I go places with her, usually, I end up on a horse or getting assaulted or, or I've been *stabbed,* and here you are that I've actually met once before, and maybe you come here every night, I don't fucking know, but maybe you can *tell* me something so yeah, I'm gonna ask questions." Her hand a fist on the table by her discarded cup.

"Every month," says Ray. "I mean, *I* haven't. Just twice. But the first Wednesday of every month, Saint Patrick's under the bridge. We'd better get chairs." He heads over to a couple of empty chairs in the ring that's filling up, chairs about them squawking on the linoleum floor as they're pulled out, pushed back, settled here and there, the men and women taking their seats, coveralls, overalls, dungarees, denim and flannel and chambray, yellow-brown boots and white-wrinkled black boots, meshback caps in their hands. "See, Open Mike," says Ray, leaning over to murmur in Jo's ear.

"Open Mike?" says Jo. A long and lanky man in a black T-shirt's clapping Twice Thomas on the shoulder.

"He's about to corral everybody, all the stragglers. Usually about twenty, maybe two dozen. Although I should say that when I say twice what I mean is this is my second time here, so I should say more like one and a third or maybe a fifth or so, and you should take all this with a grain of salt. But next..." He leans closer, those eyes bulging over a smile tucked into the corners of his mouth. "What," says Jo.

"Biscuit's about to play the piano."

A man in brown coveralls has lifted the keyboard lid of the baby grand piano and with his left hand plays a low thick chord once, then rapidly one two three, letting that last beat hang in the air a moment before snapping the lid closed and dropping the edge of the quilted dust cover back over it. They're all standing, Ray too, and after a moment Jo, and they're humming that chord from the piano, and the Soames standing there by Ysabel still sitting alone of all of them, the Soames throws wide her arms and opens her mouth to sing "Arise," and they all join in, "Arise, ye workers from your slumbers, arise ye prisoners of want! For reason in revolt now thunders, and at last we end the age of cant!"

"And then they sing!" says Ray in Jo's ear.

"So comrades, come rally," they're singing, "For the struggle carries on! The Internationale unites the world in song!"

"Brothers and sisters," says the Soames, as the echoes of the last chord of the chorus dies away, faintly ringing the strings in the closed-up baby grand. "I call this meeting of the Order of American Mechanicals United, Local Two Three Five, to order."

"I'm in your practice hall, your dojo, whatever the fuck," says Jo.

"Where *are* you, girl?" says Vincent.

Jo's brow crinkles. "Second floor? Park and Oak? Northwest corner. In, uh, in Southwest, I mean downtown. Which is whatsisname's. The Count's. No, wait – it's open. Unclaimed. Right?" Ysabel eyes closed smiles, her head resting back against the mirror.

"Where are you?" Vincent steps his left foot forward hips and shoulders swiveling head still locked his eyes on Jo. His prosthetic crooked up before him right arm loose at his side, hand canted, sword tilted up, back, away.

"Here?" says Jo, settling her knees, wincing. "Here. Standing here. In front of you."

"Where's your *feet*, girl?"

"Under my shoulders."

"Where's your shoulders?"

"Where I left them," she growls. "Edge-on. To you."

"Your hands?" he says, but she's already saying "My left hand's up and back like a queer-ass dandy pirate to balance a lunge and it itches like a motherfucker. My right hand's up, wrist in *seconde*."

"You've been reading," says Vincent. "Who? What? Naldi? Talhoffer? The Abbé?" His head up, back, his sword twitching.

"I don't know," says Jo. "I just got some books from the – "

"Forget it," says Vincent, snapping his hook. "Throw 'em away."

"I left them in Twice Tom's truck. Probably never see them again."

"Four lessons, girl! Then practice. I don't want anything else cluttering your pretty little head."

"Four," sneers Jo. "And number one's I tell you where I am."

"Number one is *knowing* where you are, girl." Vincent steps back, his left foot in line with his right. Lifts his blade to point at her. "Know it in your bones, without doubt, without fumbling for words to describe it. Know where you are. Without that, you've got nothing."

"And I wouldn't want to walk into a room like that," says Jo.

Another twist in his Van Dyke. "Lesson two," he says.

"Another question?"

"Another question. Where am I?"

"Then her sister finished us off."

She stands at the head of the low flight of stairs leading into the room, the folds of her blue-black cloak parted just over a long gown of watery mail marred by shadowy blooms of rust and here and there some broken unsprung links. On her head a plain round metal cap from which her hair does not escape. Shining around her neck a polished silver torc. "Be about it quickly, Sidney, that we might more quickly take our leave."

"Can't I take a moment instead, Linesse? To savor this strange new experience?" He looks back and forth along the ragged arc of men and women standing before him, the knife still in his hand, his hand before his face. "I've never bearded rabbits in their den."

"It's there they are most dangerous," says Linesse, but he's stepping further into the room. Jo draws herself up there between Sidney and Ysabel, her eyes wide, her breath shallow. He licks his lips. Nell looks up at Ysabel through her spectacles. Open Mike behind them squeezes his hands into fists but does not lift them.

"Well, Plain Sidney?" says Nell then. "What is her bidding? What would the Cailleach with the likes of us?"

"With you?" says Sidney. "Nothing, with you. You have this once a choice: stand up, fall back. As you like."

"We stand with the Bride," says Twice Thomas, there by Open Mike.

"Will you?" Sidney's laugh's a snapped-off syllable. "Even though she's dallied with the Axe, and sullied the gift she's meant to give the King when he returns? Put down your fists. She's in no danger. Our mistress doesn't care what lips she's kissed, though it pleases me, to use her as our bait. No," and he moves his hand then, slowly, pointing the hilt of his knife at Jo, "it's her bulldog we're about – who's killed our lady's boar, who's made her laugh most cruelly. Who has no place at her sister's court, and yet."

Ysabel says, "Dagger – Sidney – " and with a roar he steps to the right to pass Jo who rushes to block him but his next step's left, pivoting around her the hilt of his knife swinging to catch the side of Ysabel's head. Twice Thomas rushes to catch her as Jo yelling grabs Sidney's cloak hauling him back "You fucking mother-fucker" as he's stumbling bellowing "Gallowglas!" and she slaps a hand on his mailed shoulder. There is a sudden hiss. Jo screams. The tarnished metal ghosted with dew about the hand she jerks away, a ripping sound, the flesh of her palm and fingers red.

Sidney turns, slowly. Twice Thomas on his knees by Ysabel on her side her hands to her face, Open Mike over them both, fists ready. Jo stumbling back falling to the ground cradling her hand. Nell glasses clinking on the tray she hasn't put down. "It's not about *fighting* you, girl," says Sidney, but he's looking now at Nell, at the trembling tray. "It's about making you *watch.*" And then, to himself, "This farce," he says. "You all deserve what's coming."

Linesse at the head of the stairs shakes her head. "Sidney!" she cries, an admonishment.

He whips his knife around and across a short chopping swing that slams the flat of his blade among those glasses, scattering them, driving the tray from Nell's hands. A golden glittering cloud explodes around them. His other hand's aloft, holding a bicycle bell. He thumbs it, twice, chiming sharp and clear. *"You all de-serve what's coming!"* He pushes his way out of the crowd, up the stairs after the swirl of Linesse's cloak. The glittering cloud's col-lapsing, settling on the tiled floor, the shards of glass, their boots and shoes, on Ysabel a-sprawl, on Thomas's knees, his sheltering hands. Then the lights go out, and they all begin to holler at once.

"TURN UP THERE" – SUCH STEEP FREIGHT
THE PINCH OF THE TIMES – ONE HELL OF A SHINER

"TURN UP THERE," says Guthrie from the back seat.

"It's going the wrong way," says Becker behind the wheel. A flock of cellos scrapes and squalls from the stereo.

"It's on Nineteenth!"

"Which is one-way the wrong way. I'm going to go up and double back. If it's even there."

"It's there," says Guthrie, as beside him in the back seat the woman in the confetti-colored cap says "It's under the bridge. Right where it touches down." Guthrie's holding one of her hands in both of his. "I swear it's on Nineteenth," says Guthrie. "You go up too far, you'll have to come down Twenty-third, which, I mean, fuck."

"It's been there for over a hundred years," she says. "The bridge is no older than you are. They built it to close the circle but it was too late."

"You'll end up having to double back through all those, uh, parking lots. Where that company is."

"You've been there before?" says Becker. "What's the cross street? Which letter? R? S? U? What the hell is U, anyway? Is there a U?"

"I don't know," says Guthrie. "Upshur," says the woman in the confetti-colored cap. "Hurry. Hurry!"

"What's the deal with that?" says Becker, cranking the car through a quick right turn against a red light. "What is it I'm gonna spoil, anyway?" The cellos thundering now. Becker snaps the stereo off. "Huh?" She doesn't say anything. "Guthrie. What's her deal?"

"You know," says Guthrie. He's looking down at her hand in his. "She sees things, sometimes. I think sometimes that includes, you know. The future."

"The future," says Becker, stopping for a stop sign. "*This* is why you haven't been coming to work?"

"You *never* believe me," mutters Guthrie.

"Don't stop!" cries the woman. "What's wrong? Go! Go!"

"Why?" roars Becker, glaring at them through the rear-view mirror. "What's going on? Who the fuck are you, and *what* are you doing to Guthrie?"

"You – don't?" says the woman.

"He forgets," says Guthrie. "He's forgotten again."

"Forgotten what?" Becker snaps around, eyes ugly, mouth screwed tight. The woman trembles under her confetti-colored cap. "What am I forgetting? *What?*"

"Go," says Guthrie. "You'll see."

Growling Becker jerks the car into gear jolting forward into the intersection lurching to a stop as something thump-rumbles over the hood, a figure white in the streetlights.

"Shit," says Becker. "Oh, fuck me."

The woman in the confetti-colored cap screams.

"Shut up!" says Becker. "Shut her up." He climbs out of the little red hatchback. There's a bicycle on its side rear wheel canted up spinning clicking loudly, a white bicycle, handlebars twisted, flowers scattered on the pavement, over to the side someone face down, grey hoodie and grimy white jeans and black sneakers still. "Hey," says Becker. "Hey. You okay?" He steps toward the body slowly, hands held up before him. "You're not dead. Please don't be dead." Stooping over the body, reaching down for the hood. "Honestly please."

"You're far too late, my friend."

Becker looks up. Walking toward him across the intersection a big man in a dark blue suit. To either side of his mouth droop mustaches, long and grey. Behind him off to the right there above the trees behind a row of houses the swooping curves of onramps, the great towering arch of the bridge hazy in the dimming blue and gold and rose, the red-roofed tower of a church.

"Pyrocles?" says Becker.

The body at his feet scuttle-rolls away hands and feet scrabbling on pavement swarming over the bicycle hauling it upright as Pyrocles leaping forward hands up over his head swinging down a greatsword cracking the pavement striking sparks where the bicycle'd been and Becker stumbling back loses his balance falls on his ass oofing out his breath. Pyrocles takes a long lunging step swinging the sword sideways skimming the hood of the car to slice through the grey hoodie collapsing into a twist of rag of nothing at all as the bicycle riderless falls again to the pavement with a clatter and a clacking thump.

Pyrocles straightens. Wipes his hands on his thighs. "Need a hand?" he says.

"I *hit* that guy," says Becker, climbing slowly to his feet. "Where did he go? What just happened?" Pyrocles raps on the windshield of the car. "Didn't you just have a sword? Hey! Are you listening to me?" Guthrie's opened the car door, craning his head up to peer out over it.

"We must hurry," says Pyrocles. "They won't follow us into a church. There's one a few blocks that way."

"That's where we were headed," says Guthrie.

"We're not going anywhere," says Becker. "We've got to call the cops or something."

"The police can't help us," says Pyrocles. Guthrie's helping the woman in the confetti-colored cap out of the back seat.

"I can't just leave my car," says Becker.

"That car," says Pyrocles, "will kill the next person to drive it. Quickly! They never travel alone." He strides away down the darkening street, followed quickly by Guthrie hand-in-hand with the woman in the confetti-colored cap.

"Would someone," says Becker, staring after them, "please tell me what just happened?"

They're sitting again, the twenty or twenty-four of them, Ysabel feet tucked up asprawl across two folding chairs by the Soames, Twice Thomas behind them, his cap resting on his knee. Across the circle Jo sits by Ray, who's leaning over to murmur something in her ear. Open Mike stands in the center of the circle, arms wide, saying "With all due respect – "

"Seven days and a day, Brother Mike," says an old man with a big white beard, an American eagle embroidered on the back of his worn denim jacket.

"With all *due* respect, Brother Templemass," says Open Mike. "I'm well aware of our terms." He looks about the circle, his thin brows drawn together in a single line. "You've all heard Sister Jenny's report. Our reserves were depleted by the clean-up and repair of the mall. His payment for that bill was almost enough to cover the subsequent repairs to the freeway in Sullivan's Gulch. Until he covers *that,* brothers and sisters, we're tapped. I only ask that you look to the future."

"I don't like the future after we've needlessly antagonized the Duke," says a sharp-chinned woman in grey coveralls that say Jenny Rye over the left breast.

"How can even he pay such steep freight twice in a month?" says a small-featured man with fox-red tufted hair and a goatish beard.

"Seven days and a day," says the Soames. "We press the issue Sunday morning, not before. Unless – " she inclines her head, bright light sliding up the lenses of her spectacles. "Is Brother Michael's proposal seconded? That the Local seek restitution immediately from the Duke, for the repair of the freeway in Sullivan's Gulch?"

"Let me get this straight," murmurs Jo, leaning over Ray's shoulder. "They *fixed* the fucking freeway?"

"I guess so," he says.

"When?"

"I don't know."

"Because I was *there*. It was totaled."

"But it's fine now, right?"

"With that," the Soames is saying, as Open Mike takes his seat, "unfinished business is concluded. I should like to introduce our guest this evening, who has done us an incalculable honor by attending on such short notice." Jo snorts. "Our Princess, the intended Bride of the King Come Back." A rustle sweeps the room as caps are removed, heads bowed, hands placed palm down on knees. The Soames still standing says, "I've asked her to tell us of a matter that bears directly on Brother Michael's concerns. In a word, lady," turning then to speak directly to Ysabel sitting upright now, legs crossed under that voluminous denim skirt, "the Apportionment. It has been rather lean of late."

And then the Soames sits.

Ray, catching Jo's eye, hikes a brow, shrugs his mouth.

Ysabel uncrosses her legs, sits forward as if to stand, stops. Then with a deep breath pushes herself to her feet. "Thank you, Nell," she says. "This is all something of a surprise to me. I'm afraid," and then she shakes her head a little, to herself. "I can tell you," she says, "that when the King comes back, and I am sat as his Queen, you will find in me a true and constant friend."

For a moment nothing is said.

"Thank you, lady," says the Soames, "but might you speak to your mother, and tell her of what you've heard here tonight?"

Ysabel starts to say something, but does not. Her hands folded one wrapped in the other. "No," she says. "My mother knows your plight, as she knows everything that happens in her city. If your portions are lean, it is because times are lean. You've seen it yourselves – a Duke's as pinched as a charman – "

There's grumbles at that, groans. "Oh I doubt it," someone mutters. Rustling, shifting. "I," Ysabel's saying, "I don't, you must understand." The Soames gets to her feet. Ray's hand is on Jo's arm. "Brothers and sisters," says the Soames, pleading.

"Settle down!" booms Open Mike.

"I am not yet Queen," says Ysabel as the room quiets. "I am not my mother." She lifts her hands to her face, fingers fencing her mouth, and her eyes closed she lets out the breath she's been holding and lets her hands drift back down before her, once more folded together. "I can't do anything about the Apportionment, not now, not yet. But I can do *this.*" One hand unclasped slips into the pocket of her skirt to pull out a small plastic baggie, swollen with gold dust.

"What is she," says Jo.

"This," says Ysabel, "is the last of my reserves. Times are what they are. But I know the, the importance of the work you do."

"Oh," says Ray.

"And so, because I am, and will be, your friend."

"Ysabel," says Jo, but quietly.

"I offer it freely to you."

"Oh, wow," says Ray, and chairs scrape, shoes squeak, the room climbs to its feet, surges toward Ysabel, arms reach out, some push away, some are pushed, and Jo's shoving her way through the middle between Biscuit and a kid in a grey T-shirt. "Hey!" calls Ray, lost in the hubbub of thanks and pleas and cries of "Lady! O, lady!" Ysabel's stepping back from them, eyes wide, and stepping back again, hemmed in by the piano, the baggie in both hands up over her head. The Soames beside her, arms wide, "Brothers and sisters!" she cries, but they're reaching over her head. "Hey!" cries Jo, in the thick of it, "Gallowglas here! I'm the fucking Gallowglas coming through!"

"*Animals!*" bellows Twice Thomas, and suddenly it's still again.

"Little better than rude beasts!" he says.

"Tommy Tom," says someone, and "Hey, I" says someone, and "Shut up" says someone else. Twice Thomas working his way along the front of the crowd says "That's what they say about us. That's *why,* they say, they must portion it out. To each his own, they say, but on *their* terms, and in their *own* sweet time, and if they take the lion's share for their troubles, who are we to complain?" He's standing by Open Mike now, before Ysabel and the Soames. "So a Duke will never feel the pinch the way we do. That's no excuse to *prove them right.*"

"Your gift," says the Soames, catching her breath, "is very generous, lady."

"I hadn't," says Ysabel, leaning close to her, "I didn't plan on this, I don't have scales or little bags or – "

"There's glasses and measuring spoons in the kitchen," says the Soames. "Brother Michael, if you'd be so kind?"

Jo doesn't say anything in response. She straightens her right arm wrist rolling clockwise the épée in her hand a line pointing shoulder to tip at Vincent's chest. He nods and without unlocking his eyes from hers he steps his left foot out to the side his weight shifting right foot following and again. The tip of her blade smoothly follows. His left foot crosses behind his right swiftly doubling the step and twice more quickly now, his prosthetic still cocked between them, his sword still down and away. Her blade-tip swinging to follow she's stepping her left foot back to the right her shoulders swinging to stay edge-on. "What else," says Vincent.

"What else?"

"What else is here?" He lowers his left arm, relaxing his right arm, shoulders lifting and settling, his feet planted. "It's not just me, girl. There's the light." His left arm gesturing, harsh light glinting from the hook. "The shadows off to the side. The mirror. Those swords by the door behind you, ready to trip you on your ass. There's a lot in this room besides me."

"Okay," says Jo, her arm bent again, her épée back in its guarded angle, "okay. Number two is where's everything that isn't me. Got it."

"You're sure," says Vincent.

"Yeah," says Jo. "On to number three."

"So you're in a hurry," says Vincent. "Okay."

"Wait – " says Jo, but he's taking three quick loping steps to plant himself before Ysabel hitching her feet back out of his way, hiking herself up, back against the mirror. His left arm's up between them hook snapping once turning his head toward Jo his blade coming up knees settling there between Jo and Ysabel, and his smile is now quite clear and sharp. "Well?" he says. "Now what?"

"Ysabel!"

On the floor on her side in the dark her left hand held close in her right, Jo's worming around tucking as a boot crashes down next to her head as someone else trips crashing over her legs.

"Jo!"

On the floor on her knees her face in her hands Ysabel's crying out to the floor unseen, Twice Thomas huddled over her his cap long gone, gold glittering the backs of his hands. The darkness sparked by flickering spindrift swirling in the wake of scooping hands pinching fingers tumbling legs to limn shirt-creases and pant-cuffs, chair-backs and upended chair-legs, fingertips, lips, the edge of a face. "Jo!" she cries again, and "Jo!" as all about them ring sobs that billow atomies of gold, moans and cries of "No, oh no!" and "Lady, please!" and "The owr! Save the owr!" In the midst of it all stands the Soames stock still, her hands empty before her, at her feet the bent tray, the litter of broken gold-shot glass.

A click, a buzzing hum, lights flash to life in the ceiling here and there, the basement once more pinned beneath that harsh white light that silences them all. They've stopped where they are, then slowly they turn, slowly look about. Biscuit rubbing his eyes with the heels of his hands, his fingertips gleaming. Sproat curled into a ball in a litter of fallen chairs, Rye Jenny crouched beside him, her fingers in his glittering hair. Jo's hunched over an upright chair by Ysabel, on her feet, looking up to the head of the low flight of stairs leading into the room.

"Anvil," she says. "Welcome." Her voice flat and calm, her face expressionless. Her eye swollen red and purpling, a red weal down her cheek.

"Lady," says Pyrocles. "You're hurt." Behind him Becker, panting, behind him Guthrie and the woman in the confetti-colored cap.

"Sidney," she says. "The former Dagger."

"He's shown his face," says Pyrocles, coming down the stairs, reaching into an inner pocket of his suit jacket.

"He's turned his coat," says Ysabel. "Gone over to my mother's sister, and the Helm with him."

"They're the ones who've called the ghost bikes," says Pyrocles. "The church is surrounded." He's pulled out a small plastic baggie, a thimbleful of gold dust. "We only just made it." He stoops to peer at her face, working the baggie open with his fingers, but she shakes her head. "Jo's hand," she says. "She touched him."

Jo's holding her left hand tightly in her right, the skin of it tightly swollen, red, blotched here and there with black blisters. "My motherfucking Christ but he was cold," she gasps.

"Please," says Ysabel to Pyrocles, cupping her hands together. He tips the dust into her hands. "I do not know that it will suffice," he says.

She folds her hands together and lifts them to her lips, whispering something eyes closed into the steepled hollow of her fingers.

She sinks to her knees by Jo. "Hold still," she says. She opens hands over Jo's palm, and Jo hisses. She takes Jo's hand between hers, rubbing the dust into the flesh. Jo's shoulders jerk. She bends over Jo's hand and presses the palm to her lips as her heavy black hair slides from her shoulders to curtain the kiss. Jo lifts her head face clenched gasping then slowly, slowly relaxing, her breath slowing, deepening.

Ysabel straightens, brushing dust from her lips. "It wasn't enough," she says. "It'll sting, for a few days yet."

"And you've got one hell of a shiner," says Jo.

"I'll be all right," says Ysabel, and then, with an uncertain little laugh, "I can't have a one-handed knight."

"We are so sorry, lady," says the Soames. "We should never have put you in such danger." They stand together now, before the folding table laden with the coffee urn, beneath the banner with the dove, the leaves, the rainbow. Hands at their sides, folded together, clasped behind their backs. Caps on heads. "We must get you out as quickly as possible."

"Don't be foolish," says Pyrocles. "What do you mean to do? Batter your way through the cordon of ghosts? Touch one with anything but a weapon and not even your dust would be left."

"How many are there?" says Open Mike.

"Dozens!" says Guthrie, as Becker says "Ten or so."

"Eleven," says Pyrocles.

"So call for help!" says Open Mike. "A *handful* of knights could scatter them in minutes!"

"That's what they want," says the Soames. "Certainly, they could be scattered. But one or more knights would die."

"That's what they're *for,*" mutters Open Mike, as Jo's saying, "And it'd be my fault. Again. This touching thing," she says to Pyrocles, wincing as she opens and closes her hand. "Is that for everybody? Or is there a gallowglas exemption?"

"You might feel a chill," says Pyrocles.

"All right. And there's three of us here, now – "

"Four," calls Ray, sitting in a chair over by the piano.

"It would not suffice, Gallowglas," says Pyrocles. "Even if you locked arms to shield her with your bodies, they'd ride into you, knock you down, touch her. I could perhaps surprise them, attacking from inside their cordon – if I cut enough of them down – "

"There's another way," says Ray. "Bust them up without knights. Without putting any of you in danger. This church," he says, looking up at the low ceiling, "is practically smack dab under the biggest bridge in town."

"Oh!" says the woman in the confetti-colored cap.

"She's got a clue," says Ray. "What is it, folks, that lives under bridges? In fairy tales?"

THE DOORS KICKED OPEN – SIDNEY RESTS – MAYBE BLUE
A DISPUTE OVER LOSS

JO KICKS OPEN THE DOORS and runs through them onto the porch down the stairs Ray after her. Becker catches the door, watches through it as they run down the street between the boles of the great concrete pillars holding the onramps above them.

From away behind the church another crash of metal. "Back door," says Becker, and he lets the front door close.

In the basement they're mostly sitting again. Open Mike's pacing by the piano. Ysabel's turned sideways in her chair, her blackened eye faced away off toward the rack piled high with folding chairs. Beside her the Soames her shoulders to Ysabel's back, her spectacles in one hand, squeezes the bridge of her nose. "I should be out there!" cries Open Mike, pounding the quilted piano with a balled-up fist.

Twice Thomas stands and walks across the ragged arc of chairs and men and women, his cap on his head, hands cupped carefully before him. He drops heavily to one knee before Ysabel. "Lady," he says. "I would never spurn so rich a gift, but I must do something to – "

"It's spoiled," she snaps. "Gone dead. Wrung out. No better than the lint in your pocket, rabbit."

He stands then, turns, and walks away, clapping the dust from his hands.

"He was wrong," says the woman in the confetti-colored cap. She's squatting on a chair back by the coffee urn, legs folded under her orange skirt, nibbling on a donut.

"Who was what now?" says Guthrie, worrying at a thumbnail with his teeth.

"When he said there were four. There's only three from the track."

Becker's coming down the low flight of stairs. "They're off," he says. "Why isn't he back inside yet?"

"He's *enjoying* himself!" cries Open Mike, banging the piano again.

"Okay," says Becker, "where's the back door?"

Hands shoot up to point out the door behind the rack piled high with folding chairs. "Back there" says Templemass and "There's some stairs back there" says a woman in white coveralls and "Up those stairs" says Rye Jenny. "I'll show you!" says Open Mike.

"Brother Michael," says the Soames. "I thought we were to leave this to the knights."

"I must do *something!*" cries Open Mike, pounding his fist against his open palm.

"It's what they're for," says the Soames.

"I'll go with you," says Ysabel standing, walking over to Becker. "It's okay," she turns to say to the Soames, her smile hampered by the welt on her cheek. "He's my boss. And I promise I'll stay inside the church."

They're all staring at Becker. "Um," he says. "I manage a phone bank. She works there with Jo."

"I've even been given a *paycheck,*" says Ysabel, and she takes Becker's arm and walks with him toward the door behind the rack piled high with folding chairs, her denim skirts brushing the dusty floor.

In the stairwell Becker says, "So you're a Princess."

"Yes," says Ysabel.

"And Jo's your, uh, whatsit."

"Gallowglas."

"Because I keep forgetting, see."

"That happens."

"Not to Jo."

"Perhaps I don't let her forget," says Ysabel.

"Don't tell me you're paying attention to Guthrie, too."

"Some of you find it easier this way."

Becker at the top of the stairs his hand on the doorknob turns to face her. "Am I gonna remember this at all? Or tomorrow am I gonna wake up, all this, it won't even be a dream, like I shouldn't've eaten those armadillo eggs I never had."

"Open the door," says Ysabel, and he does.

The alley outside runs along the back of the church, paved with gravel, lined with a straight trimmed wall of greenery. Beyond that another ringing crash of metal, grunts and labored breath, pounding feet, and thump and tumble. "Can't see a thing," says Becker.

"He's to come back when he can," says Ysabel. "He knows he's just buying time."

"But maybe he," says Becker. "I'll just go and. Signal him. You know? Let him know. I'll stay out of sight except, I'll wave or something," and he steps out onto the gravel, heads down along the wall of greenery, bent low, looking for a gap.

"No," says Ysabel. "Don't. Stop."

Becker bent double pushes between the shrubs. Beyond a parking lot lit up a pale and buzzing white, streetlights here at the corner of the church and there across the empty lot. A half-dozen white bicycles gears clacking circle as Pyrocles his suit jacket in tatters crouches low his greatsword in both hands angled before him swinging back the tip around whipping to catch Sidney a dark shape leaping knife before him gleaming he crumples around the sword-blow driven into the pavement rolling hands flopping knife clattering away.

"Sidney," calls Pyrocles, his voice worn to a rasp. "Don't tell me you want to rest." Lurching over he plants his greatsword point-first chinking the pavement next to the dark huddle of Sidney's cloak. "Sidney?" Leaning on the hilt like a crutch he pokes. The cloak collapses.

Pyrocles looks up sharply to see Becker's face in the bushes. "Go!" he roars. "Back inside!" Tilting over alarmingly into a churning run. The keening that's been rising resolves into another dark-cloaked figure white light gleaming from a silvery helmet one arm up and back a short broad sword mouth open in a wordless howl of rage. Becker pops back through the bushes falling backwards half-catching himself rolling over to scrabble toward the door as Pyrocles crashes through the bushes big feet crunching gravel slamming fists-first into the wall of the church pushing off spinning to scoop hands on Becker's jeans the back of his plaid shirt hauling up and through the back door ajar as that short broad blade hacks through the greenery striking sparks from the ruddy grey stone. Becker in the stairwell tripping down three steps four and catching the handrail as Pyrocles crashes to the floor shoulders against the wall kicking the door shut bracing with his feet as a blow shivers it from the other side.

"Go on!" yells Pyrocles. "Take his dagger back to the Badb Catha. Tell her how you failed!" The door shudders. "You'll not cross this threshold again! *Go!*"

"Hey," says Becker, when the door is still. "You okay?"

Pyrocles on his back looks down at the tatters of his dark blue jacket his ripped white shirt the gashes hacked across his chest and upper arms oozing something thick and milky yellow. He begins to laugh. "I'll heal, Becker," he says around rough chuckles. "Glad he didn't land one of those while you were standing there."

"I," says Becker, kneeling on the steps, bracing his hands on the landing by Pyrocles, "I'm going to wake up in the morning and I won't remember anything that happened. Which I think," and he leans forward, "is the only reason I can do this," and he kisses Pyrocles on the mouth.

Pyrocles brushes Becker's cheek with battered knuckles. "I hope you remember something," he says, and he pulls Becker to him and they kiss again.

"Well?" says Jo, standing in the middle of a dark and silent street far above her the deck of the freeway raised up on concrete pillars made slender by their height, the rush of engines, rolling

tires, lights seen passing back and forth that do not illuminate what's so far below. Behind her tall grass rustles down to the river black and empty beyond. "We're out of fucking *bridge*, Ray!" Ray in the middle of the cross street hunched over hands on his knees struggling for breath. "Where's the fucking *troll?*"

"I don't, I don't know. I don't know."

"What's it look like, huh? How big is it? Maybe it ducked out for a drink or something?"

Ray's shaking his head, fishing his green bottle from the pocket of his leather jacket. "I don't know," he says, and he takes a swig.

"Have you ever even *seen* the goddamn thing?"

"It's a *bridge!*" snaps Ray. "There's supposed to be a *troll!*"

"I can't believe I listened to you," says Jo. "We've got to get back. Jesus fucking *Christ.*"

"Wait," says Ray. "Wait a minute."

"For what?"

"That?" Ray's pointing his bottle up at the cross bar high above bracing two pillars. Perched there a dark shape, a bird, much too large to be a bird, smooth rounded shoulders with not a suggestion of feathers but great angled chevrons carved in the broad breast.

"A statue?" says Jo.

The statue turns its head silhouetting an eagle's downturned profile. A blink and something that might be an eye glaring at them. Its wings open with a grate of stone on stone and flap once and settle slowly with a grinding rumble.

"That's not a troll, Ray," says Jo, subdued.

"No, but it sure as hell is something."

"You wanna climb up there? See if it wants to help us out?"

Ray grins and shrugs and his eyes slide past her over his shoulder. "Shit," he says, as the clacking sound gets louder and closer, the white bicycle slipping from streetlight to streetlight grey and black and white bicyclist hunched over handlebars lurching from side to side pumping the pedals for speed.

"Oh, hell," says Jo.

Ray pulls one more time from his green bottle then tosses it clinking to the pavement. He flings out his arms, cracks his knuckles, takes in a great draft of air through his nose, and starts to run.

The bicyclist swerves at the last instant but Ray jinks and broadsides him and the bicycle upends pinwheeling over their sprawling bodies, the bicyclist's helmeted head bouncing off the pavement, Ray's feet kicking up in the air, the bicycle crashing to the ground. Jo heads toward them as Ray rolls over on his hands and knees letting out ragged whoops of what turns into laughter. "It worked!" he cries.

Jo crouches over the bicyclist hands hovering over his grey sweater. "Hey," she says. "Hey."

"I never tackled a bicycle before," says Ray.

Jo touches the sweater jerking her fingers back then slowly touches it again. "He's not too cold," she says. The bicyclist's head shifts a little, his eyes flicker open, milky in the pale streetlight.

"Who are you?" says Jo. "What are you doing out here?"

"John," says the bicyclist. "John Milus. I'm not where I'm supposed to be."

"Where's that, John Milus?" says Jo.

"Jo?" says Ray.

"Ankeny and Sandy. Southeast. Coming downhill, making that turn – there's flowers. There's usually flowers. My sister, you know?" Those milky eyes squeeze shut, and when they re-open they're a little more clear in the uncertain light. Maybe blue. "Will you take it back?"

"Hey, Jo?"

"The bike?" says Jo "Sure. Now – "

But there's no one there.

"Jo!" says Ray. Jo stands. "Where'd he go?" says Ray. Jo grabs the white bicycle, sets it upright. Wheels it back and forth. "Jo?" She kicks one leg over the white-taped saddle and finds the white pedals with her feet. She wheels it clack-clacking around in a tight circle, reflectors smudged with white paint, white vinyl seat, grubby white tape on the handlebars. "Jo!" yells Ray. "What the fuck!"

"I'm gonna go break the seige," calls Jo over her shoulder, lurching from side to side as she starts to pump the pedals for speed.

"What will you do, girl?" says Vincent. "That's the third lesson. You're there. You forgot your Princess was in play, and here I am, between you. What will you do about it? Make your decision."

"Okay," says Jo, "I'll – "

"Don't *tell* me!"

"Okay," says Jo, "I won't."

"The fourth lesson, girl," says Vincent. "Decide. Then *do* it. Monday through Friday, here on out, that's supposed to give you the reflexes so you can put the point of that sword wherever you need it to be without thinking. It's what every fencer learns, more or less. You want to fight, you gotta be stepping through these four lessons all the time, over and over, a cycle. Like a heartbeat. Where are you? What's around you? What are you going to do? Then do it, and back again: *now* where are you? *Now* what's around you? *Now* what are you gonna do? Huh?"

"Okay," says Jo. She hasn't moved. Her knees still bent, her left hand up and back, her right arm extended but not stiffly straight, her sword canted up a little to the side.

"So *do* it already," says Vincent.

Jo drops her arm, lowers the sword. Bends down to lay it on the floor. Straightens, hands held out to either side. Looking not at him but Ysabel behind him, who's shaking her head, smiling, looking away.

"Why'd you do that?" says Vincent. "Show your work."

"I saw the way you looked at her," says Jo. "You can't even bring yourself to pretend to pretend to threaten her. Just stand in front of her like that and glare at me."

"So that's her safety. What about yours?"

"If she asked you to jump off the roof, you would," says Jo. "What'd you think I was gonna do? Attack you?"

"I thought maybe you'd try to surprise me during my little speech. That's why I went on so long." He steps his right foot forward, shifting his body, his right arm now with the sword up and out before him, his prosthetic tucked in up by his chest. "You really think you can depend on a word from her?"

"Put up your sword, Mr. Erne," says Ysabel. "We've all made our various points."

He laughs. Lowers his sword. Slashes it back and forth, the tip brushing the floor. "All right," he says. "I'll see you tomorrow. Eleven o'clock."

"Tomorrow!" says Jo.

"It's Friday, isn't it?" He walks across the room to the serried row of practice swords on the floor. "Monday through Friday. No exceptions." He lays his sword back in its place. "And bring the money."

Linesse kneels in the middle of the empty parking lot where neither of the streetlights really reaches, shapeless under her blue-black cloak. In one hand she holds a silver torc as highly polished as the one about her neck. "I've done what I can," she says, to herself, to the torc in her hand. "No one's arrived to rescue her. The ghosts remain on station, but I lost the bell when Sidney was destroyed. And there's more than one gallow-glas here." The parade of white bicycles wheels past on its way around the church. One of the bicycles breaks free, a girl's bike, a white wicker basket with plastic flowers clamped to the front, the rider in a grey skirt and a white rain slicker, arcing toward Linesse, looping a wide circle about her, then stopping, as one by one the other bicycles stop. Riders hop off their seats to stand waiting their bicycles balanced between their legs, lean their bicycles to one side, one foot on pedal, one on pavement.

Something's still clacking, getting louder, growing closer.

Linesse slowly climbs to her feet and turns to look off away toward the street where all the riders are looking. Where Jo's braking her white bicycle to a stop at the entrance to the parking lot, kicking one foot over the saddle, walking the bicycle toward them. Almost as one the riders dismount sweeping and kicking and climbing one leg over their saddles.

"Get back on," says Linesse. She walks over to the mass of ghosts the torc still in her hands. "Get back on! Keep moving! Keep watch! They'll be here any minute!"

Jo's stopped before the ghost in the white rain slicker. "Hello," she says, and "Hello," says the ghost.

"What's your name?" says Jo.

"Cindy Wojtowicz," says the ghost.

"Where do you need to go?"

"Lovejoy and Ninth. They'll take it away, but somebody always put some kind of bicycle back."

"Okay," says Jo, and the white girl's bike with the white wicker basket falls over to the ground. She plants her bicycle on its kickstand, then picks up the fallen bike and plants it, too.

"Stop!" cries Linesse.

"You," says Jo, pointing to a ghost in a white turtleneck and white carpenter's pants, standing by a slender white fixie.

"*Stop!*" cries Linesse.

"Or *what?*" snaps Jo. "What's your name?" she asks the ghost. Linesse cloak flapping mail chiming head down slams into Jo knocking her to the pavement rolling struggling to end up atop Jo kneeling on her belly one hand pinning Jo's shoulder. Her other hand shaking her sword free of her cloak, short and broad, a battered round guard rattling loosely. "Brian Northrop," says the ghost, waiting there by his bicycle.

Jo kicks her legs tries to jerk an arm free. "Stop this!" she yells. "Just go! Leave!" Linesse tosses her sword to one side, goes back into her cloak and pulls out a long knife with a single-edged blade. "You lost!" yells Jo and then she tries to tuck her chin as Linesse lays the blade alongside Jo's throat. "Damn the Mor Muman," she mutters, and tightens her grip on the hilt of the knife.

"Stop!" cries Jo.

"I'd do as she says."

Linesse is quite still, looking down at the sword-blade on her shoulder. She lifts the knife from Jo's throat and holds it up and out to her side, loosely now between thumb and forefinger. The sword taps her shoulder and lifts away, and she stands and turns to see the Duke behind her, in a deep red cardigan and a white shirt open at the throat, his longsword in one hand to his side. "I owed you," he says. "Or I'd've just lopped off your head and been done with you. But we're square, now, you and me. I know you don't have any say in the matter anymore, but have a care we don't cross paths again."

And Linesse turns and walks away quite abruptly. Jo's sitting up, coughing. The Duke extends a hand to help her to her feet. "Well?" he says. "No love for my last-minute rescue? You were expecting maybe the Chariot? I sent him down to the basement already, or he'd've been picking fights with the ghosts."

"Wise," says Jo, and then she turns to the ghost by the fixie. "Where do you need to go, Brian?" she says.

"Forty-seventh, just south of Stark," he says. "There's a tree, in the front strip between the sidewalk and the street? Just chain it up there."

"The ghosts," says the Duke, as she catches the falling fixie. "I'm impressed. Ones up front ain't moving either. I got the Mason watching just in case, but you look like you've got it well in hand?"

"Yeah, well," says Jo, looking for a kickstand. "I'm wondering if maybe I can borrow your pickup truck?"

DIRTY LAUNDRY

DIRTY LAUNDRY piled on the futon, pillows tumbled to the floor. The doors to the bulky blond wood armoire stand ajar, more clothing piled on the floor there, leaking from drawers. On the glass-topped café table a straight green glass vase full of wilting spider mums has been pushed to one side to make room for an open pizza box empty except for a couple of nibbled crusts and a litter of petals. The sink in the little hallway kitchen is lost under a pile of dirty plates, glasses, bowls, a saucepan. A key rattles in the lock. Jo limps in shrugging a shoulder out of her jacket, flicking on the light in the little hallway kitchen. She shimmies her other arm free and lets the jacket drop to the floor. Heads across the main room stumbling over the black spear-haft stretching away under the table, kicking pillows out of the way to stand by the futon, her left hand gingerly opening and closing.

Ysabel's in the little hallway kitchen looking down at Jo's army-surplus jacket on the floor by the overflowing garbage can. She starts to say, "Could you at least," but Jo snaps "Not now, okay? Not fucking now." She's unbuckling her belt. "And I don't want to hear how it wouldn't be a problem if I hadn't opened my eyes when I shouldn't have." She kicks enough clothing away to free a space on the futon by the wall.

"It was more your big mouth," says Ysabel. Jo's yanking off her jeans, wincing, shaking out her left hand. "I told you it would sting a bit," says Ysabel.

"Whatever," says Jo, squirming under the blankets. Ysabel sits in one of the spindly wrought-iron chairs by the glass-topped table. "We're going to see whatsisname, Erne, tomorrow," says Jo.

"All right," says Ysabel. "Does that mean you're going to start carrying the sword?"

"Marfisa's the Axe, right?" says Jo. "Her brother, he's the Axehandle. Not the Axe."

Ysabel looks over at Jo, half-hidden by the laundry, on her side, facing the wall. "You mean what the Dagger was saying. What Sidney was saying." She pulls a gold cigarette case from her skirt pocket. "Does that change anything?"

"I don't know," says Jo. "Does it?"

"Of course not," says Ysabel. She lights a cigarette and smokes it until it's almost down to her fingertips, and then she stubs it out in the pizza box. When Jo starts to snore, she reaches into her skirt pocket again and pulls out a small glass jar and holds it up to the kitchen light. Inside a viscous, milky fluid, frothed with tiny bubbles at the top, touched with just a hint of warm yellow gold.

He's a big man straining the shoulders of a faded plaid flannel shirt, sitting back in one of the leather armchairs beneath the large copper letters that say Barshefsky Associates: Quality Assured. Long grey mustaches droop to either side of his mouth. In one hand he holds a small notebook bound in blue leather. When the side door swings open with a sudden wash of questioning voices and clacking keys he climbs to his feet. Becker steps out into the lobby, a loose brown T-shirt over grey long-sleeved thermals, thin brown hair licked up here and there at the top of his head.

"Becker?" says Pyrocles.

"I'm, sorry," says Becker. "You're very – Do I know you?"

Pyrocles tucks the blue notebook into his shirt pocket. "Jo's told me a lot about you," he says.

"She has?" says Becker.

"Is she here today? I need to meet with her briefly on a personal matter."

"I can," Becker starts to say.

"You see," says Pyrocles, "I never did get to examine her hands."

"I." Becker looks back over his shoulder at the side door. "I'll just," he says. "I'll go see if she's, uh, if she's ready for her break."

"And I'll just wait out here," says Pyrocles.

I'm the ghost in the machine,
  I'm the genius in the gene.
I'm the beauty in the beast.
  I'm the sunset in the east.
I'm the ruby in the dust,
  I'm the trust in the mistrust.
I'm the Trojan horse in Troy.
  I'm the gin
In the gin-soaked boy.

—*Neil Hannon*

NO. 8

BEAUTY

"Let's do it in one" – His madly jerking Eyes
a Venti Vanilla Latte – a Five-dollar Bill
a (brief) Disquisition on Love – On her back on the bed in the dark
Getting Ready – Speaking Precisely – Twenty-eight thirty
the Refrigerator Light – "Draw your sword" – One Long Swallow
Something's Up – Laughing she Opens the Door
Not even breathing – Something Sharp
"Hold out your hand" – Awake, she

"**L**ET'S DO IT IN ONE," says the red-headed man, and Marfisa shrugs. He flips up the tails of his long green coat and perches on a round stool before a keyboard balanced on a couple of sawhorses. She turns to face the soft black bulb of the microphone in a spidery clamp up about her head, a circle of fine black mesh held before it on a twisty plastic arm. "Just like we said," he says, and crooks his back fingers wiggling over keys a moment before falling. Simple chords march out one by one to lay down the bones of a melody, and when they double back a little more certain she takes a breath and then another and begins to sing.

"You want us to call you *what?*" says the woman with the short dark hair, curled up in a corner of the couch along the back wall of the dim studio booth.

"The. Blue. Streak." The kid snaps off each word in its own little bubble of speech. He's wrapped around a big-bellied acoustic guitar at the other end of the couch.

"I mean for short. Do we call you, I don't know, 'The'?"

"Blue's fine," says the kid.

"She means it's stupid," says the bald man sitting on a stool before the control board. "You want to shut up a minute?" Through the thick glass wall Marfisa's holding her hands up around either side of her microphone as if to keep a candle from blowing out.

285

"What's stupid?" says the kid. "Why do we have to call *him* John Wharfinger?" The red-headed man's eyes are closed, his left hand marching still along the keys, his right hand stuttering, hanging above them, sprinkling notes. "Not just John. Always John Wharfinger."

"There's a lot of Johns," says the bald-headed man.

"Not in the band," says the kid. "And I'm not even gonna get started on *your* name."

"What," says the woman, "Otto?" as the bald man says "It's a family name. Now would the both a you shut up and listen?" He turns up the volume on the monitors. Marfisa's voice is pure and clear and cold and she's singing "There are signs in our sky that the darkness is gone, and tokens in endless array – " and it takes all she has left just to hold that word aloft, and her wide open eyes aren't seeing the foam sound baffles on the wall before her as she sways there just her curls the color of clotted cream bound in a thick rope down the length of her back. "For the storm which had seemingly banished the dawn," her voice hushed now under those implacable chords from the red-headed man's left hand, "only hastens the advent of day," and as the chords step over into a new key she lifts her head and lies her heart out: "The good time coming is almost here, oh! It was long, long, long on the way!"

"Jesus," breathes the woman.

"Wow," says the kid.

"Now run and tell 'lijah to hurry up Pomp," sings Marfisa, "and meet us at the gum-tree down in the swamp, for to wake Nicodemus today – "

HIS EYES POP OPEN MADLY JERKING ABOUT. He's stretched out on the narrow back seat his black suit coat draped over him like a blanket, squirming under it, huffing, fighting to free his arms. Up in the front seat Mr. Keightlinger leans one arm along the back of it offering a huge plastic cup filled with bright blue slushie. Mr. Charlock grabs it and greedily sucks it down with long cheek-hollowing pulls at the straw until the cup gurgles. He wedges the cup between his knees and delicately presses his fingertips to his temples, trying a number of grips, index and ring, ring and pinkie, thumbs and middle, thumbs alone, until he shivers and doubles over in a coughing fit, hacking something blue and sticky into a handkerchief. "Fuck me," he says. "It was easier when I *couldn't* get in." He sniffs, pokes the straw around the cup, slurps at what's left. "Que hora?"

"Noon's half gone," says Mr. Keightlinger.

"Shit."

"You needed the sleep. Relax. They're coming back from Erne's."

"What I *need,*" says Mr. Charlock, "is a long hot shower. Gets warm like it's supposed to today? You do not want to smell what I got going on. And the *crick* in my neck."

"Was it worthwhile?"

"Last night?" Mr. Charlock shrugs. "Whatever they had's still gone. The Chariot or whoever can mope about whichever damn door he wants and as long as I'm bounded in a nutshell done up by a joiner squirrel and drawn by a team of redundant little atomies, I can get in there whichever night you please. Just, *please.* Make it a night she's had it good and long and hard first, okay? My ribs feel like they was kicked in by red shoes."

"Oh?"

"It is positively *sticky* up there."

"I should call in," says Mr. Keightlinger.

"Because Lord knows we should fail to report their clockwork-like assignations with the dreadful Erne." Mr. Charlock drops the plastic cup on the floorboard among a litter of fast food wrappers and empty cups and paper sacks, then grabs the back of the front seat and starts to haul himself over. "Remember the, the old days?" he says. "Letters in gentlemen's magazines? Bulletins hidden, in misspelled roadside signs?" He ducks his head and rolls his back into the front seat, his feet swinging around, brushing the window-glass. "Took so long," he says, wriggling himself upright, "it's a wonder anything, we ever got anything done at all."

"We still do all of that."

"Yeah, but," says Mr. Charlock, smoothing his tie, pointing out the window toward the pay phone there by the yellow Pay Here box, "those things are fuckin' *wizard,* you know? And they're ripping 'em out. All over the place. Everybody's got the cell phones or whatever. No money left in 'em. And here's me thinking, strategizing, you know, open-ended detail that we're on, what do we do if they rip *that* one out before she moves on?"

Mr. Keightlinger opens the driver's side door with a popping squonk. "We plant a new one," he says, climbing out of the car.

"Huh," says Mr. Charlock. "I suppose that could work."

The long thin bundle in her arms wrapped in towels Jo's standing just inside the doorway, at the top of the stairs leading down by the switchback of the access ramp. She's looking out over the checkstands, the florist stand off to the side, the aisles of groceries. Signs over on the far wall say Signature Café and Great Lunches and Ready Meats. There's a very large photo of some cold cuts and cheese. The ceiling's a maze of ductwork painted white and struts and there hanging over the top of the stairs a big flatscreen television displaying in full color the entryway to the supermarket, Jo standing just inside the doorway in her care-worn jacket, army-green, eyeing the television, in her arms a long thin bundle wrapped in towels. "Maybe we should come back later," she says. "We can pick it all up after work, I guess. Except, fuck. Laundry."

"Can I at least get some coffee?" says Ysabel, her hand on the stair rail. The green sign that says Starbucks is at the other end of the store by the deli counter. A uniformed security guard's leaning on the florist's counter, laughing at something she said. The guard's shoulder patch says Safeway Loss Prevention.

"I don't think so," says Jo.

"It won't even take two minutes," says Ysabel.

"I'll just," says Jo, shifting the bundle in her arms, turning back toward the door, "I'll wait outside."

Ysabel walks down the stairs into the store, tight faded jeans tucked into oxblood boots, a brown leather bomber jacket over a tight cropped leopard-print tank top. Clear crystal flashes from the gold pin piercing her navel. Necklaces dangle and clatter, amber beads and gold links, a little golden bee, a winking rainbowed eye, a gaudy crucifix. A soft brown fedora on her black black hair. Her lop-sided grin made it so hard to win, sings a voice over unseen speakers somewhere up among the ducts and struts, all right you are, and your promises are just promises, but a sinister little wave of her hand –

The woman behind the Starbucks counter wears a dark blue shirt and a dark blue visor and a green apron and a badge that says Petra B. Her hair's short, though her bangs are long enough to brush the corners of her jaw, and her glasses have thick black rims. "What can I get you?" says Petra B.

"I would like," says Ysabel, leaning her forearms on the counter, heels of her hands pressed together, "a large," looking up at the menu board, "vanilla latte."

"Large," says Petra B. "Do you mean tall, grande, or venti?"

"Which is the large?" says Ysabel. "The biggest?"

"The venti."

"Then I would like a venti vanilla latte," says Ysabel.

"That'll be three sixty-nine," says Petra B.

"Is there more than one Petra?" says Ysabel. "Your nametag," she adds, as Petra B looks up from the cash register.

"It's my name."

"And it's a delightful name," says Ysabel. "But why not just Petra? Why Petra B?"

"We've reached the point in the transaction where you need to give me money." Petra B's smile is pursed and knowing and a dark rich red.

"Hadn't you ought to make me the coffee, first?"

"You're supposed to pay first. That's how it's supposed to go."

"But that won't do at all. What if I don't like it? You'll have my money, and I'll be stuck with a very large cup of coffee that I won't want to drink."

"Have you ever had a Starbucks vanilla latte before? Did you like it?"

Ysabel shrugs and nods her head to one side and says "Yes."

"Well there you go."

"But maybe you're not very good at making them? I'm just saying."

Petra B draws herself up and back with exaggerated dismay. "Is that what you think?"

"Tell me something, Petra B," says Ysabel, the middle finger of her right hand idly scribing a circle on the countertop. Her short neat nails painted gold sparkle under a glossy shell. "Do you think I'm beautiful?"

"What?" says Petra B.

"Am I beautiful, do you think? Am I attractive? Good-looking? Would you say, in your opinion, that I'm, well, *gorgeous?* That I turn heads and stop traffic?"

"You're, uh," says Petra B, "striking?"

"Striking," says Ysabel, a wry twist to her mouth. "That's almost as bad as handsome."

"I didn't mean," says Petra B, alarmed, but Ysabel's saying, "Let me be more direct" and she hitches up on her toes leaning heels of her hands on the countertop now lifting herself that much closer to Petra B whose rich red lips aren't so much smiling anymore, are quivering a little, her eyes behind those glasses darting from Ysabel's eyes to Ysabel's mouth and back. "Do you find me desirable?" says Ysabel, quietly.

"I don't know," says Petra B, too quickly.

"Do you want me?" says Ysabel.

And Petra B opens her mouth to say something, and maybe she's about to nod, when Ysabel tilts her head and lifts it for a kiss.

For a moment they stand there, Ysabel swooped up against the counter, Petra B arched over it, her hands held out uselessly to either side, only their lips touching, and then Petra B sighs into the kiss her shoulders relaxing, her mouth opening over Ysabel's mouth, her hands fluttering down to light on Ysabel's arm on the fleecy collar of Ysabel's jacket jerking as if burned then gingerly settling again. Ysabel breaks the kiss, and Petra B eyes closed behind those glasses rests her forehead against Ysabel's until Ysabel pulls back just a little. "Now," she says, smiling. Resettling her hat. "Make me that large vanilla latte."

Nodding Petra B steps over to the espresso machine. Ysabel stoops to peer at her reflection in the side of the cash register. Petra B's pouring clear syrup into a large white paper cup. Ysabel's smoothing a corner of her lipsticked mouth with her pinkie nail. The milk's foaming under the steam wand. "Whipped cream?" says Petra B.

"No," says Ysabel straightening, "maybe I'll put on a little nutmeg. Do you smoke?"

"What?" says Petra B. "No, I mean, I could, I guess. I've never. Here." She hands over the latte. "Will I see you again?"

Ysabel carefully takes a sip. "Not bad," she says. "Not bad. Thanks."

A hand slaps a five-dollar bill on the counter, a hand in a grubby fingerless bicycle glove. "Keep the change," says Roland. His jagged green sunglasses like pieces of broken bottle.

"Oh, no," says Petra B. "That's not necessary."

"You're not needed here," says Ysabel, her voice low, her eyes narrowed.

"Where's Jo?" says Roland.

"She didn't want any coffee. Not that it's any of your business."

"Really," says Petra B. "It's okay."

"Go on, miss."

"Go away, Roland."

"Miss, please. Take the money."

"Roland."

"It's okay. Really."

The hand in the bicycle glove crumples into a fist over the five-dollar bill still flat on the counter.

"*Chariot,*" says Ysabel.

Out on the corner before the doors to the supermarket Jo's smoking a cigarette, the long thin bundle up on one shoulder, her free hand draped over it for balance. Across the street a blocky bunker of a building, pale red brick, a sign that says Christian Science Reading Room. Down the block a construction site, a condo tower, lower levels sleeked with new green glass. A panel truck snorts past. Staples, says the big red sign on its side. That was easy. She turns just as behind her Roland stiff-arms the crashbar of the big glass doors to the supermarket bursting out onto the sidewalk to stand there in a crisp white track suit with green piping, his blue and white headphones down around his neck. "Roland," says Jo, and he looks up to see her there, "hey," says Jo, "I've been meaning to ask," and he's walking toward her, "about Ray, I mean, how do I get a hold of him," and his gloved hand's coming up balled in a loose fist, "do you have a what's that?" and is planted squarely against her chest. There's something inside. She sticks the cigarette between her lips and tugs out the five-dollar bill. "What's this for?"

"Figure it out," snaps Roland, and he walks away.

"Well?" calls Jo after a moment. "Do you have a phone number for him or something? Huh? Nice to see you too, asshole!"

"What was that about?" says Ysabel behind her, sipping from a large cup of coffee. Jo's stuffing the money into her pocket. "Fucked if I know," she says. "Let's go dump this shit and get ready for work, huh?"

In the tub Ysabel's lifting a dripping calf from steaming water, slicking it with a soapy hand. In her other hand a molded pink safety razor. On the side of the tub a translucent white teacup its rim smudged with red lipstick and a pink and white My Little Pony lunchbox. A half-smoked cigarette smolders by a black smear of ash on a yellowed saucer. "I don't know," she says, drawing the razor up along her leg. "He wanted to pay for my coffee." The door to the bathroom's half-open. Music's floating in from the main room, a guitar, a woman singing like laughing with liquid in your mouth, like you're choosing between laughing and spitting it all out. "Guess that explains the money," says Jo. "Sort of."

She's squatting on the futon sorting through wadded-up T-shirts, tossing black ones to one end, anything with color over there, a couple white ones dropped beside her. Farmers & Mechanics Bank says one, and Mykle Systems Labs says another. One of the black ones has a big red devil's face on it, sticking out his tongue. She's wearing a white one with a ragged collar and yellowing armpits that says This is Not a Slogan in scrawled Sharpie letters. "I get that he's keeping an eye on you? I get that." She frees a grey T-shirt printed with a colorful tangle of luchadores and ninjas, dithers with it a moment over the black pile before chucking it over with the colored T-shirts.

"There was a but in that," calls Ysabel from the bathroom.

"But," says Jo. "His timing? Fucking sucks. He shows up to try and buy your *coffee?* Where the hell was he when, when whatever the fuck it was tried to jump us on the MAX, huh?" She roots around one of the blond wood crates and pulls out a pair of black jeans, reaches inside to disentangle a pair of white underwear. "Damn sight more useful than a five-dollar bill. Are you gonna be in there all night? It's already ten after."

"So?"

"So they lock down the laundry room at midnight, and the Safeway closes at midnight, and we didn't go shopping before work like we were going to, and we didn't do laundry last night because you just had to see the Girl From Mars show – "

"Which was a great show," says Ysabel. Water sloshes as she shifts in the tub, reaching down for her cigarette.

"Which it was, but that's beside the point. We can't keep spending five bucks on a cup of coffee because there's nothing but dust in the Taster's Choice jar."

"It's hardly the same thing," mutters Ysabel, cigarette on her lips, lifting her other leg from the water.

"So are you gonna be getting out of there any time soon?" Jo's stuffing her piles of clothing into a big beige canvas sack. The boom box on the floor by the futon's playing a new song, a lonely fuzzed electric guitar, a woman's high and reedy voice singing if the sun shines but approximately? What a world of awkwardness! What hostile implements of sense!

"Let me ask you something, Jo," says Ysabel, slicking her calf with soap, laying the cigarette back on its saucer, taking up the molded pink razor. "Do you believe in love?"

Jo's sitting there, the mouth of the canvas sack in one hand and her white T-shirts and underwear in the other. "Do I what?" she says. "What the hell has that got to do with any damn thing?"

"It's a simple question," says Ysabel. "Do you believe in love?"

"We don't have time for this," says Jo, yanking the sack's drawstring.

"What was his name?" More sloshing. "Frankie? You never talk about him."

"Love is bullshit, okay? Now you want to get out of the fucking tub?"

"So that's a no, then?"

"It's a glandular thing," says Jo, her hands up, agitated, "that evolved so we could stand being around somebody else long enough to, to – "

"See," says Ysabel, "I think you're only saying that because you've *been* in love, and now you're not."

"I was *not* in love with him," mutters Jo, as Ysabel's saying, "Now, I've *never* been in love, yet I can't help but believe in it. I see it all around me, every day. It's why Roland does what he does."

"Never?" says Jo, still sitting on the futon, elbows on her knees. "So you and Marfisa, that was, what? You never talk about her."

"Shit!" says Ysabel. "Ow."

"What's wrong?" says Jo, looking up and over toward the half-closed bathroom door.

"Cut myself," says Ysabel.

"Well, that's what you," says Jo, and then as she's climbing to her feet "Oh, God," and stumbling over the black spear-haft on the floor past the glass-topped café table she bursts through the bathroom door to see Ysabel leaning forward in the tub one leg propped up on the rim of it looking up, licking her thumb and pressing it to a little yellowing gash on the swell of her calf there below her knee. "You're," says Jo, "you're okay."

"It's just a cut, Jo," says Ysabel, her other arm up to cover her breasts.

"You cut yourself," says Jo, still in the doorway, staring, *"I'm* here, and you cut yourself, and," but Ysabel's started laughing.

"Oh, Jo, poor Jo," she says, throwing back her head, her heavy damp black curls plopping against the water. "No no no. This is not a battlefield, sweet Gallowglas."

Jo sighs. "We, uh. Were sort of fighting."

Ysabel lifts her thumb slick with something thick and milky to her lips and licks it clean. "You thought I was done for. Gone down to dust. And you came running." She presses her thumb back against the slowly reddening cut. "You *do* care."

"I'm gonna," says Jo, stepping out of the doorway, into the main room. "I'll take the laundry down. Set it up." Rustle of cloth, jangle of keys. "Go to the fucking Safeway and put them in the dryer when I get back." She's back in the doorway now, in her careworn jacket, army-surplus green, the canvas sack slung over her shoulder. "You stay put, heal, get clean, whatever the fuck, just don't leave the apartment."

"You're leaving me alone."

"Shit's gotta get done," says Jo. "It'll only take an hour or so. And you aren't going anywhere. And you can always call for Roland if you need to, right?"

Ysabel's folded her arms on the rim of the tub, leaning her chin on her crossed wrists. "You don't have anything of mine in that bag, do you."

"I am *not* sorting your laundry, Ysabel," says Jo. "More'n half of it's dry-clean only anyway."

"Could you at least wash some of my underwear?"

Jo snorts. "I'll buy you some Woolite. You can slosh 'em around with you the next time you take a bath." She jerks open the door to the apartment and slams it shut behind her.

Ysabel reaches down for the cigarette, looks at what's left of it there between her fingers, then stubs it out on the saucer. She climbs out of the tub and heads dripping over to the bathroom doorway, standing there, staring at the door to the apartment.

Then she walks back to the tub, scooping up the towel that's draped over the back of the toilet. Patting her face, her chest, drying her hands, she crouches by the tub and opens the pink and white My Little Pony lunchbox. There among the jumbled muddle of bottles of nail polish and lipsticks pots of scrubs is a small glass jar, half-filled with a viscous, milky fluid, frothed with tiny bubbles at the top, touched with just a hint of warm yellow gold.

On her back on the bed in the dark her pale hair still in its thick rope of a ponytail draped over one shoulder soaks up what little light it can. Her knees drawn up together tipped over to one side, her little black dress rucked up about her hips, her feet bare. Her eyes closed. It's a round room with casement windows all around cranked open to the sound of rain. Cardboard boxes full of clothes stacked here and there, and more clothing strewn about the bare wood floor. The table by the bedside's a scrolled marble top balanced on a single fluted pedestal leg. A little blue glass reading lamp, dark, an alarm clock, a flimsy balloon of a wineglass with a small dark puddle at its bottom. A paperback book turned over, splayed open, says The Wounded Sky on its spine. She opens her eyes.

He's standing in the doorway, the only flat wall in the room, silhouetted by the dim light in the stairwell. His head a great dark mass, his hair in dreadlocks that hang down past his shoulders. "You're in a mood," he says.

"Go away," she says, closing her eyes again.

"Tell me," he says, "this isn't what it looks like."

After a moment she reaches for the switch on the cord of the blue glass lamp and flicks it on. "What does it look like?" she says, sitting up a little, picking up the wineglass.

"Like you've suffered some apocalypse of the heart, sister dear." His eyes are bright, his smile is gentle. "Like you've lost your one true love, who's never to return." He leans in the doorway, arms folded. His shirt's a pale pink silk, open at the throat. "Tell me you haven't gone and screwed everything up."

"You," she says, and then she downs what's left in the glass. "Of course you knew. How did you find out?"

"About the sweet moments you've stolen with our absent King's Bride-to-be? Sister love, who do you think sent her up to find you at Robin's Midsummer's party?" He comes into the room, stepping from the dim light of the stairwell to the dim light thrown by the blue glass lamp. "That first fumbling kiss is a memory I shall treasure till the end of days."

"We were found out," she says, as she takes great care in putting the glass back on the table next to the book. "Perhaps you heard? The Dagger struck at me, with a gallowglas on the field."

"Because of *that*? I'd heard he just went mad, and's been exiled for it." He sits on the bed beside her, his hands in his lap. "Unfortunate you were there when he snapped, and thanks to grace and luck and running shoes the Chariot was there in time."

"The Chariot, who as much as threatened *me* with banishment, if I so much as spoke with her again."

"And it's him says who's to be denied the bread and salt and oil, these days? I hadn't known."

"He *knows*, brother. He saw us, together. The Dagger knew. The Duke knows." She takes a wobbly breath. "The Gallowglas..."

"Ah," he says, his hand on her knee. "Sister mine, a secret everyone knows but none dare speak of is still a secret *kept*. The Princess will be Queen soon, and were you still her paramour – well. There's power to be had, in forcing others to speak around a thing like that."

Eyes closing, she shakes her head. "No, brother dearest. The tower's ruined. It won't help." She lifts his hand from her thigh. He jerks it from her grasp, looks away from her, out an open window at the rainy night. "It's cold in here," he says. He stands and cranks a window shut, moves over to the next. "You should have a care," he says, his back to her. "Remember, an axe is useless without its handle." But her breathing's settled into sleep.

Wrapped in a Spongebob Squarepants towel Ysabel crouches by the futon fingers hovering over the buttons on the boom box, stabbing suddenly at the one that says Eject. The tape drawer pops open. She pulls out the cassette and tosses it to one side, then clatters through a shoebox full of tapes, pulling out a smokey clear one that says The Weasley Variations in tidy white-inked letters. She drops it in the drawer, snaps the drawer shut, presses the button that says Play. Thundering drums and a squalling guitar and a man singing somewhere under it all they hit you at school, they hate you if you're, and "Shit!" says Ysabel, slapping the button that says Stop. Her fingers hover again until she finds Rewind and holds it down until the tape stops. She presses Play. A jangling guitar's followed by drums, then bass, then a man's voice declaiming there are no angels left in America anymore. They left after the Second World War, heading west. Ysabel stands and still wrapped in the towel half-dances over to the glass-topped café table, grabs the empty pizza box and the tall green glass vase, stuffs the pizza box in the garbage can in the little hallway kitchen, sets the vase in the sink. "They kept heading west, to who knows where," she sings along with the tape, dancing into the bathroom.

Wrapped in the Spongebob Squarepants towel Ysabel's standing by the glass-topped café table looking it over, a box of matches rattling in her hand. Three lit candles, one tall and white and skinny, one short and red, its wall of crinkled wax collapsed to one side, one in a glass chimney covered with praying hands and a bleeding heart wrapped in thorns and the faces of saints. Before them the small glass jar half-filled with something milky. Thickly fuzzed guitars seep from the boom box, and someone's singing when you clean out the hive, does it make you want to cry? Are you still being followed by the teenage FBI? Ysabel's in the kitchen, dropping the matches on the counter, pulling a round yellow bowl out of a cabinet. She sets the bowel on the table by the jar, steps back, head cocked. Shakes her head. Takes the bowl away, comes back with a wine glass. Sets it on the table by the jar. "No," she says, taking the glass away. She comes back with the bowl. Sets it down. Picks it up again. "Shit," she says.

The Spongebob Squarepants towel wrapped about her waist Ysabel's peering at herself in the bathroom mirror, smiling, frowning, wiggling her eyebrows. Music's drawling in the other room, a dark voice chanting the lower the sun, the longer the shadows become. She pulls a dark red lipstick from the My Little Pony lunchbox and paints her lips, smoothing a corner of her mouth with a pinkie nail, then suddenly daubing one nipple, then the other. She leans back wet hair heavy on her shoulders, looking herself over. Her grin slides into a scowl. She throws the lipstick into the sink, jabs her fingers into a jar of Vaseline, smears the color from her lips. "Fuck," she says, reaching for the toilet paper.

Ysabel naked sits on the carpet her back to the bulky blond wood armoire, her hair tied back in a simple tail, her head in her hands. The boom box is silent. The candles still burn on the table. She leans to one side and pulls a shimmering white slip from the laundry spilling out of the drawers of the armoire, turning it over in her hands, fingers worrying at a faint ivory stain, a smudge of something red at the neck. "Dammit, Jo," she says, dropping it on the crumpled cloud of frothy lace beside her. "Would it have killed you." She finds a pair of grey yoga pants and sniffs them, her face souring, shakes them out, kicks one foot into them and then the other.

The laundry room is brightly lit and steeped in the susurral static of tumbling soaking churning clothes, three dryers on the back wall, one set to spinning, five washers in a line, two with their lids up. Ysabel in grey yoga pants and her leopard-print tank top, her armload of shimmery satin and frothy lace, stands before one of the open washers, running a finger along the text printed on the underside of the lid. "Need some, uh, help?" says the man standing in the doorway.

"Which of these is the dry cleaner?" says Ysabel, without looking up from the lid.

"There, ah, none of them," he says, frowning. He wears a neat reddish beard and a navy blue hoodie that says Beloit College. "You'd have to go to Bee's, I think they're the closest."

"How long does it take to dry-clean something?" says Ysabel, looking up at him.

"I think," he says, "they've got same-day service, but, you know, they're not open right now, can I help you? With anything?

Do you have any, other, laundry in here? I'm gonna have to lock this up in about an hour."

"I think Jo's got her stuff in the washers here, but she'll be along soon to do whatever needs to be done to it."

"Jo. You're staying with Jo? In four-oh-seven?"

"Yes," says Ysabel.

"Could I, talk to you? Just for a minute. About Jo. I mean, it's irregular, yes, you wouldn't have to answer my questions, if you didn't want to, but I'm trying to help your – "

"Who are you, exactly?" says Ysabel.

"Oh! Tim. Tim Carroll. I help manage the building, do some counseling, for our residents – "

"Counseling?"

"A lot of our folks are on assistance of one sort or another, we help them navigate the paperwork, can we go to the office? It's a little more, ah, private – "

"These are *private* questions?" says Ysabel, stepping around the line of washers.

"Well, it's a little more discreet? Than the laundry room?"

It's a small office, tucked behind the front desk up by the racks of mailboxes in the lobby. Tim squeezes between the desk and the wall and drops into a swivel chair, careful of the teetering stack of bankers boxes in the corner. "Go ahead," he says, gesturing, "take a seat, just close the door first, it's harder if you do it the other way around." He's opening a drawer as she pushes the other chair in the room to one side to make room for the door to swing shut, and he looks up from the yellow legal pad he's pulled out to see her pushing the chair back to make room to sit, and his eyes fix on the crystal flashing from the gold pin piercing her navel. "Your questions?" says Ysabel, sitting down, draping her armload of lace and satin over her lap.

"How long, ah, have you known Jo?" he says, looking up to her sidelong smile.

"I don't know, exactly," says Ysabel.

"Well how long have you been staying with her?"

"I couldn't precisely say," says Ysabel.

"Maybe a guess? Did you know her in school? Has it been years? Months? Weeks?"

"What time is it?" says Ysabel, sighing.

"Quarter past?" says Tim. "Eleven?"

"Then I have known Jo Maguire for thirty-three days, one hour, fifteen minutes. Thereabouts."

He picks up a pen, puts it back down again. "Okay – "

"I can't be more exact."

"That's, okay." He leans back in his chair with a grinding squeak. "Could you maybe, *guess* then, how long it is you've been staying with her, I mean, you *are* staying with her, right?"

She shrugs. "Half a day less?"

He sits up again. "Ah."

"Oh?"

"Where were you, staying before?"

She waits until he's looking her in the eye again. "With my family. Here in town."

"Did you, run? Away?"

"You haven't even asked my name, Mr. Tim Carroll."

"It's not, I don't need to know that, you're not one of our residents. Not really. This is about Jo."

"It's all been about me, so far. Not run, no. I'd say it's more like I was pushed."

"Because of Jo?"

Her smile widens. "Not in the way you're thinking."

He's looking down at the empty pad again, fiddling with the pen he hasn't uncapped. "And, ah, you're employed?"

"I work with Jo, yes."

"You help with, the rent? Groceries? Like that?"

"I am apparently paying my way," says Ysabel.

"Ah," says Tim.

"That's the second time you've uttered that terribly freighted syllable, Mr. Tim Carroll."

"Jo," he says, tapping the pen against the pad, "receives a voucher, from the Housing Authority, to assist her with rent, she was very lucky to get it. But one of the conditions of the voucher is, she's to report any change in the size of her household, that would be you, to the Housing Authority, in writing. And one of the conditions of the voucher is, she's to report any change in her household's, *income,* in writing. To the Housing Authority."

"And we need to write a letter?" says Ysabel. "You've got the pad already. That's so kind of you."

"It's not, ah, it's been over a month. There's nothing to be done now, they'll review the case, but I'm afraid Jo's going to lose her voucher."

"Because you think she doesn't need it? Because I've changed her situation?"

"You'll have to leave regardless. She was also supposed to inform us, that she had someone living with her. Which is grounds for eviction."

Ysabel gathers up the froth of lace and the shimmering slip from her lap with a rustle and lays them on the pile of papers by her chair. "You weren't entirely honest with me, Mr. Tim Carroll."

"I, it's not like I – "

"You had an ulterior motive that cut against our best interests. Had I know that, I would have declined to answer your questions."

"I have a responsibility – "

"Yes, to your residents, to, what was it you said? Help them navigate these rules and regulations?" She leans forward, her elbows on the desk, her hands lightly on the legal pad. "It's a very," he's saying, "the rules," as she says "Tell me something."

"They're very strict," he says.

"What was the first thing you thought when you saw me in the laundry room tonight? The first thought that went through your head? Was it, I'd better ask her my questions while I've got the chance? Was it gosh I hope she smiles at me?" She sits back in her chair. "Was it, I wonder if she's wearing any underwear?" Her flip-flops flap to the floor. She kicks her bare feet up to rest on the edge of the desk. An anklet golden shining, a silvery gold-tinged ring about a middle toe. "Why don't you take off that sweatshirt, Tim?" Her toenails painted gold and sparkling under a glossy shell.

"This is improper," he says, the bottom of his hoodie bunched in his hands.

"You knew that from the start," she says, hooking her thumbs in the waistband of her yoga pants, pushing them over her hips and down her legs. Dropping them on the frothy pile of lace. "Do you think I'm beautiful?"

And he nods, slowly.

"Then please take off your shirt." By the time he's struggled out of the hoodie she's skinned off her tank top. He's wearing a brown T-shirt that says Chewie is my Co-pilot. She's stretching, her arms up, undoing the tie about her fall of thick black curls. "Now," she says, standing. "Let's think a moment." Sitting on the edge of the desk her back to him, pushing her chair back against the door with a foot. "What can be done?" She spins on the desk scooting forward a little and spreading her legs to rest her feet on either arm of his chair. His mouth open a little eyes wide staring at the crystal flashing from the gold pin piercing her navel. "Jo is my very good friend," she says, and then she takes his head in her hands. "She takes good care of me, and I will do no less for her." She bends to kiss the top of his head. "So how do we keep these terrible things from happening?"

"I don't," he says, and she pulls him to her, resting his head against her breast. "Don't say don't," she says, softly, her lips against his ear. "Say can, Tim. Say will."

Jo sets the shopping baskets she's carrying in either hand on the floor before the shelves of canned beans. She pulls down a couple with blue labels that say Black Beans. Eighty-nine cents says the price tag. "Buck eighty," she says to herself, putting a can in either basket. "Plus twenty-six fifty, twenty-seven, twenty-eight uh, thirty." She pulls a grubby little white pad from a pocket of her army-green surplus jacket, fishes up a grease pencil from another pocket, crosses something off on the pad. "Twenty-eight thirty," she says again. "Dairy." She picks up the shopping baskets each maybe half full, a couple of onions in one, a couple of potatoes in the other, a box of rice balancing a jar of coffee. She heads up the empty aisle toward the front of the store. Music's floating down from the unseen speakers up among the ducts and struts, a lazy, loping beat, drink this to put out the flame, drink this, it tastes like vanilla. Aside from the clerk at the lone lit-up checkstand the only person at this end of the store is a woman with long black hair and a loose blue skirt, looking over the frozen pizzas at the end of one of the aisles. Jo heads over toward the dairy display. "Fucking Woolite," she says to herself, stopping, setting the baskets down. Pulling out the pad and pencil to make another note.

"Gallowglas," comes a voice behind her.

Jo looks over her shoulder.

It's Orlando standing by the freezer full of pizzas in his blue sarong, his white half-unbuttoned dress shirt, his long black hair draped over one shoulder. "Where's the Princess, Gallowglas?" he says, and though his voice is soft it carries.

"Oh, fuck me," says Jo, looking past him. The clerk's gone from the one lit-up checkstand. The florist counter's dark, and the deli counter too, and there's no one, no one in sight at all, not even at the tables by the Starbucks counter.

"You're alone here?" he's saying. He puts the box of five-cheese pizza back on the freezer shelf. "How fortuitous. So am I." His hand a loose fist out to his side turning a curl of light in the air between them as he draws his arm back to himself, and it's gone so suddenly still, no more bleeps from the registers, no squeak of a shopping cart's wheels from the next aisle over, even the compressor in the freezer's rattled to a stop, and the music's gone away. "Go on," says Orlando, settling the hilt of his Japanese sword in both hands. "Where's yours?"

"Fucking fuck me hell," says Jo.

THE REFRIGERATOR LIGHT – "DRAW YOUR SWORD"
ONE LONG SWALLOW – SOMETHING'S UP

THE REFRIGERATOR LIGHT as he opens the door shines dimly on her there in the saggy blue chair in the corner, curled up in a long pink T-shirt, her book in one hand, a finger keeping her place, the flimsy balloon of a wineglass in the other. "Hart and hive, girl," he growls. "You spooked me."

"Agravante woke me," says Marfisa. "I couldn't get back to sleep."

"Sleep can't stand me," he says, closing the refrigerator. He's leaning most of his weight on a black-handled blue metal four-legged cane. "Been at each other's throat for years." He shuffle-clomps over to the counter, reaching for a light switch. Halogen spots under the upper cabinets flash to life. "Can't remember who started it. But a lovely girl like you? How could sleep resist your charms?" His dressing gown's a deep rich blue, unbelted over pale blue and pink checked pyjamas.

"There's plenty enough who can," she says, lifting the wine-glass as if to sip from it, but turning instead to set it on the narrow kitchen desk. "Why should sleep be any different?"

"Troubles of the loins, is it?"

"Of the *heart,* Grandfather. Please."

"Ah. Love." He snorts. "Something we didn't have in our day. Never saw the use of it. Now *beauty?* Oh!" Both hands on his cane he tips his head back wizened face lit up by a beatific smile, ivory hair a wild crown. "Why once I razed the towers of Heigh Pareval and salted the foundations of her walls because her Queen thought to keep her three most beautiful boys from the eyes of the world." His shaggy brows come together and his smile droops, his eyes look away as his bobbing head begins to shake from side to side. "Or was that your grandmother, rest her teeth? I get confused."

"You always told us it was Grandmother went a-Viking," says Marfisa.

"So she did. So she did. And I stayed home to bake the bread."

"Didn't you love her, Grandfather?"

"I was *bound* to her, girl. Ties of toradh. Great weighty chains of obligations first forged when the world was young. And hound and hawk I wanted her, yes, I did, still do. I close my eyes," and he does so, "and I can see her as I saw her first, the day we met, coming out of the kitchen in my flour-dusted apron, that greatsword in her hands – " He opens his eyes. "The ache in my bones," he says. "The ice in my belly. The sight of her like poetry, standing my hair on end." He pounds his cane against the floor. "Love had *nothing* to do with it. Leads to sitting around in the dark waiting for someone else to do what needs doing, or so it would seem." She smiles at that, a little. "Should have bound you over to someone long ago, girl. Removed any uncertainty and doubt. Let you get on with the important things."

"It would have weakened our position. Agravante's said so."

His bobbing head's shaking again. "There's not world enough, nor time, for *love*. Now. I'm going to tell you a secret." He leans over his cane at her, but he's smiling at the refrigerator. "There's a corner of a sheet cake in there. Big blue flowers. I'll cut you off a slice."

"Thank you, Grandfather," says Marfisa.

"It's *terrible*," he says with great delight. "The frosting's nothing but sugar and some awful chemical color cooked up in a lab."

Jo between her baskets of groceries both hands held up away from herself eyes locked on Orlando there by the freezer full of pizzas his sword in his hands. Neither of them's taken a step. Two whole aisles between them. "If I don't," says Jo, then what, I automatically lose? Forfeit or something? All my offices become yours, is that it?"

"You mistake the situation, girl," says Orlando. "This is no duel. This is murder."

Jo takes a step or two back. He doesn't take a step forward. "Either," she starts to say, and swallows, and tries again, "either way you get the Princess, right?"

"This isn't about her." He resettles his grip on the hilt of his sword. "Tell me something, girl, before I kill you, and tell me true." He takes a step, just one. "Do you love him?"

"I," says Jo, as she starts to frown, to shake her head, and taking another step back she carefully says "I already answered that question."

"Not to me you haven't," says Orlando.

"Yes!" cries Jo, her voice ringing in the empty supermarket. "Yes! I love him! I miss him! I'm," and she's interrupted by a sudden hitching sob of a breath, "I'm very fucking sorry. Like I already. Fucking. Said. What do I get, this time? My groceries? That it?"

"Do you pity him?" says Orlando, the hilt of his sword rattling in his hands.

"What?" says Jo.

"Do you pity him? Because of his leg?"

"His *leg?* I don't – "

"His leg! That you broke on the hunt so that now he must limp like a beaten dog." Two steps, his arms going up and back, the blade like a beam over his head. "Do you *pity* him? Is that why you love him?"

"I'm not talking about the Duke," says Jo, her voice gone quiet.

"I am."

"I don't love the Duke," says Jo.

"Liar." He brings the blade down before him pointing with the slight curve of it toward the tip. "Do not think to talk your way out of this."

"Why should I," she says. "One cut, and you're done for."

"So here we are," he says. "Draw your sword."

"Yeah," says Jo. "About that." Glancing over her shoulder. The stairs behind her, the switchback of the access ramp, the doors outside filled with blank black night.

"You won't make it, girl," says Orlando.

"Probably not," says Jo, and she starts running. To the side. Down the aisle. Toward the back of the store.

Orlando bare feet padding swiftly blade swung up above his head past the empty aisle the abandoned baskets of groceries around the corner to see Jo halfway down its length before the shelves turning her arm whipping up and out and again, blue cans flying at him one two. He sidesteps ducks head canted and a third's spinning through the air right at him. He brings his blade down in a short swift chop. Two halves of the can spinning away to either side, top and bottom clattering against shelves falling a spill of black beans spattering the floor. Jo's running away down the aisle turning at the end of it.

Backpedalling Orlando his white shirt splashed with purple at the front of the supermarket again past the abandoned baskets of groceries peering down the next aisle over. No sign of Jo. He stands unmoving eyes closed head tipped down, listening, his blade in both hands held before him. Away down the aisles a squeak, a clank. A pat, pat of footsteps, slow and careful. He opens his eyes, looks to one side, the stairs, the access ramp. To the other, the deli counter, the Starbucks counter, more doors blank and black. "You can't wait me out," he calls, and then quickly bare feet whispering he's off down the aisle.

She's crouched at the end of it climbing to her feet as he comes around the corner and she flings another can at him and he swings a spray of tomatoes over his head can-top and bottom clanging away and as she turns to run back up the aisle she throws one more can from the clutch in her arm and he twists his followthrough torquing his blade to slice sideways at it. It's a longer can than the others, skinnier, wobbling as it spins at him, a yellow plastic cap on one end.

There's a loud whoomp and a clattering crash of falling cans and jars and maybe shelves and a bellow of rage and pain. Jo's up the next aisle over, looking back, setting the cans she's carrying back on the shelf, another blue can of beans, a red can of tomatoes, and another longer, skinnier can, topped by a yellow plastic cap. Easy Off Oven Cleaner, says the label. Heavy Duty. Contents under pressure. "Question number two," she mutters to herself. "What's *around* you, *asshole.*" Music's coming from unseen speakers up among the struts and ducts, Ray-hey, ey, Uncle Ray! Scanner's bleeping at the checkstand, security guard's looking about as she bursts from the aisle, running along the front of the store toward the stairs. "Hey!" he hollers.

"He's got a sword!" yells Jo. "Something exploded!"

"Shit," says the guard, looking down the aisle, hand going to the club at his hip, looking back toward her, but she's already up the stairs and through the doors.

Laughing she opens the door to the apartment. "Jo?" she calls, standing there in the little hallway kitchen. She's holding a manila envelope in one hand. "Jo!" Out in the main room on the glass-topped café table three candles unlit. Before them the small glass jar, half-filled. She plants a kiss on the envelope and drops it on the kitchen counter.

In the bathroom water's filling the sink. She's standing before the mirror looking herself in the eye. She shuts off the faucet, dips her hands in the water, splashes her face, wincing. Runs wet hands through her hair, pulling it back, tight against her skull. Her lips unpainted a thin straight line. Her eyes blink once. She lets go of her hair and scoops up more water, splashing her face again, gasping, then grabs the hem of her tank top and lifts it over her head. She carefully plucks the grip from the gold pin piercing her navel and sets it crystal glimmering on the edge of the sink. She peels off her yoga pants and leaves them on the floor by the toilet.

She doesn't turn on the boom box.

She relights the candles, puts the matches back on the kitchen counter, shuts off the light in the main room. Stands before the table head bowed a moment in the flickering warm light. "All right then," she says, opening her eyes. She take up the jar and unscrews its cap, setting it on the table, lifting the jar to her nose. Her face settles into such a contented sigh. "Oh," she breathes, and "wow." She lifts the jar and nods to the windows before her filled with the lights of the city at night, then turns to her right, lifting the jar and nodding to the wall over the futon, its collage of post cards and scraps of paper, scribbled post-it notes and pages ripped from magazines. She turns to face the wall behind her, lifting the jar and nodding to the blond wood armoire, the clothing littering the floor, then turns to her left, lifting the jar and nodding to the bathroom door and the little hallway kitchen and the door to the hallway beyond. "What's freely given," she says, quietly but clearly, "I freely give. The price of it's too dear if licked from thorns." And lifting the jar to her lips she pours the milky fluid down her throat in one long swallow.

She sways, lips shining –

Slowly turning, she puts the jar back on the table –

A loud clink. Lifting her hand too rapidly away in surprise –
"Whoa," she says with half a laugh, rolling over to sit up
among the tangled blankets on the futon.

Her hand to her chest thumb stroking the notch in her clavi-
cle. She wipes her mouth clean with a finger and one hand on
the pillows. She licks her fingertip. Another half laugh, shaking
her head, rolling over to sit up among the tangled blankets on
the futon. She lifts one leg into the air toes curling and "Oh"
she says her hand suddenly on her belly her belly rippling like
water under a sudden gust of wind.

Climbing to her feet she stumbles over the black spear-haft
on the floor stretching beneath the table arms out to catch herself she rolls over with a half laugh in the tangled blankets on
the futon groaning, clutching her stomach shaking like sand
after heavy footsteps.

"Whoa," she says, her laugh a wetly hacking bubbling cough.
Letting go of herself slowly, hands on the edge of the futon now.
"First step's a doozy." She pushes forward to climb to her feet
when her belly roils like a sack full of snakes and her groan's
through gritted teeth. Rolling over in the tangled blankets on the
futon on her hands and knees as something yellow and wet spurts
from her mouth strings of it clinging to her lips. "Oh no" she says
in a small weak voice, clutching her clenching gut until bucking
suddenly she heaves up a gout of vomit white and wet and tinged
with yellow and red, slickly shining in the candlelight slopping
over the blankets, another wash of it spattering the wall with clusters of tiny pearly curds. She lies there on her side her breath gone
quick and shallow. "Help," she says so quiet, and then she folds
over herself like a kick and tumbles from the futon to the floor.

"This is all terribly basic and very well as far as it goes," says
Mr. Charlock, digging with chopsticks for a piece of pork.
"Divinational time is orthogonal to pseudo-time, sure." Beside
him Mr. Keightlinger's chewing a bite of egg-salad sandwich,
his elbows up on the steering wheel. "What they don't seem to

appreciate, thinking of the apex of what they call vertical time as some synchronous slice of the godhead," he takes a pull from a bottle of soda and sticks it back between his knees, "anyway, thing they don't seem to understand is, you've made it, you're swanning about where everything just *is* in perfect harmony and synchronous bliss, well great, but you still haven't solved the fucking problem of nirvana, that one eternal unanswerable question: what happens next?"

"Nothing," says Mr. Keightlinger, thoughtfully plucking a shred of greasy lettuce from his beard.

"*Nothing!* Nothing fucking happens there! Because it's all happy and perfect and as it should be and you don't *want* anything and you don't *need* anything, because bliss is instantaneously everywhere, so nothing ever *changes*. Nothing happens. You are. Effectively. Dead. There's a reason they call it heavenly." Mr. Charlock pulls a half-eaten egg roll from a paper sack. "And I don't know about you, but dead is the *last* thing I want."

"I would have to agree," says Mr. Keightlinger, popping a potato chip into his mouth.

Mr. Charlock taps his temple with the chopsticks. "*Fuck* enlightenment. I *like* having fallen from stuffy old perfect grace, being locked up in this box of bone, quote unquote trapped in this ugly old world where I want things and need things and get to fucking *do* things. Where things *change*. You know there's a *reason* Western civilization took over the fucking world. We *harnessed* that shit. We gotta see what happens *next.*"

"Lights out," says Mr. Keightlinger, setting what's left of his sandwich on the dashboard.

"Really?" says Mr. Charlock, scrunching down to peer up through the windshield at a fourth-floor window of the building opposite. "I dunno. Looks like she's got candles going in there. She got something on the side with somebody in the building?"

"You'd know."

"Christ, don't remind me. Just tell me, again, why we aren't up there snatching her right the hell now."

"Observe," says Mr. Keightlinger, scooping the last bits of chip from the bag. "Do not engage."

"He wants the Princess in December, why's he hire us in June? The hell? She is up there, alone, utterly and completely naked, not even a fucking dreamcatcher on the wall, her bodyguard stormed off who the hell knows where, I bet she hasn't even locked the goddamn door. Ripe and ready and this could be over in five minutes none the wiser, but we gotta sit on our tuches and observe and not fucking engage." Mr. Charlock sets his carton on the dashboard chopsticks clattering. "Something's up. Can't you feel it?" He lifts his feet up to the seat squatting up and twisting over the back of it. "Whole tight thing, back of your neck?"

"Where are you going?" says Mr. Keightlinger.

"To check it out," says Mr. Charlock, climbing into the back seat.

"Mr. Charlock," says Mr. Keightlinger, leaning abruptly to avoid one of Mr. Charlock's kicking black wingtips.

"Keep your tie knotted," says Mr. Charlock, lying down across the seat. "I ain't engaging. Just observing more closely. Fuck tha thirteen-twenty, right? Twelve-sixty forever."

"I have no idea what you're talking about," says Mr. Keightlinger.

"What's endearing is you think I do," says Mr. Charlock, closing his eyes. "Wakka-ding-hoy." He folds his hands on his chest.

Mr. Keightlinger picks up the soda bottle Mr. Charlock left on the floorboard. He takes a swig. Rubs the back of his neck. "Tight?" he says. "You feel anything? Whoops. Heads up." He reaches into his jacket and pulls out a pair of classic black sunglasses. The left lens covered with spidery words written in white ink. He puts them on. Outside across the street in the rain Jo's running past, stumbling to a stop at the doors to the lobby of the building holding onto the handle, throwing back her head to whoop with delight as she hauls the door open. Mr. Keightlinger purses his lips, leaning down a little, looking up through the sunglasses from Jo crossing the glass-walled lobby toward the elevator along the building above. He whistles softly. "Mr. Charlock?" He leans back. "Mr. Charlock." Mr. Charlock moans. "Wake up, Mr. Charlock," says Mr. Keightlinger. Mr. Charlock's hands have come unclasped and wave about before his face. His eyes still closed. "Whole building's ringing," says Mr. Keightlinger. "You'd best come back."

Mr. Charlock begins to scream. Mr. Keightlinger opens his door with a sharp popping squonk as Mr. Charlock arches his back heels drumming as Mr. Keightlinger climbs out of the car and leans his seat forward to shove his way through grabbing Mr. Charlock by the shoulders. Mr. Charlock's voice scraping out of his throat as Mr. Keightlinger swings his big arm in that narrow space to slap him, hard, and again. The scream cuts off.

"You all here?" says Mr. Keightlinger, rain plopping on his broad black-suited back.

"Anybody," says Mr. Charlock, and he coughs, "this side of the river the *least* bit sensitive's gonna have *such* the headache tomorrow." His hands up to either side of his face he brings them down staring at the darkness spotting his fingertips. "Wow," he says. "I never bled from my ears before."

LAUGHING SHE OPENS THE DOOR – NOT EVEN BREATHING
SOMETHING SHARP – "HOLD OUT YOUR HAND"

LAUGHING SHE OPENS THE DOOR to the apartment. "Ysabel?" she calls, standing there in the little hallway kitchen. Out in the main room three candles still burn on the glass-topped café table. Before them a small glass jar, uncapped, empty, sides filmed with milky residue. "You wanted a little atmosphere?" Jo flicks the light switch. The shoulders of her jacket and her short brown hair are dark with rain. Her face screws up. "Jesus, the *smell*," she says. On the carpet bare feet bare legs stretching along around the corner Jo's suddenly darting forward to see Ysabel naked on the floor by the futon head to one side eyes open mouth slack black curls smeared and wet. Jo hands over her mouth eyes wide. "Ysabel?" Her voice gone quiet, and then, coming back, "Oh fuck oh fuck. Ysabel. What have you done? What," kneeling by Ysabel's side hand over Ysabel's throat under her matted plastered hair, "did you take," reaching instead for her wrist, the arm flung to one side over the futon, stopping short and coming up to her own face, reaching down again to peel the hair from Ysabel's throat and breast, her thumb then fingers feeling for a pulse just below the corner of Ysabel's jaw when Ysabel's mouth sucks down a thinly ragged breath. Jo shrieks her hand jerking back up in the air. That breath escapes in a gentle sigh and is followed by another, deeper, bubbling in the pit of it. "Fuck," Jo's saying, "Jesus fuck," almost a sob, "what did you do what did you do." Reaching for Ysabel's flung-aside arm, pulling it close, looking to the crooks of her elbows. "What did you do." Jo stands, looking about the room. By the candles on the table the jar still filmed with a milky residue.

She snatches it up and holds it to the light, brings it to her nose for a sniff. A slime of vomit clings to her hand, and she sniffs that, her face screwing up again. "The fuck *is* this stuff? *What did you do?*"

Another ragged breath Ysabel's back arching one arm reaching up her hand a claw, her other arm clutching her belly eyes wild red-rimmed looking for Jo. "Oh fuck," says Jo, dropping to her knees again by Ysabel as Ysabel's arm reaching for Jo grabbing at Jo's arm Jo's hands hanging useless, "I don't know," and then finally Jo reaches out and pulls Ysabel to her, "what's happening," Ysabel's breath now coming in short and shallow pants, "Ysabel, say something, please," Ysabel's head settling on Jo's shoulder the claws of her hands relaxing one loosing its grip on Jo's shoulder falling away slowly slumping the arm to the floor as she sags in Jo's embrace. "Ysabel. Ysabel, please. Breathe goddammit. Breathe. *Breathe!*" Jo leans back. Ysabel's head slumps forward and Jo catches her chin lifting up and back Ysabel's eyes closed now her jaw slack once more. "Ysabel!" Jo shakes her. Ysabel's head flopping back and forth loosely on her neck. "Oh God Ysabel you stupid. Stupid fucking goddamn Ysabel you stupid, *stupid,* stupid – " Jo slaps her. Lifts her head. Slaps her again. "Fuck!" Pulling her close, holding her tightly her head again on her shoulder, "Oh God I don't know I don't know." Rocking back and forth. "I don't know what to do, Ysabel, I don't know what to do, I don't, I don't." Slowing. Jo leans back away again, lays Ysabel's body gently down supporting her shoulders, her head. "Roland," says Jo. "Roland." Ysabel laid out on the floor by the futon Jo smoothing her hair back straightening her arms. Ysabel's belly shivers. "Oh, God," says Jo, and she does not brush the fluttering skin with her fingers. "Roland," she says, and she stands.

Jo savagely twists the handle of the window cranking it open leaning against it with her shoulder. "Roland!" she cries. "Roland! *Roland!*" Leaning out over the faux balcony hands on the flaking white railing. *"Roland!"* Screaming into the rain. "Woot!" cries someone outside unseen. In the parking lot across the street a big man in a dark suit's standing next to a black car looking up at her. "Roland," she says again, her voice faltering. "You useless sonofabitch. Five fucking dollars and you can't, you can't fucking *hear* me when I *need* you, Roland! *Roland!*"

A block or two away a car's honking a screech of tires and coming around the corner there a figure all in white streetlight glinting from green piping flashing from jagged green sunglasses like pieces of broken bottle running across the street under the window and there's a banging down there and a yell and the sound of breaking glass. Jo steps back from the window knuckling her eyes. She finds the spindly wrought-iron chair by the table and falls into it as footsteps shake the hall outside. He doesn't knock. The door bangs open and he's there, past the little hallway kitchen and standing before her in the main room, one hand stripping off his sunglasses, one hand knocking the blue and white headphones from his ears. Not even breathing hard. Rain shining in the white-blond fuzz of his hair.

"She's naked," he says.

"She isn't fucking *breathing,*" says Jo. "She took something. I don't know, what is it you people take. It isn't heroin. She fucking overdosed on *some*thing – " He's by the table looming over her snatching up the small glass jar, turning it over in his gloved hand, watching the milky residue roll down the sides. "Who gave this to her?" His voice quiet, strained.

"I don't know. We have to get her help, Roland. I don't know who to call or where – "

"Who *gave* this to her?"

"I don't know!"

"You *must* know. She's your *responsibility.*"

"Roland, please," says Jo, still sitting in that spindly chair. "She's dying."

He closes that jar in his fist and stoops to pick up the Spongebob Squarepants towel from the floor. He drapes it over Ysabel's body, then sits on the edge of the futon, dragging his gloved hand through the foul spew puddled among the blankets. He lifts his slimed hand holding something pinched, a pearly curd. He squeezes it until it bursts in a sudden puff of ashy dust that hissing he shakes away, beating his hand against the blankets. He rips the velcro on his glove and peels it off, dropping it in the vomit. "Is this it? The only bed?"

"Nah," says Jo, "there's another one in the bathroom. *I'm kidding.*"

"Then help me strip this one," he says.

Jo gets up from the chair and sets the pillows to one side and together they bundle the blankets together, the sheets, Jo wadding them into one of the blond wood crates at the foot of the futon. The futon itself is stained, an irregular dull grey patch soaked through the white ticking. "Help me lift her up here," says Roland.

"That isn't puke," says Jo.

"Careful." Roland takes up Ysabel's shoulders cradling her head as Jo hooks her hands behind Ysabel's knees. They lay her on the futon close to the wall, away from the stain. "She's so *heavy,*" says Jo. Roland's resettling the towel over Ysabel's body. "Who gave her the jar?" he says.

"I can't suddenly remember something I never knew," snaps Jo.

"This is important, Jo." Sitting there at the head of the futon, hands on his knees, one bare, one still gloved.

"So's *this!*"

"She's not in any danger of dying. Not the way you think. Was there anyone at the grocery store today?"

"She's just gonna wake up, is that it? Nothing but maybe a terrible hangover? Blinding headache? Shivers and shakes and babies on the ceiling? What are we *talking* about here, Roland?"

"Anyone at all that you recognized, today?"

"What the hell with today?"

"She *did* it today," says Roland. "You left her *alone,* today. At the grocery store."

"This is *not,*" says Jo, but Ysabel's hand lifts a little fingers trembling and her chin tilts mouth opening around a gurgling sip of air. "Hell," says Jo, when Ysabel's hand settles palm up now, "if it's me leaving her alone, then maybe it was somebody at the Queen's dinner party? Or the siege at the church last week. Or hell maybe it was you gave it to her while I was off hunting the boar with the Duke. Somebody could have dropped it off tonight while I was out getting jumped – "

"To*night?*" roars Roland.

"Shit's gotta get done! She wouldn't get out of the fucking tub! And what the fuck would it matter me leaving her alone? Did *I* know she wasn't supposed to get a fucking jar of something? Somebody walks up and hands a jar of something to her and what do I say because did anybody *tell* me? *Jesus,* Roland, *what* do we *do?*"

He's looking down at his bare hand picking at the velcro straps of his remaining bicycle glove. "I need a knife," he says.

"What?" says Jo.

"A carving knife. Steak knife. Something sharp." She's looking at him blankly. "I can't use my sword, Jo. Never mind." He heads for the little hallway kitchen, opening drawers, rattling through cutlery.

"What are you," Jo tries to say, and then again, "what are you going to cut." Staring down at Ysabel's body, at the towel trembling, rippling over Ysabel's belly. "Roland? What the fuck are you going to *cut?*" He's standing by the glass-topped café table holding the long thin blade of a knife in the flame of the tall white candle. "Jesus Roland," says Jo getting up from the futon, grabbing his arm, "what are you *doing* – "

"If you struggle," he says, "a cut will destroy her." He holds the knife up. The blade smoked black, the edge of it glimmering sparking red here and there.

"What are you *cutting,*" says Jo, not letting go of his arm.

His headphones clack together around his neck as he shifts in Jo's grasp. "She tried to turn the medhu," he says, his voice flat. "She failed. It's gone bad in her and must be cut out."

Jo lets go of his arm. "Tell me you're not going to hurt her."

Roland takes a step toward Ysabel's body on the futon. "I must," he says. "Try your best to remember that this is chirurgerie. Not battle." He kneels beside her, heedless of the stain.

"Wait," says Jo. "Don't we need bandages or something? Boiling water? I don't – "

"Sit," says Roland. "Please."

"Okay," says Jo, and she sits in the spindly wrought-iron chair. Roland the knife in his gloved hand reaches for the towel with his bare hand and lifts it from Ysabel's body. The muscles in her stomach bunch and relax, bunch and relax. He leans over her bare hand gingerly just below her breasts on the arch of her ribcage knife point-down in his gloved fist tip of it there by his bare thumb. Jo closes her eyes squeezes them shut then opens them just as Roland punches the tip of the knife through Ysabel's skin.

Jo gasps knuckles to her mouth. Ysabel's shoulders jump neck arching and no sound is coming from her open mouth. Roland crouching bare hand shivering drags the knife from her sternum down and down through her navel opening a yellow line that gleams that shines that dims filling with something darkening reddish brownish black that overflows in runnels slow and thick like syrup down her flanks her hips jerking one of her arms flopping and from the back of her throat now a keening grating groan her head tipping over her chest rising around a great sucking draught of air and Ysabel begins to scream.

"Help me." Roland's tossed the knife to the floor and is wrapping his arms about Ysabel's kicking legs. "Her shoulders." Jo's up from the chair and kneeling by Ysabel's head knocking from side to side eyes open as she screams. "Let her cry!" Jo's hands leap from Ysabel's face. "Let her cry," says Roland hoarsely. "Help me turn her. On her side." Ysabel's belly clenching at the bottom of her scream a bubble brown and shining slicked with red and yellowed black swelling from the wound as Jo shovels her hands under Ysabel's back and when they lift her and turn her it bursts spattering the wall the futon Roland's crisp white track suit hissing and steaming Jo's jeans her jacket sleeve her face a weight of it slopping from the wound oozing across the futon between them splashing the carpet with great thick plops staining Roland's spotless white running shoes. "Hold her," he says, standing. Ysabel's legs gone limp now. Her scream crumbled into sobs. "Hold her." Jo awkwardly shifting her hands her grip into a hug Ysabel reaching for Jo's arms pulling Jo close, "Jo," she's saying in among the hiccups, "oh Jo."

"Shh," says Jo. "You're gonna be okay. It's gonna be okay." She's looking over at Roland as she says this, Roland tugging at a zipper on a white nylon pouch. "Okay," says Jo. "It's okay."

"The wound," says Roland. "Hold it shut. We must close it." Jo's staring down at the ruin of Ysabel's belly edges of the cut hanging slackly gleaming oily in the light and streaked with hints and blots of greens and blues, purples, reds and yellows, the stain on the futon spread before her now a fan of seeping darkness wetly plop of fat drops here and there still falling to the carpet. "I don't," says Jo, and then, "there's nothing," and then, "there's nothing there. Is there." Her hands stained the color of liver. Her jacket cuffs soaked. Ysabel's wet eyes gently closed.

"This'll be enough," says Roland, pulling a plastic baggie from the nylon pouch. "This might be enough." A thimbleful of gold dust in one corner of it. He looks up at Jo cradling Ysabel in her arms her hands slipping in the dark mess of the wound Ysabel's eyes closed tightly now biting her lip. "Jo," he says. "Jo, you'll need to." Holding the baggie out to her.

It takes a moment before she looks up at him. She says, "I can't."

"There's not much here. You've the keeping of her. It'll mean more, from your hand – "

"Roland, I can't. I'm not, I don't, I don't have the – "

"The what?" His voice rising, no longer ragged. "The honor? The devotion?" His face softens. "Jo," he says. "Hold out your hand."

She holds out her hand, reaching across Ysabel's body. He pours the dust into it.

"Oh," says Jo. "Oh wow."

"Quickly," says Roland.

Jo carefully lowers her hand glowing enough to light up that darkness as she presses it flat against the wound Ysabel hissing

rigid and trembling as Jo draws that hand up along the wetly
open edges of the wound and where it passes all that's left behind's a whitish line of scar. Jo strokes Ysabel's belly again and
even the scar puckers away, the dregs of the stain on Ysabel's
skin dissolving in sparks of color, and when Jo closes her dimming hand in a fist and opens it again no longer glowing at all
it's been scoured clean. Ysabel's twisting in Jo's arms laying her
head against Jo's chest. "I'm so," she's saying. "Sorry. I never."

"Shh," says Jo. Then, "I think she's asleep."

"She will for a while," says Roland. "You'll want to get her
off that bed."

"Yeah, well," says Jo, slumped against the wall unmoving,
"the smell alone. Christ how am I gonna clean this up."

"You must burn it all," says Roland, sitting heavily in the
spindly wrought-iron chair. "Nothing but bad luck and night-
mares will come of it now."

"What," says Jo, "even the carpet? I think, I think they're
gonna have a problem with that." Laying her head back, eyes
closed. Ysabel's head slipping from her chest to her shoulder.
"Could you maybe find an uncursed blanket or something? I
don't wanna disturb her."

"Oh," says Roland. "Of course." Standing and rooting about
the scattered laundry, he scoops up the Spongebob Squarepants
towel and shakes it out, holds it up, eyeing both sides. He
spreads it over them both, Jo on her side, Ysabel asleep in her
arms. "There," he says. "There." Jo's closed her eyes.

"You guys gonna buy me a new bedroom set or what?" she
says, her voice thick with sleep.

"You *must* learn to take this more seriously," says Roland, and
Jo snorts, shaking with quiet giggles. Roland straightens, frowning. "You *do* realize," she says, when she can, "how funny that is."

"Yes," says Roland. "I think I do." Jo's quivering giggles re-
double. Roland turns and sits heavily in the spindly chair. He
fingers the stain on the knee of his crisp white track pants, a
purplish brown that fades to yellow at its edges like an old bruise.

When Jo begins to snore lightly, he gets to his feet and heads
into the little hallway kitchen and stoops to knock on the cabinet

door under the sink. He knocks again. He looks up, straightens and knocks on the cabinet door up above the refrigerator. As he's doing so he's looking down at the sink full of dirty dishes. "Oh," he says, shifting the handle of a frying pan caked with leftover refried beans. "I see." He looks about the main room, Jo and Ysabel asleep under the thin towel, the appalling stain splattered across the futon and the carpet, the pile of ruined blankets and sheets kicked to one side, the drifts of Ysabel's dirty laundry here and there about the room. The black spear-haft stretched on the floor under the glass-topped café table. The dead candles. He steps into the room and picks up the knife from where he'd tossed it, then heads back out again, switching off the lights as he goes.

Awake, she

AWAKE, SHE sits upright blankets falling into her lap. One hand to her breast one to her belly, tangled black hair slipping over one shoulder in a matted clump as she holds herself. Something scrapes. Something's sizzling. Her mouth opens around a word. She tries again: "Jo?" she says.

Jo pops around the corner from the little hallway kitchen, spatula in her hand. "You're awake," she says. "Did I wake you? How you doing?" She's wearing boxers and a loose black tank top.

"Thirsty," says Ysabel, her voice rough and weak. Jo busies herself in the kitchen with cabinets and the refrigerator as Ysabel leans back closes her eyes pulls the blankets to her chin.

"We only had the two eggs left," says Jo. Ysabel opens her eyes and takes the glass of water. "I cut 'em with the can of cream of mushroom. Campbelled eggs, which I used to have when I was a kid." She's setting plates on the blankets by Ysabel, greyish yellow glops of egg, black-cornered toast. "Only I think the ratio of egg-to-soup needs to be higher. But you can soak the toast in it, which is good because the bread's pretty stale." Ysabel's handing back the glass, empty, tugging the blankets back up to her chin. "You want a shirt?" says Jo.

Ysabel shakes her head. "These are new," she says. The top blanket's a woolly plaid in black and red and orange-browns over a maroon thermal blanket.

"They replaced the futon, too," says Jo, forking up some runny egg. "With a mattress, but whatever. No idea how they did it while we were sleeping on it." The carpet where she's sitting's no longer stained, but bleached almost white in big round spots. "Dishes weren't done, though. And your clothes are still all over the place." She scoops some more egg onto her toast, looks at Ysabel. "I went ahead," she says, "and called us out sick to work. Stomach flu, I said."

"Jo," says Ysabel. "What did you do to me?"

"What did we," says Jo. "We saved you, Ysabel."

"I don't know about that." Ysabel's slumping, folding about herself.

Jo says, "What the hell was that stuff" as Ysabel's saying, "I feel, I feel lighter. Empty. Emptier. As if something were missing." Holding herself tightly under the blankets. "I'm cold."

"Roland said it turned on you. It went bad. And we had to cut it out of you."

"What does *he* know."

"More than me."

Ysabel reaches our from under the blankets and takes Jo's hand. "I never meant," she says, and she squeezes, lets go, pulls her own back under the blankets. "It's a mystery."

"Well, yeah," says Jo.

"I mean it might have been working. Maybe that's what has to happen. Every single, every time." Curled about herself she rests her cheek on her knees. "I don't know."

"What are we talking about?" says Jo, her hand on Ysabel's shoulder.

"What does the Queen do?" Ysabel sits up, Jo's hand falling away.

"Your mother? I don't — "

"Why is she the Queen? Where does the owr come from, Jo?"

"The owr?" Jo frowns. "Roland said a different word. Began with an em."

"Medhu," says Ysabel. They sit there a moment, Ysabel on the bed, Jo beside it, eyes locked, plates forgotten.

"So you," says Jo, "the Queen takes this," and there's a knock on the door. "Fuck," she says. The knock again. "Hang on," says Jo, getting to her feet.

"Jo," says Ysabel, "wait."

"Just a minute," says Jo, heading into the little hallway kitchen, opening the door to the apartment. Marfisa's there in black boots and a dark blue trench coat, her hair about her shoulders a loose cloud of curls the color of clotted cream. "Jo Gallowglas," she says. "I will not come in."

"Okay," says Jo.

"Marfisa," calls Ysabel weakly from the bed.

"I would have you know," says Marfisa, "that come the Samani, when our Queen with her hand gives you a sword and names you a knight, I will then have you offered grease and ash and sugar that your body might prove the merits of my quarrel: you are a false knight, and in no wise fit to bear blade or office."

"You're," says Jo, "you're talking about a duel."

"I would not have anyone say you were surprised. In seventeen days, I will take her from you. Whether you choose to fight or not is of no concern to me." Marfisa turns and walks away down the hall, toward the elevators.

"Marfisa!" calls Ysabel, her voice still rough, still weak. "Axe!"

Park that car.
Drop that phone.
Sleep on the floor.
Dream about me.

—*Emily Haines*

NO. 9

GIUST

MARFISA FALLS sprawling greaves striking sparks from the bricks sword bouncing from her hand clattering away as she clambers after it sandal-soles slapping for purchase when the kick catches her in the gut lifting rolling her arms tucking about her head tumbling after the blade that skitters down the slight slope toward the glass doors away across the plaza. Cries from the crowds on the great sweep of steps, the low walls to either side of the brick-paved plaza, the balconies hung with banners slack in the still night air, the hawk and the hound and shining above them both in the harsh white light the bee. On her side Marfisa her head cradled one curled arm eyes swollen shut yellowing lip split the ravages of a blow. Leaves of her armored skirt askewed a dent bashed into the edge of her breastplate crimping broken links of torn mail beneath dug into ripped silk and an ugly, milky wound. Groaning rolling her free arm over she plants her hand by her face. Names are cut into the bricks beneath her fingers, James Elkins and Michael Lynn Tinnin and Marie Equi. The crowd gone quiet again. The footsteps nearing echo starkly, sharp metallic clacks. Muscles clench under a darkening bruise she pushes herself up hissing armor chiming to her hands and knees and stooping into loping strides arms back and wide for balance footsteps ringing faster now behind her and louder, closer, there the sword her hand on the hilt lifting turning swinging to catch the blade sliced

325

at her knocked to one side ducking her shoulders beneath the slice her arm slipping up under the massive gauntlet driving her sword inside to stop suddenly screeching blade-tip caught against the greened bronze disk strapped to his bare chest.

He staggers back one step, two, his battered boots heavy on the bricks. The painted skull-mask swallowing half his head its up-turned mane of black hair rippling slowly in some unfelt tremor of wind. Beneath the crudely chiseled mask-teeth overhanging his lips twist in an ugly smile. She's half-bent over still her sword yanked back before her at an angle shoulders heaving with the ef-fort of dragging in gulps of air one slow tentative step at a time backing away chime and smack of skirt and sandals in the breath-less air of the plaza ringed by hundreds of people limned by sharp white streetlights, hundreds of mouths half-open waiting to howl or cheer or gasp or cry again. His free hand wrapped in a knotted leather thong pressed to that greened disk his sword twirls once in his gauntleted hand that mask lifting black mane floating weirdly in the light and the empty shadowed holes where eyes should be looking away from her crouched before him looking up and over the balcony above the glass doors where the banners hang limply hound and hawk and bee and beneath them the Queen in her black dress standing, behind her on the balcony Jo in a simple dress long and grey with yellow piping, her hand white-knuckled in Ysabel's white-knuckled hand.

"End this," says the Queen.

"You're changing the subject," says Jo, pushing through the crowd after Ysabel who's through the door and darting to the right, singing "Ever survive, ever so I, honest of mind most of the time!" Twirling arms flung wide in her bulky pea coat. "Ysabel!" calls Jo. "The line's gonna be fucking ridiculous."

"So?" says Ysabel. "I want a donut."

"I asked you a question."

Ysabel's smiling eyes shining, black curls swept back beneath a grey watch cap. "Could it possibly be more important than a chocolate donut with chocolate frosting and those horrible little chocolate cereal puffs all over it?"

"I said wouldn't it be better if she won."

Ysabel's smile sloughs away. Jo there before her the crowd pressing about them, Jo shoulders hunched hands stuffed in the pockets of her careworn jacket grey-green in the lurid neon light, cuffs of her baggy houndstooth pants rolled over her mismatched Chuck Taylors. Jo saying, "You could go home, or at least a fuck of a lot closer."

"You'd be *dead,* Jo," says Ysabel.

"Which is a downside," says Jo, looking to one side.

"And I'm fine, here, with you. You know?" That smile slinks back. "I've seen more shows the past couple of months than I ever saw in a year with Roland."

"Ten dollar covers," says Jo, "and shitty well drinks. For this I'm supposed to beat your girlfriend in a sword fight."

"*Ex*-girlfriend," says Ysabel.

"I hit her with a sword – if I manage to hit her with a sword – that's it, right? A duel counts? She'd be gone, like Tommy Rawhead." Ysabel nods. "I don't want to do that again," says Jo.

"If you don't – Jo, that's *why* she'll kill you. And not just beat you. To be sure."

Jo's shaking her head. "I could just not. Say no when she gets in my face. Drop the sword. Walk away."

"But," says Ysabel, "your *honor* – "

Jo barks up a bitter laugh. "*Fuck* that. Seriously. I'll be able to walk, is the thing. And anyway I don't give a shit about my honor, remember?"

"I said," says Ysabel reaching up as if to touch Jo's face, "you held it lightly enough." She stops, lowers her hand. "I was wrong. Wasn't I."

"Let's, you've got to be freezing." Jo's looking at Ysabel now, her legs below her short pea coat in black stockings whorled with fronds of clocking. "You forgot to wear pants again."

Ysabel claps her grey-gloved hands. "I know what to do!" She grabs Jo's hand dragging her back through the thinning crowd spikey heels clicking on the sidewalk. "Whoa," Jo's saying, and "what the hell" around the corner past the club Ysabel saying "It's literally I mean just two blocks away, I can't believe I didn't think of this before" at a half-run across the street and through a narrow empty parking lot, under a colonnade and over the light-rail tracks to stomp to a stop in a little cobbled plaza. Another colonnade freestanding across from them says Ankeny Square in mottled gold letters rimmed with old water stains. Behind them a grand old building, laser-printed signs saying No Sitting or Sleeping in Front of the Windows taped over and over to the glass along the first floor. In the center of that plaza a dead fountain, a low octagonal pool. Two caryatids in the center of the empty pool stand back-to-back a great basin held over their heads. "Do you have a penny?" says Ysabel.

"A penny." Jo flips open her jacket to dig in her pants pockets.

"Any coin will do. But a penny's best."

"You gonna chuck it in and make a wish?" Jo drops a penny into Ysabel's outstretched hand.

"Something like that," says Ysabel, holding it up between them. "Okay," she says. A metallic clang somewhere behind her, then a rising gurgle. "Tell me. What is it," and she takes a deep breath, "what do you like best about, our situation." The spout in the basin is trembling.

"Our situation."

"If – if you were to walk. What would you miss the most?" Water's bubbling up and out of the spout, splashing into the basin. More clanking, and the bubbling redoubles.

"The promise," says Jo. "I made a promise, and I'm keeping it. And I don't want to break it now or fudge it, and get out on a technicality. You know?"

"I," says Ysabel, "okay." She nods quickly, shivering. "It *is* cold." Water's seeping out over the edge of the basin, here and there and there, drips becoming trickles that spread into falls joining all around the rim to become a glimmering curtain splashing into the dead dry pool. Ysabel's unbuttoning her coat.

"Ysabel?" says Jo. "What are you," and then Ysabel's handing her the coat. Tugging off her cap. Holding out her hand, turning and lifting a foot up onto the edge of the pool. "I want to do this before it gets too deep," she says.

"You're nuts," says Jo, helping her step up onto the edge.

"Not my rules," says Ysabel, and she steps gingerly into the water. "Oh, fuck me, it's *freezing.*" Hugging herself in her minidress shining silver and white wading a couple of steps up to the waterfall. "Ysabel?" says Jo, but Ysabel ducking her head and closing her eyes steps through the water with a shriek. "Ah geeze," says Jo, holding the pea coat. Behind the waterfall Ysabel's reaching up to grab a caryatid's upturned arm, stepping onto its plinth, balancing on her toes against the statue ducking under its arm to press the penny to its expressionless lips, to whisper something in its ear and follow it with a kiss, to drop the penny in the stony drape of scarf across its impassive breast. Stepping off the plinth and ducking back through the waterfall, gasp and sputtering, leaping tottering up on the edge of the pool as Jo reaches up to help her down.

"There," says Ysabel, brushing water from her face as Jo wraps her in the coat. She huddles into it. Jo rubs her arms. "That's that," says Ysabel. "Say yes if she challenges you. Fight her if it comes to that. It'll all end up okay."

"Yeah?" says Jo. "What'd you wish for?"

"I can't tell you that!" says Ysabel. "It wouldn't come true. Surely you must know *that* much at least."

He's stepping out – a Boon – his Treat
something Wet & Ruined

He's stepping out of the elevator before the doors have fully opened, ducking his white-hatted head and lifting a white and ivory brogue over the inner doors opening vertically, swinging his shoulders draped in a long white coat to sweep through the outer doors opening side to side. Behind him a big guy and a little guy in black suits and skinny black ties, the little guy on his heels, thinned hair vainly trying to launch a curl between his brow and the top of his skull, a fiendish little basket-box in his hands carved from a single chunk of dark red wood. The big guy gives the chain that opens the doors one last tug and follows them. His beard's the color of mahogany and bushy enough to bury the knot of his tie.

The floor about them wide open and dark, plastic sheeting hung here and there lofting and popping in occasional gusts of wind. Bright light from caged lamps leaves deep pools of shadow in corners and along the white-patched drywall. On a folding chair sits a man in a soft blue suit his arms folded, his white hair touched with gold in dreadlocks hanging down about his face, brushing his shoulders, "Leir," he says.

"Viscount Pinabel," says Mr. Leir, doffing his hat. His face quite young beneath all that white unruly hair. "I hope the season finds you well? Above us ascends a woman of good face and habit; two men strike at her, and their blows bring about comeliness, beauty, but also all manner of strife and treachery, deceit, detractation, and perdition."

"Charles. Wentworth. Leir," says Agravante, and plastic sheeting rustles in a sudden gust. "Tell me why I am sitting in a half-finished building."

Mr. Leir smiles, hands his hat to Mr. Keightlinger, then slips his coat from his shoulders. "Such a quaint superstition," he's saying.

"I told you to *tell* me," says Agravante. "What went wrong?" Plastic rustles and pops again.

"To believe that, because one knows the full and true name of a thing, or a person," says Mr. Leir, folding his coat and draping it over Mr. Keightlinger's outstretched arm, "one might then control it. As if all that I am, my blood, my bones, every book I've read, the sandwich I had for lunch and the two thousand dollar shoes on my feet, the old friends I've loved, and betrayed, the vectors of every desire and necessity that have brought me here to stand before you at this moment – as if all that could be summed up and bent to your will with twenty letters written on a piece of paper filed away in the Breathitt County Courthouse."

Agravante's standing, chair pushed back. "I don't *care* about your shoes" he's saying but Mr. Leir folds his arms there between Mr. Keightlinger and Mr. Charlock and says "Oh, but you should. It's *precisely* the knowledge of these little things that grants us the control we seek. That you, for instance, Viscount," and he untucks a hand to begin ticking points with his fingers, "chafe under the thumb of your grandfather, that you've no stomach ever to try and sit the Throne yourself, that you've set aside money and property in an attempt to position yourself with respect to those you see as most likely to become the King Come Back, that – and this may seem the *important* fact, but it's not, for you are prudent and adaptable though your current suppositions in that regard are wrong, all wrong," and four fingers ticked off Mr. Leir now folds three back and lifts his index finger, a final point, "no, the important fact for our purposes here and now is that despite your care and preparation you'll be terribly surprised by what your sister plans to do in two weeks' time." Mr. Leir spreads his hands, and all about them plastic sheeting billows out, blown taut. "Is all that somehow wrapped up in a name I've known for years – Agravante Pinabel, Axehandle to Her Majesty's Court?" He shakes his head. Mr. Keightlinger's impassively keeping watch over the hat in his hand. Mr. Charlock's holding that basket box up and out and away from himself. Agravante's slowly sitting back down. "A name however true and full," says Mr. Leir, "serves merely to marshal these facts, to bring them to the forefront of my thoughts when I require."

"You spoke," says Agravante, "of my sister. And a terrible surprise."

"But one year and one day ago, Viscount," says Mr. Leir, "you asked me to intercede on your behalf with certain powers to ensure the success of a construction enterprise." Looking about the unfinished floor. "These riverfront condominium towers, which were presented in every particular detail drawn up in meticulously beautiful plans."

"Tell me what you know of my sister, sorcerer!" says Agravante, and all about them the plastic's snapping taut again, and the lights tremble in their cages splashing shadows about.

"These buildings," says Mr. Leir, "are not the buildings those plans described. Not in every particular detail."

"You," says Agravante, "you must mean, you can't possibly." Plastic rustles, flutters, collapses. "Elements had to be changed, I was told, yes, you'd be mad to think – "

"Compromise," says Mr. Leir, "is ever the death of art. Had *those* buildings been built, the ones presented to me last year in those plans, the ones on whose behalf I interceded – your success would have been assured." He beckons to Mr. Charlock, who steps up with that fiendish little basket-box. "I have fulfilled my end of our agreement. You in turn did deign to grant a boon."

"I did," says Agravante, quietly.

"I would have you take this from me, Viscount," says Mr. Leir, lifting the box from Mr. Charlock's grasp. "Keep it safe and undisturbed until I ask that you return it. Tell no one that you have it. If you fail me in this, know that not even the grave would keep me from making my displeasure known." Harsh light shines from where it's caught in the polished gloss of the dark red wood. "If it is in your power to do this thing for me, our agreement is satisfied, and we will be quits."

Agravante puts a hand on the box but does not take it. "You must tell me, sorcerer, what it is my sister's planning to do."

"Please," says Mr. Leir, smiling. "Call me Charles."

"Hup," he says and she steps forward knee bending deeply sword flashing forward and down whipping to thwap against the red heart pinned to the dummy before her. Her trailing leg a long straight line from planted foot to hip her off arm flung back along it. "And up," he says, and she pulls back settling her weight on that planted foot knees bent a little, sword-arm crooked the blade at a slight angle before her tip about the level of her eyes, off arm tucked close to her dingy padded jacket empty hand held palm out before her chest. "Hup," he says, and she lunges wrist flicking blade down whap against the red heart, "and up," he says, and back she settles waiting. "Hup," he says again, and then "okay," he says, "okay," thoughtfully stroking his salt-and-pepper Van Dyke. "Tell me what you're doing wrong."

"She's chopping," says Ysabel sitting back to the mirrored wall, not looking up at either of them but down at the small thick book in her lap, legs curled under the stiff pleats of a corduroy skirt.

"Please, lady," he says. "Less kibitzing. But you were," he says. "Chopping."

"Yeah," says Jo, standing relaxed upright looking down at the épée in her hands. The bell of it dull and dented, the hilt wrapped in grubby red tape.

"What have I told you about chopping?" He steps over to the rack of foils by the dummy and wraps his fingers around a complicated grip with odd bends and hooks like some obscure medical instrument. "Not to do it," says Jo, as he plucks the foil from the rack and swivels to glare at her down the wiry length of it scored with dings and nicks its dull black rounded rubber tip shivering there before her eyes. "This is a *needle,* girl. Not a damn cleaver. The reason the tip of it's padded is that's the part that's *dangerous.* You chop like that and all the power in your legs and hips and arm is wasted. All you bring to the table's the flick of your wrist. Not nearly enough. And if you do wind up for a decent cut," he swings the blade back and up and over his head, elbow up and out to one side, "you pull your blade away and leave yourself wide open for acres of time. Anybody could step in here and do whatever the hell they wanted and my one way to stop 'em's otherwise engaged." He lowers the blade en garde and then with a little fillip of a salute dips the tip to the floor. Jo's saying, "I guess I'm just, I keep thinking of how Orlando was coming at me."

"Mooncalfe's on a katana," says Vincent, tip of his sword whicking over a ragged x of blue tape on the floor. "Anybody uses a katana's a damn fool thinks a saber's really a scalpel. Every now and then, someone like him's crazy enough to pull it off."

"Marfisa wields a rapier," says Ysabel.

"Well, yeah," says Vincent. "Many knights do." Looking back and forth, from Jo's suddenly pursed mouth to Ysabel still not looking up from her book. "Four times out of five a heavy old-school Italian rapier beats a jumped-up Ginsu knife, all else being equal. Something you want to tell me?"

Jo shakes her head. Ysabel turns a page.

"*God*dammit," snaps Vincent, turning away, slashing at nothing. "*What* have I told you about keeping a low profile?"

"She pounded down my door while I was making breakfast in my underwear," says Jo. "That low enough for you?"

"It's okay, Mr. Erne," says Ysabel, setting her book to one side, as Vincent's saying, "You aren't nearly ready. Not nearly."

"It's *okay,*" Ysabel's saying.

"The Axe is *fast,* lady. She's beaten the Chariot, three for three." He turns back to Jo. "You *cannot* keep this shit from me, girl. The hell were you thinking?"

"She hasn't formally challenged Jo yet," says Ysabel. "Just said she would. At the Samani," and Vincent's saying "Okay, well," as Ysabel says, "Besides, I made a wish."

"I," says Vincent, and he swallows a grimace, not looking away from Jo. "Okay. Well. When she pops the question, then, you dumb enough to say yes?"

"The fuck do you care?" says Jo. "I say yes, I'm dead. I say no, I'm out. Either way you lose your two hundred bucks a month."

No one says anything. No one moves, until Vincent slams his rapier back onto the rack. "Lady," he says, hand braced on the edge of the rack, "please. Leave. Take your gallowglas with you." His shoulders rise and fall around a sigh. "Come back Monday." Jo's kneeling over by the door, shoving her épée into its soft leather sheath. Bundling it up in a couple of folded towels. "Before somebody says something we all end up regretting."

"Honestly, the two of you," says Ysabel, walking towards the door. "I *made* a *wish.*"

"That's a pepper bacon with cheese basket and a Black Forest shake, a colossal basket and a Pibb Xtra, two regular burgers no ketchup and a large Diet Coke, an Oregon Harvest with cheddar basket and iced tea. Those regular burgers want any fries?"

"Nah," drawls the driver, leaning out his open window. Slap 'em up and shake 'em up and then you know, says the car radio over a loping beat. Let 'em off the flow then bait 'em with the dough, you can do it funk or do it disco. The fat man in the back seat leans forward a little face still hidden in the shadows back there. "Get us some a them sweet potato fries. My treat."

"You want a large order?" says the speaker on the post by the lit-up menu board.

"Sure," says the driver. His chin is enormous, stained by red and green and orange light from the menu board. His eyes are very small and sleepy.

"Thirty dollars thirteen cents," says the speaker. "Pull up to window two."

"Ha," says the fat man, settling back as the driver puts the car in gear. "Tell him there's a boom in child prostitution, when he show up at the stroll give him lead restitution." Singing over the radio. "Ha!" Slapping the beat on bare knees below the ragged hems of his cargo shorts. The girl in the back seat by him sits pressed close against the door her elbow on the window-ledge, head in her hand, light from the drive-through window sliding across her closed eyes. Her hair scraped down to patchy stubble around a floppy mohawk. "Put a fifty in the barrel of a gun, yeah he try to suck it out well you know this one!" Shifting back and forth, scraggly hair wobbling as he bobs his head. Up front the driver's leaning over, poking the guy in the passenger seat, hand out, palm up. "The fuck," says the guy in the passenger seat. "His treat. He said." Dark hair hanging lankly down to his shoulders. Windbreaker zipped all the way up to his narrow throat.

"Timmo's only picking up the fries," says the driver. "Ante up."

"Five million ways, motherfucker!" bellows Timmo, shaking the back of the passenger seat. "You catch Mel's, too. You owe her I'm pretty sure. I know you're good for it." Grumbling to himself the guy in the passenger seat digs through his pockets. The clerk's handing drinks through the window and the driver hands the shake back to Timmo, then takes some money from the guy in the passenger seat and hands him a couple of large paper cups. "They used to call it Mr. Pibb," he says. "Pibb Extreme's a dumbass name."

"Call it whatever the fuck you want," says Timmo. He jabs a straw into his shake and takes a slurp. The driver's taking bags from the clerk and dropping them in the lap of the guy in the passenger seat, who's holding those cups up and out of the way. "We good?" says Timmo. "We good? Let's go, let's go, we divvy it up back at the house. Come on Abe let's go already."

"Problem," says the driver.

"What problem," says Timmo, leaning forward. Beside him the girl's stirring, lifting her head, opening her eyes. In front of the car a figure one hand on the hood long black hair lofting in a gust of wind face hidden in the shadows flung from headlight beams. "Fuck her," says Timmo. "Gun it."

"I ain't running her over," says Abe.

"Him," says the guy in the passenger seat.

"Him?" says Timmo. "Frankie? You *know* this fucker?"

The figure's walking beside of the car now, trailing that hand along the fender. White dress shirt half-unbuttoned, black hair settling about his shoulders. One eye's not lost in shadow but hidden under a black eyepatch cupped there beside his sharply angular nose. "Go," the guy in the passenger seat's saying, "go, go! Go!" Leaning back away from the door as the figure lifts a pale hand to knock on his window.

"He's in it," says Mel, scratching at her mohawk. "He's one of them that's in it."

"You want to tell me about this, Frankie?" says Timmo.

"Ho," says Abe. That pale hand's around a hilt now, rough black cloth wrapped over a bone-white grip, the butt of it tapping against the glass. "Shit!" Frankie's saying. Abe's got a gun in his hand, an ugly little revolver, barrel barely long enough to poke out over the knobby finger curled around the trigger. "Put that fucking thing away!" says Frankie.

"Well maybe you ought to get out of the car and talk to him," Timmo's saying. "Seems to me this is all on you and none of ours."

"You can't just leave me here," says Frankie. Timmo shrugs. "How the fuck am I getting back?"

"When you do," says Timmo, reaching up to snag the bags of food from Frankie's lap, "you best come talk to me." The barrel of Abe's gun pointing at Frankie's belly now. "Fuck," says Frankie, yanking the handle of his door, shouldering it open. Even as he's putting his feet on the pavement something grinds and chunks in the car and as he's turning to close the door, "Hey!" he yells, it leaps away engine snarling red lights flaring as it slows suddenly whipping right and squealing away down the street. "My burger!" he's yelling. "You shits!"

"Frankie," says Orlando, his sword held low at his side.

"Fuck you," says Frankie, turning to walk away. He stops mid-step. The bare tip of the blade's resting on his shoulder. He turns back, ducking out from under the sword even as Orlando's lifting it and pulling it back. "You're her ex, Frankie. Jo Maguire. Jo Gallowglas. You know a great many things about her, I'm sure. You know whom it is she loves."

"What?" says Frankie.

"Before," says Orlando, "I would not have cared how she was removed from court, so long as she was removed. But now – " He scratches his cheek by the eyepatch, tugging at the skin there a glimpse of something wet and ruined beneath. He lifts the sword with his other hand. "I cannot allow Marfisa to kill her in a duel. Not now. Not before I've had a chance to do terrible things to her." He strokes Frankie's cheek with the dulled back of the blade. "Things you will help me with."

"Kill?" says Frankie, voice a squeak, eyes on the sword there brushing his face. "Duel?"

RAW GREEN PEAS – THREE QUESTIONS ONLY
"SUBPARAGRAPHS AND SHIT" – TARNISH

RAW GREEN PEAS at the bottom of a teacup set to one side of the scarred linoleum counter. A fat red candle slumped in on itself guttering in a pool of melted wax, a couple of blue-tipped matches scattered before it. A blackened matchstick smoking in a shot glass blazoned with a Tlingit eagle. An old key blurred by rust, a splintery chopstick, a damp bus transfer in a plastic pot that says Oxygen Bleach Cleanser. A threadbare little rabbit on a leash of string nibbles at a page ripped from a pornographic magazine. More pages spread across the linoleum, lozenges of skin like brushed suede, like toasted caramel, like slick beige plastic. Gauze like drying sea-foam, lace like rotten ice, black vinyl shining tight. "Salt," says the woman sitting at the counter. The rabbit-string tied about her wrist. She flicks her head from side to side and wrinkles her nose. "Dried sweat." Hunched inside a sweater the color of flour, a floppy black hat pulled low over her yellow hair. Under the brim her eyes squint milkily.

"Okay," says the man sitting on the stool across from her. His coat is long and camel-colored. A derby reddish brown in one gloved hand, his other on a soft brown briefcase flat on the counter, buckles undone. A wooden cane leans against the counter, its handle a stern, rough-hewn hawk.

"Sea air," she says, "and bleach, and. Jelly?" That head-flick again, annoyed. "Old socks. Corn chips."

"Suggestive," he says. "First question, then?" She nods once, sharply. "How old are they?"

She shrugs, hat-brim dipping to meet her shoulder. "Old and old, Leo. Twenty-two days? Twenty-three?" On the wall behind her a number of paintings, one of spaceships on black velvet rigged with blinking lights, one with a shimmering tumble of light suggesting a waterfall behind translucent plastic. The tinny whine of its little motor in the silence. He sets the derby on the counter next to the briefcase. "Not old at all for a magazine," he says then, "not especially." Tugging his gloves off a finger at a time. "But old and old indeed for a bit of byblow."

"I didn't say it was byblow," she says, tugging the rabbit's string.

"Didn't ask," he says, stirring the pages about. "Three weeks ago the Princess and her guardian were attacked on a MAX train that came to a stop about a chain away from where this bag was finally found."

"Finally?" says the woman, rubbing the rabbit's nose.

"I didn't hear the details at first, didn't bug me for a while, I've been busy. Duke stuff. So Northeast went for somebody. So Northeast got distracted and didn't go hard. Happens all the time. Right?" He tugs one of the pages from the spread. "Only Northeast has plenty and plenty of monsters. Northeast doesn't need to make ugly hollow men from dried jizz and bad dreams." On the page in his hand a girl lying back tight orange jacket unzipped short skirt flipped over her belly dark stockings gartered halfway up her long long thighs striped underwear stretched taut between spread knees. "This is wizard-stuff. Witch-stuff. Red-blooded fool-stuff."

"You get three questions," she says, hauling the rabbit into her lap. "Not a lecture."

"I'm not the only one can put two and two together on this, Miss Cheney. Of course, most of them will think *I* commissioned the hit." He lays the page back on the counter. "I tell the Queen to make the Gallowglas a knight, she says no, this thing happens, the Gallowglas steps up. Voila! Her royal hand is forced. Looks nice and neat to the politically unsophisticated."

Her eyelid trembling she says, "You're trying to clear your name."

"Haven't the chance of a hope in hell, there," he says. "But forget the two shits I could give what people are saying. I want to know what they're *doing*. Second question. Who's touched this bag but me?"

Her mouth jumps open, snaps shut. The rabbit starts squirming. She leans over to let it down from her lap. "I couldn't say," she says, straightening.

"You couldn't say," says the Duke. "Well. There's a number of reasons maybe why you couldn't. You failed, say. It's beyond you. Or you can, but. You're under a geas. It violates the strictures of a promise you've made to someone else." His elbows on the counter, his chin in his hands. "The moment I ask whether or which, there's my third question. At least it's not like you could've, and chose *not* to, papered it over with rhetoric – " He smiles. "I almost said 'right?' then, with a questioning lilt like that. Boy, *that* would've been stupid."

"Ask your third question," she says, hat-brim hiding her eyes and her nose but not her soured mouth.

"What have you got in your pockets?" says the Duke.

She tips that floppy black hat back, her milky stare aimed squarely at him. Reaches down shifting her bulky sweater to dig into a pocket and come up hand closed around something she carefully places on the flesh-colored pages. Lifts her hand away. A little toy car, silver and green, sheened with weak afternoon light strained through the tall dusty windows behind him.

"The Chariot," says the Duke. "Can't say I'm surprised."

"It's not what you think," says Miss Cheney.

"Didn't ask," he says, setting the toy car to one side, scooping up the pages limp and slick, heavily awkward. "I find it's best when consulting an oracle to know what you want to know going in. Saves on sleepless nights afterwards, whittering over ambiguities."

"You'd know more," she says, head ducked again, "if you'd asked anything else with your third question. The tenth word on page twenty three, sixth book from the end. The name of my rabbit. When next you'll see the Bodach Glas," and the Duke says "Don't" as he's stuffing pages into the briefcase, and she says "Who'll win the duel between the Axe and the Gallowglas," as the Duke's saying "Don't even make a," and then he stops, one hand still holding the briefcase open. Frowning he says, "The who the what now?"

"Come back Monday," says Jo as the elevator doors close. "Monday's the fucking day." One hand carrying a long thin bundle wrapped in towels. The other's holding a foil-wrapped burrito in a red-and-white check paper boat.

"The Samani's not till midnight," says Ysabel, nibbling on a salad roll wrapped in rice paper.

"Great," says Jo. "Plenty of time for a pep talk before I stand up and get myself killed."

"It's not like you were going to learn that much in the next few days," says Ysabel. "What?" The elevator doors open and Jo stomps out and down the orange-carpeted hall. "You'll be *fine,*" says Ysabel, following after. "You have to trust me on this."

Jo's unlocking the apartment door, burrito in her other hand, bundle leaning against the wall. "*I* don't have a problem trusting you," she says, opening the door. "It's my lizard brain." Looking back at Ysabel. "Gets all fight-or-flight just thinking about it." Stepping in her leading foot slips forward suddenly and she falls back on her butt.

"You okay?" says Ysabel.

Jo sits up still holding the paper boat, inside it still the huge burrito wrapped in foil. "Ow," she says. On the floor a manila envelope with a label that says JO MAGUIRE 407. "The fuck?" says Jo, climbing to her feet.

Ysabel squeezes past her there in the little hallway kitchen, out into the main room past the glass-topped café table to crank open the window. Sits on the floor tapping a cigarette against a gold cigarette case. Still in the kitchen Jo's tugging a binder-clipped bundle of paper from the envelope, peeling up the first page or two with one hand, picking at the foil wrapping her burrito with the other. Ysabel lights her cigarette, then leans back to breathe smoke out the window, smoothing the stiff pleats of her corduroy skirt.

"Well," says Jo, letting the pages fall from her hand. "Shit. Turns out you aren't a houseguest. Turns out you're a member of my household. And because I didn't inform them of a change in the size of my household, they have no choice but to revoke my housing voucher."

"We weren't supposed to get that," says Ysabel. "Don't worry about it."

Jo looks over at her, eyebrows up. "We weren't supposed to get this."

"Yeah, he said there was plenty of time yet to stop the notice going out and there shouldn't be any hiccups. I guess he was wrong about – "

"Would 'he' be," says Jo, flipping up a couple of pages, "Tim Carroll?"

"Yes," says Ysabel.

"Who's no longer employed in a management capacity at the Gretchen Kafoury Commons?" says Jo.

"Well," says Ysabel, sitting up, "okay, but he gave his word. And he wrote it all out and gave me a copy. I didn't want to worry you, is – "

"That'd be," says Jo, flipping to another page, "the agreement should in no way be considered binding, and then it goes on to list all the, the things it's in violation of." She flips up another page, and another. "Subparagraphs and shit. It's an impressive list." She looks up from the document. "What the hell did you *do* to this guy?"

"Jo," says Ysabel, "I – "

"Christ, it never occurred to me I had to tell you not to talk to the fucking landlord about how you live here. I never thought you'd even *see* them without me around. Hell, that you even had the slightest idea what they were *for*."

"Do we need to," says Ysabel, leaning forward, "leave? Now?"

"Thirty days," says Jo, stuffing the document back into the envelope. "Gonna be one hell of a Thanksgiving."

"Well, then, there's time," says Ysabel, standing, flicking her cigarette out the window. "I just need to, I guess, talk to whomever's his boss – "

"You need to not, okay? Just," both hands on her head pushing her short hair back, "don't. Okay?"

"Jo, I can fix this," says Ysabel.

"How?" says Jo, throwing her hands in the air. "You gonna do somebody else what you did to Carroll that got him fired? That stirred up all this," picking up the envelope, "shit?" Dropping it to the counter again. "Is that how you're gonna fix it?" Ysabel's looking down, away, hands useless at her sides. "Make another goddamn wish maybe?" Ysabel slams her eyes shut, and her hands ball into fists.

"Tell him to stay down," says the man kneeling in the shadows.

"Stay down, Mike," says the very small woman standing by the gunmetal desk. Her face worn, her cheeks round and ruddy even in the dim light from the reading lamp on the desk.

"Not," a groan from the shadowed floor, a bubbling cough, and then "not a problem."

"I don't understand, sir," says the very small woman. A thin chain about her neck holds a pair of spectacles she lifts and fits over her eyes. "What offense have we caused?"

Something small and glinting arcs from the kneeling man that she catches awkwardly against her chest, a small glass jar, empty, filmed with some whitish residue. The spectacles fall from her eyes. She pinches the bridge of her nose. Sets the jar on the desk by the overflowing in-box. "You must be running low," says the kneeling man. "Send for a bucket, to catch what's spilling from him." He shifts, lifts an arm a wet sound slicing his hand in the light from the desk lamp, grubby fingerless bicycle glove, heavy golden pommel a sword gleaming swiveling in the light to point at her and sink back into the shadows again.

"I imagine you laughed long and loud together when she came to you with this," she says, "and told you what I thought I'd planned with her. But then you went and poured it straightaway into the Queen's pots. We're all running low these days, and watery-weak, and sour, waiting for a King who hasn't come."

"The Princess did not laugh at you, Soames," says the kneeling man. "The Princess is, *naïve.*" Shifting, standing, his face rising up into the light. "That jar was empty when I found it." His hair a close-cropped white-blond fuzz. About his neck a pair of blue and white headphones.

"Then she turned it," whispers the Soames, hands clasped before her face.

Roland shakes his head. "It went bad on her. I had to cut it out."

"You – " Her face gone blank, head pulling back and up as her shoulders sag. "You could have destroyed her. You may well have crippled her."

"Then there will one day be another Princess," says Roland. "But had she been found poisoned? Or had your mad plan worked, and she'd turned it on her own, usurped the Queen – "

"A Queen who's let this city starve," says the Soames, suddenly fierce.

"You'd rather see it ablaze?" says Roland.

And as suddenly she sags again. "I suppose, then," she says, "it's to be exile for us both." She picks up the small glass jar, turns it over in her hands. Roland in that slice of light says nothing. "Oh," says the Soames, setting the jar back on the desk. "Of course. You'd have to clap the Princess in irons, too. Whatever treason we've committed's just as much on her head." One hand up in a fist before her mouth. "There'll be a fire, won't there. We'll have been tragically trapped by the blaze. Working late, as we were, no one else to hear our cries for help."

"I must make certain, first," says Roland, looking down at the shadowed floor, taking a step back, and another. "Your name is Open Mike, isn't it." Both hands on the hilt of his sword.

"Yeah," says Mike from the floor.

"Forgive me, Open Mike," says Roland, lifting his sword above his head.

Mike retches. Something splatters. Both of the Soames' hands up over her mouth. "Fuck you, boss," says Mike.

Roland brings the sword down in a sudden savage chop.

The Soames shakily says "Tell me, sir. Will you next go to burn down the Axe's house, and strike her brother's head from his shoulders? She has tarnished more than the Bride's name in the eyes of the King, if he ever does come back – "

"Would you have those as your last thoughts, Soames?" says Roland, straightening.

"No," says the Soames, "no," and then as he tightens both hands on the hilt of his sword, "I had a dream, last night. Tell me, sir, are you young enough that you have always slept, and dreamed?" Roland doesn't nod. He doesn't shake his head. "I can remember when we didn't need such things," she says. "When I have them they are so terribly vivid, but so weightless, so inconsequential – last night I was somehow back in my little mountain hut. I could see the colors of the mismatched glazes of the tiles pressed into the mud walls so very clearly. Someone was serving me chestnut cakes hot from the griddle. Wrapped in wet leaves the way we used to, to keep them from scorching. Over and over they dropped to the table before me, and I peeled them and gobbled them, down every one."

When she does not say anything more, Roland says, "Stand to the side of the desk there, Soames Nell. And lift your chin."

"I should have known," she says, her words just loud enough to be heard. "They are the blandest things you can imagine, with not even a pinch of salt to be found." She steps away from the desk, hands at her sides, head high. Not looking at him. "But how I've missed the taste."

"My blade is sharp, and I am strong," says Roland. "If you do not flinch, it will be clean and quick." Lifting his sword, arms back and to one side. "Forgive me."

AN INDECISIVE CREAM – A CHANGE OF CLOTHES
ONE HELL OF A CUE – THE SOUND *&* THE LIGHT

THE OFFICE PAINTED AN INDECISIVE CREAM just big enough for a desk and a couple of chairs. Neither of them sitting. Jo's leaning against one of the closed doors still in her careworn jacket, army-surplus green. Over her shoulder a poster, a photo of the full moon that says Shoot for the moon... Even if you miss, you'll land among the stars. "You can't *do* this to us," she says.

Becker shrugs in his big flannel shirt, half-sitting on the edge of the desk. "My hands are tied. Client pulled the survey early. Tartt's as pissed as any of you and now Sales is out there scrambling," he jerks a thumb over his shoulder at the other closed door behind him, "because there's nothing in the hopper till Pet Depot comes back online in a couple of weeks."

"Come on, Becker! You got three people out there dialing a bee-to-bee right now. Give us a couple of phones. You know me and Ysabel can rack up completes like nobody else." Becker shrugs again, runs a hand through what little of his hair is left. "Becker, come on! You need the numbers."

"I need reliable people is what I need," says Becker. "You and her, you knock off early, you don't show up – "

"I call! I give you notice!"

"You play by the rules, yeah," says Becker. "And I can cut you slack on a night shift. But for the commercial stuff I need people in seats I know will be there. I mean, are you ever even conscious at six in the morning?"

"Fuck you, Becker," says Jo. "You know the shit we have to deal with."

"I know the what now?" says Becker.

"Fuck it," says Jo, slumping against the door. "Never mind."

"The job's unreliable, Jo. You know that. We had a good run but there's always downtime. Pet Depot's a sure thing in a couple of weeks. Until then, you know, apply for unemployment, hang tight, go find something else, I don't know. I can't tell you what to do here."

"It's just one more goddamn thing I have to – "

The door behind Becker pops open and a woman sticks her head through topped by a tricorn hat edged with frilly lace and red ribbons. "Arnie, I need that old WinBank file. I think it's on top of the monitor there?"

"Sure, Donna," says Becker, "just a second."

"Oh," she says, stepping through, seeing Jo. "Sorry. Didn't know you had someone in here." A garish red low-cut blouse that's slipped from both her shoulders held up by a shiny black corset. She points a short plastic cutlass at the desk. "Actually, I left it right there. If you could just." Becker scoops up the file and hands it to her. "I'll get out of your hair."

"Scrambling, huh," says Jo as the door closes.

"Halloween party," says Becker.

"Yeah? What are you going as?"

"Isn't it obvious?" He spreads his hands grinning ruefully. "Phone room supervisor."

Jo splashes water over her face, runs wet hands through her hair. Hangs a moment over the sink hands braced to either side. "Come on," she says to herself. "Come on. You can do this. Whatever the fuck it is. Do it." Pushing up and there she is in the mirror over the sink. Short brown hair water-darkened, slicked back. Muddy eyes to either side of her nose, that nose, flat cheeks warmed by big round yellow bulbs around the mirror, mouth a thin flat pale-lipped line. The cords in her throat leap out, fall back as she swallows. A simple dress long and soft, heathery grey, yellow and white piping down either side. Splashed water mottles the fabric of it here and there. A black bra strap peeps out to one side. She tucks it back with her thumb, scoops up more water, splashes her face again, slicks her hair again, stops there both hands on her head. "Okay," she says. "Okay." Shaking water from her hands. On the floor by the stainless steel bathroom stall tangled clothing a pair of jeans one leg flung out a grubby T-shirt a blue sweatshirt half inside-out a careworn jacket, army-surplus green. Atop the pile in its soft leather sheath the bell of it dull and dented her épée. She squats there, roots around, comes up with one and then another of a mismatched pair of Chuck Taylors, black and white, toe swaddled in grubby duct tape. She's tugging one open loosening the laces when she stops, sets them both by the épée on the pile of clothes. Stands, flexing her bare feet against the wide white tiles. The nail of her left big toe a dead grey ridge.

Up a narrow high-walled switchback staircase of poured concrete Jo pads into the darkened coffee shop chairs upended on tables all about the lights above all dim in pale glass globes like emptied honeycombs. On all sides the walls are windows floor to ceiling filled beyond with a mass of milling shifting waiting people half-seen in the confusion of light-struck reflections and shadows dazzling the glass. Past a dim glass cabinet filled with signs for pastries and donuts by empty plates the Queen in her black dress stands by a rack of CDs under a sign that says A Wynters Nightes Pastime. Her hand on Ysabel's shoulder leaning forward to tell her something, their two dark heads bent together. Cardboard ornaments red and white that say Hope and Faith and Wish hang on strings from the rafters all about them. To one side a man in a black suit hands behind his back chin restless between the high white gateposts of his upturned shirt-collar. A chair's been set down by a table for an old woman in a glittering gown and jacket of pink and red and white her glossy white hair done up in an elaborately braided bun. Past them all the barista bay where under the weak light on the counter is laid a sword.

The scabbard plain and black with a beaten metal throat and chape the color of thunderclouds. The hilt of it simple and straight, wrapped in dulled wire, the quillions clean straight bars almost as long together as the hilt. Over and around them a glittering net of wiry strands that meet in thick round worked steel knots all gathered together in a single cord swooping down the length of the hilt to end at the great silvery clout of a pommel.

"Whoa," says Jo approaching, more a breath than a word.

Behind the counter the big man straining the shoulders of his soft blue coat says, "Welcome, Gallowglas." About his mouth gently smiling droop two long grey mustaches. "As my Queen has asked, a sword made to your hand."

"Is it okay?" says Jo. "To look, I mean? It's not like a bride and groom thing, right?"

"Feel free," says Pyrocles. He takes the hilt in one hand and the scabbard's throat in his other and tugs free about six inches of blade. The surface of it polished shining but within deep waves of dark and light steel chase the spine of it. "The steel was folded over eleven times," he says.

"That's, ah, that's good, right?" says Jo.

His smile widens. "This sword was once a leaf spring from a 1972 Buick Skylark," he says. "The car belonged to Peabo, an old friend of the mechanicals, though never a member of their union. It was a beautiful car, a lovely deep red color, and he took great pains to keep it so." He sheathes the sword with a whisp and a snick. "It never went as fast as it wanted."

"You mean you made this from a car?"

"Part of a car," says Pyrocles.

"Wow," says Jo.

"Aren't your feet cold?" says the Queen, her black dress rustling up to them.

"Majesty," says Pyrocles, ducking his head, and "Ma'am," says Jo.

"Thank you for your hard work," says the Queen, "it is we are certain a fine blade and true, Anvil. If you would take your leave. Now," she says, turning to Jo as Pyrocles ducks his head again and steps out from behind the counter. "Let's be straight about something. You are only being granted your spurs ex officio. The moment my daughter tires of this dalliance, and sets you aside, is the moment you will no more be welcome in this our court."

"I wouldn't dream of imposing, ma'am."

"And yet you would say yes." The Queen lays a hand on the sword's scabbard. "These decorations," she says, looking up a moment at the ornaments. "Do you people not know what season it is?"

"I'm surprised they waited till Halloween, honestly," says Jo.

The Queen smiles. "Our daughter will gird you herself with her own two hands, before," she says, and wraps her pale hand about the black lacquer scabbard, lifting it. "I find it helps to keep the fumbling to a minimum during the colée. When you hear the trumpets." Turning she rustles sword under her arm to the front doors of the coffee shop, where Pyrocles and the man in the black suit push them open. The crowd settles and grows still out there as she walks through them around the glass-walled coffee shop to a balcony lit up with harsh white lights under banners slack, a hawk, a hound, a bee.

"You look beautiful," says Ysabel. Her gown a clattering fall of amber and gold beads over a short ivory slip. In her hands she holds a limp black belt.

"You got a strange idea of beauty," says Jo, lifting her arms as Ysabel wraps the belt loosely about her hips. "We're both gonna be chilly out there."

"It's not that cold tonight," says Ysabel. "And it won't take long. She will strike you gently on the shoulders, three times."

"You went over this already." Outside they're cheering something the Queen has said to them.

"She will tell them all to remember your honor and your bravery." Jo rolls her eyes at that, and Ysabel jerks the belt tighter, an admonishment. "She will tell you to remember your oaths and obligations, and she will ask that you hew to the Apportionment and likewise to keep all our feasts and revels. And then she will tell you to rise, lady knight."

"And then Marfisa calls me out."

Ysabel adjusts the angle of the belt. "Do you believe me? Do you trust me?"

"That it's all gonna work out fine?" Jo shrugs. *"Something's got to go right today."* Outside a sudden rush of trumpet notes, a fanfare harshly bright as the spotlights. "That's one hell of a cue," says Jo.

"You will not lose," says Ysabel, both of Jo's hands held tight in her own. "You will not destroy her."

"Okay," says Jo, nodding. "Okay."

"I'm right behind you." She opens the door before Jo, and outside the crowd begins to applaud as Jo walks through them around the glass-walled coffee shop to the balcony under the banners. Ysabel stands and watches, holding the door still open.

"Hey, Ys," says a voice from the otherwise empty shop, and she jumps and lets the door swing shut. She does not turn around. Quiet and calm and flat she says "You son of a bitch. Where the fuck have you been."

"The Gallowglas has coarsened your tongue." A deep voice, rough, slurred a little. "Is that any way to speak of Mother?" Maybe a shadow by one of the pillars between dazzled crowd-filled windows shifts something that might be a head, a shoulder.

"I have been left here alone without you," she says, something filling swelling her words until they almost burst, but he says "You love her, don't you?" and she stops. Leaning her head against the glass. "And she doesn't know, does she?" he says. Outside more applause shakes them all like wind.

"You know what that would cost me," she says, quiet and flat and calm again.

"She's." A little hitch in his breath that might be a chuckle. "She's surprising."

"She's fierce," says Ysabel. "And so loyal and true and so," and she stops to let the air out of her words again, "beautiful," she says, "but Mother told me I will not be the one to break her heart. She's seen it, she says."

"Pay no attention to what Mother says." The shadow leans back, folding itself into the sharper shadows of pillar and rafter and window frame. "The next few weeks will be hard," he says, his voice fading, falling away. "Harder than what went before. But I promise you this – "

She looks up. Steps over toward the pillar. There's nothing there, nothing at all. But outside the crowd's gone still, stock still and silent.

Ysabel pushes open the doors walking out along the side of the glass-walled coffee shop the clatter of the beads of her gown startling in the silence of the crowd all about her peering and craning to see what can be seen in the plaza below. Clear as a bell then the Queen says, "If this is a joke, it is in poor taste."

Pushing between the last few people Ysabel steps out onto the balcony there beneath the banners where Jo's standing looking down at the sword hooked to her belt. No one is looking at Jo, or the Queen, or at Ysabel even as they step out of her way. Everyone in those still and silent crowds on the great sweep of steps to the right, the low walls to either side, staring at the figure in the center of the otherwise empty brick-paved plaza, a broad-shouldered man in leather trousers and battered, dusty boots. Broad leather straps about his shoulders fix a greened bronze disk over his bare chest. A mask white and blocky crudely painted with thick black lines to resemble a grinning skull hides his face. An upturned mane of black hair rippling slowly in the otherwise still air. His arm outstretched he holds in his gauntleted right hand the hilt of a longsword pointed at the crowd on the low wall there, the crowd that has pulled back away from where the sword is pointing to reveal Marfisa standing in her breastplate and her armored skirt and her greaves.

Ysabel takes Jo's hand.

Marfisa steps down from the wall and pulls her sword from the air sandals slapping the bricks as she strides toward the masked man who settles on slightly bent knees both hands now on the hilt of his sword held ready.

He falls backward ripping the sword from her hand the sword that's buried half its length or more through his side at an angle to burst its glittering tip from his back scraping against the brick as half on his side he tries to roll over push himself up throwing his gauntleted hand across his body for momentum. The upturned mane of black hair about his mask falling gently as if dropped to settle about his shoulders. Marfisa panting plants her sandaled foot on the bronzed disk strapped to his chest and pushes his body back against the bricks. Wraps her hand about the hilt of her sword and wrenches it free. She says something to him that is lost in the cheering and whooping and the thunderclap rush of applause sweeping the crowds all about them. Steps back and offers her left hand. He takes it in his bare hand, and she pulls him to his feet.

"Well fought, O Axe," calls the Queen effortlessly over the roar of the crowds, settling them all and quieting them again. "We had not thought to celebrate this investiture with a passage at arms. Your willingness to rise to this unknown warrior's bait is most commended. And as for you, sir." No hint of a smile upon her face. "Your sense of humor is perhaps too rarified for an audience so large. The office of Huntsman is anathema to us – take solace, then, in this: should I in some dark day that's yet to come seek out a knight to fill that role, all you've done tonight is to remove your name from our consideration." Until now, perhaps, that relaxation of her mouth, the settling just of her chin. "Whatever that name might be. *My city!*" And she throws wide her arms as if to take them all in. "All of you who call these streets your home. When first we came here many years ago we brought with us a light that had not shone until that day, a color that had not before been seen. We said an unspoken word, and made music where once had been only silence. Tonight!" Sweeping through the crowd another sound, the rustle of hands in pockets, of plastic baggies in hands, of candy-tins and cigarette cases, pill bottles and ampoules, of gel caps snapped between thumbs and forefingers, as hands lift up above their heads glittering and gleaming with golden light that shines and builds and fills the empty brick-paved plaza. "Tonight, my people! Lift up your voice with mine and show this world that light has not gone out!"

And behind her Jo caught tight in Ysabel's embrace her chin on Ysabel's shoulder says, "I didn't lose," All about them the crowds have begun to sing, a slowly rising nameless vowel that rises till it slips dizzyingly at once into an ululation ringing back from the buildings towering over them. And Ysabel in Jo's ear says, "Nor was she lost."

Leaning back in Jo's arms Ysabel begins to sing with them all, with the Queen, another round of that simple swooping phrase from a thousand throats filling the plaza and the streets about it, the blocks beyond, all glowing now with a golden hazy light that drifts in curls and tendrils like a fog, clinging to streetlamps and neon signs. Jo reaches out away from Ysabel for a droplet of it skirling up out of her grasp, light tumbling and eddying the wake of her hand. The bricks beneath her feet have taken on a dull red glow as falling light seeps into them. The ivy twined about the pillars smolders with a green and yellow light. The pillars themselves gleam as if newly made, and the green band about the coffee shop sign too bright to look upon rings an unbearably portentous sigil of a mermaid mired in black ink.

"Let's go dancing!" cries Ysabel, and Jo begins to laugh. All about them the song falling away as people take down their hands from the lofting light, a shirtless boy in a three-piece suit, a heavy-set woman in cycling tights blazoned with angry cartoon cats, an old man in a cardigan and plaid pyjama pants leaning on the shoulder of a woman in a shiny yellow sou'wester, putting away bottles and vials and cases and little plastic baggies, cupping still-glowing hands like candles to their chests, a man in a peppermint seersucker jacket stuffing his hand into a pocket that becomes a dim lantern, and one by two and three they turn and take their leave.

BARE BRANCHES TOSS AND CLATTER, DEAD LEAVES patter down the street before sudden gusts of wind. Candles and Christmas lights wink and flicker from every window of the big white ramshackle house on the corner. A thin young man pushes open one of the two front doors and staggers onto the porch, letting out a burst of music, a fiddle, sharp popping drums. Rings glitter from his fingers as he beckons to someone inside. His black T-shirt says Bobu Magurasu in white letters. "See," he's saying loudly and then he shushes himself. "I think I know."

"What?" says the woman following him onto the porch. Her serape striped in browns and yellows. On her head a confetti-colored patchwork cap.

"Why it was three. Why it was only three." Guthrie leans close and whispers, "I think I'm just like you."

"There's an easy way to find out," she says.

Inside the big front room the drum kit set up between the fireplace and the keg. The drummer's head sweating as he works furiously over a snare drum, throwing off parade-ground fusillades. A red-headed man kneels before him swaying, sawing a soaring theme from his fiddle. Behind him on a stool a kid clutching a big-bellied acoustic guitar taps his foot. A woman with short dark hair one hand on the neck of a bass guitar the other on Marfisa's shoulder leaning close together singing into the same microphone, "Suntower, asking – cover, lover – June cast, moon fast – as one changes – " Marfisa swallowing a laugh as she fumbles a couplet. Her armor gone she wears a tight red dress, quite short. In one hand a flute. A dozen people or more pressed close together along the wall below the stairs heads bobbing tossing a feathered headdress a big black hat jeweled hands and bare hands and hands smeared with clayey colors waving in time, someone tossing gauzy scarves by Roland in a green track suit with white and silver stripes scowling as a boy in a brown bomber jacket his hair a matted pompadour pushes past him up the stairs where Becker in his big plaid shirt sits leaning back against Pyrocles a step or two above him soft blue jacket somewhere else his pale blue shirt unbuttoned over a white undershirt. "Of course it's Yes," says Becker.

"What?" says Pyrocles leaning over him, smiling between mustaches a-dangle.

"Yes!" laughs Becker, settling back against him. "Yes I said yes. A thousand times yes!"

In the bright toothpaste-colored kitchen Jo's wedged into a corner by a big blue garbage can overflowing with empty bottles brown and green, hugging herself in her long grey dress her sword about her hips. Ysabel before her beaded gown clacking side to side a cigarette tucked between two fingers of the hand wrapped about her wineglass. With a crash the band in the big front room takes up the soaring theme, bass and drums now churning under fiddle and flute and over them all the clear crisp vamping guitar folding in on itself. "I want to dance!" cries Ysabel.

"You didn't tell me *she* was gonna be here!" snaps Jo.

"I didn't know," says Ysabel, waving the wineglass between them, slopping red wine to the floor. "She isn't going to – Jo, you don't have anything to worry about – "

"Because it's Robin Whatsisname's house, right? And nobody *ever* gets hurt in Robin's house." Shivering her hand on the hilt of her sword she pushes out from the corner past Ysabel walking a little wobbly to the fridge. "I need another cider."

"Are you," says Ysabel, taking a drag from her cigarette, "aren't your feet cold?" Jo's bare feet filthy on the black and white check floor by the fridge without looking back she lifts a hand middle finger extended and Ysabel shrugs and stubs out her cigarette on an empty bottle in the garbage can. 72, says the label. Absinthe Verte de Fougerolles. That soaring theme has collapsed out in the big front room and from the wreckage a calypso beat's assembling itself with what sounds like a real steel drum. Jo closes the fridge bottle in hand and turns to see Becker there in the doorway, gawping at her. "Oh, hey," he says, "oh, hey, I'm sorry."

"Don't," says Jo, padding across the kitchen towards him.

"No, really," he says, "you have to remember. I forget. I didn't remember any of this, or about you, or, or. I didn't remember him, can you believe it?"

Jo takes the empty bottle from his hands and tosses it into the garbage can. "Don't." Hands him her unopened bottle. "I, uh, I had no idea you were."

"Were what?" says Becker, twisting off the cap. Swallowing some cider.

"Gay," says Jo.

"Well, yeah," says Becker, wiping his mouth with the back of his hand. Guthrie bursts into the kitchen one hand held before him in the other, headed for the sink. Yanking the faucet on he shoves the hand under the water yelling "Oh, ow, oh!" The woman in the serape and the confetti-colored cap drifts into the kitchen saying "You did want to know."

"You *bit* me!" The water's running red from his fingers. Becker shaking his head looks back to Jo who isn't paying attention to what's going on by the sink at all but staring out into the big front room where Ysabel's dancing by the red-headed fiddler pounding steel-drum sounds from a little keyboard. The bassist and Marfisa singing into the same microphone again, trading verses and la-la-las, "We got a million dollars worth of ethyl gas, and a reservation for the room!"

"Hey," says Becker, leaning close to Jo. "Like I say, I'm sorry. I'll see what I can do to get you guys on the bee-to-bee – "

"No you won't," says Jo. Not looking away from Ysabel dancing. "You'll forget you ever said that come the morning." One hand on the hilt of her sword again. The heel of her other hand rubbing an eye. "I'm gonna go find somewhere to lie down. If she comes looking for me. Okay?"

To the right of the door to the kitchen a dark hallway passes under the stairs. Jo heads down it one hand brushing flocked velvet wallpaper. In gaudy frames hang old paperbacks brightly colored with titles that say Go-Go Sadisto and Game Finger and The Merciless Mermaids. Past a closed door painted white with a sign that says Sorry We're Closed. The music's dissolved into a great thunderous drone lit up by stabs of tinny brass. Past photos now in clear glass frames of fruits and vegetables, close-ups in black and white of glossy curves and roughly pitted skin and strange hollow shadows, past a closed door painted white with a sign that says Sorry We're Closed. Jo turns unsteadily music whooping and lurching around her. The kitchen a few steps back short stretch of hall green-black flocking sprawled across the dark magenta wall. One closed door, white-painted, with a sign.

Turning back. Pinned to the walls now scraps of parchment inked with illuminated letters, strange fleshy creatures crawling through the typographic underbrush. The next door down's ajar, a puddle of warm light seeping out along the floor. A small room lined with books from floor to ceiling on dark wooden shelves lit up by unobtrusive spotlights. More books in roughly neat piles on rugs by a couple of wing chairs and narrow end tables bear up under the weight of more stacked books, leather-bound and dust-jacketed some wrapped in clear plastic, paperbacks tucked here and there and some books blankly featureless in wraps of plain brown paper. Jo steps carefully among the books bare feet sinking in the Persian rug, stopping to dig her toes in it eyes closed. Before her the broad high oxblood back of a tufted leather sofa pulled before the flickering glow of a fireplace. Something cracks and pops. She opens her eyes, steps up to the sofa one hand on the back of it. The Duke is kneeling before the hearth in a red-and-brown striped jacket, feeding kindling to a slowly dying fire. "Hello, Sir Jo," he says.

"Oh," says Jo, "I didn't know," turning to leave as he says "A little loud and crowded out there, huh?" and then reaching for his cane, pushing himself to his feet, "Oh, no, don't worry about it. Feel free. Goodfellow's house, right?" Scooping his long brown hair up away from his face. "Wouldn't dream of telling someone where to go in it." She's still got a hand clamped on the back of the sofa, leaning against it now. "You okay?" She shakes her head, quickly. "Come on, come on. Sit down. Where's the Princess?"

"Dancing," says Jo, taking his hand over the sofa, stepping gingerly around it. The sword catches as she tries to sit and for a moment she stands there blinking at it until he helps her sit side-saddle knees tucked up toward the arm of the sofa. "Sorry I couldn't make it to the colée," he's saying. "I heard there was a crasher. You look awful."

"I'll be fine," says Jo.

"Hey," says the Duke. "Hey." She looks up at him. "Where's your shoes?"

Jo's laugh is low and shaky. "In the bathroom of the Starbucks on Pioneer Square. Along with my pants and my jacket and my smokes and," she laughs again, sharper now, more certain, "my *other* goddamn sword and I can*not* be doing this again."

"Okay," says the Duke, and "Sorry" says Jo and "No, no," says the Duke, "don't apologize, it's okay," turning to poke at scraps of kindling with his cane.

"I didn't mean to," says Jo.

"Of course not," says the Duke. "Actually, I have a confession –
I came here tonight to ask you something." The copper ferrule
scrapes against the hearth. "The Queen's dinner, when I set this
whole misbegotten juggernaut alight. You said you'd lose a challenge, throw a fight, if that's what the Princess wanted. Yeah?"

"I did," says Jo, "but – "

"Hang on," says the Duke, waving a hand, "that's not the
question I wanted to ask. My question, and it's basically moot because you didn't lose, hell, it didn't even happen, but humor me.
This duel that was supposed to happen tonight. You and the Axe,
who's out there singing like butter wouldn't melt on her mike.
You two cook that up so her and the Princess could get back together, only crazy mask-guy jumped the queue and queered
your play? Because, and don't let this affect your answer in any
way, I'll be really fucking pissed if you did."

"I lost my job today, because of this," says Jo. The Duke looks
over his shoulder at her, his face shadowed. "Last week," she
says, "I learned I'm getting kicked out of the only apartment I
can afford downtown. And I wouldn't have had to cook anything
up with anybody. If she had stepped up to me, I could have just
said no." One hand on the throat of the scabbard. "Fucked off."
The other on the hilt. "Dropped the sword and walked."

He steps away from the fire. "I would have been incandescent
if you'd done that."

"Like I care."

He's leaning on that cane over her, the rough-hewn hawk at
its head caged in his fingers. "She wants the Princess, she'll
come at you again. You gonna hope crazy mask-guy keeps
coming back? Maybe drop the sword then if he doesn't? Why
wait? Go on. Fuck off now."

"You aren't listening," says Jo. "I lost my job. I lost my home.
All because of this promise I made that I'm going to keep. And
if the Axe or anybody, or you, comes up to me and says I can't
do this, I'm not fucking worthy – " She looks down, then back
up at him. "I'll cut you and, and, I'll watch you go down to
fucking dust."

"Okay," he says, and then he stamps his cane once against the floor. "Good," he says. "Good."

"Good," says Jo flatly. "This is good."

"Good that you know it. Good you can say it." He leans the cane against the sofa. "Good that it scares you." He's unbuttoning his jacket. Her hand relaxes on the hilt she does not let go. "Yeah," she says. A sharp breath in through her nose. "Well."

"Here," says the Duke. "Sit up." Jo doesn't as he wriggles his jacket down his arms. "You look chilly. I'm trying to do a chivalrous thing here." She reaches up then, takes his jacket, drapes it about her shoulders. Scoots closer to the arm tucking her feet under herself as he swings around to sit heavily next to her. Wincing he rubs his thigh. "There's aspects," he's saying, "advantages of knighthood, of which I do not think you've taken account. Along with the weighty responsibilities. You were knighted banneret, which is the Queen fucking her daughter over, keeping you out of the Apportionment. Since you got no patron, and nobody obliged to give you medhu. There's nothing I can do about that. But I can," reaching into his vest pocket, "give you this." Plucking out a gold credit card. "Go on. Take it."

Gingerly she does. "This," she says, "that's my full name." Turning it over in her hand. "And my signature."

"Wouldn't work otherwise," says the Duke. "And it's a lovely – "

"Jo will do just fine," says Jo. Turning the card back over again. "This is a thing, isn't it."

"Verily," says the Duke.

"Bank of Trebizond?" she says, tripping over a breathless little laugh.

"I wouldn't buy a car with it," he says. "But otherwise. And you'll never see a bill."

"I don't, I don't know what to say," says Jo. "I mean thank you, yes, sure, thanks so much, but I – "

"Tough, isn't it," says the Duke. "These new problems that suddenly overwhelm you. Whatever shall you worry about now. However fill your days. Oh!" Lifting a finger. "The apartment you might yet lose. That card won't help much there, but I might have a word with the landlord?" Smiling. "Some folks say I can be persuasive. You don't consider him a friend, do you?" Jo laughs. "Put it away, don't lose it. Obviously. But I want to have a look at your sword." Jo tucks the card into her bra, then unhooks the scabbard from her belt. "Draw it," says the Duke. "I trust you."

She tugs the sword free a clean quiet scrape of steel against leather and metal the blade ringing faintly still as she turns it and holds it in the air before them firelight licking the dark whorls within its polished gleam. "May I?" says the Duke, holding out his hand.

"Okay," says Jo, handing the hilt over to him. "I trust you."

He tips the blade down, then back up again. "Nice," he says. Leaning the blade away from her, laying it flat against his other arm, leaning over to peer along the length of it. Jo watches with a quizzical smile. "The Anvil's a fine smith," says the Duke, lifting it again and leaning it the other way over her lap, flat against the arm of the sofa. "He's signed it, here." Pointing to a crude little sigil stamped into the thickness of the blade above the quillions, a simple block shape with a horn to one side, the suggestion of a foot. "You ever figure out your banner, he can stamp it here," rolling the blade over, "mark it as yours. What's so funny?"

Jo's smiling broadly, shaking her head. "You."

"Moi?" The Duke rears back, hand to his chest.

"You. You're a piece of work, you know that? You set your goons on us, you shanghai my ex-boyfriend into a stunt that could've gotten him killed, you drag me on a hunt for a goddamn boar that could've gotten *me* killed, you insult me, you fuck me over, and you think you give me a gold card and maybe call the Housing Authority for me that means you still got a chance."

The Duke still smiling licks his lips and lets loose a quiet little laugh. "No," he says, "no, what's funny is this. What's funny is you get Tommy Rawhead killed. You let the boar loose in the first place and you nearly got *me* killed hunting for it and you broke my fucking leg. You lose me the Dagger and the Helm and when I reach out to you nonetheless as a newly dubbed knight, a member of the fraternity, you spit on my gifts and threaten my life and yet still, somehow, you're the one who thinks you have a chance."

Shoulder to shoulder neither of them not smiling Jo leaning a little closer the Duke lifting his head Jo frowning a little over her grin and about to say something when she closes her eyes for a swift soft kiss. "Huh," she says, her nose by his. "I guess I do."

"What a coincidence," says the Duke. They kiss again.

"Enough!" roars Roland sword in hand the audience in the big front room falling back with shrieks and screams scrambling from dancing to running and ducking. The band stuttering to a stop the drummer and the bassist and the fiddler still singing "When we are Queen," their doo-doo diddle oo-doos tumbling away into the tense shocked sudden panting silence. Marfisa lowering the tinwhistle from her lips glaring at Roland glaring back at her. "Enough," he says.

Ysabel grabs his arm jerking it to one side and he tugs against her but does not push her away. "Please!" she's saying. "Chariot! Put it away!"

"This madness of hers must stop," he's saying. He's lowering his sword. She lets go of his arm. Marfisa's standing still her arms at her sides whistle loosely in one hand. "If her brother were here," says Roland.

"He isn't," says the short man all in black, pushing through the audience. "Is this now to be your party trick, sir?" His dark beard neatly trimmed a whisper of curls just past stubble along the line of his jaw. "Put up your sword."

"They sing treason, Goodfellow – "

"This is a free house, sir," snaps the short man all in black. The band looking back and forth at each other sharply, except Marfisa who doesn't look away from Roland. "All may speak freely here. And no metal's drawn in anger. Not here. I would not have it."

"It is an insult," says Roland. Ysabel beside him shaking her head. "To the Queen, the Princess – "

"I do not wish to ask again, sir," says Robin Goodfellow, raising his hands arms out palms down a placatory gesture. The nail of one little finger a long curled black thing. "Not in my own house."

Roland's turning the blade back lifting the hilt with a sigh when Marfisa begins to sing in a high voice roughened by adrenaline, "There will be more dancing, and less worrying," and Roland face twisting hauls the sword back up and out again, and Marfisa's singing "more singing and less hurrying" as Ysabel cries "No!" and steps between them as a man in a grey flannel jacket calls "Princess!" and a woman in ragged white lace sleeves her hands before her screaming mouth and the bassist slinging her guitar up before her body steps up and a shirtless man turns and pushes back through the crowd and another man and another and a woman and more on his heels toward the front door banging open before them all and Roland stops his thrust just short of Ysabel's throat his face stricken. Marfisa finishes in a sing-song voice, "but everything will still get done on time, when we are Queen."

"Princess," says Roland, and his hand is empty now.

"You stupid, stupid fool," she says. "It's just a song."

"Is it?" says Marfisa behind her. Ysabel turns. "Is that all it is, Princess? Just a song?"

"You're just singing a song!" says Ysabel. "To call it *treason* – "

"It's just a song," says Marfisa. "Then these must be just words. This bread, that you have made for me."

And under her wild black curls Ysabel's face has suddenly gone pale. "No," she says, her voice quite small and far away. "Don't."

"The bread that you have made for me!" cries Marfisa, and the crowd's gone still and silent in that room. "I spit it out. Why shouldn't I do this?"

"Because I ask you not to?" says Robin, but Marfisa's saying, "It isn't the song, it's not the song at all. It's me. I'm the insult that cannot be borne. This salt that you have given me."

"Marfisa, please," says Ysabel, and "That's not true!" cries Roland.

"I spill it, and grind it in the dust!" says Marfisa. Ysabel grabs her shoulders. "Please!" she cries. "I made a wish!"

"Did you?" says Marfisa, quietly. Behind her the drummer's gone the stool behind the drum kit tipped over on the floor. The kid and the bassist to either side of her watching wordless guitars hung useless at their sides. "Did you wish that I'd win the duel? Did you wish we could be together again?"

Ysabel's slowly shaking her head. "I wished," she says, "that you wouldn't be hurt." And then she says, "Either of you."

"Either of us," says Marfisa, and she takes Ysabel's hands from her shoulders and holds them a moment. "Well I'm not hurt," she says, and kisses Ysabel's fingers. "And she isn't even here. This lamp you have lit for me."

"As you love me," says Ysabel.

"I smother it," says Marfisa, "and it gutters, and goes dark."

She steps back from Ysabel then hands lifting into the air together drawing them apart right hand on the hilt of her sword left hand falling away from its tip as she swings it about once switching her grip both hands on the hilt now blade turned around and point down. She drives it with a great crack and a flash of light into the floor of the big front room.

"There," she says, a little shaky, smoke drifting about her blade stuck upright through a scorched black mark. "I'm done. With all of you."

And she walks past Ysabel away from the band and past Roland and past Robin his head in his hands and past the crowd stepping back and away as she passes them up to the open front door and through it out into the night.

"WHAT WERE YOU THINKING?"

"WHAT WERE YOU THINKING?"

Ysabel stands on the sidewalk arms akimboed, face hidden in the shadows under the streetlights. A thin mist not quite rain seeps slowly out of the air to sheen the pavement and the cars parked up and down the street. Jo still in her long grey dress barefoot sheathed sword in her hand comes down the steps from the porch of the big white ramshackle house on the corner, its windows behind her all lit up with candles and Christmas lights. "I was thinking," she says, "we'd take a taxi. Borrowed a phone from the drummer. I mean even if I was ready to walk home like this, you wouldn't make it in those heels."

Her beaded gown clattering Ysabel folds her arms together as Jo steps onto the sidewalk. "How are we going to pay for a taxi?" she says.

"That's supposed to be *my* line," says Jo, holding up the gold credit card. "So maybe I'll cop yours and say don't worry about it."

"Where did you get that?" says Ysabel, taking the card slowly from Jo, turning it over and over again.

"The Duke gave it to me. Said it was one of the – "

"The Duke?" says Ysabel, sharply. "The Hawk was here? Tonight?"

"Yeah," says Jo. "I was talking to him, in the library. Which is where I was I guess when the whole thing happened, which, I mean, I'm sorry, but – "

"This is a big deal," says Ysabel. She isn't looking at the card. She's looking away across the intersection at a darkened green house on the opposite corner behind a low stone wall.

Jo's hugging herself tightly, shivering a little. "Yeah," she says, and lets out a shaky little laugh. "If it works like he says it really changes *every*thing. We'll be taking a lot more taxis, you know?"

"We could," says Ysabel, holding the card out to Jo. "Did you fuck him for it?"

Jo doesn't take the card her hands still tightly holding her bare arms. "He gave it to me because I'm a knight now," she says, her voice leashed tight, her breath a clammy cloud about her face.

"Wonderful," says Ysabel, letting the card fall to the sidewalk. "Did you fuck him because you're a knight now?"

"What the hell," snaps Jo, stooping to collect the card.

"Don't tell me it's none of my business, Gallowglas." Ysabel grabs Jo's arm and hauls her around, upright. "The Duke would sit the Empty Throne." Jo shakes her arm free. "If he survives he'll be the King. He'll have me as his Bride. He'll send my mother off to Gammer-hood, or worse."

Jo says nothing, fingers curled around that gold card.

"Do you love him?" says Ysabel.

Jo's laugh is short and flat. "No. Don't be – "

"Do you love me?"

Jo shivers. Wraps her arms back around herself. "You, you didn't," she says, "you said," and then a deep sharp breath in through her nose. She closes her eyes. "I thought you understood," she says in a small and quiet voice, and then she opens her eyes. "Not like that. Ysabel, I'm sorry, I'm not – Ysabel!"

Ysabel's very slowly falling sinking to her knees there on the sidewalk as with sharp cold popping sounds fat raindrops start to splat about them. Jo kneeling there by Ysabel who's on her hands and knees saying "Harder than what went before" to herself and then, looking up at Jo with blank dark eyes, she rocks back and says, "There." Her hair gone flat in the thickening rain. "So nice and neat," she says. "You're his. And now I'm yours."

"What?" says Jo Maguire.

Here may you keep your arms from rust,
  May breathe your war-horse well;
Seldom hath pass'd a week but giust
  Or feat of arms befell:
The Scots can rein a mettled steed;
  And love to couch a spear:-
Saint George! a stirring life they lead,
  That have such neighbours near.

—*Sir Walter Scott*

NO. 10

SURVEILLING

WHISTLING TUNELESSLY – UP THAT HILL – SUNLIGHT SOFTLY
ALMOST A VACATION – FENNEL & SORGHUM
EVERYTHING IN THEIR POWER – THREE MEN STANDING
NOT ANY COURTESY – HIS FILTHY MIND – WHAT THE LORD REQUIRES
GROANING THE SHAPE – TÊTE-À-TÊTE – "YOUR REASON FOR LEAVING?"
MARKING THE SPOT – MR. CHARLOCK SITS – THE SWORD IN THE FLOOR
BAKER, JULIET, INDIA – THE WOMAN KNEELING BY THE TUB

WHISTLING TUNELESSLY he crosses the street hands in the pockets of his black leather jacket. Jogging the last few steps before the light changes his pinkish-orange hair bobbing. The sky above is dark and starless, heavy and low where it isn't lost in the streetlight glare. The little corner parking lot is crammed with a half-dozen food carts shoulder-to-shoulder with signs that say El Brasero and Potato Champion and Whiffies Fried Pies. He squeezes between a couple careful of power cords and a water line wrapped in insulating foam and knocks on the back door of a silvery cart trimmed in purple and green and gold. The cart lurches. "Fuck off," calls someone from inside. He knocks again. The door's wrenched open enough for a man to peer out. "It's five o'clock in the fucking," he says. "Jesus, Ray." Wrapped in a shapeless brown corduroy coat. Tuft of beard leaning sideways off his chin. "I don't do breakfast. You know that."

"Like I could pay if you did."

"Don't do charity neither," says the man in the corduroy coat.

"Relax." The man in the black leather jacket pulls his other hand from a pocket. "Just need some water and a pot." He's holding three eggs still speckled with bits of feather and chicken shit.

Three eggs in fizzing water in a red saucepot on a bluely glowing propane stovetop next to the big empty griddle. Ray in his black leather jacket leans back against a wall papered with lists and recipes scrawled on index cards, grimy menus, a photo of the man in the corduroy coat wearing a bowling shirt and dark glasses, smiling, thumbs up by the sunlit cart. He's up in the narrow nose pouring coffee from an orange thermos into white paper cups. Leans over to hand one back steam billowing in the sharp light of the electric lamp hung over the griddle. "Oh, hey," says Ray. "Thanks."

"I'm a cheap sonofabitch and an uncharitable bastard," says the man in the corduroy coat. "I ain't inhumane."

Ray sips his coffee, the sets it on the griddle and pulls a green glass bottle from his jacket. He pours a slug of something colorless into the cup.

"Jesus, Ray," says the man in the corduroy coat.

"Ain't neither of us slept yet," says Ray, "so it's still way the hell after noon." He takes another, slower sip. "And the essences of juniper and coriander really bring out the floral notes of a good arabica blend. How's tricks?"

"Can't complain," says the man in the corduroy coat, yawning hugely. "Drunk people need their fried starches, but damn. I get stuck cleaning up till the crack of fucking hell. You?"

"Ah, you know," says Ray. He takes the bubbling pot off the lit eye, sets it on the griddle, slaps a lid on. "No job. No prospects. Stealing eggs from somebody's backyard coop. Haven't kicked a cat yet, though. So I got a ways to fall yet."

Ray leaves the cart with a brown paper sack and a covered white cup. He darts across the empty street against the light and runs more quickly across the intersection with the yellow light, waving at a bus lumbering down the dark street toward the corner. He pulls a handful of paper slips, bus transfers in muted reds and oranges and greens, and rifles through them one-handed till he finds a short one, greyish yellow. The bus snorts to a stop and he flashes it at the driver, then heads for the back, past the only other passengers: a man in a powder blue tuxedo, his collar open, his bow tie unclipped, and a figure anonymous in a bulky black parka and a green meshback cap pulled low that says PC-815 over the bill.

The bus climbs slowly past apartments and restaurants a hardware store and a wine shop, a bakery, a comic book store, a tented farmer's market and a woman setting out signs that say Open, Blood Oranges, Two Ninety-nine. Crowning the hill a funeral home behind a majestic sweep of lawn. Down the other side the street falls through thickening blocks of two- and three-storey buildings that push right up to lightening sidewalks through a welter of power lines and phone lines. Stoplights click and change over empty intersections. Maybe thirty blocks away the street climbs again up to the colonnaded porch of a big yellow house its windows dark in the lap of a much larger tree-shadowed hill. Off away behind it all, orange light's leaking through cracks in the soft grey ceiling of clouds.

Someone pulls the cord and the bus shudders to a stop by a dark movie theater with a big sign that says Bagdad in ornamented letters. The man in the tuxedo gets up and carefully hands on the backs of the seats makes his way off. Morgan Stewart's Coming Home, says the unlit marquee. Adventures in Babysitti. Barbarella 1100.

Maybe ten blocks shy of that big yellow house up on the hill the bus turns off the street, and Ray yanks the cord. He gets off at a corner stop by an empty parking lot. The sign above it says F.O.E. East Portland Ærie No. 3256. His footsteps echo as he heads back to the street and continues up it past the last of the two-storey blocks. A barista's setting out a sign that says Albina Press. Up past blocks of one- and two-storey houses now, still dark behind hedges, under skeletal trees. When the steepening street reaches that big yellow house with its colonnaded porch and a sign out front that says Western Seminary it doglegs around it and up and up past more dark houses until it ends finally in a great grass berm, blocks long to either side. Ray climbs it up a narrow flight of cracked concrete steps to a low stone wall topped by an arrow-tipped wrought-iron fence. Past the fence under buzzing street-lights an enormous open reservoir half-filled with black water untouched by the orange glow that's still threatening somewhere away behind the hill. Across the reservoir a crenellated pump-house like a tower without its castle. Beyond it the hill continues to rise, the houses left behind now, dark trees rooted in black shadows all about. Another flight of concrete steps much longer and much steeper than the last. At the bottom of it Ray drains his paper cup of coffee and chucks it into a garbage can. Paper bag in hand, shoulders set, head down, he starts up that second flight, slowing, huffing as he nears the top. There's another low stone wall, another wrought-iron fence, another crenellated pump-house, oval instead of blocky. Another open reservoir, inky and vast. Ray stoops there at the top of the steps, hands on his knees, hair flopping over into his eyes. The buzz of the streetlights cuts out, and he is left alone in the gloom, his breath loud and rough in the silence. He straightens, turns, looks back.

Past the dizzying fall of steps past the squared-off reservoir below past the trees and houses the street stretches away stop-lights winking yellow to red, flanked on either side by more streets, more blocks fixing the gentle rumple of the land with streetlights and porch lights, storefronts and signs, the straight-lined grid in turn gentled by dark-shadowed clusters and thick-ets of trees, all of it lipped by a low ridge maybe thirty blocks away. Past that ridge shreds of fog lick up lighter than the clouds above, the unseen river bracketed north and south by the great arch of one bridge, the sweep of another, the cars so far away just crawling white lights and red lights. Past that rippled curtain then the towers of downtown and a thousand thousand windows filling with an uncertain light, yellowish blue without a hint of green, and the corners and edges and frames of those windows have all of them caught hesitant sparks of orange.

Ray sits on the top step and pulls three eggs from the paper bag. He rolls one between his knee and the palm of his hand, crushing the shell, and peels it, watching the city before him tip over into daylight. The light in all that glass firms up into a softly greyish white just brighter than the lightening clouds above, still touched with blue and yellow blushing about those smoldering orange edges and corners. He eats his egg and begins to peel a second. One of the towers stands alone, away from the others off to the north, its reddish amber glass framed by dark pink stone still dim, un-touched by lightening day. Digging in his pockets Ray pulls out a paper packet that says Salt and rips it open, pouring it out in a pile on his palm, sprinkling a pinch of it over the peeled egg. That lone tower glimmers and suddenly every pane of glass in the building flares with smoldering orange light that grows and spreads as he lifts the egg to his mouth and somewhere up behind him the clouds break open and the morning light rolls down over the city, the wave of it washing out all those little lights down the street and up the ridge, the shreds of fog between the bridges tattering, melting away, the cloudy light filling those thousands upon thousands of windows in the towers blown out by orange and yellow and red. And the lone tower's glass is filled with all those colors and more, golds and roses, purples, pearly whites, even clean pure lines of the greens and blues that only shine at sunrise and sunset, and its dark pink stone gleams now as behind him the sun mounts and the morning takes hold. He climbs to his feet one hand shading his eyes against the glory.

"I knew it," he says. He laughs and spins around once on the top step. "I *knew* it!" Backing up a couple of half-dancing steps he drops a shoulder and cocks his arm and spinning around once more and again he hurls the third egg away off the hill toward that burning tower, that blaring slice of sunrise cut into the dark hills away across the river. It spins from his hand a tiny shadow lost in all the dazzle and never comes back down.

SUNLIGHT SOFTLY – ALMOST A VACATION
FENNEL & SORGHUM – EVERYTHING IN THEIR POWER

SUNLIGHT SOFTLY drifts from skylights through the atrium pale, brighter though and whiter than the sconces warming shadows about the outer walls. Wooden doors under a sign that says Council Chambers swing wide and a robot steps through, a man in a robot suit made of blue and grey plastic shells articulated about knees and elbows, a grey grill of a mask on his blue crash helmet. A woman in a broad-brimmed bonnet and a black-and-white striped swimming costume takes his arm, smiles coquettishly into a hand mirror as someone snaps a photo, then tucks the mirror away, reaching for a green rainshell held out to her by a man in a grey flannel suit and an elaborate red-and-purple headdress. A bald man in a white vest leans on a cricket bat, speaking animatedly to a man in a red striped shirt with white collar and cuffs. Flash and flash again, more photos. A little guy in a black suit and a skinny black tie pushes free of the crowd and heads toward an office across the atrium. What hair he has is lankly grey, clumped about his ears and struggling to launch a curl between his brow and the top of his skull. He's taking off his sunglasses, careful of the twirling owl's feather tied to one side. Glaring sourly at the man in the red striped shirt walking towards him. "The fuck was that about?" says the little guy, tucking his sunglasses away in a jacket pocket.

"Comics Month," says the man in the red striped shirt. His tie is much the same red as the stripes. "They do charity work." Behind him the man in the robot suit's shuffling into an elevator.

"Which means fuck-all to me," says the little guy. "And has zilch to do with riverfront condos."

"Schedules change," says the man in the red striped shirt. "You're not exactly the easiest people to get hold of." Tipping his wrist to look at his watch, heavy and gold.

"I need a phone," says the little guy, and the man in the red striped shirt pulls one from his pocket and flips it open. The little guy stares at it. "Something secure," he says. "A goddamn landline." Pointing at the door to the office.

"You can't go in there," says the man in the red striped shirt.

"Sure I can," says the little guy.

He sits in a swivel chair tipped back his worn black wingtips crossed up on the desk, handset of a phone held up before his face, earpiece against his forehead, saying "Completely. Fucking. Useless" into it. He's wearing the sunglasses again. "Next meeting's on Tuesday," turning the handset around, tucking it between ear and shoulder, "but we damn well better get this off our plate before then. We are stretched thin. Again. He's gotta understand – " Leaning forward to brush something from his shoe. The man in the red striped shirt watches him through the glass in the door. "He's gotta figure it out, he keeps distracting us like this, the work's gonna suffer. And we *know* who's fucking with Southwest's condos, I mean, come *on* – " He tips back further in the chair. "Whatever. Whatever. Sure, sure, sure. I'll fuck around at this legwork I'm *so* good at and keep doing as he says and you run after our targets all by yourself on another interminable shopping spree down Spendy-third or whatever. Yeah. Great fucking plan." He slams the phone down in its cradle. "Shit," he says, taking off the sunglasses, digging at his eyes with his fingers and his thumb. "We need a goddamn day off."

"Count it out again," says the man in the shapeless green coveralls. He's looking at the floor and his hands are clenched in trembling white-edged fists.

"Look at the ballots, Tom," says the man in the brown coveralls. On the folding table under a felt banner of a rainbow and a dove, there by the coffee urn and a plate piled high with donuts, three stacks of roughly torn paper slips. One has maybe a dozen, one has maybe three or four, one is piled sloppily high, maybe a hundred, maybe more. The man in the brown coveralls stirs the big pile with his hand. "Even if we miscounted and there's a couple votes for Jenny in your pile or hart and hive, a vote for me lost somewhere in here." He lifts a few slips, lets them flutter back to the table. "We've spoken, Tommy Tom. Loud and clear. You are the new Soames."

The man in the green coveralls lifts those white-edged fists to his mouth as all about them men and women in coveralls and dungarees, denim jackets and flannel shirts, in blues and soft worn reds and rugged greens and browns, meshback caps in hand, nod or duck their heads or lift free hands in sketchy salutes, so many of them there's no room for the chairs pushed back against the walls, folded and piled high on a rack shoved over behind the baby grand piano. They're murmuring "Soames" or "Soames Thomas" or "Oh indeed" or "Go get 'em!" or "Twice Thomas, aye."

"Go get who?" says the man in the green coveralls, opening those fists, folding his hands together. They all about him fall silent at that, and look away. "You can't mean what I think you mean." Stock still, only his head moving, turning enough to take them all in. "If you did, if you do, you should not have chosen me." Spreading his hands. "Nell, Soames Nell, and Open Mike. My good, my old friend, Open Mike. They were destroyed in a horrible accident. A fire unforeseen. There is no one to get."

And after a long still moment a small and quiet voice from the crowd says, "They were executed."

"Were they?" says the Soames Thomas. "Was there a trial? Did the peers speak with one voice before us to order them cut down?" And hands turn hats over at that, and feet step to one side or another. Back by the table the man in the brown coveralls starts to scoop up the ballots, but freezes when the Soames says "Now if you mean that they were *murdered...*"

The whole room's gone still. The Soames looking down but not at his fingertip worrying an old cut on the back of his hand. "Have a care," he says, "before you say a thing like that." His voice gone soft and gentle. *"Think,* long and hard. If that is what you mean to have said," and he looks up, then, at them all, "you leave us with no choice. We'll none of us have any choice at all but to turn our tools to weapons again, and once again march forth. But not against the Silk-Stocking Mob, or vigilantes got up in olive drab. Not against Mecklem and Meier, not against Odale and his Red Squad or Marchant and Bacon and Stroup. We'd march against our Queen and her six dozens, and they would destroy us all."

When no one says anything at that, the Soames turns to the man in the brown coveralls behind him. "I'm glad, then, that's not what was meant," he says. "Go on, Biscuit."

The man in the brown coveralls goes over to the baby grand piano and lifts the keyboard lid. He plays a low thick chord once, then rapidly one two three, and lets that last beat hang in the air. "Arise," says the Soames Thomas, his voice breaking on that word, but they all join in and together begin to sing.

"Now *that's* what I'm talking about," says the little guy, coming barefoot from the bathroom, wrapped in a white towel. "Ten hours sleep and this is as close to a vacation as we're *ever* likely to get on this gig." He climbs up onto one of the two queen-sized beds and scoots back against the padded headboard. He reaches for the remote on the nightstand. "Don't," says the big guy.

"Don't?"

"Still tuning up." His black jacket draped over the back of the chair the big guy's sitting at the round table by the big picture window at the front of the room. Spread out on the table a map. Plastic letters scattered across the map, refrigerator magnets in bright and simple colors, a yellow Y at the edge of downtown, a blue P over the freeway, a red Q above them, an orange B on the other side of the map away across the river, down by 39th and Hawthorne. In his hand another letter turning over in his thick and hairy-knuckled fingers, another B, a green one. "What's that for?" says the little guy.

Mr. Keightlinger looks down at the letter in his hand. "Bunny," he says. He snaps the letter onto the map at the foot of the northern freeway bridge over the river. Mr. Charlock snorts. "You think they're involved?" Twirling the little sprig of hair curled almost precisely between his brow and the top of his skull.

"Don't know," says Mr. Keightlinger.

"Sure we do," says Mr. Charlock. "It's Southeast, fucking with Southwest. Mechanicals ain't even in the mix. I'm telling you, if Leir would just listen to us on this," and Mr. Charlock leans forward, blotting his forehead dry with a corner of the towel. "Instead of riding us for something proofy he can take to fucking Agravante. Christ, man!" Mr. Charlock slaps the bedspread. "You're fucking with the vacation vibe here. Put it away so we can watch us some teevee."

Mr. Keightlinger says, *"I* don't know." The letter he's turning over in his fingers a purple M. He looks up, over at Mr. Charlock, beard lopping over his shoulder, and snaps the letter down on the map. Lifts his fingers, turns to look, "Huh," he says. The M in the middle of an empty arc of land up by the airport, near the slough.

"Well, hell," says Mr. Charlock. "We gotta go get you a couple more packs of letters so you got a full set of seventy-two for the – "

"Fifty-six," says Mr. Keightlinger.

"Actually, fifty-seven," says Mr. Charlock. He starts counting off on his fingers. "Prince, Huntsman, Luthier, Outlaw, uh, Bullbeggar, Dagger and Helm – "

"Axe," says Mr. Keightlinger. He scoots the M to one side, slides it back. "Huh," he says again.

"Yeah, right, her, whatever, okay," Mr. Charlock's saying. "Let's get everybody pinned down on the damn map, you're gonna ignore the one guy's got motive and opportunity."

Mr. Keightlinger starts to say "More than," but the rainbow pile of letters to one side of the map is trembling, shaking, clattering.

"Feature or bug," says Mr. Charlock sharply, pushing himself to the edge of the bed. "Feature or bug?"

"No," says Mr. Keightlinger, not looking away from the buzzing letters.

"You close it off yet?"

"No," says Mr. Keightlinger. One of the letters twitches its way out from under the settling pile and spins to the edge of the table, a red numeral two.

"No you ain't closed it off," says Mr. Charlock, hopping off the bed. "Shit." Quickly quietly heading to the door his back to the wall beside it, one hand retucking the white towel about the round hard swell of his belly, the other up by his head, two fingers curled back against his palm, two fingers extended, thumb cocked. Mouthing a silent shush he reaches for the doorknob. A sudden jerk and the door's open and he steps to block the doorway finger-gun leveled in the face of the man standing on the sidewalk just outside the room, a man in a grey suit and a white shirt buttoned all the way up to his throat, dark face stretched by a faltering smile, one hand up for a knock that never had a chance to land. "The fuck are you?" says Mr. Charlock.

"Charley," says the man. His eyes crossed looking at the fingertips just a couple inches from his nose. "Doc Charley, man, it's me. Bottle John."

"You better hope you got something better than that," says Mr. Charlock.

The man leans his head to one side eyes jumping as Mr. Charlock's fingers shift to follow. His smile opening up again. "I'm gonna reach into my jacket, pull out something to demonstrate my good intentions." The arm that had been up to knock is lowering slowly, carefully. "I'm gonna do it nice and easy. I remember what it is you can do with that." His hand slips inside his jacket. Mr. Charlock hikes up changing the angle of his fingers cocking his thumb back a little further. Carefully, slowly, the man's lifting his hand from his jacket. He's holding a tube of toothpaste. Natural Care Tom's of Maine, says the round white logo. Nature's Antiplaque Toothpaste with Propolis and Myrrh. Fennel.

"Toothpaste?" says Mr. Charlock.

"Fennel," says Bottle John. "Come on. It was all I could find."

"Toothpaste," says Mr. Charlock. "You think maybe I got too much sorghum on my biscuits?"

"Man, you told me I ever run into you again," says Bottle John, still standing solidly in the doorway, his hand still between them, still offering up the toothpaste, "you'd be an asshole." Looking past the finger-gun in his face into Mr. Charlock's eyes, squinting against the weak light from the colorless evening sky. "And here you are. Said I should remember to bring you some fennel. And I ought to – "

"I *know* what I told you to tell me," snaps Mr. Charlock. "Or maybe it's I know what it is you want me to *think* I told you to tell me, so that much of whatever you're cooking is coming up fine, pal. Kay. Mr. Kay!"

"Yes." Mr. Keightlinger's picked up the red numeral two.

"I ever talk to you about Goose City? Ever say anything about Sergeant John Wesson of Echo Force? The aluxob, and the jungle?"

Mr. Keightlinger says in a soft little sing-song voice, "The jungle's full of tiny eyes, the jungle's full of creeping feet." He sets the numeral two on the map, there where Sandy springs from Burnside and Twelfth. Mr. Charlock still squinting retucks the towel about his belly, finger-gun still aimed at Bottle John's face. Bottle John's smile has floated off. He shrugs and slips the toothpaste back into his jacket. "I saved your life down there, man," he says.

"Yeah, well," says Mr. Charlock, lowering his arm. "*I* saved the whole fucking world. You still owe me." He shakes out his hand, four fingers and a thumb. "So you're for real, or you're so damn good it makes no never mind. Whaddaya want."

"Well," says Bottle John, "it's me, and it's my brother Ezra." He steps to one side. Across the street behind him a luridly orange car with a dusty black ragtop. Beside the car a man his arms and legs a jumble of pipes in a grey suit dropped into a wheelchair, white shirt buttoned all the way up to the dove grey bow tie under his chin. Hands and eyes too big for the rest of him, hands folded together in his narrow lap, eyes behind thick black horn-rimmed spectacles. "Got one a them mutually beneficial arrangements to talk about," says Bottle John.

"Huh," says Mr. Charlock. "Okay." Hitching up his towel again. "Tell you what. You wait outside a minute, let me get some pants on, we'll go get some Vietnamese sandwiches, maybe, sit down, see how this goes."

Bottle John's smile is back.

"No offense," says Bottle John, looking down at the map on the table, the letters spread across it, piled next to it, "but you ain't the Dr. Kilo I remember."

"Different lodge," says Mr. Keightlinger without looking up. A long sandwich still wrapped in white paper by his elbow on the table.

"Mr. Kay has some pungent opinions on the topic of serving one's country," says Mr. Charlock, plucking some cilantro from his lip. "How many callsigns you guys end up using, anyway? At least up to Dr. Mike, right?"

"Nah," says Bottle John, sitting heavily in a chair by Mr. Keightlinger. "Em was a Doc Munroe, for reasons that don't bear going into. Last one I knew of was Dr. Oscar." He pushes the last of his sandwich into his mouth with his thumb.

"Damn," says Mr. Charlock. "Y'all did babysit a bunch of us."

"It is nice, to catch up with old friends," says Ezra. A yellow wrapper spread across his lap that says McDonald's over and over. A bite or two of cheeseburger left.

"But boring for those who aren't," says Mr. Charlock. "I hear you. Maybe you should let on what's up with this arrangement, and how it gets to be mutually beneficial."

Bottle John screws up a white wrapper in one hand, flicks a shred of carrot from his knee. Looks up at Ezra looking back at him, their mouths pursed with the same contemplative twist. "I knocked around a bit, you know?" says Bottle John. "After I left the service. Needed some time." He shrugs. "But what we did in Echo, man, it was *hard,* but it was *good,* right? And doing good, you get that itch? So." He chucks the wadded-up wrapper, banking it off the wall into the wastebasket. "Figured out a way, with my brother, to do some good. We, ah, well, basically, we walk the earth."

"The good Lord," says Ezra, "tells me where things need doing. And we go, and we do them."

"The Lord," says Mr. Keightlinger.

"God," says Ezra. "Our Father Almighty, Maker of the Heavens, and of the Earth." Folding the McDonald's wrapper precisely in half and half again.

After a long thin moment Mr. Charlock tucks a sprig of hair behind his ear and says "Just what the hell is it God needs done in Portland fucking Oregon?"

"Helping you," says Ezra.

"Help," says Mr. Keightlinger. He picks up his sandwich.

"Us?" says Mr. Charlock.

"Your boss," says Bottle John, as Ezra says, "Your employer, Mr. Leir? Has set you a certain task. We're to do everything in our power to assist you in accomplishing it."

"*Are* you," says Mr. Keightlinger, looking up from the map, and Ezra sighs waspishly and says "The Lord has told me," and "It's cool," says Mr. Charlock, loudly. "We're cool. Mr. Kay. Dr. Kilo." He snorts. Mr. Keightlinger takes a big bite of his sandwich. "Thing is," says Mr. Charlock, "you basically got two options to choose from – "

"Charley!" says Mr. Keightlinger around his mouthful of bánh mi.

"We're. Cool," says Mr. Charlock. "One of 'em's a long-term surveillance gig. The other one's more immediate, more goal-oriented, a favor for one of Mr. Leir's, ah, business associates." He waves a hand, smiling wryly. "I don't suppose the good Lord gave you any specifics?" Ezra doesn't say anything. He doesn't smile. Bottle John just barely shakes his head. "Whichever," says

Mr. Charlock. "We're kinda doing a general overview strategy thing tonight – "

Mr. Keightlinger slaps his sandwich down on the table, stirs through the pile of letters, picks one up.

"So maybe you come back, in the morning? We'll have some waffles, figure this out. Truth is, we're spread a little thin. You help us with one, you help us with both. That good enough?"

"Sounds good," says Bottle John, climbing to his feet. Mr. Keightlinger slaps the letter down on the map, a purple o, up north past the red Q, but it scoots away as he lets go. He snatches it up, sets it down again, waits a moment before lifting his hand. It slides smoothly away from him across the river and north, up and up, faster, off the map, over the edge of the table falling unheard to the carpet.

The orange car noses out of the side street by the motel, then whips into a tight left turn past a sign that says Executive Lodge – Your Home Away From Home. Ezra in the passenger seat his knuckled forefinger against a temple, muttering something under his breath. Bottle John gnaws at a thumb, wrenching the car one-handed through one right turn without signaling, and then another, against the light.

"I am assured," says Ezra, opening his eyes, "we are not being followed or watched."

"Don't matter," says Bottle John. "They didn't buy it."

"We weren't selling anything, John."

"They did not for one minute believe we just dropped in out of the fucking blue to help them with whatever the hell it is they are doing."

"But we will, John," says Ezra. Bottle John slows the car, stops at a red light, a five-way, a six-way intersection at the top of a low hill. Spread before them the towers and lights of the city against the darkening sky. "We will do exactly as we have said. If it went against God's will, it would not be in our power." Bottle John's looking about, eyeing the signs over the intersections, the lights, the flow of traffic. "But, yes, in their suspicion," says Ezra, "and their paranoia, they will – you want that street, over there, not the immediate right, but the orthogonal – "

"You mean," says Bottle John, flicking on the turn signal, "the regular right. Not the hard right." Looking sidelong over at his brother backlit by yellow flashes.

"In their suspicion," says Ezra, "they will take steps. Even if they do not go directly to the sorcerer Leir, they will do something that reveals to us some weakness we can exploit."

The light changes. Bottle John guns through the intersection. "I want to go down a couple blocks, right? To double back."

Ezra's taken off his spectacles, he's wiping them with a handkerchief. "I wish you would wear a tie, John."

"Ezra," says Bottle John, taking another right turn, "I told you. I'll wear the suit. I'll pack my shirt in, I'll button it all the way up." He jerks the car to a stop, yanks the gear shift into reverse, throws an arm over the back of the seat. "But I ain't wear the damn tie." He looks back through the rear window as he eases the car into a parking space by the sidewalk.

"It would promote a more uniform appearance," says Ezra.

Bottle John turns off the engine. A block or so away, rising up above the building beside them, the sign that says Executive Lodge – Your Home Away From Home. "Oh yeah," says Bottle John. "We doin' good."

"Yes, John," says Ezra. "We are."

THREE MEN STANDING – NOT ANY COURTESY
HIS FILTHY MIND – WHAT THE LORD REQUIRES

THREE MEN STANDING around an upturned oil barrel, a weathered grey plank laid across the top. All of them their dark hair tightly curled and closely cropped, all of them wearing dull grey coveralls with short sleeves and lots of pockets. One of them's holding a tool of some sort, a toothed wheel, a crank, edges blurry with rust, and he's saying something to the others but it's drowned out by the voice of an unseen narrator, by the dissident socialists of New Britain, retains a peculiar brand of socialism that is about as inefficient as socialism has ever been, yet Moambans seem to like it and feel a strong sense of attachment to their community and their island. One of the others takes the thing and points to where the wheel joins the crank, and they all laugh. His coveralls unzipped to the waist, underneath a T-shirt printed with an enormous stylized smiling man, the eyes squeezed to joyous slits. Mr. Charlock sitting at the edge of the bed isn't watching the television. He's watching Mr. Keightlinger's back. Mr. Keightlinger his half-eaten sandwich still by his elbow watches the letters on the map. There's a glass of water by the sandwich.

"Okay," says Mr. Charlock. "What. So you think I'm a total amateur, is that it?"

The water inside the glass is trembling. The glass itself is buzzing faintly. Without looking up from the map, Mr. Keightlinger puts a hand on it to still it.

"John knows how I work, okay? He knows the drill. So him and me go out tomorrow watching the Bride, you stay here and tinker with your map and keep half an eye on that *thing* in the chair." Leaning hands on his knees glaring at Mr. Keightlinger's broad back. "End of the day you have what we need to get this Agravante thing off our backs, the Bride won't have upped and run off to Seattle while we weren't looking, *and* we'll help out an old buddy of mine." On the television a strip of sand white-hot in harsh sunlight cut by a straight sharp line of shadow, a naked man on his back, feet and shins reddening in the sun one arm over his eyes, skin painted with stripes and jagged shapes of fluorescent green and pink and yellow. His pooled white hair paler than the sand. His other hand idly stroking his stiffening cock. Remains very humid, the narrator's saying, and near thirty-two degrees Celsius at all times. Nudism, though not universal, is widely practiced and quite obvious in all public places. I have no difficulty telling the girls from the boys there!

"That's like a, a win-win-win," says Mr. Charlock. "Well? Mr. Keightlinger? You trust me? Dr. Kilo?"

Mr. Keightlinger looks up from the map beard rustling against his shirt as he turns to say, "Don't call me that." The glass is buzzing faintly again.

"Do you trust me?" says Mr. Charlock.

Mr. Keightlinger lifts the glass of water and with his free hand catches the purple o before it can scoot off the table. "With my life," he says.

"Your *soul*, bucko," says Mr. Charlock. "Else this whole thing falls apart." Shaking his head. On the television a leathery hand netted with small white scars delicately adjusts some beads strung on a complex swirl of wire. "I'm insulted, really, is what I am." Mr. Charlock lies back, hands laced behind his head. "As if I'd believe Bottle John Wesson had a brother all this time and never told me."

Ghostly gliding through the dark gully down train tracks bare feet balanced on a single polished rail that faintly shines in citylight reflected from the unseen clouds above. Naked but for a wide white cartwheel ruff about her throat. She's been splashed with something that's dried in crusted white swathes along her flanks and arms, her belly, her back. She stops suddenly still balanced on that rail. "Step out," she calls. "My lady knows you are here, and would have you come before her."

A man steps from the low trees to one side of the tracks, a man in a blue and black sarong and a loose white unbuttoned shirt. "The rain's stopped the while," he says. His hair is long and dark and gathered in a single braid down his back. A black patch covers one eye. "I thought I'd take a walk." He turns back to the trees, crooks a finger at them. "You seem to have come uncapped." The leaves shake and rattle, and a branch cracks loudly.

"Mooncalfe," says the woman in the ruff. "I'd always thought you mad, not cruel." Another man stumbles from the brush, dark hair a tangle about his head, pale blue windbreaker smeared with grime.

"Oh I am mad," says the man in the sarong, grabbing the other man's hand. "Mad as you've made me. Lead on, Linesse."

A little further on and one side of the gully falls away a clearing then, and far beyond and below a highway and streetlights and bright-lit signs. A figure looms anonymous and impassive in a crude and blocky suit of wicker armor, head hidden away behind a great woven barrel of a helm. With a rustling rattling creak it lifts out an arm holding a long rattan pole to bar their way. At one edge of the little clearing a plain white sheet tied to tree branches and stakes driven into the ground. A movie flickers against it, a close-up of a kitten rubbing back and forth against a man's unshaven cheek, a sudden cut to a crush of people in a subway stairwell that fades to blood cells coursing through a vein. A woman laughs. She sits in the grass facing the screen, her back to them, wrapped in a tattered black cloak. Two children, toddlers, wrestle in the muddy leaves beside her over a broken plastic fire truck. She lifts a gnarled grey stick, smooth and dull as driftwood, and the armored figure lowers its arm, pulling the rattan pole back against its body.

"Congratulations," calls Orlando, and the woman cocks her head at that. "On finding a court of your own, out here in this counterfeit wild."

She props a hand on one crooked knee. "And to you," she says, grunting, pushing herself to her feet, "now that you might see the truth of things direct. There's something about you." She holds that stick up before him, a white-blue spark glimmering at its end.

"Eyes," says Orlando, "eyes buzzing about me. I'd not have them see where I go, or the company I keep."

"A courtesy!" She steps then from him to the man beside him hugging himself tightly in his windbreaker. "No one does me any courtesy. I know this man." She draws back, the stick flaring, harsh blue-white light filling the clearing. "Kitchen knight!" she cries. "Boar-bane!" The man in the windbreaker cringes his face in his hands. Something's growling in the darkness beyond the screen, where figments of cars chase each other against the heavy flow of traffic up a freeway. Orlando's drawn his sword and holds it blade-down at his side. "Do nothing," he says.

"Not any one thing?" she says, her stick still spitting light.

"He is in my keeping," says Orlando, "and has been almost a week now. But – " The other man looks wildly about at that, from Orlando to the palely naked woman beside him, the figure in wicker armor, the toddlers sitting frozen in the clearing, holding either end of the fire truck between them. "I don't," he's saying, "you can't," and Orlando cuffs him on the back of his head and says, "I would bargain with you, lady."

"No courtesy is ever done to me," says the woman in the cloak. The harsh light from her stick dimming. "He's not so much. Barely a mouthful. No boar-bane he, it was the girl did for my poor Erymathos. The one my sister's taken to her bosom."

"And he's the key to her," says Orlando. "Frankie Reichart, who's held the Gallowglas, and whispered her sweet nothings."

"Christ you fucking asshole you can't *do* this – " and then Frankie stops, Orlando's hand a fist now in his hair, tugging. Orlando's sword still pointed at the ground as he leans close, nose to ear. "I do what I want," he says. "Well, lady? Somewhat more valuable, perhaps, than you'd thought a moment before?"

"I need no such key," she says. Orlando smiles. "Perhaps," she says, "Linesse," she says, "my ugly duckling would like a gallowglas of her very own." Linesse in her ruff hands at her sides says nothing. "But such a jape is not worth all *that* much to me."

"Oh," says Orlando, eyeing the toddlers on the grass, "just one of your byblows."

In his grey suit holding a newspaper up over his head against the rain Bottle John jogs the last few steps up to the orange car parked by a low white building that says Auto Upholstery over the door. The daylight all about him directionless and grey. He sets a cardboard tray with a couple of covered cups of coffee on the roof of the car but doesn't open the door just yet. Down the sidewalk some empty tables under unfurled black umbrellas that say Captain Morgan. Parked by them a reddish brown car with a black stripe down its side.

Inside the orange car Mr. Charlock is slumped in the passenger seat, his head pressed against the window, tongue lolling in the corner of his half-opened mouth. Left eyelid twitching over

a white eyeball. One hand jerks up swiveling about as Bottle John
settles in the driver's seat, then falls back against his chest, fingers
trembling. Bottle John sets the coffee cups on the dashboard, tugs
one free, wipes rainwater from the cover before taking a hesitant
sip. His face screws up and he wipes his lips with a thumb, putting
the cup back, tugging the other one free. The whole time he's
watching Mr. Charlock twitching and shivering, his jaw working
now, mouthing soundless words with jagged shapes. His hand
jerks up again, makes a fist, he's biting his lip, sniffing the air,
doubling over suddenly in a coughing fit, reaching for the dashboard, clinging to it, hauling himself up against it from some deep
well. Bottle John nudges the cardboard tray along the dash until it
brushes Mr. Charlock's hand. "Coffee," says Bottle John. "Black.
Fuck-ton of sugar." Mr. Charlock scrabbles for the cup, yanks it
free slopping coffee steaming on his hand, wrenches it around and
pours most of it down his throat in one long swallow. Lifts the cup
away wobbling teeth clenched behind clamped lips the cords in his
neck standing out eyes bulging rolling turning to settle on Bottle
John watching from the driver's seat. Mr. Charlock lets out a little
puff of a cough and grabs a quick breath and then with a sigh he
relaxes, slumps, face gentling, eyes closing, hands settling in his
lap, wrapped around the cup of coffee. "Thank you," he says.

"And?" says Bottle John.

"And what?" says Mr. Charlock. "They're just, they're just
talking. The hell else you gonna do at a strip club at eleven in the
morning?"

"Man walks into a strip club with three women like that,
doesn't matter what time it is. You're gonna have thoughts."

"Well stop," says Mr. Charlock, rubbing his eyes. "It's distracting."

Bottle John leans an elbow on the steering wheel and says, "You
picking up what *I'm* thinking? Man, that is downright unsettling."

Mr. Charlock's digging at the corners of his eyes with his fingertips. "Don't work like that," he says, tugging his cheeks
down, prying his eyes wide open.

"Like what," says Bottle John.

"Like what you're thinking," says Mr. Charlock. He blows out
another sigh and tips back his cup of coffee, draining the rest.

Pulls off the top and tips it back again, shaking loose some sugary sludge from the bottom of the cup. "I just know you, John. You got a filthy mind."

"You can call it filthy if you want," says Bottle John, peering through the windshield at the nondescript black door past the umbrellaed tables. The neon sign at the corner of the building says Cocktails in big red unlit letters. Devil's Point. "What I'm thinking is downright beautiful."

"Yeah, yeah," says Mr. Charlock, shaking more sludge into his mouth.

"So this it? You go from saving the world to sniffing psychic panties?"

Mr. Charlock leans over, thwaps Bottle John on the shoulder. "How many ops we do together? And you still fuck that up?"

"Jesus, man, come on – "

"It is sloppy thinking, is what it is. You're still hung up on Foxtrot and her fucking mentalist bullshit."

"She was pretty impressive, you gotta admit – "

"She had long legs and an ass that looked great in ACU pants," says Mr. Charlock, and Bottle John snorts. "She also had," says Mr. Charlock, "a line in cold reading and parlor tricks that propped up a gift she did *not* understand. You think of it like psychic fucking powers, you're working the wrong model. You're thinking it's rational, it's repeatable, it makes some kind of sense. That it'll behave." Bottle John's looking down, away, at his coffee, taking a sip. Mr. Charlock leans close, ducking his head, trying to catch Bottle John's eyes. "That it's a science, but it *ain't*. It's an art, okay? Doesn't make any fucking sense at all. Doesn't have to. It is right and true in a way that doesn't give a shit about you and if you do not respect that it will get you killed."

"Yeah," says Bottle John. "You just pissed because she whipped your ass at poker."

"Who's sitting here, huh?" says Mr. Charlock. "Who's sitting here in the car next to you, and who's buried three miles deep under Jo'burg? Tell me that." Bottle John takes another drink of coffee. "Poker," says Mr. Charlock, reaching into his jacket.

"I'll show you some fucking poker." He's got a couple of playing cards and he hands one to Bottle John. The King of Clubs.

"What's this?"

"Lick the back of it and stick it to your forehead." Mr. Charlock licks his card and sticks it there just under his lank grey curl. The Queen of Diamonds. From another pocket he's pulling a folded-up square of glossy paper, an ad ripped from a magazine, a sleek sports car with smokey glass and a rounded roof. "Come on, come on. They'll be leaving soon." He licks his thumb, smears saliva along the top of the ad, leans up to stick it against the windshield.

"The hell you doing?" says Bottle John.

"Orange car?" says Mr. Charlock. "Couple guys in suits? Pretty fucking noticeable. They look this way coming out, they'll see a happy loving couple in a nice grey Audi."

"Loving couple, huh," says Bottle John, eyeing the red queen stuck to Mr. Charlock's head. "That make you the girl?"

"Fucking hell," says Mr. Charlock, snatching the card from his head. "Operational security, nimrod!" Rubbing his knuckles across the queen's face, then licking the card and putting it back in place. "No stupid questions while I'm working." From another pocket now he's drawing out a pair of classic black sunglasses, an owl's feather tied to one side.

"Aw hell man," says Bottle John. "I hate that thing."

"It hates everybody," says Mr. Charlock, putting them on. "Lick it and stick it already."

Bottle John licks the back of his card and sticks it to his forehead. "The hell you chasing out here, anyway?" he says.

"Ain't it obvious?" says Mr. Charlock. He's grinning now. "Ultraterrestrials from Sefirah X."

The green B up on Swan Island now in a channel of milky sunlight from the curtains opened not much more than a handspan. The red Q lit up still on the corner of Everett and 20th. Out of the light on the other side of the map the orange B and the yellow Y together there where Foster Road begins to slice diagonally across the regular grid of streets. A clink and a rattling buzz as the purple o under an overturned water glass beats itself against the table. "That's quite distracting," says Ezra. Mr. Keightlinger looks up from the map but doesn't say anything. He taps the glass. The buzzing stops.

The wheelchair back in the dark alcove by the bathroom Ezra's leaning heavily on the nearer bed, sliding with uncertain steps closer to the table so he can peer over Mr. Keightlinger's broad back at the map. "I can help, you know," says Ezra.

That broad back hunches in a shrug.

Ezra sits on the bed, lifting his legs to resettle his feet in shining black shoes too large for the rest of him, like his hands, like his eyes behind those spectacles. "Your name starts with a P," he says. "But it doesn't sound like a P. The Lord has whispered your name to me, though I could not catch it. Your partner, Dr. Charley, though. The Lord has said nothing to me about him. Butterscotch?" A couple of yellow-gold candies dandled in the big pale palm of his hand. Mr. Keightlinger shakes his head, the clumsy club of his ponytail waving back and forth. Ezra unwraps a candy and pops it into his mouth. "We have no quarrel with you," he says around the candy clicking against his teeth. "Some might open the book and cite Exodus, chapter twenty-two, verse eighteen: Thou shalt not suffer a witch to live." He smiles to himself, big hands folded together in his narrow lap. "But I have seen too many things in this world to forget the unknowable, the constantly surprising majesty of God. He truly works in mysterious ways, and even one such as you, and your partner, and your deviltry, can all be part of His plan." He sucks on the candy, works it between his teeth. In the glass on the table the o is buzzing again. There's a crunch. Ezra lifts his eyebrows in a little sigh, chews, swallows. "I can be so impatient sometimes," he says. "What the Lord requires of me already is more than I could ever ask of myself. I have learned not to presume what *else* I might do, to fulfill my part in His plan. I hardly even witness, anymore." He's toying with the second candy in his palm. "My younger self would be so disappointed in me." Unwraps the candy, pops it in his mouth. "Such a hard lesson to learn, for something so obvious. That nothing in this world is pure. Especially oneself."

Mr. Keightlinger taps the glass again and the buzzing stops. He opens his mouth and pulls out a pink plastic x. He wraps his fist about it and closes his eyes and sweeps his fist over the map, back and forth, in and out of that pale band of light, slowing, his fist opening, the x taken gingerly between thumb and fingers, eyes still closed the hand lowering to place the x just so. Opening his eyes. Hand hovering over the pink x there by the river at the bottom of the map, where the street grid curls around a lakelet just south of a skinny, claw-shaped island. The rest of the letters scattered well above and around it, turning and twitching in place. The yellow Y and the orange B together sliding down Powell toward Thirty-ninth, wobbling a little over a crease in the map. Mr. Keightlinger stands and scoops up a ring of keys from the top of the television set.

"Are we going somewhere?" says Ezra.

"No," says Mr. Keightlinger, opening the door.

"But," says Ezra pushing himself to his feet, leaning heavily on the bed, "I don't understand. What am I to do?"

"Answer the phone," says Mr. Keightlinger. "If it rings."

GROANING THE SHAPE – TÊTE-À-TÊTE
"YOUR REASON FOR LEAVING?" – MARKING THE SPOT

GROANING THE SHAPE on the futon rolls and twists and hunches up suddenly. A head appears shrugging off a rumple in the covers, tousled hair thin and wispy, a man on all fours somewhere under the crazed tangle of quilts and blankets and sheets, reds and oranges and greens and pinks and blues, midnight blues, patches of iridescent blue like feathers, like eyes, a ripple of blue like a warm clear tropical sea, stripes of cloudless sky blue. He's crawling toward the edge dragging the whole mass of color with him, and he stops, tries kicking himself free. A foot shakes loose, a bare leg, falling over on his side wrestling free of the striped comforter his hip his chest his shoulder and arm. Tugging a stretch of sheet back over his nakedness he reaches up over his head feeling about the floor to one side coming up with a pair of blue jeans belt still looped and green plaid boxers still tucked inside. Kicking, squirming, he gets both feet free and up in the air and into the legs of the jeans and rolling over on his belly gets the jeans up about his hips. He tugs a corner of a sheet from his waistband before buttoning and zipping and buckling. Up on his knees now reaching back over the edge of the futon for a thick soft shirt in a sunset plaid. "Wallet," he says, patting his pockets, "wallet, good, keys. Keys. Shit." Looking about the long narrow room, running a hand through what little of his hair is left. "Shoes. Shoes." Futon's at one end. A long table runs the length of it, stacks of binders and loose paper atop it lit up from behind by fluorescent lights through greenish louvered windows. The floor of broad wood planks chipped and scratched but clean, uncluttered. He snaps his fingers, leans down, reaches under the futon and comes up with an old brown shoe. Shakes it. It jingles. He smiles. The door opens.

The man there's big, broad, a loose yellow slicker draped over him shining with rain. Long grey mustaches droop to either side of his mouth. A white paper bag and a cardboard tray with a couple of paper coffee cups. "I was going to wake you with burritos," he says.

"Yeah," says the man on the futon. He buttons up his shirt. "Breakfast, that's – thanks."

"Brunch," says the man in the slicker.

"Shit," says the man on the futon.

"You said you wanted to stay awake as late as – "

"Yeah, I'm sorry, what time is – "

" – as late as you could – "

" – what time is it?"

The man in the slicker sets the bag and the coffee on the table. "After lunch," he says.

"Shit," says the man on the futon, stuffing his feet in his shoes. "I've got to call the office – "

"You called them. You called them already."

The man on the futon runs his hand through his hair again. "I don't," he says. "I don't remember doing that."

"About sunrise," says the man in the slicker. "You left a message."

The man on the futon pushes himself to his feet. "I don't remember doing that. I don't remember – anything. I must've, had something fierce to drink last night – "

"Not really, no," says the man in the slicker. "Coffee?" He tugs a cup free from the tray.

"No, sorry, it's just – I don't remember. A thing. About last night. I don't remember meeting – "

"It's all right, Arnold," says the man in the slicker.

The other man stoops, picks up a blue rainshell from the end of the futon. "What, did you get that from my driver's license?" He pulls it on.

"You're right," says the man in the slicker. "Becker. I'm sorry."

"I should, ah, go," says Becker, sidling toward the door. "Make sure everything's okay, that is. I don't usually call out, I mean – "

"Pyrocles," says the man in the slicker, stepping out of his way.

"Pyrocles," says Becker, standing beside him a moment. Looking out the open door down a narrow metal staircase bolted to a concrete wall, a dark cave of a garage opening below, racked drawers of tools and parts standing here and there. "Where," says Becker, zipping up his jacket, "I'm sorry, where am I?"

"Fourteenth and Everett," says Pyrocles. "Northwest."

"Okay," says Becker, nodding. Looking away. Stepping abruptly past Pyrocles and heading down the stairs, one hand on the rail, not looking back.

"Perry comma Yizzabel," says Mr. Charlock. "Age unknown."

"Okay," says Bottle John. "Looks early, mid-twenties to me."

"Does she," says Mr. Charlock. "Daughter of Perry comma Duenna, age ditto. Father died some time ago, don't know when. Name unknown. There was a brother but he ran away some time ago, ditto ditto ditto."

"So you been following this girl for four months, five months, and you don't know a goddamn thing."

"No, no, no," says Mr. Charlock, and then he sighs. "Well yes. But." He hitches forward, leans closer, wriggles a bit, unbuckles the seatbelt. "It's like," he says, "I think it's like, well, a story."

Bottle John drums his fingers on the steering wheel. "A story," he says.

"Well okay like it's always been there, waiting," says Mr. Charlock. "And then when the right person comes along, it begins, okay? And when it begins," tapping his finger against his palm, "she's always already just past twenty, twenty-one, okay? Her mother's always already wealthy and, and spending all her time doing whatever it is she does all day, and her father's always already been dead for however long, and her brother's always already long since run off, and then when it's done, whatever it is – "

"She always making out with hot blond chicks in the front seats of muscle cars?" says Bottle John.

"What?" says Mr. Charlock, leaning forward, rubbing at the condensation fogging the windshield before him. "Shit."

"Other two ain't even gone five minutes," says Bottle John.

"Hope this isn't offending your new-found Bible-thumping sensibilities."

"Man, *fuck* you," says Bottle John with sudden heat. "Do not lump us in with that ignorant cracker bullshit. You could be singing show tunes in the shower with your Dr. Kilo and I wouldn't give a good God damn. Me and my brother, we are serious. We are here to do His will and to fight evil on this earth, you hear me? And whatever the hell else that might be," pointing out the windshield at the reddish-brown car parked half a block away along the cross street, "it ain't evil."

"Don't be so sure about that," mutters Mr. Charlock.

"What?"

"Your brother," says Mr. Charlock, slumping back in his seat. "How come you never talked about him?"

"I told you about Ezra," says Bottle John.

"You never mentioned a brother, John," says Mr. Charlock.

"Man I got five other brothers and three sisters and with the nieces and nephews all told I figure they make up about half of Judson by now. I got razzed so hard, remember, hauling their pictures out all the damn time?" Leaning forward pressing against the dashboard. "Mom and pops coming up on their fiftieth in a couple years oh come on baby, don't lie her down, don't lie down." He slaps the steering wheel. "Shit. Can't see a fucking thing now."

"Put it our of your head," says Mr. Charlock. "Just, stop. Stop thinking about it. Seriously."

"Well there she is out here where anybody can see. Like this guy, the jogger? He's about to get an eyeful."

"That's no jogger," says Mr. Charlock.

"What?" says Bottle John.

Outside the man in the green track suit's slowing as he comes up to the reddish-brown car, calling something out. Two heads appear, blond, brunette, two figures sitting up in the front seat of that car. "She is *dangerous,*" Mr. Charlock's saying. "This is why. I told you not to engage but if God forbid you talk to her, if you bump into her on the sidewalk and you catch her eye and you let slip the slightest hint, the least little clue that you, *want* her, that's it. It's over." The man in the green track suit's leaning both hands against the roof of the reddish-brown car saying something very earnestly through the half-open passenger-side window. "She'll have you on all fours baying at the goddamn moon if she thinks she can get a laugh out of it."

"Make her sound like every woman I ever went out with," says Bottle John.

"Grow up," says Mr. Charlock.

"Your reason for leaving?"

Thin black hair hanging down about his face black-nailed hands one over the other glittering with silver rings, ankhs and snakeheads and dice. "They, uh," he says, "ran out of work." His voice deep and silky around that catch.

"What sort of work?"

"I, uh, called people. On the phone? And asked them questions."

"Telemarketing?"

"Oh no, no." Rearing back, looking up now at the woman behind the counter. His black T-shirt says Kurtzberg Krackle in white letters. "Surveys. Stuff like that. No sales. But. But I do have sales experience. Retail. It was a grocery store."

She chuckles. "You've had experience with a mop." He frowns. "Clean-up on aisle seven?" He's still frowning. "Because you have to be okay with cleaning up the private booths from time to time."

"That's okay," he says, "I mean it's," and then he stops and says "Oh. Um."

"Yeah," she says. "Um. That a problem?" She has a silvery ring in one nostril and a silvery ring through her lip and she's wearing a red-and-blue striped polo shirt that's a size or two too small. A roll of belly lops out from under the hem of it over her big black belt.

"They actually," he says, "go, in there, and – "

"*Private* viewing booths," she says. "What do you expect? You're gonna get jerkers in the aisles, too. Guys who don't wanna pay for a private booth. Maybe the library's too public for 'em. They find a case they like and take it off to a corner somewhere out of the way." She pats the computer monitor on the counter beside her. "They never think about the security cameras. Or maybe they do."

He says "So you have to go and – "

"Oh, there's no go," she says. She grabs the microphone on the swivel stand next to the monitor and thumbs it on and says "We put the fear of God in them" in a voice that booms out over speakers throughout the store. "Hilarious," she says, letting go of the mike, "the way they spook and run. You sure you want this job?"

He says, "There's a paycheck, right?"

She shrugs. "How'd you hear we were hiring?"

"She told me," he says, pointing. Over across the store past the black wire racks filled with DVD cases in greens and oranges and magentas and lots and lots of tans and beiges and pinks with signs here and there that say Anal and Anime and Asian and New Releases there's a row of thin white mannequins in teddies and merry widows and spangled pasties and absurdly short schoolgirl kilts. In front of them a woman in a yellow raincoat and a brick-colored poodle skirt over patched jeans and a bulky sweater dotted with knitted sheep. On her head a confetti-colored patchwork cap. She's leaning close, almost but not quite touching a glittery tassel.

"Your girlfriend told you to get a job in a porn store," says the woman behind the counter.

"I, uh, I guess so," he says. He's looking down at his hands again. One fingertip wrapped in a dingy wad of bandaid.

"You guess she told you?" She's leaning her elbows on the counter, her chin in her hand. "Or you guess she's your girl-friend?"

"It's," he says, "complicated." He sighs and shrugs, skinny shoulders up about his ears. He shivers and rolls his head from side to side, settling his neck. "She told me I get the job, which is good, because it's important. Is what she told me."

"Did she now," says the woman behind the counter.

Mr. Keightlinger gives the chain one last jerk and winds it off, then steps off the elevator. The floor beyond unfinished, open, steel beams and white-patched drywall, plastic sheeting hanging limply gently pattering with rain. "Wonder who Joe is," he says. He heads over toward the nearest plastic sheet, brushes it with one hairy-knuckled finger. "Really," he says. He reaches into his jacket, pulls out a pair of sunglasses. The left lens is covered with spidery words painted in white ink. He puts them on and lifts the plastic aside.

Twenty or thirty floors below the river unruffled by the rain the bridges over it marching out ahead of him one by one into the deepening afternoon gloom until far-off the great arch of the northern freeway bridge winking with red and white lights. To his left the cluster of buildings downtown, the brick tower, the high white tower with narrow dark windows, the grey and white tower topped by a sweeping wing-shape, a rooftop garden in its shadow. Past them away and beyond a lone tower of ruddy amber glass framed by dull pink stone all of it smeared against the dark and rainy hills beyond.

"Wrong side," says Mr. Keightlinger, letting the plastic fall. "Should have said something."

He heads across the open empty floor toward the other side of the building where the plastic sheeting soaked in soft grey light glows against the shadows. The sound of the rain louder here and under it the hissing rushing of freeway traffic. "Armenians?" he says. "That doesn't matter." And then, "Under his collar. On his back?" He looks over his shoulder, still wearing the sunglasses. "You're not making any sense." Mr. Keightlinger lifts the plastic aside. "He's on his own," he says, then pushes under it and steps out to the very edge of the floor.

The river below, hills to his right dark with trees and studded with houses, the freeway sweeping past and around a dark shoulder lit up with headlights and taillights, to his left low bluffs and trees, a busy street along the river's edge, more houses. A curl of island like a claw ahead of him, like an arrow pointing at him scrimmed with black-green trees and dotted with the battered yellows and oranges of construction equipment, gantries, cranes. Past it the left bank rising a bit and there in the trees the sky-blue wall of some long flat building an eagle painted spreads it wings over a long and rickety staircase that tumbles down to the water.

Mr. Keightlinger lets the plastic fall behind him, lowers his sunglasses, tilts his head, taking in that far-off blue wall, the bluff, the dark trees, the houses about. Just past the island a sudden confusion of lights, a ferris wheel, a snaking curl of roller coaster but he's looking above it, past it. Lifting the sunglasses back into place. "Okay," he says. Shifting the toes of his black shoes hanging over the long fall to the unfinished street below he licks a finger and then throws his arm out, pointing. A rush and a sodden bang, far-off, a smudge of pink light blooming in the air out there over the houses past that sky-blue wall. It smolders there, flickering, dying as pink-white sparks pop from it cooling to yellow and orange and red and nothing at all as they fall.

"Sonofabitch was right," says Mr. Keightlinger, and his bushy beard shifts to one side in a small smile.

"The strong wind blew," says Ezra, and his big hands locked about the edge of the table he lifts it just with a grunt and lets it fall shaking the letters scattered across the map. "And when Peter began to sink he called out and the Lord held out His hand." Again, and the letters tumble and fall away, all but the pink x stubbornly fixed there by the river at the bottom of the map, where the street grid curls around a lakelet just south of a skinny, claw-shaped island. "And I say glory to You O God," his voice rising, "who created the angels, O ruler of æons, the heavenly chorus of æons sings praises to you." The pink x lightening now, lines and streaks of white slashing across it as he shakes the table a third time. "I call to my hand now all those made righteous by their struggles, and in memory of St. Cosmas and St. Damian," and then he staggers back from the table as a thin wisp of smoke begins to curl from under the x and the map beneath it darkens. "The cherubim," he says, hushed now, breathless, "praise God, and the chorus of angels praises the thrice-blessed church, and the brotherhood of saints blesses the King Christ, our Lord..." The x softening, sagging, shining white-hot as a lick of flame ruffles the air above it. He rubs his jaw with his big hand smiling now, sagging, a sharp-edged bundle in his grey suit. "Oh my brother," he says. "Oh, we have them."

He pushes himself back up until he is sitting again on the edge of the bed his hands folded in his lap his head bowed his eyes closed and he takes a deep breath. The only sound in the room the crackle of the dying fire eating a hole in the map. "Hear me my Father," he says, his voice a whisper now, a breath just barely falling from his barely parted lips. "Father of all fatherhoods, of infinite light, make them all worthy to receive Your baptism of fire, and release them from their sins, and purify them from their transgressions, yea, hear me my Father as I invoke your imperishable names, the names that are in the treasury of light," and he stops a moment, licks his lips, eyes still closed, and he says "Azarakaza A," and then he says "Amathkratitath," and then, his voice catching, growing louder, stronger, he says "Yo" and "Yo" and "Yo" and "Amen, amen" and shouting now he says

"Yaoth Yaoth Yaoth Phaoph Phaoph Chioephozpe, Chenobinuth, Zarlai Lazarlai Laizai – "

MR. CHARLOCK SITS – THE SWORD IN THE FLOOR
BAKER, JULIET, INDIA

MR. CHARLOCK SITS on an empty phone book binder at the bottom of a phone booth, knees drawn up, arms drawn in, green-grey handset pressed to his cheek. "Jesus they was all over town today," he says. "Bus down Hawthorne and they head right to the fuckin' Duke's, breakfast with him, and then it's off in his car for a tour of all the hotspots in Southeast. I'm telling you – listen." He leans against the side of the phone booth. "If it had just been you and me, or just you, and me off at another goddamn council meeting – " He knocks the handset against the side of the phone booth. "Yeah whatever," he yells into the mouthpiece, then tucks the handset back against his cheek again. "How was working with the so-called brother?"

He slumps against the back of the phone booth listening. Over his head a sticker half peeled away says that someone unreadable's got a posse. Next to it a sticker in the shape of a taxi cab. Call Radio, it says. Someone's scribbled a monster in black ink, big head looming out of the taxi window, one hand on a gear shift spearing the taxi's hood. Mr. Charlock shivers suddenly, sits bolt upright. "Shit. Seriously? All right. All right. And what did I tell you? Fucking Southeast. Oh don't give me that we both know it's him. You owe me ten bucks. I don't care, you owe me ten bucks on general principle!" He sits back, smiling broadly. "Yeah. What? Sellwood. I told you, all over fucking Southeast. Yes, Sellwood. I don't know, this crazy-ass place on a vacant lot by the river. All windows and doors and scrap lumber and shit." His smile's leaked away now, he's hunching forward. "I don't know, a couple blocks away. I had to find – I had to find a phone." One hand on the jamb of the phone booth pulling himself to his feet. "A what? Blue building? By the river?"

Outside the phone booth at the edge of the parking lot an empty school and past the school looming over the trees a big blocky building with one wall the color of a high blue sky. Up in the clouds above and behind it a fading pinkish tinge, a glimmer, a few last dying sparks arcing toward the ground a couple of blocks away.

"Shit," says Mr. Charlock. "That was you? I was looking for a fucking phone, not – " He turns back to the phone booth. There's no phone inside the booth. The cord from the handset's stuffed through a hole in the booth where the phone used to be. "It's a – it's a fucking coincidence is all. Yes. Okay even if it isn't because of the Duke and the Bride so fucking what. It still has nothing to – it couldn't possibly have anything to do with John or his so-called – well sure. Come on down! What the fuck." Mr. Charlock yanks the cord out of the hole in the phone booth and stands there a moment, handset in his hand. He wraps the cord about it, stuffs it in his pocket. "Shit," he says again.

He turns abruptly, heads down the sidewalk. Up in the sky the pink blush almost gone. He reaches as he walks for the knot of his tie and yanks to loosen it. Unbuttons the top button of his shirt.

Mr. Keightlinger hands the phone back to the young man in the navy suit, who hangs it up on its cradle on the empty desk of glass and blond wood in the middle of the glassy lobby. On easels scattered about are renderings of a completed building, photos of smiling men and women, floor plans in white ink on blue paper. Penthouse, says one. 2200 Square Feet says another. "That was, that was odd," says the young man in the navy suit.

"Joe says hello," says Mr. Keightlinger.

The young man's face brightens. "Oh! Joe. Right! Did you get what you needed? Everything fine? Anything else?"

"There are no coincidences," says Mr. Keightlinger, turning and walking away.

Parked on the street outside a black car dimly through the sea-green glass. "Ross Island?" says Mr. Keightlinger to himself.

"Sellwood? Ross Island." Pulling the ring of keys from his pocket as he pushes open the lobby door.

It's a short straight sword, the blade of it two fingers wide from the guard down its visible length, the hilt of it wrapped in white leather worn and yellowed with long handling, quillions and pommel heavy and plain, struck with cold silvery gleams even in the warm lamplight. The floor where it's been thrust is singed, the scratched wood black and rough like charcoal in a neat ring about the upright blade.

"It's good that you have come," says the short man in the doorway, dressed all in black, black jeans, black boots, a tight black turtleneck. "As you can see, dancing's a bit awkward, since your sister left." His beard a whisper of tamed curls just past stubble along his jawline.

The man beside him says nothing. A head and a half taller at least he's wearing grey flannel pants flecked with white and black and pink and a bulky blue sweater. His white hair touched with hints of gold, hanging in tangled dreads down past his shoulders. He walks into the room and over to the sword, stepping carefully about it, kneeling beside it. Brushing his fingers along the plain and heavy pommel lifting his hand away sharply. Stroking his chin. "It's hers," he says.

"Your pardon, Axehandle," says the man all in black, "but that was never in doubt."

"It's hers, Goodfellow," says the man with the dreadlocks, standing. "I can't just take it."

"Nor can you leave it here, sir. All due respect."

"Think of it," says Agravante, one hand filliping the air, looking for the proper phrase, "as a conversation piece. The stories you can tell. The sword, in your ballroom."

"There's but one story to be told about that," says Robin. "Sir. And everyone already knows it."

"She will come back," says Agravante. Looking at the sword again. Walking about it. "She will come back, and when she comes through that door – " pointing at the front door there past the stairs " – and takes up this sword again – " He lets his arm fall. *That's* the story," he says to Robin. "You couldn't risk missing *that.*"

Robin stands in the doorway his arms folded not leaning to either side. "All are welcome in my house," he says. "If she were to come through that door I'd poor her a dram with my own two hands to hear where she'd been. But she left her sword there and she walked away, alone. She's leigeless, houseless, flagless now. Her meaning was quite clear."

"She still has a brother," says Agravante, quietly. And then, "Think of it as a favor done for me, and a boon I – "

"I owe no one any favors," says Robin, quickly. "In return, I ask that none are owed to me." Somewhere back behind him in the house a burst of laughter, "No no, wait!" calls someone, and with a wheeze and a thump some skirling driving music launches itself from several rooms away. Agravante shrugs. "Then here it stays," he says, "and I owe you nothing for it. I cannot draw that sword."

"You mean you will not," says Robin. "Sir."

"And because I will it not, I can't," says Agravante, headed away from the sword in the floor, up to Robin in the doorway. "Draw it yourself, if you like. I'll just collect my coat now, and be off, after thanking you for a lovely afternoon."

Robin steps to one side, and Agravante's past him, walking back into the house, back toward the music.

"Blast and rot," says Robin Goodfellow.

Two residential streets, lined with parked cars, a simple intersection, the pavement of it painted in a great circle stretching from corner to corner in yellows and whites a sunflower faded by weather and traffic opening under the darkening sky. Houses sit comfortably at three of the corners lights aglow against the gathering night, and at three of the corners there by the sidewalks stands have been built, little kiosks of scrap lumber and windfall painted in primary colors dimmed with age. Library says a sign over one, and old paperback books are stuffed on a shelf behind a spotty glass door. Tea says a sign over another, and a couple of thermoses and some old mugs and cups and tins and cans of tea on shelves beneath.

At the fourth corner a high red gate freshly painted, white lights strung about it. Two old paned windows hang in the air to either side of it from wires just visible strung from tree branches and the gate itself. Beyond a ramshackle confusion gathers itself from windows and doors and bare wood, roofs of tin and translucent plastic aglow with lamplight, the trees of the lot winding in and out of the structure built around them. One of the cars parked near the gate is reddish-brown, and has a black stripe down its side. A block or so away the orange car with the dusty black ragtop. Bottle John sits behind the wheel, looking at the folded phone in the big pale palm of his hand. Stuck to the windshield a page torn from a magazine, a photograph of a man in hip-boots and a hat strung with fishing lures leaning on the fender of a new pickup truck. "Let's hope you're right," he says to the phone, and he tucks it into a jacket pocket. Leans forward reaching behind himself to tug out a snub-nosed revolver, almost as small in his hand as the phone. He looks it over, cracks open the cylinder to check the bullets, counting them off under his breath. Snaps it shut. Sets the revolver on the seat beside him, under a fold of his jacket, looking back over his shoulder as he does so. Mr. Charlock's coming down the street toward the car.

Mr. Charlock opens the passenger-side door but doesn't get in. He squats and fiddles with the side of the seat until it leans forward, then climbs into the back seat, wrestling the door shut behind him. Pulling the seat back upright.

"You get done what you needed to get done?" says Bottle John.

"Yeah," says Mr. Charlock. "I'm just gonna have a lie-down for a minute or three." Settling himself on the narrow back seat, rolling over on his back knees up, stretching out his legs as far as he can.

"Mind if I yammer at you?" says Bottle John. "While we're watching?"

"Got something you want to get off your chest?"

"Something like that," says Bottle John, lifting the fold of his jacket away from the revolver on the seat.

"Knock yourself out," says Mr. Charlock, closing his eyes, folding his hands upon his chest.

"You know I left the service a couple years ago," says Bottle John. "But I didn't exactly leave under color of law, you know?" Gingerly he picks up the revolver. "It's not that they consider me AWOL or nothing, just they think I'm still somewhere I ain't. See I was at Dome A."

"Yeah?" says Mr. Charlock.

"You been out the loop I'm sure. Dome A. Bottom of the world, man. Bottom of the fucking world." He tucks his finger into the trigger-guard. "The Kunlun Station. Joint op with the PLA's Third Research Institute? They'd been, *hearing* things. In the ice. They had their people, we scrambled a full troop. And three Doctors, man. Three of you fucks. Baker, and Juliet, and India." The gun trembles in his hand. He wraps his other hand about it to steady it, still it. "You look in our jackets," he takes a deep breath, "I'm sure you'll see something about a transport chopper going down in Afghanistan or some such. No survivors. And you know I still got no idea whether we managed to save the world down there or not? Some days I don't think I made it out. Some days I think I'm still down there and all this is me just dreaming away whatever it is I got left. Anyway." He lifts his arm suddenly turning to point the gun over at the back seat. There's nothing there but an empty black suit, a white shirt, a skinny black tie still looped under its undone collar.

Bottle John blinks.

"Aw, *hell* no," he says, yanking open his door, kicking himself out of the car in a scramble gun up pointed still at that empty back seat. Standing slowly, looking about, the gun not wavering now, steady, solid.

"Hell no," says Bottle John again.

Out in the intersection a block or so away the rainless air above that painted sunflower's shivering, rippling, a blur of heat, and from it faintly a howling burst of trumpet-song, of wind-song, a roar of lions and of fire. Bottle John's head whips back and forth, the roiling air, the orange car, "God dammit," he says, darting toward the car, pointing the gun behind it, coming around it to point the gun at the sidewalk on the other side. No one's there. Light pours from the hole in the air over the sunflower now, light and feathers, a great wing unfolding and another, and another, the intersection filling with sunlight. "Sonofabitch," mutters Bottle John. He starts to walk toward to the sunlight, looking back as he does, his gun still aimed at the car. *"Son*ofabitch, we ain't ready, we *are not ready,"* breaking into a loping run, skirting the intersection filled now with bright hot light and wings and in among the wings are opening slowly eyes the color of shadowed earth and polished wood and dried dead grass and desert skies. He spares it one last look before turning and bulling his way through the red gate.

Grey-white smoke drifts from the smoldering table up in sketchy whorls to melt into clouds that hug the ceiling. He sets the phone on its cradle on the nightstand and pushes himself upright, then leaning heavily one hand on each of the queen-sized beds makes his way down the narrow aisle between them. "Do well," he says, puffing with the effort. "Do well, John. Do well." Stopping at the foot of the beds, upright, carrying his weight in his legs mostly now, not his arms. Across the smokey room in the dark alcove by the bathroom his wheelchair waiting. "Anaharath," he says, closing his eyes. "Ashbel and Baara. Cuth-Cuthah." Crooning the names, lifting his hands from the bedspreads, standing now on his own two feet. "Elealeh and Esh-ban. Ur, Uri, Uriah, Urim! Zephath and Zephon, Zethar, Zuph!"

The bathroom door bursts open smashing into the wheelchair knocking it back against the sink. Bright fluorescent light slashes through the eddying smoke. Ezra's eyes open shocked and he topples arms waving for balance catching at but missing the end of either bed as he turns and falls to the floor. Mr. Charlock steps naked from the bathroom through that slash of light one hand lifted thumb cocked two fingers curled back two fingers pointed at Ezra's stupefied face. "You," gasps Ezra, "how – "

"I'm a magician, you dumb sad fuck," says Mr. Charlock. "You think you fooled me for a minute?"

"Please," says Ezra, squirming over on his belly, "please set aside your rage – we're here for the sorcerer, Leir, not you, not your partner. There's still time – " Hands planted on the floor pushing himself half upright lifting one of those hands to Mr. Charlock, imploring, "Please," he says. "Please, get down on your knees, before the Lord in His majesty, and His wrath. *You still. Have. Time.*"

"Yeah?" says Mr. Charlock, lowering his hand just, thumb still cocked. "Leir? You think Leir is anywhere near *any* of this shit?"

"But – " says Ezra, and Mr. Charlock lifts his hand again and says, "Shut up. Hold still. This is gonna fuck you up something fierce."

THE WOMAN KNEELING BY THE TUB

THE WOMAN KNEELING BY THE TUB wears nothing but a pair of narrow black-rimmed glasses. Her chin tucked she's looking only at her hands folded one over the other in her lap. On the white tile floor beside her an oval copper tray and on the tray a gold plate and a bone knife, a white plastic funnel, a rehoboam pitcher filmed with a milky residue. Beside the tray a stack of thick white folded towels. The bathroom about her's large and lined all in tiny white hexagonal tiles, the lines of grout gone dark with age and grime. The tub sits on its four clawed feet on a low blocky pedestal at one end of the room, beneath a window of frosted glass, blackly blank in all that white.

Her nose twitches shifting her glasses. She doesn't lift a hand to scratch. Her face has been carefully painted, her lips an exaggerated Cupid's bow in a thick bright red, her eyelids brushed with gold over dark long lashes. She blinks. Her nose twitches again. She doesn't look up. Her hands don't move from her lap.

The tub filled almost to the brim with water motionless strung with ropes of something viscously white. A woman stretched on her back submerged eyes closed her black hair drifting loosely tangled curls about her head and shoulders, tendrils looped over her face, her breasts, along her arms. Her hands float limply either side. A bubble of air creeps from one nostril to shiver a moment before its release, blundering up and up through fronds of dark hair and strands of white stuff slowly, so slowly, until wobbling it reaches the surface of the water clinging there to its underside a moment before breaking the silence with a tiny crack. The woman by the tub blinks rapidly behind her glasses but does not lift her hand, doesn't turn her head. In the tub the Queen's hands move now, slowly, stirring, tangling, shredding the ropey strands to milky clouds about her fingers. Her head rolling slowly, so slowly from one side to the other, eyes still closed, lips parting just enough to release a mouthful of smoke, reddish, brownish black, and where it billows in the water the milky ropes pull back, away, break apart in the water that's begun to slosh against the sides of the tub, water with a greasy sheen. The Queen's eyes open then in the water, in shock, in terror as her mouth opens around a great gout of the stuff pouring out of her. One hand breaks the surface of the water with a splash reaching for something, and the woman kneeling by the tub does not put out her hand to grasp it, does not look up. The Queen braced on an elbow now hauling her hand back down out of the useless air pushing arcing her back up and up the water sliding from her face pulling her hair back with the weight of it her mouth still open throat jumping eyes still open searching as water streams from them as that stuff the color of old blood drips from her mouth and nose down her cheeks, her throat, across her breast and shoulders. The water in the tub darkening, clearing. A tearing retching gasp and the Queen begins to breathe, head jerking, chest heaving, a foot squeaking against the tub as she tries to brace herself, and the woman kneeling by the tub has closed her eyes, and her hands in her lap are folded together.

"Anna," says the Queen. "A towel."

And now the woman by the tub leans forward, lifts a towel from the pile and shakes it open, handing it to the Queen, who wipes her face, her mouth, her chin and throat. "These will have to be burnt," she says.

"Ma'am," says Anna.

The Queen stands, letting the soiled towel fall to the tiles. Anna hands her up another, and she scrubs at the sticky stuff along her shoulders and arms, her breasts and belly. "Sluice it clean. Do not let it into the drains. Pour it into buckets and tell Cragflower when you are done. He'll know where to take them." She drops the towel and lifts a foot to the edge of the tub, and Anna kneeling again dries it with another towel. "Ma'am," says Anna. "All of it?"

"It's gone brackish, and sour," says the Queen. "We must simply gather more and try again." Her foot cleaned and dried she steps to set it on the tiled pedestal, and lifts her other foot dripping from the tub.

"There's nothing to be done?" says Anna, rubbing it clean.

The Queen kneels there on the pedestal beside her, plucks away the stained towel and drops it to the floor beside them, takes Anna's face in her hands. "Scrub yourself when you are finished," says the Queen. "Be most careful and thorough. I'll not have you sickened."

"Ma'am," says Anna.

Surveil has encountered the same kind of critical resistance that was once accorded to other back-formations, such as *diagnose* and *donate*. It remains to be seen whether it too will eventually come to be regarded as useful and unexceptionable.

—the *American Heritage*®
Book of English Usage

NO. II

ROUNDS

THE LIGHT FROM THE TELEVISION – WHAT TIME IT IS – "IS IT THE MONEY?"
WHAT THEY'RE GETTING – LITTLE MORE THAN A CLOSET
WHY HE'S DOING IT – MADEMOISELLE JULIETTE – "I AM THE HOUSE"
WHAT THE STARLING DOES – TITS & ASS & OH – "WHAT I THINK IS MAYBE"
MODERN AND MORE EQUITABLE – THE STRONG HAND
ON THE STRAND – UNRESERVEDLY – ROUNDING A CORNER
NEXT THURSDAY – NO HULLABALOO – TO HAVE GONE DANCING
LIKE BUBBLES – "SIR? SIR?"

THE LIGHT FROM THE TELEVISION flickers over tangled blankets in the otherwise dark room. It's a large flat-sceen model hung on the wall over the blond wood crates at the foot of the futon. On the screen a man in a white top hat and tails is dancing before a gospel choir as a couple of men in orange jumpsuits wheel about him on skateboards. If you don't come see me today, says the television, I can't save you any money. Someone's snoring lightly. At the foot of the futon a tumbled pile of empty shoe boxes, a couple that say Converse, a larger one that says John Fluevog. An orange carton of cigarettes ripped open at one end. Djarum, says the label. 76. The commercial ends with a fanfare and the light from the television changes. A man in a dark suit's scooping cat food from one can into another in a minty pastel kitchen. He's humming along with the soundtrack. A shot of a marmalade tabby pawing and mewling at the louvered kitchen doors. The snoring hitches and stops and a bare foot kicks out from under the blankets as Jo rolls over on her side. Wrapped in a clean white fluffy robe loosely belted falling from one shoulder. Oh the cat's hungry, right, right, says the television. I'll fix you dinner just as soon as I get me a smoke. Jo takes in a deep fluttering breath and the snoring starts again. At the head of the futon a low shelf painted white, a glass ashtray with three or four butts, a low thick-bottomed tumbler, a slick of something amber left inside. A half-dozen DVD cases most still saying Security Device Enclosed along the side and three books lying flat, the top one with a receipt tucked inside. A sword in a plain black scabbard, its guard a glittering net of wiry strands about the hilt, its pommel a great silvery clout. Someone moans.

The bathroom door is closed. Inside it's dark but for three candles on the back of the toilet. Ysabel on the bathmat in black lace underwear curled on her side her hair a great black tangle spread across the grimy tiles her arms shivering clenched about herself. Gasping. A sob, and another. Her lips move, and she licks them, swallows, her cheek against the tiles she says her voice a breath, "Could I enchant, and that it lawful were," and maybe she coughs, or laughs, and then she says, her voice worn thin, "her would I charm, softly, that none should hear – "

Standing leaning against the sink her hand held up before her reflection shadowed and colorless. Her forefinger and middle finger together, extended, glistening in the candlelight. She presses her fingertips to the mirror and with a squeak draws them across the bridge of her reflection's nose leaving a smeared and blurry wake obliterating the eyes. "Fuck the sager sort," she says, shaking her head, her reflection turning away, falling as she sits on the bathmat, the smear left behind, snagging the candlelight. Ysabel leans over to twist a knob on the baseboard heater and then wrapping her arms about herself lies down again her back to it as a mosquito-whine climbs a couple of notches and something somewhere inside it begins gently to buzz. She closes her eyes, her mouth set in a straight flat line. From a hook on the closed door hangs a clean white fluffy robe, the belt of it dangling from one soft loop to draggle on the floor.

The light from the candles caught in that smear on the mirror flaring, popping. On the floor Ysabel doesn't stir. Four sparks, five, left glimmering on the mirror, pulsing a little against the candles' flicker, fading. Falling away from the mirror three specks of glittering gold dust, four, drifting down and down to settle there on the edge of the sink. One of them and another landing in droplets of water still standing by a faucet, where they blacken and are gone.

"I don't know," says Jo in her white robe sitting on the futon, eating garish orange cereal from a yellow oblong plastic bowl. On the large screen on the wall behind her a cartoon girl in chaps and cowboy boots and a long white scarf soundlessly fires her outsized handguns at a giant robot.

"Is it ten o'clock?" says Ysabel. In her black underwear curled into one of the wrought-iron chairs, heels on the cushion and arms about her shins. On the glass-topped café table an empty pink oblong plastic bowl and an open cereal box that says OJ's. "Half past ten?" Her cheek on her knees.

"I have no idea," says Jo. Her voice rough and slow. "Maybe. We were out late."

"Is it almost eleven?"

"God*dammit*, Ysabel," says Jo, leaning over, grabbing a glassy black phone from the shelf at the head of the futon. She thumbs the only button on its face. "Quarter of ten," she says. "Okay? Happy?" Tossing the phone back onto the shelf.

"He said you could go back on Monday," says Ysabel, turning her head, her chin on her knees now. Looking out the window. "And we didn't go back on Monday." Jo's scooping up more cereal. "Or Tuesday, or Wednesday, or Thursday – "

"There's a point?" says Jo, thumbing some milk from her chin.

"You said you wanted to learn from him. You wanted to learn how to use the sword."

"Are you hungry?" says Jo. "Aren't you cold?" Ysabel's resting her cheek on her knees again. "I was thinking," says Jo, "I don't know. Maybe it'd be smart if we both used a little time to cool off. Him and me."

"Does he know that?" says Ysabel.

"Jesus, would you put on a fucking *shirt?*"

Ysabel doesn't move, and Jo looks away, looks down, sets her bowl on the shelf. On the television behind her the girl in the chaps and cowboy boots is silhouetted by an enormous orange explosion. "As you wish," says Ysabel then, and she unfolds herself stretching her arms and legs and still sitting bends to grab a plain white T-shirt from the floor, tugging it out from under the black spear-haft that lies under the glass-topped table. Jo's leaning across the futon, digging through the clothing stuffed in the blond wood crates, sitting back with an armload of stuff, all black. Scooting off the futon holding the robe closed as she climbs to her feet. Ysabel watching as Jo walks past, into the little hallway kitchen, clothing bundled under one arm. "You never used to get dressed in the bathroom," says Ysabel.

"You never used to sleep in the bathroom," says Jo, closing the door.

"Is it the money?" – What they're getting little more than a Closet – Why he's doing it

"Is it the money?" says Ysabel.

"What?" says Jo. "No. Pick out anything you want. Whatever. I don't care." Clacking dresses from one side of a rack to the other without really looking at them. Her coat of soft and butter-colored leather beaded still with raindrops.

"No," says Ysabel, "I mean, was the money why," turning a pair of boots over in her hands, worn brown leather, sharp toes, high heels. "I could have given you whatever you wanted, you know? Whenever. Whenever you wanted it." She's wearing a white trench coat unbuttoned over a tight T-shirt dress printed with a blond Batgirl in purple and grey. "Before I gave it all away." She puts the boots back on the shelf above the rack.

"It," says Jo. She stops flipping through dresses. "What about whatever we needed? Huh? What about what we needed? All those times I'm giving you shit for buying peach ice teas we couldn't afford, you ever think of saying oh, hey, wait a minute, here's twenty bucks I got in my pocket? It." She pulls something off the rack, a sundress, blue and yellow checks. "What do you think, huh?" Holding it up in front of herself. "Too summery. Yeah." She slaps it back on the rack. "You did it the one time. You gave Timmo the money for the fake ID. You told him to spend it all in one place. Why'd you tell him that?"

"Jo," says Ysabel.

"How long did that money last in his pocket? How long before he reaches for it and it's gone?

"Jo," says Ysabel, "that card is the same thing."

"The hell it is," says Jo. "It's still right here, in my pocket. Hasn't turned to dust or ashes or leaves or whatever the hell."

"What about the – "

"How long was it in his pocket? How long would it last in mine?" Jo heads to the next rack down, running her hand clack-clack along the hangers.

"It's just drawings on paper," says Ysabel. "Easy to make."

"Easy come, easy go. How long? Timmo didn't come out yelling after us about ripping him off so it's at least, what, half an hour? Long enough to buy breakfast, maybe, instead of bitching about cold pizza? Only our waiter goes to settle up and he's short because one of his twenties ain't there anymore, gone to moonbeams or cobwebs or whatever the fuck."

"That card is a promise to pay," says Ysabel, following after down the line of racks. "But you aren't going to pay, are you."

"I hope to hell not," says Jo.

"So who is? How is that any different?"

"Because it's all, I don't know. Between banks. Numbers in a computer. And anyway banks don't beat the shit out of who-ever's standing next to them when they suddenly figure out their wallet's lost weight."

"Is that how it works?"

"I don't know. You tell me." Jo holds up a shirtwaist dress in black and grey with pink and white dots here and there. "What do you think. Demure rockabilly?" She shoves the dress back with a rustle. "You wanted to come here. Find whatever it is you want, I don't care. I'll go look at some T-shirts maybe." She turns, heads off down the rack toward the other big room.

"You should talk to him, Jo," Ysabel calls after her. Jo stops, turns her hand on her hip, that buttery coat falling open over her satiny black slip, her skinny black jeans. "He told you it was because you're a knight," says Ysabel.

"It's my due," says Jo.

"The Chariot doesn't have a card like that," says Ysabel.

"What," says Jo, walking back down the racks toward her, "he gets by on his charm? I think you're missing the point. If this card works and so far it has, then *we* don't have to. Okay? No more calling people at random to ask what they think about this ballot measure. Or the last time they went to the fucking Pet Depot. Or how happy they are with their checking account. Okay?"

"So it'll keep us from getting evicted?" says Ysabel.

"He's working on that too," says Jo.

"You've got to *talk* to him," says Ysabel. "What can he possibly do that I couldn't?"

"Well," says Jo, "right off the bat I bet he ain't gonna try to sleep with the night manager."

Ysabel looks away at that, then starts walking, down the racks, past Jo. "You have to know what you're getting us into," she says, heading into the other big room. "Where are you going?" says Jo, trailing after. Past racks of old silk-screened T-shirts and pants, coats and jackets, a display of white knee socks printed up the sides with slogans that say Whisky and Bacon and Kosher and Brooklyn. Past the cash registers, day-glo colored burlesque posters hanging above on the high red walls. "Ysabel?" Past the last rack of clothes, a giant stuffed tiger lounging on the top shelf, pushing through glass doors out into a colorless day soft with rain. Ysabel stops a moment and pulls a crumpled white fedora from under her arm, shakes it out, looks at it in her hands before settling it on her head. Jo grabs her arm. "What the fuck, Ysabel?"

"We're going to go see the Duke," says Ysabel. She points down the street, past signs that say Bread and Ink and Bagdad and Naked City and Nick's Famous Coney Island. "Three blocks," she says, and she turns and starts walking.

"Ysabel!" calls Jo after her. "Jesus. It's raining!"

"It's Portland!" Ysabel calls back. "It's always raining!" Waiting for a car to turn past her, then stepping out across the side street. "Except in the summer," she says to herself. "When it goes to the weird desert place." Jo trotting after her, bare-headed, hands jammed in the pockets of her coat.

Stepping through the propped-open double doors into the black-and-white tiled foyer Jo's brushing rainwater from her short dark hair. "You cheated," she says.

Ysabel one white boot already up on the first wide white-painted step doesn't turn, but stops, one hand on the crown of her white fedora, and says, "That's a serious accusation."

"It was all about this. You didn't want to go shopping at all."

"This," says Ysabel, taking off her hat, glancing back over her shoulder. "Of course I wanted to go shopping."

"And you just happened to take us somewhere a couple blocks away from the Duke's place." Jo's looking about the foyer, the wide staircase, the sign beneath them that says India Oven, the bouquet of tie-dyed T-shirts hanging in the doorway opposite. "This is the Duke's place?" A man's ducking under the T-shirts. "Ladies," he's saying, "excuse me." His hair richly red, flopping from a high widow's peak. "You can't, ah, you can't go up there." His vest a dull brick, his shirt a dingy gold, his knitted tie is brown.

"How was I to know," Ysabel's saying, turning now, taking her foot off the step, "you were going to pick a fight about him?" The man with the brown tie's brought up short, eyes widening, jaw slackening. "Majesty!" he says, and then, quickly, "Highness, no, I – "

"Highness, good," says Ysabel, as Jo starts to say "I wasn't picking a." Ysabel walks past her, up to the man with the brown tie. "The last person," she's saying, "to mistake me for a queen had to give up her sword. Etiquette is *so* important."

"Highness," says the man with the brown tie, and he swallows, "he's engaged. He's not to be disturbed."

"But surely," says Ysabel, smiling, walking past him, behind him, around him, "he'd not say no to his Princess, nor his paramour."

"His *what?*" says Jo.

"Will *you* say no," says Ysabel, her hand on his shoulder, "to your Princess?"

And he bites his lip and doesn't nod, but doesn't shake his head, either.

"We'll show ourselves up," says Ysabel.

The stairs double back and end in a white landing on the second floor that opens through wide double doors on an empty echoing ballroom. A row of folding tables lined with glass pipes in delicately jeweled colors under buzzing fluorescent lights. Jo stands in the doorway looking back and forth between the ballroom and the landing. "Well?" she says.

Ysabel standing by a humming bright Coke machine points to an unmarked white door on the other side of it.

"This?" says Jo. "Are there more stairs, or something? Is this his place? There's no bell. Do we knock?"

Ysabel shrugs. "Why not open the door and see," she says, and Jo puts her hand on the faceted glass knob and turns it and opens the door.

The room beyond is little more than a closet and to one side of the door there's a mop bucket with mop propped inside. In the corner past a rack of cubbies stuffed with spray bottles and cartons of light bulbs and wrapped bundles of paper towels under looped hanks of orange extension cord there's the Duke in an unbelted dressing gown crowded with paisleys of purple and maroon and gold and brown looking down hair hanging in his eyes at the woman kneeling before him his hands on her head fingers in her shining blond hair undone and splayed down her bare back and down a burning heart in a glistering starburst of red and yellow rays criss-crossed by the black strap of her satiny thong and he's looking up eyes opening over an opened mouth twisting a slash of a grimace eyes narrowing "Get out!" he roars. "Close the damn door!" The woman sitting back on her heels the bottoms of her bare feet smudged with dirt one hand up before her mouth as Jo slams the door shut. She looks over at Ysabel who's biting a knuckle and trying not to smile.

"The fuck was that?" says Jo.

A rustle a thump a clatter and footsteps approaching the door from the other side. "You did *not* just open my door!" says the Duke. "You did not just open my door without knocking or announcing yourself or I will have the Stirrup's guts for my garters I assure you."

"I, ah," says Jo, looking from the door to Ysabel and back again, and Ysabel's examining the Coke machine now, and Jo scowls. "I'm sorry," she says. "I didn't know. We'll just, we'll go, okay? I'm sorry."

"No, no, no," says the Duke, and there's a grinding sliding sound and a sharp clap. "Don't go, don't go. You're fine. Stand over there."

"What?" says Jo. "Stand where?"

"Not you!" calls the Duke. "Not you. You're fine. There's a password. Which I'm gonna impose on the Princess, because she knows it, and she fucking knows she knows it. Okay?" Something on the other side of the door falls with a fluttering crash. "You ready? Highness?"

Ysabel steps back from the Coke machine, her eyes on the doorknob. "Yes," she says. Jo's glaring.

"Duncan will be one man," says the Duke.

"And," says Ysabel, "Farquahr will be two."

"Okay," says the Duke. "Okay."

"Go on," says Ysabel.

"Fuck you," says Jo. "You do it."

"Okay," says Ysabel, and she puts her hand on the faceted glass knob and turns it and opens the door and steps through into a dark hallway that opens into a room filled with soft light from tall narrow windows hung with white cloth shades pulled low. The Duke in the middle of the otherwise empty room, his dressing gown belted, his feet bare. "Highness," he says. "What a surprise. So good of you to come. Don't look out there."

Jo reaching for one of the long white shades stops her hand in the air and looks back at him. "It's still a bit raw," he says, and he shrugs, his face kiltered with an apologetic smile. "Don't know what you'd see out there. Highness!" His smile tightens. "How *wonderful* you're here. You should have had someone call."

"It was something of a whim," says Ysabel.

"She said she wanted to go shopping," says Jo.

"You had questions about the card," says Ysabel, and then to the Duke, "What do you think about her coat?"

"It's nice," he says, "I like the outfit, it's – "

"I think it's a bit ostentatious," says Ysabel.

"I did not have questions about the fucking card," says Jo.

"You wanted to thank him for it, then," says Ysabel.

"Ysabel you were the one who stalked out of the store all of a sudden and I had to chase you down the street because, because – "

"Because?" says Ysabel, but Jo doesn't respond, she's staring over past Ysabel at the doorway and the Duke's looking down, rubbing his forehead. Ysabel turns to see the woman in the thong leaning in the doorway, hugging herself, one hand up pushing her slippery blond hair out of her face. "Leo," she says.

"What a great idea!" cries the Duke. "I'll find a shirt, you find, some clothes, and we'll all go together to get some brunch. Okay? My treat."

The Duke drains the juice from his wineglass, daubs his lips with his thumb, sets the glass on the table, looking across the table at Jo the whole time. She's looking down at her plate, tearing a bite from a thick slice of bacon specked with crumbs of black pepper. He shakes his head, forks up a bit of omelette. "You really don't get it," he says.

"She can be quite oblivious sometimes," says Ysabel, sipping coffee, sitting next to Jo on the bench before the rain-dappled window.

"What," says Jo. "It's good bacon." She finishes it off, scoops up some scrambled egg. "Anyway *I'm* not vegetarian."

"He doesn't like it," says the blond woman, swirling a bit of waffle around in a pool of deep purple syrup. "When you eat meat," she says, popping it into her mouth.

"So?" says Jo.

"Actually," says the Duke, "it depends." He turns in his chair, lifts his empty glass, wobbling it at the woman over behind the counter loading up plates of bagels and scones and bialys. "How about you?" he asks Ysabel.

"You're asking," she says flatly.

"Why not?"

"What?" says Jo, frowning.

"What what," says Ysabel. Untouched on the plate before her a couple of bean cakes under poached eggs, a tidy pile of mango salsa to the side. "Follow her needs must I," she says, almost to herself.

The Duke sits back. "No shit," he says. Ysabel doesn't take up her fork, doesn't sip more coffee. On the dull red wall above them hang calligraphic cartoons, a lowercase d playing itself like a drum, an S playing itself like a bass fiddle. Jo's looking back and forth between them, and across from her the blond woman in the grey chauffeur's uniform jacket buttoned up to her throat is finishing off her waffle. "Doesn't matter," says the Duke. "You know why I'm doing this?"

"Because you would be King," says Ysabel.

"I *will* be King, Princess. And you my Queen." He leans forward, elbows on the table. "Did you know the Soames had gone?" Ysabel looks up at that, eyes wide, face paling. "You didn't," says the Duke.

"What's her name, Nell?" says Jo. "Where did she," and then she stops and says, "Oh."

The woman from behind the counter sets a fresh glass of juice by the Duke. "Anything else?" she says.

"Nearly a week now," says the Duke, shaking his head. "Offices burnt to the ground, and her and one of her lieutenants inside. Maybe more, who can keep track these days. They went and picked a new one already the other night." He lifts his glass in a little salute. "Long may he chair."

"My mother," says Ysabel, and Jo lifts a hand, holds it hesitating over the fist Ysabel's made, "would never have – "

"Which makes it worse," says the Duke. "Much the worse, if someone else is meting out such fates, and she won't stop them. Or can't."

Ysabel opens her fist, then picks up her fork, and Jo lowers her hand. Ysabel cuts a bite of bean cake and egg, yellow yolk seeping out over her plate. "And so it's all down to your grace," she says.

"You see anyone else?" says the Duke. "Tell me something, highness. Why did you go to see the Soames last month?"

"She invited me," says Ysabel.

The Duke snorts. "And there's me, always asking the wrong question." He reaches down into the pocket of the tweed jacket draped over the back of his chair and there's a slippery rustling sound and he drops a big clear plastic bag in the middle of the table, the mouth of it sealed with a purple zip-lock. Inside in turn maybe a dozen little plastic baggies each twisted tightly about a thimbleful of golden dust, and each even in this weak light glitters through the cloudy layers of plastic. Gold sparks set to dancing in the glasses. "You know what that is, highness? That's Southeast there before you, or what of it that's left. My fabled treasuries and storehouses gape before you." He lays a hand on the bag. "Not enough to fill your breakfast plate."

"You are famously profligate," says Ysabel.

"Is *that* what they're calling it," says the Duke. "Well even a grasshopper might one day learn to husband grain against the coming winter, highness, but when winter comes every blasted month – " He lifts his hand away. "Your mother's late. Again. And yet." He picks up the bag, hefts it in his hand a moment. "Meet their needs must I." He tucks it back into the pocket of his jacket. "Come along with me."

"What?" says Ysabel.

"As I am about my business today. The both of you. Come see what I see as I choose the which of my people might divvy up these last few moths from my wallet." He looks over his shoulder, catching the attention of an older man weaving between tables with a coffee pot, and he makes a scribbling motion in the air. "Well?" He lays his hand on the hand of the blond woman beside him. "You mind going to get the car, hon? While I settle up?"

MADEMOISELLE JULIETTE – "I AM THE HOUSE"
WHAT THE STARLING DOES – TITS & ASS & OH

MADEMOISELLE JULIETTE n'a pas vraiment la tête, that voice slinking out over the driving beat, choisir entre Montague, Capulet, two women on the stage that fills one end of the dark red room, the same high white wigs piled atop their heads, the same blued eyes under elaborately painted brows, the same striking noses, very similar breasts bared over embroidered corsets, long wide-hipped skirts parted before like curtains over the same frothy confusion of lacey underwear and garters and stockings, all dusty pinks and ivories and pale blues and paler golds. Stepping daintily back and forth to that enormous beat hands out to either side just so, one of them holding a fan, the other a handkerchief. Cette commedia del'arte n'est pas assez déjantée sings that slinking voice, and they dip and sashay in unison stepping free of their skirts leaving them upright and empty behind, long legs bare hips turning and ducking and stopping then one of them tilting her head back the other looking over her shoulder. "Jackie!" she yells over the beat. "Jackie the goddamn *lights!*" And then a smile blooming her voice climbing, cooing, "Leo!"

"Ettie, darling," calls the Duke, there by the bar. "Could we?" Waggling a finger in the air at the music.

"Jackie!" she bellows. "Cut it!" The other dancer's stepped down from the stage, she's wriggling her way into a long sheer robe, careful of her wig. The music stops mid-Juliette. A woman pops up from behind the bar, spiky red hair and a faceful of freckles, a sleeveless black T-shirt and skinny arms festooned with tattoos. "You want it again from the top?" and then her scowl unfolding eyes widening her voice a shriek, "Jessie!" Planting her hands on the bar she hops it in a single practiced bound. "Goddamn girl!" Dodging tables past the Duke and Jo and Ysabel to swallow the blond woman in the grey chauffeur's uniform jacket with a spinning, staggering hug.

"Leo, chér," says the first dancer, one hand on the column of chain at the corner of the stage, turning and stooping to lower a stockinged leg. Arms out for balance she totters toward them on thick-soled high-heeled shoes. The other dancer sitting unstraps her shoes, sets them on the table before her, white with whorls of gold. On the stage behind them the skirts still standing empty, flared shells of starched linen and ribbon and lace.

"Ettie," says the Duke again. "Chrissie. A delight to find you here."

"They've given us a night, mon chér," says Ettie, leaning to kiss his cheek as he takes her into a one-armed hug. "Burlesque in the round." Her voice jerks from coo to growl. "If we can ever get the cues straight." In the reddened gloom by the pool table Jackie's laughing at something Jessie's said.

"If I might present," says the Duke, "Jo Maguire." Leaning on his cane one arm still about Ettie's shoulder. "And of course the Princess."

"Enchanté," says Ettie, offering her hand. Chrissie in her robe coming up on stockinged feet. Ysabel with a smile tucked in the corner of her mouth takes Ettie's hand and Ettie with a half-twist turns it lifts it to a lipsticked kiss on her knuckles. "It's so sophisticated," says Chrissie, her hands on Ettie's hips. "How you've revived the pomp of a royal court the way you have." Ettie straightening says, "The etiquette." Chrissie's chin settles on Ettie's shoulder. Their wigs rustling brush together.

"Indeed," says Ysabel rubbing her knuckles with a thumb.

"You must come see our show," says Ettie, and "Oh, you must," says Chrissie. "We're premièring a piece from our new collaboration."

"But minus our collaborators," says Ettie.

"The Dispute d'enfants après jeux," says Chrissie.

"They wouldn't fit," says Ettie. "Orchestras, you know."

"What are you up to now," says the Duke.

"Didn't we tell you, chéri?" Ettie steps out from under his arm, and Chrissie as she says "We call it Pictures at an Ecdysis" steps one arm about the Duke's waist now, the other still about Ettie's, Ettie who's saying "We wanted to call it Strippers at an Exhibition," her arm settling on Chrissie's shoulders. "Mæstro Vajda's a bit squeamish. But so are the subscribers. He has his point. Just think of it – the SÏurs Limoges – the Oregon Symphony Orchestra – the Schnitz!" And the Duke looking from one to the other his smile growing. He says, "But you need help."

Chrissie squeezes against him. "Are we so obvious, mon grand?"

"'Help' is such a vulgar word for it," says Ettie.

"Tell you what," says the Duke, lifting Chrissie's hand from his hip taking it in his own. "Have your people call my people."

Scooping Ettie's free hand up along with it. "While they're distracted, we'll sneak off for dinner somewhere." Kissing their
knuckles each in turn. "Just the three of us. But later!" Taking
a heavy step back from them both. "Is the Starling back there?"

They look at each other, Ettie and Chrissie, and then Chrissie
says, "Yes."

"She is," says Ettie.

"In the which case," says the Duke, taking Ysabel's hand,
"the Princess and I should excuse ourselves."

"Whoa," says Jo, pushing past Jackie and her tattooed arms,
Jessie in her grey jacket, planting herself there between the
Duke and Ysabel, and Ettie and Chrissie arm-in-arm. "Easy,
killer," says the Duke. "No hanky-panky. I promise."

"Where she goes I go," says Jo.

"And here you are!" says the Duke. "And we're gonna walk
through that door over there. Back in five minutes. Not even." He
shrugs. "What could I possibly manage to do in just five minutes?
Shut up, ladies." Ettie and Chrissie snort precise little giggles.

"Jo," says Ysabel.

"If you won't trust me," says the Duke, "trust your boon."

"Jo," says Ysabel again. "This is just part of his little show.
Let him have his fun."

"Yeah, I wouldn't have put it that way," says the Duke, "but
okay. And you have your fun. While we're back there, bar's
open. Whatever you want. It's before noon but it's not like
you're driving anywhere anytime soon. Everybody!" Taking in
the sweep of glimmering glass on the wall with a sweep of his
cane. "Drinks on the house!"

"Really," says Jackie, tattooed arms akimbo.

"I *am* the house, baby," says the Duke. "And the house is feeling famously profligate today. Princess?"

Lurching he leads Ysabel toward the nondescript door by the
stage as Jackie hops back over the bar. Jessie settles herself on a stool.
Chrissie murmurs to Ettie, "What do you think? Four digits?"

"Five," says Ettie.

"You always did like one-stop shopping," says Chrissie, letting
go of Ettie, pulling her robe more tightly about her, walking over

to sit on a stool next to Jessie. Jackie's pouring from three bottles at once into a silvery cocktail flask.

"It's a little Marie Antionette," says Jo. "Don't you think?"

"What?" says Ettie in her stockings and garters and her thick-soled shoes and her embroidered corset. She reaches up to loosen the wig, lifting it from her head. Yellow hair severely straight slithers down to her shoulders.

"Wouldn't you want something more medieval? The song." Jo takes her hands from her pockets, folds her arms in her butter-colored jacket. "Montagues. Capulets."

"You've obviously never tried stripping in a kirtle," says Ettie, setting her wig on a table.

Past the nondescript door a short and narrow hall, dark, one end another door half-opened on white light and papers stacked high atop an old grey metal cabinet. At the other end a dim room, small, walls painted black, a sliver of mirror, warm pools of light. The Duke stops there between leans on his cane close to Ysabel as her eyes flick from his to his lips and back again, but he's looking down the short length of that hall to the dim room. "Just," he says, "Starling's – well. He's a little odd. Don't, ah – "

"Don't be rude?" says Ysabel.

"Okay, sure," says the Duke. "Don't be rude. Wait." He's looking at her now, and her eyes flick again, his eyes, his mouth, the door they just stepped through, his eyes. "We were both oblique at brunch," he says, "so let's run through it again. You asked."

"Yes," says Ysabel.

"And she said no."

"She said no," says Ysabel.

"See," says the Duke, looking down at the tip of his cane, "what I don't get is why you'd ask. I mean, you must've known – "

"Why'd you sleep with her?"

He looks up again. "She said that."

"Did she lie?"

"Tell me something else," says the Duke. "When you ate the tongue. What did you see? Oh come on." Ysabel's drawn back against the wall, looking down, away, her white hat in her hands. "I *let* you have his tongue. I let you have his tongue because I knew you couldn't resist eating it. I knew when you ate it you'd see what's to come. I wanted you to see that." He's even closer now. "What we all know will be. Tell me!" She's looking at him now leaning over her. "You saw me as King, didn't you. The banners of hawk and hive together over the city. A new day dawning."

"I saw," says Ysabel. Not looking up. "I saw myself as Queen. I saw Jo, at my side."

"Yeah, well," says the Duke, stepping back. "I was obviously out that day when you looked in. Taking care of business!" He taps his cane against the floor. "Always taking care of something."

The dressing room, small, dim, painted black so many times the regular lines of the cinderblock walls are soft and blurry. Under one of the mirrors surrounded by stickers and photos a short red velvet chaise, on the chaise a figure in sweatpants and a large black hooded sweatshirt, the hood pulled up, looking down.

"Starling," says the Duke.

The figure doesn't move, the head doesn't lift, the hood doesn't fall, the hands don't shift from the lap. "Your grace." The voice is rich but worn and ragged.

"You never miss a Friday."

"Or a Monday. Or a Thursday." One of those hands now dips a moment into the shadows under that hood, then comes back down between the knees. A big hand, the back of it snarled with thick veins, the nails short and flat, painted red, the enamel chipped and flaking. "I am so sorry, your grace. I am not myself today."

"No need to apologize," says the Duke, squatting. "No, your grace, please," she murmurs, but he's shaking his head, putting a hand in the pocket of his tweed jacket. "I have something for you." Pressing into those hands a little baggie twisted round a thimbleful of gold dust. "Better sometimes than never," he says.

"Does he always bring it to you himself?" says Ysabel in the doorway.

"Highness!" cries the Starling, hitching up from the chaise, dropping to one knee by the Duke slowly straightening, standing. "I was so wrapped up in pity for myself I did not see you there."

"The Princess has kindly agreed to come about with me on my rounds," says the Duke.

"His grace can be quite persuasive," says Ysabel.

"His grace can be quite cruel, in his kindness," says the Starling. Turning, lifting herself to sit on the chaise again before the mirror. "We're opening soon," she says. "I must prepare myself. I thought it best to go on early today. When it wasn't so busy."

"Show us," says the Duke.

Ysabel in her white coat in the doorway, the Duke leaning against the dulled black wall, the stern, rough-hewn hawk at the head of his cane in his hands. Her hood turns away from them both, looking to the litter of makeup vials and jars on the little stack of shelves bolted in the corner by the mirror. "Quite cruel, your grace," she says.

"Show her," says the Duke. "Show her what you do with her mother's gift."

The Starling picks up a jar filled almost to its wide-mouthed brim with a viscous, milky fluid, touched with just a hint of gold. "I cannot but as you ask," she says, handing the jar to the Duke. "In answer to your question, highness," she says, setting the little baggie on a shelf, untwisting it open, "no. He does not. Not every time." Dipping finger and thumb to pinch up some dust. "Usually, his man Sidney came to me. The Dagger." Holding up that pinch, taking up a tube of lotion with her free hand, deftly opening the tube and squirting a dollop in the palm of the hand with the pinch. "Sometimes as often as once a week, or even every few days. He could be quite – boisterous. Enthusiastic. He often told me how beautiful he found me." Letting the dust drift from fingertip to lotion shining white in her palm. "He would not have liked to see me as I am today."

"He was an oaf," says the Duke. Both hands on the hawk again. He's tucked that jar away somewhere. "I should've listened to you."

"I never said a word against him," says the Starling. The fingers of that hand lit up a little, calluses and creases picked out in sharper shadows now.

"Well," says the Duke. "Still. I should've listened."

Those hands pressed together now rubbing the lotion front to back, criss-crossing, the sleeves of her sweatshirt sliding away as she rubs lotion along her wrists, her forearms, her hands again, and the Starling says, "But his grace does come from time to time." Her hands smoother now, more slender, longer perhaps, her nails definitely longer, and a glossy, flawless red. "I am honored when he does." She lifts her hands to her face there under the hood and holds them still a moment.

"An artist of your talent honors us all," says the Duke.

"But I do wish you had warned me," says the Starling, pushing the hood back, sweeping out a wave of black hair glossy in artful tangles. Looking green eyes up into the mirror at Ysabel looking back at a reflection of herself, a little older, the nose a little wider, the chin more prominent. The red smile hesitant. "Please," says the Starling. "Forgive me. It is – something of an homage, intended with the utmost respect – "

"Why," says Ysabel, there in the doorway, "why must I forgive such flattery?"

"Red Ruth?" says Jo. On the bar before her a shot glass half-full of something clear and colorless. Jackie shrugs her tattooed shoulders. "It's in England somewhere," she says. "Saw it on a map once. Said to myself, that's a bad-ass stripper name." She holds up a hand. On the stage a man in jeans and a morning-coat holds an umbrella strung with little white lights. He's singing over a roughly strummed guitar Narcissisma, Narcissisma as Ettie and Chrissie in shimmering haltered gowns and opera gloves dance a foxtrot about him. Narcissisma is the pride of Pomona, he sings, and Jackie slides a couple of dimmer switches on the console sitting on the bar, and lights dim and shift on-stage from yellow and red to blue as the white lights strung about his umbrella flare. Pomona, Pomona says she looks like me, but she will look like you when I'm set free. "I used to do this pirate thing," says Jessie, turning back from the console. "Back when it was big."

"Sisters, huh," says Jo, watching them twirl into a dip onstage.

"The twin thing," says Jackie.

"It's a license to print fucking money," says Jessie. She shoves a glass rattling with a few loose ice cubes at Jackie. "Pour me another one, babe."

"Diet Dr. Pepper on the house," says Jo.

"Maybe you don't have to drive, but *I* do," says Jessie, smoothing the front of her grey chauffeur's jacket. She takes the glass of soda from Jackie. Jo says, "So what was your name?" and Jessie sets the glass down unsipped and squeezes her eyes shut and says "Oh God it was so fucking emo."

"Oh please," says Jackie.

She's got no braids in the inkwell, no money on the prize, the man's singing as Ettie or Chrissie slips a glove from Chrissie's or Ettie's arm. Ain't got no boyfriend behind her that she can't hypnotize.

"Rain," says Jessie, opening her eyes.

"Rain?" says Jo.

"I moved up here from San Diego, okay? I had this idea I'd spend these long lazy afternoons in a hot tub in a cabin in the woods with candles and wine and a good book and it'd be raining all the time on a tin roof or something. So I was Rain, okay?" Swaying back and forth nose to nose Ettie and Chrissie gloveless undo the straps to each other's gowns. Narcissisma is the pride of Biloxi, sings the man in the morning-coat. Biloxi, Biloxi says she's not your kind, but Narcissisma gives me peace of mind. "So fucking romantic," says Jessie.

"If there's somebody in the hot tub with you," says Jackie.

"Speak for yourself. Let me tell you something." Jessie leans over, puts her hand on Jo's. "It's the music, okay? Picking your songs. Everything else, it's just tits and ass and your oh face. You gotta get the music right." Ettie and Chrissie hold their last pose forehead to forehead arms about each other's necks and then one of them turns away suddenly saying "Thank you, Jeff. Can we run that again? To get the lights right?" as the other works her gown back up in place. "And if you really want to tell them what it's all about," says Jessie, "there's only one song to dance to."

"What's that," says Jo, her hand still under Jessie's.

"Eleanor Rigby," says Jessie.

"What I think is maybe" – Modern and more Equitable the Strong Hand – on the Strand – Unreservedly

"What I think is maybe this time Jo comes with me," says the Duke, his arm hooked over the headrest, looking over at Jo and Ysabel in the cramped back seat. "If you're worried about the Princess, killer," he says, "don't. Everybody knows my car. Just about the safest place in the city – especially in my demesne? Back seat of this very automobile." He gets out of the car, levers his seat-back forward, leans in to offer Jo a hand. Ysabel scoots over as Jo climbs out and follows her, hauling herself out of the car. "Thought I'd sit up front, with your driver," she says to the Duke's arched eyebrow. "More pleasant place to spend the five minutes or so you'll be inside."

"You guys were gone at least twenty," says Jo, looking at the brick block across the street. Over the front door square in the middle of the façade a small model of a three-masted sailing ship, a little red metal banner frozen in a snap of wind. Letters carved into the lintel below say Vitula Arms.

"An exaggeration," says the Duke. "Shall we?"

As she slides into the front seat Ysabel says to Jo, "Don't forget." She pulls the door shut against the gently seeping rain. Watches Jo jog and the Duke hop limpingly across the street and along the sidewalk to the building's front door. The Duke reaches past Jo to open it for her. "How long have you known him?" says Ysabel.

The door closes, Jo and the Duke inside. The woman behind the wheel in her grey chauffeur's cap and her grey chauffeur's jacket looks over at Ysabel sitting beside her. "About a year almost?" she says. "More than that. First time I talked to him was around Christmas last year, but I'd see him at the club before that."

"Is it a little stuffy in here?" Ysabel works one shoulder then another free of her white trench coat and wriggles it off. "The heater's been working overtime." The blond Batgirl bunched up in the wrinkles that crease her tight T-shirt dress. "Mind if I crack a window?" The woman behind the wheel shrugs, and Ysabel cranks the window down a bit. "That's better, don't you think?"

"You're going to marry him, aren't you."

"I'm the Bride. I have to marry someone."

Wavering rain glazes down the windshield before them. "I'm not just his mistress," says the woman behind the wheel.

Ysabel props her elbow on the seat-back, rests her head in her hand. "I'm not the one you should be telling," she says.

"He knows," says the woman behind the wheel, looking Ysabel in the eye from beneath the brim of her chauffeur's cap.

Ysabel says, "Oh, this will be fun." Reaching along the seat toward that cap. The woman behind the wheel pulls back a little, away. "I think," says Ysabel, "you missed a move or two in the game."

"What game?"

"Tell me," says Ysabel. "Do you think I'm beautiful?" The woman behind the wheel catches her breath. "Ah," says Ysabel. "Did he tell you what that means?"

The woman behind the wheel frowns, and starts to shake her head. "I," she says, "don't know what you," and Ysabel shushes her, shifts closer along the seat to her, says, "It's all right." Takes off the cap. The woman doesn't pull away this time. "You already answered," says Ysabel, leaning in to kiss her mouth.

Jo leans back, opens her eyes. Hands on the Duke's hips. "I wasn't expecting that."

"Really?" says the Duke, hands on her shoulders. He leans close, forehead brushing hers. "I've been wanting to do that all week."

They kiss again there in the foyer, the door closed behind them. The Duke pulls back suddenly. "You didn't call," he says.

"I don't, I don't have your number," says Jo.

"You didn't ask."

"I didn't know you had a number to ask for," says Jo. "Anyway you're a Duke. What are you waiting around for the girl to call?"

"Is this not a modern and more equitable age? Are we not now either of us capable of waiting for a phone call?"

Jo smiles. "You make it sound so romantic."

"Is that a good thing?"

"Is that really a conversation you want to be having? Here? Now?" The walls of the foyer a yellow floating dimly in the shiftless cloudy daylight. "Isn't there a thing we're supposed to do? Or go? Or was this just, what?"

"You can think of something more important?"

"Okay," says Jo, and she takes a step back. Hands still on his hips. "Okay." His hands fall to her sides, the pale leather of her coat. "Then first things first." Brows puckered. "I need you, I, sorry. But. I need to know what the deal is with her."

"The Bride?" says the Duke.

"*Jessie*," says Jo. "Your, your driver." Ahead a long dark staircase leads to the apartments on the second floor. "I had," she says, "the most awkward conversation with her, back at the club. I don't know what to say. I don't know what she knows, what she thinks is going on, I don't, I don't know what I know. I don't know – this morning." She looks down at her black boots on the threadbare rug, his worn brown brogues, the scratched copper ferule of his cane. "Was that something you wanted to do all week, too?" Lifts her head to look him in the eye. "Or was it just an itch, and we walked in while you were getting it scratched."

It's a long thin moment before the Duke says, "I'd like to," and then he coughs to clear his throat. "Object. I'd like to object to the framing of that question – "

"Yeah?" says Jo. She doesn't let go of him. He doesn't let go of her. His laughter's soft and brief and he looks away a moment with a puckered smile. "I have a question, too, long as we're all trying to figure out what it is we're standing in." Looking her in the eye. "Where were you during the coup? The *attempted* coup."

At that Jo steps back again and lets go, and his hands fall away, find the stern hawk at the head of his cane leaning against the wall. "What?" she says. "Coup. I don't – "

"Did her highness not receive a jar or bottle or vial of medhu from the Soames Nell?" says the Duke, and Jo's shaking her head, slowly. "Come on," he says. "Did you or did you not go to visit the rabbits? And did she or did she not suddenly have such a flask, after your visit?"

"She didn't say where she got it," says Jo. "I didn't ask her where she – "

"And did she or did she not try to turn the medhu once she had it?" Partway along the hall beside that staircase burns an incandescent bulb, but its light doesn't seem to fall anywhere. "Fact you're not asking me what that means is enough to tell me she did." The Duke shifts his weight, rubbing his leg, wincing as he says "Catch up. She'd done that, turned the medhu to owr, that's Queen-stuff. She'd done that – not that she *could,* not without a King, but if she'd gone and usurped the rightful ruler – " His cane raps smartly against the rug – "that's a coup."

"But she can't do it," says Jo. "Right? So what's the problem?"

The Duke looks away a moment, the rustle of his tweed jacket loud in the foyer. "Do you know, Jo Gallowglas, the one thing that's more upsetting to order, and routine, and a regular day you can take as it comes, than scarcity?"

"I bet you're gonna tell me," says Jo.

"Abundance," says the Duke. Leaning heavily on his cane he sets off down the hall.

Jo watching doesn't follow, doesn't move from her spot by the door, lifts a trembling hand clawing slowly into a fist opening her mouth finally calling out exasperated "Duke!" and hurrying after. He's saying "a consummation devoutly to be wished, but there's gotta be a strong hand on the plow."

"Yours," says Jo.

The Duke turns there in the narrow hall lifting his cane the stern hawk up by his smile. "You see anyone else?" The door they're standing beside opens suddenly. The woman in the doorway has long loose hair the color of steel and she wears a thick cardigan over a blowsy white chemise. The light behind her grey and chill. She wraps her arms about herself and shivers a little. "Your pardon, your grace," she says. "I couldn't help but hear you in the hall, your voice, and thought, now why make him knock, and wait?" There's laughter behind her, and the sudden pound of footsteps, "Gotcha!" cries a girl, and "No! No! No!" cries another, and "No fair, Thya! No fair!" The woman in the doorway sighs and smiles tightly. Her cheeks blotched, her eyes rimmed red. "Girls!" she bellows. The giggles stifle. "Granddaughters," she says. "But if you'd like to come in, your grace, I'd – "

"Not today, Nan," says the Duke.

"Well if you're in a hurry I understand, there's a lot of folks waiting themselves I'm sure – "

"Not. Today," says the Duke again, and she blinks as his words sink in, the blotches fading suddenly from her cheeks gone pasty white. "It's just," says the woman in the doorway, "even a *pinch* – with the Samani already this week and all – "

The Duke lays a hand on her folded arms. "You got a little set aside," he says. "You're gonna have to make it do till next time."

"Next time?"

"The very next. I swear it."

There's a toppling crunch of crockery and a mighty splash and shrieks of laughter now. "Girls!" bellows the woman in the doorway. "Artemita! Thyatira! Dionysia! Meganissi!" Turning in the doorway to glower back into the apartment. "You put that back right *now!*" The Duke grabs Jo's hand and yanks her after him further down the hall. "Wait," says Jo, "wait!" The door slams shut behind them. The Duke lets go. "If it's such a problem," says Jo, looking back at the closed door.

"You really want to be having this conversation right now?" He knocks on the next door down, two sharp raps with the head of his cane. "Right here?" The door opens, the frame of it filled with a huge figure of a man in a yellowed shirt and an unbuttoned charcoal pinstripe vest. Heavy eyes and a wrinkled daub of forehead planted in a nest of wiry hair, all grey and peppery black and coiling sprigs and shoots of white. A plump-bowled meerschaum pipe juts from somewhere below the eyes. One furred-knuckle hand swallows the doorknob, and leaned against the jamb the other's not a hand but a hand-shape, cast in bronze and beaten with whorls of puckered dots. "Your grace," says a thick-napped voice around the stem of that pipe.

"Coffey," says the Duke.

"Wasn't expecting yez. Come in, come in. Mind you step." He backs away and they step through, the Duke, then Jo, into an airy little room with white walls and pale blue carpeting, a long and angular sofa, a low shelf buried under a great bouquet of wild-flowers. By the flowers a little stir of knickknacks, a glass ball with a wooden salmon suspended inside, a leather tobacco pouch, a ring of keys, a small framed photo of a bare-shouldered woman looking away from the camera, one hand up as if to hide her wrinkled neck. On the wall above a plain and simple compass rose in red and black, and the portrait of a jowled and scowling president from many years before. There's a muffled thump from somewhere on the other side of that wall. Coffey waves at it. "All hours those girls drive old Nan hard," he says. "What brings yon by." His brass hand tucked under his arm.

"Lewis David Coffey," says the Duke, "might I present the Gallowglas – "

"You might," says Coffey.

" – the, ah, the newest knight," says the Duke, "at court."

Coffey takes the pipe from his mouth. The bowl of it's a mer-maid running a comb through her hair. "You want a medal for that?" he says to Jo, who's still standing by the door.

"No," says Jo.

"Good," says Coffey. "They don't alot me to give out the medals." The pipe-stem's back between his teeth. The Duke's handing him something, a little plastic baggie. "What is it you're looking at?"

"It stopped raining," says Jo.

"Was it raining, then?" says Coffey, tucking the baggie into the pocket of his shirt. "Go on," he says, and Jo gingerly walks across the parlor toward the great picture window in the opposite wall.

There are no trees in the window. There are no houses, no cars. There's nothing but a seamless haze of blue-white sky over a yellow-grey strand, dull under light that falls from no particular direction. Beyond it out and out to a sharp edge stretches a cold and restless grey-green sea. The Duke watching smiles as Jo eyes wide lifts a hand to her mouth and "Oh" she says. "Oh wow."

"Articulate, these new knights," says Coffey.

"Look down the beach," says the Duke. "Back toward the front of the place." Stepping behind Jo, looking over her shoulder, pointing. "See them?"

A snap of white in the wind a long loose gown caught tugging against her legs and her back Ysabel her face in her hands stands barefoot there her black hair streaming before her a flag in all that wind. Beside her looking out to sea one hand on Ysabel's shoulder Jessie in a grey houppelande too heavy to billow her blond hair wrapped in a wimple. Her other hand on a pole planted, a banner above them both, orange with a russet hawk. "Oh I can smell it," says Jo. "The ocean." Ysabel and Jessie stand there unmoving, only the wind, tugging banner and hair and gown.

"Well it's right there," says the Duke.

"Yez might well to look yonder," says Coffey. He's holding out a pair of binoculars. The Duke drops a plastic bottle of something viscous and milky into his jacket pocket so he can take them. Coffey's brass hand points to a fishing trawler stationed not far off, someone in dark rain gear at the prow, watching the women on the shore.

"Duke," says Jo, pointing back up along the strand. He lowers the binoculars. A low two-wheeled car drawn by two slow-stepping horses trundles along the sand toward Jessie and Ysabel. Standing in the car one hand on the slack reins a figure in a long gleaming hauberk and a polished silver breastplate chased with green, face hidden by a slit-eyed bucket helm. Above the car a banner, white with a yellow bee.

"See?" says the Duke, handing the binoculars back to Coffey. "I knew we were being followed."

"Hey," calls the Duke, lurching onto the sidewalk. "Chariot."

Roland in the rain his hands in bicycle gloves on the roof of the car across the street, the reddish-brown car with the black stripe down the side. He's saying "Princess, please" through the half-open window. Ysabel in the passenger seat leaning down a little back against Jessie looks up through the window at him and shaking her head she's saying "Go, just go" to Roland.

"Chariot!"

Roland looks up to see the Duke stepping into the empty street, to see Jo in the doorway under the small model of a three-masted sailing ship. He looks back down into the car and says "Please come with me."

"Chariot!" The Duke leans on his cane in the middle of the street and mutters "What am I, chopped liver?" to himself.

"Roland, it's okay," says Jo on the sidewalk. "We don't need any – "

"*You!*" Roland pounds the roof of the car and inside it Jessie flinches. "A month ago he had you chased through the street like dogs and now you ride about with him in his *car?*" Coming around the front of it to stand there his green track suit dark with rain. "You have the *keeping* of her! She is to be *safe* in your hands! That is your *office!*"

"You want to talk safe," says the Duke, "as in houses, as in better than sorry, as in questions that aren't, well – where were you the night those two got jumped on the train?"

Roland's face jerks, goes quizzical, chin lifting, his hands in those gloves balling into fists and opening up again.

"Cat kitten in your mouth?" says the Duke. "Your zeal in keeping the office you lost to the Gallowglas is well-known. It's well-nigh a *joke*. Half of everybody figures it was you under the Huntsman's mask, losing yet another duel to the Axe." The rain's stopped. It's all gone terribly still. "The Princess calls, she *coughs* and you come running. Except." Water beads the shoulders of the Duke's tweed jacket. The blacktop under his feet gleams wetly. "That one night."

Roland says "This is none of your – " and the Duke cracks his cane-tip against the pavement and the sound is thunderous. "I.

Am. Not. Finished," he says. Pursing his lips. "Best I can figure," he says, "it was shame." Roland repeats the word, "Shame," in an oddly lilted voice. Jo's watching him, watching them both, the Duke impassive, Roland trembling there at the edge of the street. Ysabel leaning over Jessie both of them watching through the rain-flecked driver's window.

"Yeah," says the Duke. "Maybe you were so ashamed at paying off an Old Town witch to concoct the fucking ambush that you couldn't show your face to save the day – "

"*Liar!*" roars Roland stepping out into the empty street, jabbing a finger at the Duke who cracks his cane-tip against the pavement again. Roland jerks to a stop still pointing at the Duke in the middle of the street. The Duke says, "Are you so sure of that, knight?" In the car Jessie's face is in her hands. "Would you have it proved upon my body?"

Roland lowers his hand slowly, open, loose, the palm facing the Duke, there by his side he stretches it and begins to close his fingers about something, the air, when he stops. Eyes widening just he's looking past the Duke who turns then to see Jo, stepping off the sidewalk, into the street, her butter-colored coat flapping, her face firmly flat, her cold eyes squarely aimed at Roland. "Go on," she says, her voice clipped. Between them now. Roland's hand closed in a fist as she steps right up before him. "Do it. None of this fucking around. Go on!"

"Jo," says Roland, trying to get by, "take the Princess, go, I'll find you – "

"He's goading you, you dumb sonofabitch!" Jo blocks him, arms at her sides, ducking her head to keep his eyes on her. "You're dumb enough to fall for it, then go ahead, but let's do it right, okay?"

Roland steps back from her now, his hand still closed in a fist about something that isn't there. "I did not do what he says I did."

"I don't care!" cries Jo, and Roland's mouth curls and sets and he holds his fist out at his side and he says, "I do," and light begins to leak from whatever it is he's holding.

The Duke says, "I'm sorry, Chariot."

Roland shivers opens his fist with a silent flash. There's nothing there. "What?" he says.

Jo's turning now to look at the Duke, both hands still on his cane, hair limply damp. "I voiced my suspicions," he says, voice calm, cool, "I spoke in hypotheticals, and did so without thinking. Your anger is entirely justified, and for it I offer a complete retraction, and apologize, without reservation."

And no one moves, and no one says anything more. Somewhere blocks away a car alarm begins to whoop. The slow rain's seeping down around them again. Roland says to Jo, "Please go to the car, and take the Princess back – "

"Just go," says Jo. "Get out of here. We're fine." He's shaking his head about to say something. "I know what I'm doing," says Jo. And Roland's mouth curls again, and sets, but he ducks his head. Off away down the street a couple of cars are headed their way. The Duke's taken a couple of steps toward his car, one hand out now to Jo. She doesn't take it. Roland turns and with a little skipping jump sets off across the street, down the sidewalk, at a half-run now around the corner and out of sight.

The Duke lowers his hand. "Took you long enough," he says.

"Shut the fuck up," says Jo. Digging in the pockets of her coat she comes up with an orange pack of cigarettes.

"Your concern," says the Duke. "Touching." He limps over to the car. Jo follows him, cigarette in her mouth, stuffing the pack back, coming up with a silvery lighter. "I had to know," says the Duke. Jessie's climbing out of the car, levering the front seat forward. "I could give two shits," says Jo, fumbling the lighter, clicking and clicking it again before it strikes.

The Duke leaning on his car shakes his head. "You are not doing that in my car," he says.

"Then we can fucking wait five minutes," says Jo, and she takes a long drag and blows smoke out into the softly falling rain, "while I settle my fucking nerves."

The Duke watches her smoke a moment, Jessie standing there beside him, then he ducks down. "Princess," he says. "Could I maybe reclaim my seat? This leg."

"Actually," says Ysabel, leaning back against the passenger door, "if you wouldn't mind riding in back?" The blond Batgirl smiling from her tight T-shirt dress.

The Duke sighs. "Today," he says, "is a day for capitulation."

ROUNDING A CORNER – NEXT THURSDAY – NO HULLABALOO TO HAVE GONE DANCING – LIKE BUBBLES

ROUNDING A CORNER the houses to one side fall away and there past a drop a sheen of still water and just past it low buildings a bright red roof like a circus tent a spindly Ferris wheel and a snaking curl of roller coaster. Across the river behind it all the hills of trees green-black and brown and orange dotted with houses and lights just starting to come on and then they're past the gap and trees and houses take up that side again. "What the hell?" says Jo, craning her neck. The Duke beside her shifts, looks back as well. "Some kind of mini Disneyland thing down there by the river?" Endicott's always back in time, sings a voice over a driving beat and popping guitars. Endicott's not the cheatin' kind.

"Oaks Park," says the Duke. "You never been to Oaks Park?"

"Never heard of it," says Jo.

"One of the delights of my demesne," says the Duke. "We should go sometime. The rides are closed right now, but they got the rollerskating – hey, hon, turn right up there. I want to see something."

"Fun?" says Jo, as the car slows, turns. "You're asking me out on a date? We're gonna put on rollerskates and listen to Journey?"

"Why not?" says the Duke, looking back through the rear window. Endicott keeps his body clean. Endicott don't use nicotine.

"Would this be before or after the wedding?"

He looks away from where they've been, looks at her, crammed into the corner of the back seat in her butter-colored coat, arms folded tightly about herself chin tucked behind her shoulder one eyebrow hiked over cold and muddy eyes. He sucks his teeth. "I don't know. What do you think, Princess? A solstice wedding?"

From the front seat without turning Ysabel says, "Why don't we see if you survive the Throne before worrying about setting a date?"

The Duke snorts, turns to watch out the rear window again. "Feel the love in this car," he says.

"Should I head on to Next Thursday now?" says Jessie.

"What?" says the Duke. "Yeah, just, find a cross street and cut on up. We're good."

"Thursday which?" says Jo.

Two residential streets, lined with parked cars, a simple intersection, the pavement of it painted in a great circle stretched from corner to corner in yellows and whites a sunflower faded by weather and traffic opening under the colorless sky. Houses sit comfortably at three of the corners windows lit here and there against the rainy gloom, and at three of the corners there by the sidewalks stands have been built, little kiosks of scrap lumber and windfall painted in primary colors dimmed with age. Jo's standing by a sign that says Central Square over a bulletin board papered with note cards and post-its and photos and laser-printed flyers, guitarist sought, vegan nanny, found one cat, feng shui process development. Ysabel in her white trench coat stands with Jessie by a sign that says Tea over shelves laid with a couple of thermoses and some old mugs and cups and tins and cans of tea.

"Central Square," says the Duke, standing by the reddish-brown car. He lifts his cane and points to the fourth corner. "And the Next Thursday Teahouse."

At the fourth corner a high red gate freshly painted, white lights strung about it. Two old paned windows hang in the air to either side of it from wire just visible strung from tree branches and the gate itself. Beyond a ramshackle confusion gathers itself from windows and doors and bare wood, roofs of tin and translucent plastic aglow with lamplight, the trees of the lot winding in and out of the structure built around them.

"Your demesne contains such wonders as we'd never dreamed of, Duke," says Ysabel.

"Yeah," says Jo, to herself.

"Go on in," says the Duke. "We're expected. We're always expected." Ysabel takes Jessie's hand and they walk across the sunflower toward the red gate. Jo angles toward the Duke still standing by his car. "Caught up yet?" he says, leaning on his cane.

"With what?" says Jo. "It's been a long day."

"With the *point,*" says the Duke.

"Yeah, yeah, the glory and the majesty of you," says Jo. "We're all impressed. What?" at his look askance. "You own a strip club. You own some coffee shops. You're down with the anarchist bicycle collective and you support cartoonists and you take care of the old folks and what, you built this place with your own two hands?"

"I made it *possible,*" says the Duke. "Everything you saw today, I made all of it possible. I didn't *make* any of it, I cleared the way and kept it safe so it could get made at all."

"You," says Jo, looking at his hands wrapped about the hawk at the head of his cane, "you should do earnest more often," she says. Looking up. "It's good for your eyes."

"Go on," says the Duke. Flexing his fingers. "I need to take care of something."

Jo heads toward the gate, but stops just past the front of the car. "Hey," she says. "What – what do I call you? I mean, Duke, hey Duke, it just seems a little weird."

"Most," says the Duke, limping around to the back of the car, "usually address my grace."

"Your grace," says Jo, smirking.

"Go on," says the Duke. "Check it out. I'll be there in a minute to show you the good bits."

As she walks through the gate he pulls a single key from a pocket and opens the trunk. He leans in, wrestles a box to one side, reaches for another one toward the back, stops, sighs to himself, opens the first box. Inside maybe ten or so large plastic bags sealed with purple zip-locks. Two or three of them each filled in turn with a dozen little plastic baggies twisted tightly about thimblesful of gold dust, the rest fat with loose dust, untwisted, lighting the trunk with a fitful mimicry of daylight. He pats one, shakes his head, closes the box up shutting the color away. Reaches for the second box, lined with a garbage bag, and tries to tug it toward him but it's caught. He reaches down, works something free, sets it to one side, a mask that could swallow half a head, white, crudely painted with thick black lines to resemble a grinning skull, a mane of long black hair dangling limply from it. Tugs the second box closer. Inside a glass jug sloshing with something viscous, white, frothed with a sheen of bubbles, a hint of warm yellow gold. From his pockets come jars and bottles and he sets them in the trunk there by the box. He uncaps the jug and starts pouring them in. As each is emptied he drops it in the box, in the garbage bag lining among other emptied bottles and jars. Some blank, unlabeled, some with labels worn away. Snapple. Fiji Water. He caps the jug again, shoves the box back in place. Clasps his hands together looking it all over for a moment. Then he shuts the trunk.

"Where is everybody?" says the Duke. He hangs his coat in a cozy little antechamber lined with Persian rugs. The only other coat hanging there's a white trench coat, a white fedora on the hook above it. The light from ropes of white bulbs strung and tangled all about is dim but everywhere. The thumb-sized wodge of dust in the baggie he pulls from inside his jacket can't quite manage to sparkle. "Hello?" he calls, tucking the baggie into the pocket of his collarless yellow silk shirt. Heading out into an uncertain room, angles and openings on all sides, the light still dim but all about. A rushing wash of sound, branches tossed by a wind heavy with water that's not yet fallen as rain, lifting and rattling the tin sheets nailed above. His cane-tip dimples the rugs laid one on the other on another under his feet.

"Leo," says the man stooping to peer through what's yet another doorway. "I'm so glad you could come."

"Quiet night," says the Duke.

"We," says the man unfolding himself into that uncertain room, "were supposed to have had the hearing yesterday." Slip-on jogging shoes, loose grey sweatpants, a dark grey fleece pullover that says Tartans with a logo of a Scottie dog. "We spread the word to think of the Teahouse as - closed, this weekend." The pullover's zipped all the way up to his chin. His face all cheekbones and nose and eyebrows jutting. He's wearing a black watch cap. "Win, or lose. I didn't want a lot of hullabaloo."

"But you didn't have the hearing," says the Duke.

The gaunt man shakes his head. "Been a bad week, Leo," he says, and he holds up a hand, "it's all right. Tonight it's better. I'm okay. Okay." His hand in a black knit glove, fingertips removed. "It's been put off till next week."

The Duke puts a hand to the pocket of his shirt. "I've got some more, Michael," he says. "It'll help."

"We'll talk," says the gaunt man. "About that. But Jasmine's down, from Seattle?"

"We don't want to impose – "

"No, no. Lauren's here, too. We're having an, an early supper. In the Heart. Just – try to keep it down?"

"Keep it," says the Duke, and then, "oh. Of course." Smiling. "Early. How can you tell in here?"

Another wash of almost-rain rattles the roof above them and Michael looks up, lays a gloved hand on a bare joist. "I should have torn all this down at the end of summer," he says.

"We'll talk about that," says the Duke.

"Your friends are on the Smoking Porch," says Michael.

Cigarette clamped in her mouth unzipping a long white boot Ysabel says "What do you think?" She tugs her boot off, points her foot, flexes her toes. Jo still in her butter-colored coat sits at the other end of the long low sofa, cigarette in her hands, hands dangled between her knees. The porch about them open on three sides, the roof held up by columns of peeled and polished unplaned branches. Past them over the tops of trees a grey stretch of river shining with what daylight's left. "It's incredible," says Jo. "I had no idea any of this was down here. He must've been building it for years."

"Not what I meant," says Ysabel, unzipping her other boot, pulling it off. Jo looks over her shoulder. By the back wall Jessie in her grey chauffeur's jacket hands behind her back is looking over a wall of stained and faded snapshots of people all of them taken in this room, with cigarettes, cigars, pipes in their hands, their mouths, a hookah stem, cigarette butts and cigar butts pinned in and around among the photos. Wind washes around the porch, tugging smoke from their cigarettes, the trees about them rolling like waves. "I think you have a thing for blonds," says Jo quietly.

"Jealous?" says Ysabel, turning to stretch her legs down the length of the sofa, bare toes painted with gold glitter not quite touching Jo's coat.

"I can call a cab for us whenever," says Jo.

Ysabel shrugs. "As you wish." Pulling her legs back curling arms about them chin on her knees. "But that wasn't what I meant either."

"You're gonna marry him," says Jo, and Ysabel lowers her knees to sit tailor-fashion, tugging her T-shirt dress down to cover her lap, stretching out the smiling blond Batgirl. "When the King comes back," she says, absently stroking her belly, "then I will be Queen." Leaning forward suddenly, reaching along the back of the sofa for Jo's shoulder, the loose mass of her hair falling over one shoulder as she ducks her head, trying to catch Jo's eye, Jo head down grinding her cigarette in the ashtray beside her. "What do you think of him?" says Ysabel. "Now that you've talked to him. What do you think of what you've gotten us into?"

Jo turns to look at Ysabel, and "There you are!" cries the Duke, in the low wide doorway to the porch. "I swear this place gets bigger every time I come." Ysabel sits up, stubbing out her cigarette on the burn-scarred arm of the sofa. Jo's looking down again. Jessie presses against the Duke and he pulls her into a one-armed hug. "We've pretty much got the place to ourselves tonight, which, unexpected, but hey, gift horses, whatnot." He lets go of Jessie, stumps a little closer to the sofa. "Anybody hungry? Jo?" Ysabel's stretching her legs out again, lying back again, tugging down her dress again. Jo shrugs. "There's at least a couple of kitchens in here," says the Duke, "usually stocked with this or that. We could assemble a picnic supper? How about it? Up for a quest?"

"Sure," Jo's saying, climbing to her feet. She heads past him into the low narrow hall lined with more rugs along the walls and black-light tapestries and ghostly batiked scrims. He pauses in the doorway, looks back, at Jessie, at Ysabel's hand on the back of the sofa. "We'll be back," he says, "but minutes in here sometimes seem like hours? And vice-versa. Part of its charm."

"Well," says Ysabel, as the thump of his cane recedes. "I wanted to go dancing."

"Well, talk to Leo when they get back," says Jessie.

Ysabel sitting up leans over the back of the sofa chin on her folded arms. "Leo," she says. "I see why he has you wear that jacket. You have fantastic legs. No, I wanted to go dancing just with you."

Jessie says, "That'd be nice."

"Nice," says Ysabel. She tips her head back smiling looking up at the bare rafters roof rattling in another gust. "I wanted to go dancing with you," she says, "in a room full of men we didn't know. I wanted them to race each other to the bar to buy us drinks." Jessie's taken off her cap, she's holding it in her hands, her back to that wall of photos. "I wanted," says Ysabel, stretching, "them to be thinking of what they'd've been thinking they'd get to do to us," and then she turns and lies back down along the sofa, "while the whole time we'd've known what we'd be doing to each other."

Jessie doesn't take a step toward the sofa. She doesn't take a step toward the low wide doorway. Ysabel's legs appear lifted straight up from the sofa bare feet pointed. "We would have pretended to go to the bathroom together," she says, "and left them to fight over the bill." Her hands appear working a scrap of black lace up the length of those legs. "In the elevator it would all have been too much." Jessie lets her cap fall to the rug. "The doors would've opened," says Ysabel, pulling one foot free, then the other, "and a couple of men would've been standing there, staring, and we'd've run down the hall to our room, laughing." She lets the underwear fall from her hand behind the sofa, lowers her legs, hooking the one over the back of it her foot restlessly turning. "We wouldn't've made it to the bed," says Ysabel. Jessie stoops to pick up the underwear, stands, one hand on the back of the sofa. Ysabel sprawled along it the blond Batgirl lost in the wrinkles of her rucked-up dress and flashing there from the gold pin piercing her navel a bit of crystal. "And somewhere in all of that," she says, "you'd've told me your name."

"Rain," says Jessie.

"Rain," says Ysabel, holding up a hand. "Come here, Rain."

"Michael St. John Lake," says the Duke. "He was an architect or something? I don't know." He's sitting at a picnic table painted with rainbowed swirls of graffiti.

"I got a can of sardines," says Jo, kneeling next to some shelves built into an angle of this room where a slope of ceiling abruptly meets the walls. "And some pita chips. Stale pita chips."

"Any glasses?" says the Duke. On the table five or six bottles, round and square, clear glass and green glass and deep deep brown. "Goblets? Paper cups?"

"No, no, and no," says Jo, standing. She pulls her butter-colored coat from one shoulder, the other, lets it slide down her arms, drapes it over the shelf behind her.

"Decided to stay awhile?" says the Duke, as she sits across from him. He sweeps a hand over the bottles. "Lady's choice." She grabs a clear bottle and surprised he says "Whisky."

"Did you?" she says, offering it to him, and he shakes his head and grabs a short fat bottle too dark to see through. "Gin for me."

"So this Michael," she says. "St. John Lake." Unscrewing the cap to her bottle. "He's not like you. Right?" She takes a swig. "He's more like me."

"In a world," says the Duke, uncorking his, "where there's only two types of people, sure. He's more like you." He sips from his. "Anyway. I heard about his ideas for suburban piazzas from somebody, I don't know, and I thought – "

"Piazzas?"

"Central Square," says the Duke. "With the street painting and the corner kiosks and anyway I wanted to see what one looked like, and have I told you you have nice shoulders? Because you do. They're nice. You should wear stuff that shows them more like that. So says me." Jo's looking down, away, she takes another quick drink from her bottle. Her satiny black slip with simple ribbon straps no wider than a finger. "Why don't you ever ask direct questions?" says the Duke.

Jo looks up, sets her bottle on the table. "I – "

"No you don't. Not when it matters."

Jo rests her elbows on the table. "Okay," she says. "Sometimes," she says, looking at him through the thicket of bottles. "It's like, if I did, about some stuff, sometimes, I think, I think you'd all just. Pop. Like soap bubbles."

"People, like me," says the Duke. Jo nods. "Well," he says. "I'd like to think I'm a wee bit more substantial than that. Go on. Try me."

"Okay," says Jo, chin in her hands. "How old are you?"

"That's a terrible question!" cries the Duke, rearing back. "How old am I. How fast is speed? How far is deep?" He takes a sip from his bottle and then leans forward both hands on the table. "I'm young at heart," he says. Sits back. "Try again."

Jo pulls something from her pocket, a wad of money clamped in a medium-sized binder clip, and opens it just enough to slip a gold credit card free. "Who pays for this?" she says, and she puts it on the table between them.

The Duke nods. "Better," he says. "Better." The card there gold and bright against the green and purple swirls. "You do," he says.

"You said I'd never see a bill," she says.

"You won't," he says. "You already paid for it." He moves a bottle from between them, then another. "I confess," he says. "It would've been a minor breach of protocol, but I went to them to see about a modest line of credit for you." He slides the card back across the table to her. "Imagine my surprise to find you already had quite a substantial account." Jo's shaking her head, saying, "I don't have any idea," and the Duke takes her hand in his, leans forward, says "Careful, careful. Some things *do* pop like bubbles. Maybe you wrote something on a piece of paper and burned it. Maybe you answered three questions from a stranger. Maybe you whispered it into a tin can under a bridge, I don't know, but don't, don't tell me. Don't ever tell anyone what you said. Understand?" Jo nods. The Duke sits up a little. He doesn't let go of her hand. "I maybe should have said something," he says. "But, ah. I didn't."

"That's," she says, "Your grace, it's – thanks. Thank you."

"Leo," he says. "Call me Leo." He frowns, looks over his shoulder. "Did you hear that?"

"What," says Jo, "like a – roar?" Her hand is empty. "Leo?" There's no one sitting across the table from her.

"SIR? SIR?"

"SIR? SIR?" says the guard. "What's your name, sir?"

"Ray," says the man in the black leather jacket.

"Just Ray?" says the other guard on the other side.

"Well it's not Ray Lemon or Ray Limeade or any other lame Sprite knockoff if that's what you mean." His bulging eyes are bloodshot, wet. His pink hair draggled into strange dark colors by the dim light in the lobby. "Who," he says, "who lives on the top floor?"

"What?" says the first guard.

"*Who,*" says Ray. "A couple days ago I saw it all from the volcano." He lurches toward the other guard and they both skip back keys a-jangle saying "Whoa, hey, whoa" and he stops, holds up his hands. "I *know,* okay? What has to happen. Only I really *need* to know who's up there. Before I go." He turns. They're standing before a computer screen in the wall under a sign that says US Bancorp Tower. Touch screen for individual listings. "Okay? This thing is all *alphabetical,* not whatever it's *geographical.* You know? And I really want to know who's up there before I go. I mean that bang? There was a loud bang over across the river. Did you hear that bang?"

"Sir," says the first guard, "we're going to have to ask you to," and the other guard's saying "The 142nd."

"What?" says the first guard.

"The Air National Guard," says the other guard. "Sometimes they do flyovers? Maybe he heard a sonic boom."

"Man, *do* not answer their questions, okay?" says the first guard.

"But it's dead simple," says Ray. "Who lives up there?"

"Fuck this," says the first guard. "You watch him. I'm calling CHIERS." He stalks off, keys ringing like bells.

"If it's who I think it is," says Ray, slumping back against the glass-covered wall, "oh God if it's *what* I think it is." Head in his hands, knees bending, falling slowly, slowly to the floor.

"It's okay, man," says the other guard. "They'll take care of you. Get you dried out in nothing flat."

"Oh no," says Ray, "oh no no no," hands scrabbling like turtles as he fails to push himself back up, "oh no that would be a disaster."

"It's okay," says the guard. "It's all gonna be okay."

I had no ambition beyond life's daily round and
the weekend celebration of it.

—Eddie Campbell

The text has been set in Tribute, a typeface designed by Frank Heine from types cut in the 16th century by Françoise Guyot; specifically, a specimen printed around 1565 in the Netherlands.

Kɪᴘ Mᴀɴʟᴇʏ lives in Portland, Oregon, with a cartoonist, an aspiring large and exotic animal veterinarian who loves animals, and (at last count) two cats and one hamster.

He may be contacted via email at kipmanley@yahoo.com. His general-interest website is available for viewing at www.longstoryshortpier.com.